W9-ACO-722

THE CONJURER

WRITTEN BY

CORDELIA FRANCES BIDDLE

WITH STEVE ZETTLER AS NERO BLANC

A Crossworder's Delight

Another Word for Murder

Wrapped Up in Crosswords

Anatomy of a Crossword

A Crossworder's Gift

Corpus de Crossword

A Crossword to Die For

A Crossworder's Holiday

The Crossword Connection

Two Down

The Crossword Murder

ALSO BY

CORDELIA FRANCES BIDDLE

Murder at San Simeon

Beneath the Wind

THE CONJURER

Cordelia Frances Biddle

Thomas Dunne Books

St. Martin's Minotaur

New York

This is a work of fiction. All of the characters, organizations, and events portrayed in this novel are either products of the author's imagination or are used fictitiously.

THOMAS DUNNE BOOKS.
An imprint of St. Martin's Press.

www.thomasdunnebooks.com
www.minotaurbooks.com

ISBN-13: 978-0-312-35246-2
ISBN-10: 0-312-35246-8

First Edition: February 2007

10 9 8 7 6 5 4 3 2 1

For Steve

husband, partner, and dearest friend,
with my love and admiration always

Acknowledgments

Many thanks to my wonderful editor, Marcia Markland, and her equally perceptive assistant, Diana Szu. Their enthusiasm and energy in bringing *The Conjurer* to life has been an inspiration and a joy.

One who never turned his back but marched breast forward.
Never doubted clouds would break,
Never dreamed, though right were worsted, wrong would triumph,
Held we fall to rise, are baffled to fight better,
Sleep to wake.

—ROBERT BROWNING, *Asolando*

THE
CONJURER

A River in Flood

THE TWO DOGS STARE DOWN into the river. In their intense concentration, they neither move nor whimper, while their brown fur, wet and bemired with hunting, appears all of one color with the earth like two animate objects formed from the flinty Pennsylvania soil. The older dog shivers and finally relinquishes his post, curling himself into a woeful ball on the frost-hardened hilltop, but the pup remains seated, gazing fixedly at the turbulent rapids as they roar past the riverbanks below, sending up mud-filled foam and sprays of dirt-gray water that almost scream out power and vengeance. The Schuylkill in flood is a terrible place: twice as broad as it should be, the waves so relentless they appear likely to crest over the high hill itself. The island that sits in the midst of this part of the stream is already drowned; only the top halves of its trees remain, leafless black limbs like arms thrust upward in supplication.

As the young dog watches, entire tree trunks and mangled fence rails thunder past, the power of the surge so great that each sodden piece of wood is repeatedly plunged below the surface to then repeatedly shoot back up into the air. The pup scans these projectiles with apprehensive eyes, although he never follows their course for more than a yard or two. What he desperately searches for should be directly below his resting place.

He sniffs the air, briefly pricks up his ears, then flattens them again. It is bitterly cold, and the dogs have remained atop the steep rise for a long time. Their coats no longer emanate heat or the steamy moisture of warm bodies accustomed to racing across fields at their master's call. The old dog groans from his icy bed, then closes his eyes. The pup turns briefly toward his companion, his allegiance torn between love and duty. Then he also whimpers and lies down.

"WE REALLY SHOULD consider proceeding with luncheon, Mr. Simms. I'm sure Father simply lost track of the time." It's Martha Beale who makes these twin statements, although her tone lacks conviction. Her stance is also hesitant: a tall figure cloaked in a blue cashmere gown. Despite its lilac satin trim, its tight bodice and white lace, its long sleeves equipped with two *à la mode* pouffings, Martha is scant competition for the opulent red velvet swags that drape the parlor's cherrywood portal. Not that it would enter her mind to attempt such an outrageous act. Ladies, she's been taught, must be discreet additions to their habitations, speaking only when necessary—and then with decorum and tact.

As a result of this rigorous schooling, even the requisite underwiring of her costume, the whalebone corset and stiff crinoline underskirts, fails to make her an impressive figure when compared to the excesses of Beale House: its room upon room overflowing with torchères of bronze and alabaster, with Turkey carpets, marble urns, and dense suites of black walnut furniture. All new, of course, just as the country estate in the wooded and ravined land that stretches west of the city of Philadelphia is new, and built in the most fashionable and ornate of Gothic styles.

"You know how unhappy Cook becomes when the schedule is forsaken . . ." Martha adds, keeping her polite gaze upon her father's confidential secretary, who remains seated beside one of the parlor tables, his attention devoted to the newspaper in his hands.

"As you say, Martha" is Simms's sole response.

"Surely Father won't mind if we commence without him." She attempts a small laugh, hoping to sound assured and competent, but the effort merely makes her seem younger and less experienced than her twenty-six years would suggest. "Especially if he's had a successful morning's hunting. Besides, he must have packed some nourishment in his creel. Biscuits and cheese, at least . . ."

She pauses, again at a loss. How long has it been, she wonders, that Owen Simms has been part of the household? Fifteen years? Sixteen? She knows it was well before she achieved adulthood, and because of this fact it seems that he has always been here, and that her behavior with him has never climbed out of an uncomfortable and tongue-tied infancy. Or perhaps her reaction simply reflects the great man he serves. ". . . And we both know how fond Father is of tramping into the deepest reaches of the forest—"

"As you say."

Martha suppresses a sigh as she considers the response. *As you say,* not *as you wish.* And *Martha,* rather than *Miss Beale,* which would be fitting and right given her age. If she were married, perhaps . . . but no, there's no use in starting down that long and tortured road. At her advanced years, it's doubtful she'll ever participate in wedded life. The rules of social conduct are strict in 1842, but doubtless they've always been so. "I'll inform Cook, then, shall I?"

Owen Simms merely nods. Seated within a pool of light cast from a nearby paraffin lamp, he should appear lesser than the standing Martha, but the very opposite is true; and he seems as authoritative and commanding as the granite bust of a Roman senator: each chiseled curl in place, the watchful eyes full of self-satisfaction and pride. "The decision is yours, of course, Martha. This is your father's house, after all. And you, naturally, are its hostess. Matters of dining and so forth must be left in your capable hands." With that remark, Simms returns to his newspaper. He doesn't wait to see if his master's only child stays or leaves, and so Martha Beale makes one more foray into conversation, affixing a masterful smile she doesn't remotely feel. *Capable hands!* she thinks, and her cheeks involuntarily redden. She has no idea whether Simms means the words as a compliment or a critique.

"Good. Let us dine. Father certainly wouldn't wish us to go hungry."

Then she walks away to tell Cook that they will sup without awaiting her father's return. But this small moment of autonomy doesn't engender a sense of dignity or ownership. Instead, Martha feels utterly immaterial; and her body as she crosses the broad foyer and turns down the corridor that leads to the kitchens and pantries is self-conscious and stiff.

IT'S THE HEAD gardener, Jacob Oberholtzer, who finds the dogs, so cold the old male can scarcely move, while the pup recognizes the servant and barks often and noisily without once forsaking his sentry station on the hill. Oberholtzer drags the old dog up by the scruff of his neck and propels him forward by pumping his shivering sides as though they were bellows. "Come," he orders in English, although that's not his native tongue: "Come, dog."

The old male weaves unsteadily forward. The pup remains behind. "Dog, come!" Oberholtzer yells, but the pup refuses to move. The gardener swears in *Plattdeutsch;* the pup barks; the old dog wavers, and Jacob, his teeth chattering viciously, his hands and nose nearly numb, storms back to the site overlooking the swollen Schuylkill. He makes a grab for the pup, but the pup leaps away, whining and nearly plunging backward down into the madly rushing river.

The value his master places upon these two makes Oberholtzer hesitate; he can't risk losing one of them to the gray-brown waves that tumble past the rock-strewn bank. In pausing, Jacob looks beyond the recalcitrant animal, beyond the frost-flattened scrub of the hillside, beyond the tangled trees that lead into the wilder parts of the forest. The daylight is fading fast, and the landscape and waterscape taking on a leaden hue: sky, earth, water, river boulders of the same dead color that presages snow. Oberholtzer swears again, and in giving voice to his frustration and his wrath finally sees the creel and rifle dropped among the stones at the Schuylkill's swollen edge. Premonition paralyzes him. His legs, accustomed to hours tramping the Beale estate, refuse to move. His mind, trained to take orders without asking questions, panics. He stares down at the valuable gun, shouts his master's name, turns his head from the roaring river to the nervous dogs, then nearly runs from the scene.

MARTHA IS READING in the parlor when Oberholtzer barrels through the front door of Beale House. Naturally, she assumes it's her father, at long last returned from his shooting excursion. She thinks the noise and the stomping, the rush of servants clattering into the foyer, are in answer to his immediate needs: a warm jacket to replace his cold outer coat, slippers in place of boots, a soothing glass of port wine. She never imagines it's Oberholtzer who has engendered this commotion; servants enter through the rear of the house, and a gardener, rarely at all. Only people approaching the Beales' social status are admitted through the main door. With her book resting on her lap, she composes herself in the attitude of calm and cheerful anticipation her father would expect.

But it's not Lemuel Beale who enters the room; rather, it's Owen

Simms. "Your father seems to be missing" is what he tells her; his tone is as measured as always. "Oberholtzer found the two dogs and then spotted your father's hunting equipment at the river's edge."

"Missing?" is all Martha can think to reply. "But that's impossible, Mr. Simms. Father cannot be *missing*. He must have walked further upriver, or down. Or perhaps he entered a crofter's cottage to escape the chill, or found a farm wagon to carry him home. Late as it's become, Father would never—"

"And left his dogs behind? And his percussion rifle?"

Martha has no response to these queries other than to utter a gentle "But there must be a logical explanation . . ." Then she attempts a lighter tone. "And you know how fond Father is of logic—"

"Martha, the Schuylkill's in full spate, and with the river flooded, the current is exceedingly treacherous. If your father slipped on the rocks—"

Martha sits straight in her chair; the book is now clenched in her fingers, and her breathing has grown shallow and quick. "I'm sure that as soon as Father returns home, he'll be able to provide us with a—"

But Simms interrupts her. "If he lost his balance and fell, Martha, the current would—" He doesn't complete the sentence, and Martha stares into his eyes. Her ears begin to buzz with noise while her mind's eye begins to create an awful picture: the rapids, the treacherous terrain, her father venturing one precarious and fatal step . . . Then her brain blacks out the image; and she pinches her lips and wills her breaths to slow.

"Did Jacob search the shore?"

"He called your father's name repeatedly. There was no reply to his entreaties. The light had grown exceedingly dim, which prevented him seeing into the distance."

"And where is Jacob now?" She stands, all at once galvanized into action. Her rise is awkward, far too unrehearsed and ill considered to be the graceful motion of a proper lady, but the change of posture surprises both her and her father's secretary with its unaccustomed vigor.

"In the servants' kitchen."

"And Father's dogs?"

"Surely we should not fret over mere beasts at a critical time like this, Martha."

Her shoulders stiffen, and her longish face with its aquiline nose also hardens while her gray-green eyes turn dark as slate. She resembles her father at this moment; a younger version, naturally, but someone equally tenacious.

"The dogs were out all day, Mr. Simms. They must have become quite chilled, especially old Tip, who's grown so lame."

Martha takes a firm step forward and is again astonished at her own resolve. "We must gather a search party, and plenty of lanterns and torches to light our way through the wooded terrain. I'll fetch my mantle and bonnet while you assemble the servants." She turns to leave him, but Simms stops her.

"I cannot permit you to endanger yourself in such a fashion, Martha. Your father would never forgive me. It's exceedingly cold; the icy ground is treacherous; you're liable to do yourself harm. We'll search tomorrow when we can better watch our footing. And as you yourself just now stated, he may have taken refuge, or found a wagoneer—"

"It's my father's safety and not his daughter's that's at issue here, Mr. Simms," she counters with the same determination. "You're the one who employed the term 'missing.' My father's only fifty-one, as you well know. He's in the best of health. If he fell into the water as you just suggested, he would swim; he would call out; he would save himself." Martha stops herself. She can hear how emotional she's grown. Such a display would not please Lemuel Beale. "And my father will never forgive *me,* Mr. Simms, if I neglect my filial duties. Now, please assemble the servants. And let us bring some fortified wine and warm clothes with us, should we find he has endured an unfortunate accident."

THE CRUNCH OF boots on frozen earth is the dominant sound. There are no words, no coughing, no whistling, no throats cleared, just the slap of leather marching across the ice-coated soil. Accompanying this merciless noise is the quick chuff of wool rubbed against similar pieces of cloth: knees and cuffs of trousers, coat sleeves, and Martha's long pelisse hurrying over the ground. Like the others, she grips a lantern whose flame sizzles and flares in the bitter air. Beside her is Jacob, leading the party. "There, Miss Beale." He points to the rise. "Dogs there. Basket, rifle below." It's the first time since departing Beale House that anyone has spoken.

They descend to the river's edge, stumbling and slipping on the bank's slick stones. The lanterns bob uneasily as arms and bodies struggle to keep balance. The fires hiss, adding to the noisy suck and pull of the water speeding past. Martha finds herself forced to shout. "Show us the place, Jacob."

Sure enough, there's the creel. Jacob points to it proudly. "And the rifle?" Owen Simms asks, but Jacob's hand merely indicates an empty nest of rocks.

"There's nothing there, man!" Simms's sharp inflection bears the mark of his anxiety.

Martha turns to Jacob, lowering her light so that it won't glare into his eyes. "I know you to be a loyal servant to my father, Jacob. Perhaps you were mistaken about seeing the weapon?"

"Jacob see." He points again. Martha follows the gesture.

"Perhaps a wave carried it off?" she offers.

"And not the creel, Martha?" Simms interjects. "Surely the water would more readily sweep away a wickerwork object than one fashioned of metal."

Martha has no response; Simms is correct, of course. She studies the forsaken creel, the empty rocks; beyond them the night-cloaked river seems to spread out endlessly, an ocean of murderous rapids and currents without landfall or hope of salvation. She feels as though she were standing at the last known edge of the universe. Tears start into her eyes, then freeze upon her cheeks.

Shakily she lifts her lamp and extends her arm, hoping its gleam may cast light farther afield, but the fire cannot penetrate the inky blackness. She sees only the chilblained faces and frightened eyes of her father's servants.

"And the dogs were up on the hillock, Jacob?"

"Yes, miss."

"Not here beside the water?"

Jacob glances at the promontory. "Watching."

Martha turns her back to the hilltop, staring riverward as she imagines the dogs did. What did they see? she wonders. What might they have heard? Why would they so diligently wait if it were not for the imminent return of their master?

"This is a futile effort, Martha," Simms tells her as he pushes through the huddled throng. "It's far too dark. We will continue our hunt tomorrow."

"No, Mr. Simms. We must search the shoreline tonight—all night, if need be. If Father did lose his footing . . . if . . . if he were carried downstream before struggling free of the current—"

"Martha, I beseech you; listen to reason—"

"I am, Mr. Simms!" Martha fights back. "I am heeding the voice of my own heart."

"Then let me go on alone with the other men, and you return to the warmth and comfort of your father's house."

"I cannot permit that, Mr. Simms." Then she adds a more diplomatic "Surely you must understand my sentiments."

Martha doesn't wait for a reply. Instead, the grim party moves forward one by one, boots bumping over the riverine rocks while the lights jostle flame into the night. The color is a vibrant white, and in the frigid air seems to become compacted and brilliant like molten glass thrust into chilled water. There's little sound save for the searchers' nervous breaths, the course chafe of their clothing, their shoes abrading the ground, and, far off from Martha, a number of grumbled curses. Her father might give employment to many, but he's not a man blessed with either love or fidelity in return.

She walks apart from Owen Simms, urging the others on by example as they scan the water's edge, the lesser streams that cut a meandering path into the larger river, the glades that suddenly appear within the forest, the underbrush where a spent body might lie in exhaustion and desolation. Nothing. No sign of dislodged creek pebbles, no clutched-at and broken branches. As far as they tramp there's no sign of Lemuel Beale.

Finally, Martha stands erect. The little group has traveled a mile and a half only, an arduous journey that has consumed half the night. "We'll go home," she announces in a subdued and hopeless voice. "Perhaps my father did gain the opposite shore. Perhaps the current was running so fast he was carried several miles toward Philadelphia before freeing himself. Mr. Simms and I will contact the local constabulary in the morning. They will have further plans, I'm sure." Then she extends her hand to each of the servants. "I thank you," she tells them in a somber tone. "You have performed a great service tonight. I will make certain my father learns of your generosity."

DAWN APPEARS GRAY and bleak. Above the fanciful turrets and gables of Beale House, above its freshly quarried stone and tall tracery windows, its balconies, its verandas and parterre gardens, the threat of snow lowers in the sky. Martha rises after a brief and sleepless night, although she doesn't ring for her maid to assist her in her morning ablutions. Instead, she laces her corset herself, slips into her endless underskirts, and pulls on the same cashmere dress she wore the day before. Owen Simms will remark upon her negligence, but Martha doesn't care. In fact, she experiences a brief glow of rebellious anger at her daring.

Then her mind immediately retreats to duty; and she picks up the silver-handled tortoise-shell brush and begins attending to the long chestnut-colored hair that's her secret pride. She counts the strokes as she goes: ten . . . twelve . . . twenty . . . before her hand stops midair. *What use is dressing my hair?* she demands in growing bitterness and wrath. *What use is a silk cap trimmed with lace and flowers? Or finding my satin slippers? Or donning the gold locket Father gave me? What use is breakfast, or conversation, or practicing my daily notes on the piano? What use is this room? This handsome house?*

Martha stares at the brush in her hand, then swiftly returns it to its mates: the comb, the buttonhook, the pot of lavender-scented cream. Her fingers are shaking uncontrollably. Her chest is now heaving also, and she places a hand above her heart to steady herself. *Father doesn't approve of theatrics,* she repeats under her breath.

Then she walks to the frost-clouded windows. The vista of frozen lawns and fields marching imperiously toward the river is absolute. In the somber light, the Schuylkill's frenzied state lies hidden beneath a veneer as slick and brutal as steel.

"Father," Martha murmurs at length; as she speaks the name she realizes that it's inconceivable that Lemuel Beale should be gone.

Beale House

FOR TWO FULL DAYS, MEMBERS of the day watch have scoured the grounds of Lemuel Beale's country estate; and the news of their search has spread to and inflamed the city proper. So renowned a person doesn't vanish without causing a good deal of speculation among citizens both affluent and not. Naturally, a tragic fall into the Schuylkill is the most obvious answer to the financier's peculiar disappearance, but other tales are beginning to surface.

Beale is rumored to be a hard man with a penny; it's further acknowledged that he's a difficult taskmaster both of himself and others, that the clerks in his employ are often disgruntled with their master's many demands, that he has a habit of keeping his underlings on tight and unhealthy leashes. Finally, the origins of his wealth itself become subject to conjecture, because Lemuel Beale is that great rarity: a millionaire, one of only ten such fortunate men in the whole of Philadelphia. New York, the city's northern cousin, can boast a mere five in all of its boroughs. And how, people are beginning to ask, in the midst of the great depression that President Andrew Jackson precipitated and that currently holds the nation in its terrible sway, can men like Beale continue not only to survive but to thrive? Perhaps there's more to the financier's disappearance than meets the casual eye.

Martha, sequestered at her father's country house, hears none of the gossip that washes over the city. Instead, she astonishes herself by becoming the calm center of the storm of apprehension that grips Beale House. By those who make the arduous journey west from the city on visits of either official investigation or personal condolence, her behavior is deemed "admirable" and "stoic" and "brave."

Privately, she knows none of those words are true. As she dresses each morning and undresses each evening, she realizes she resembles nothing so much as her clothing. A well-crafted exterior concealing the limpest and most flimsy of interiors: lace and flannelette, velvet and watered silk. *If it weren't for this stiff corset, these hoopskirts and well-rolled seams,* she tells herself, *I'd collapse to the floor in a useless puddle. It's fortunate my feet are hidden from view and can tap out their distress in private. Who would have ever imagined that fashion could serve a practical purpose?*

"No, Mr. Kelman," Martha now states in the same measured tone she's been relying upon for two long days, "I cannot believe my father has what you refer to as an 'enemy.' A serious competitor in the marketplace, perhaps, or even several. But that's not what you're suggesting, is it?"

Martha and her unexpected guest are in the formal withdrawing room, a large and high-ceilinged space where her father habitually receives his visitors and which today she's commandeered for her own, reasoning that the twin Parian marble mantelpieces surmounted by tall looking glasses in appropriately dark and polished frames better match the seriousness of the situation than the more private parlor. It also seems to her that the drawing room lends an unspoken air of support, as if her father were present and admonishing her to behave with dignity and stamina.

The man called Thomas Kelman regards Martha Beale in thoughtful silence. His stance is official and polite, his legs planted firmly on the Nankin blue carpet, and his back to the nearest fireplace as though his body has no use for heat. He has explained to her that he's an assistant to the mayor of Philadelphia, although in what capacity he hasn't indicated—nor has Martha inquired.

"You're implying, sir—if I understand your words correctly—that my father's disappearance may not be due to some . . ." Here Martha's voice wavers, and her lips momentarily quiver. ". . . Some accident involving a fall into the river."

"It's speculation merely, Miss Beale. And I apologize for introducing it." As Kelman speaks, his long fingers tremble slightly at his sides. Arms straight, shoulders straighter, he has a military bearing that almost negates the poet's hands.

Martha acknowledges the apology in silence while her brow furrows with worry. "I can only repeat what I previously told you, Mr. Kelman: that the police captain and the members of the day watch who searched the area mentioned nothing of an unusual nature. My father went hunting, as is his wont, in the neighboring forests and along the Schuylkill's banks. And the captain's assumption, which he assured me was based on many years of experience with the river at flood strength, and the frailty of—" Her words cease; she lowers her head; within her shoes her toes have curled themselves into knots.

"Miss Beale, are you quite well?"

Martha nods once but cannot make herself reply. She wills herself to breathe in and out while the icy rain that's been intermittently spattering the now dusk-dark windows grows to a malign gust, rattling the glass in their solid wood casements. She listens to the doleful racket before continuing. "In my heart, Mr. Kelman, I cannot imagine my father dead . . . cannot even imagine him gone from this house—not for a mere journey of a week or so; I was accustomed to those absences . . . but for all time? That, I cannot accept. I simply cannot." She pauses again, then notes that Kelman's body has gradually shifted from shadow to light, and that the scar she previously noticed on his left cheek now appears in greater relief. It's as if he were entrusting her with his most precious secret.

"It has been two days, Miss Beale," he says gently. "Two days in most inclement weather."

"But such occurrences do happen, Mr. Kelman, do they not? If my father were . . . if he were wounded and struggling . . . if he were carried downriver—even toward the Delaware—his escape from the torrent and thus to land wouldn't be easy. But he's a strong man; and the forests on both banks are dense, and might provide adequate shelter."

"That's true, Miss Beale." Kelman hesitates. "But the river and climate are exceedingly cold."

Martha glances again at his scar. She has a sudden and shameful desire to touch it, to touch his face and his wondrous hands. Instead, she cleaves to her air of studied detachment. "So I have been repeatedly cautioned, Mr. Kelman. Not even my father could survive in the river for more than a few minutes' time." Then she gazes at her visitor full in the face, behavior that seems as wanton and reckless as her previous wish. "But if Father did escape, could he not have found a cave in which to take refuge? And isn't it possible that he's there now? Delirious from the chill he must have taken . . ."

Her words again trail off; and Kelman waits for a moment before continuing.

"I apologize again, Miss Beale, for my lack of delicacy. But a man as important as your father . . . Well, we must examine every aspect of the situation." He looks to her for comprehension, but she remains motionless in her chair.

"I appreciate your thoroughness, Mr. Kelman," Martha murmurs at length, although the tone has grown hollow, and her posture appears resigned rather than grateful. "But I wonder, if this were not the case of a wealthy and illustrious man, but rather that of a destitute person, would so much attention be paid . . . especially by an assistant to our city's mayor?"

The thin line on Kelman's cheek turns a bitter pink while his black eyes cloud. "Police procedure dictates scrupulous equality in dealings with those of both great and lesser birth, Miss Beale."

She stares at him in surprise. The sentiment is a far cry from those she's heard espoused by her father and Owen Simms. "Do you also adhere to this policy, Mr. Kelman?"

"I do."

She doesn't respond. What is it in his tone, she wonders, that so resembles reverence? It isn't the stentorian theatrics of Dr. Percival at St. Peter's Church or the rumbling incantations of the famous Bishop Fosche; instead, it's a pure sound, unrehearsed, heartfelt, clean. She feels herself blush; this time she doesn't bow her head.

"As long as I can recall, Mr. Kelman, my father has been a successful man of affairs . . . an increasingly successful man. In answer to your previous question: Yes, I imagine it's possible he became unpopular with some of those who considered themselves his competitors . . . perhaps even some who are not American born. My father, as you may know, has had many successful enterprises issuing notes against foreign currencies: Spanish and German specie and so forth. However . . . however, I don't believe civilized persons—no matter what nationality—kill one another."

The scar on Kelman's cheek again reddens with emotion. Martha clasps her hands in her lap and shifts her gaze to the floor. When she next speaks, her tone is subdued. "Do you ever work among the poor?" she asks.

The question seems to take him by surprise. "Among them? As a city official, do you mean, Miss Beale? Or are you referring to service with one of the charitable institutions?"

"As anything you wish."

His answer is slow in coming. "I'm in contact with people of differing means, differing social and economic histories, differing educations." He pauses and gazes at the sleet-coated windows. "Philadelphia's police departments, as you know, are many—representing many districts. The night watch, the day watch, the turnkeys, lieutenants, and captains of each division have their hours filled up with larceny, vagrancy, the receiving of stolen goods, threat of riots, bloody competition between fire brigades, and so forth. If there's a death from unnatural causes, I'm often summoned, Miss Beale," Kelman concludes, then hesitates again. He hadn't intended a dissertation on the inadequacy of a decentralized constabulary in an expanding city. He looks at her in her chair, then rapidly glances away. "This isn't a conversation I would normally have with a lady, Miss Beale."

She stares up into his face. "Are ladies then excluded from tragic ends?"

The thin scar flushes hot; the black eyes flash. "All types and conditions of men—and of women—can meet a brutal death, Miss Beale."

She doesn't speak. She recognizes something deeply personal in his response; and women of her social sphere are strongly discouraged from soliciting private revelations—even from their husbands. "I should like to work among the poor, Mr. Kelman," she offers in quiet apology. "Not in a policing capacity such as yours, of course, but as an aide . . . someone bringing a measure of solace . . ."

"What they need is food, Miss Beale." He speaks the words rapidly and without thought, then attempts to remedy the rashness of the statement. "And comfort, too . . . I should imagine."

A half-smile briefly lights Martha's face. "You're direct, Mr. Kelman. An admirable trait. It's one Father greatly admires." She flushes again, looks toward the windows again, then returns her gaze to Kelman, attempting a self-deprecating laugh as she does so. "My father forbade me to join a humanitarian mission. Perhaps he, like you, realized my lofty goals would make paltry fare for empty bellies."

Kelman is silent. Martha realizes that he's berating himself for his impulsive speech. It's something she's often done herself. "The city sympathizes with you in this time of travail," he says at length.

This time she smiles in earnest. "Less direct, Mr. Kelman. But more politic."

"I hope you understand that my queries into his disappearance are *pro forma*, Miss Beale?"

She nods. The fleeting look of pleasure that suffused her face is gone. "If the household staff can assist you in any fashion, Mr. Kelman, they'll be only too happy to comply" is all she says.

"Comply with what, Martha?" The heavy drawing room doors slide open at that moment, causing the fires in the double grates to flare in alarm, and Kelman and Martha to turn in surprise as though caught in some clandestine act. Owen Simms strides into the room. "I'm Mr. Beale's confidential secretary. I was in town attending to his affairs; if not, I would have been here to greet you sooner."

"And I am Thomas Kelman." Kelman nods politely, although his eyes remain observant and impassive.

"Mr. Kelman has been dispatched from the mayor's office, Mr. Simms—" Martha begins.

"Yes, I know." Simms doesn't sit; instead, he walks to the fire beside which Martha sits, warming his hands behind him while he continues to regard Kelman. "I've heard your name mentioned before now." He glances briefly at Martha before resuming his speech. "The local day watch searched the shore and woodlands exhaustively. I fear that no trace of Miss Beale's father was found."

"I'm aware of that fact, sir. There was also mention of a missing percussion rifle?"

"'Stolen' might be the more appropriate term, Mr. Kelman. And by the very gardener who purported to 'find' Mr. Beale's effects—"

Martha interrupts. "That's conjecture only, Mr. Simms. And quite unfair to poor old Jacob."

Simms regards her in an avuncular fashion, then lets that indulgent glance travel to Kelman. "Miss Beale has an exceedingly kind heart, as you must have noted."

Martha inadvertently bites her lip but doesn't otherwise respond. "It's not kindness, Mr. Simms," she insists at length, and then turns to Thomas Kelman. "I simply do not believe Jacob would steal from my father."

"He's a fortunate man to have your trust, miss."

After another hesitant pause, Martha speaks again, her words now clearly articulated and assured. "I asked the captain in charge of the day watch if he would send members of his force to areas further down the river—"

"Martha, my dear, I—and many others—have already explained the situation to you," Simms interposes. "Further down the river are the separate communities of Gray's Ferry and Southwark, each with their own day and night watches. The captain to whom you spoke has no jurisdiction there—"

Lemuel Beale's daughter ignores the interruption. "Mr. Kelman suggested that Father might have met with some . . . some malicious intent." She glances up at Kelman in appeal. "And he does have jurisdiction, do you not, sir? You can order a search in those other parts of Philadelphia, as well as in the nearer forests, can you not?"

"Oh, Martha, let us be reasonable," Simms interjects. "Your father isn't hidden in some hermit's cave. Nor has he been deliberately dispatched, as your visitor may have attempted to imply. Believe me when I tell you that I know far more about your father's worldly affairs than you. He has no mortal enemies; his methods have always been above reproach. Painful as it is, we must accept the obvious evidence we have: the falls in terrible torrent, a stumble upon the rocks . . . We can only pray that his end was quick."

But Martha doesn't heed this plea. "Will you help me find my father, Mr. Kelman . . . ? Living or not, as may be?"

WE CAN ONLY *pray,* Martha thinks as she clambers into her canopied bed that night. As sacrilegious as the notion is, the idea of prayer as solace and solution brings not one speck of relief. *Besides, what should I pray for?* she asks herself. *Should I do as Mr. Simms suggests, and beseech God to grant that my father's demise was mercifully swift? Should I not beg for a miracle instead? Or yearn that Father be immediately restored to his home? Or perhaps I should wish that he'd never gone hunting in the first place!*

Martha shuts her eyes, although not in piety. Instead, she's willfully closing out her thoughts as she moves her toes across the cold sheets and sniffs at the comforting scent of starch and the flatiron. She might as well be an unhappy ten-year-old instead of a lady of twenty-six.

Then suddenly panic catapults her back into her adult self. *If Father is truly gone, then what of his affairs?* her brain demands. *How will I manage them? How will I deal with Owen Simms? If I haven't the faintest notion of how to order my own existence, how can I hope to run the business of a successful man?* Worrying thus, Martha collapses into sleep.

But dreamland proves no more peaceful a place. A tomb springs up before her closed and sleeping eyes; it's a cave dug into a hillside, and two girls are trapped within its rocky walls. Near them, lying on a stone bed and wrapped in a gray and flimsy winding sheet, is a corpse. Martha knows it's her father, although she cannot see his face.

She also understands that she's the younger of the two children imprisoned in that inhospitable place. "There, there, don't cry," she hears her taller companion say. "Mary, my dearest, don't you cry—"

"But I'm Martha," she protests with the high-pitched whimper of someone very young.

Dressed in a plain gown of old-fashioned cut, the older girl turns her back in irritable contempt. She doesn't respond to Martha's weeping pronouncement but instead embarks upon a remarkable transformation: growing gray-haired and stiff-boned beneath garments that also alter, leaving her clad in a rough woolen tunic and heavy felt shoes.

Martha witnesses this change with dismay though little surprise. "I liked your other dress better," she states, then adds a vigorous "And I'm not Mary. I'm—"

But the old woman interrupts with a bitter "First me, then you!"

IN HER FATHER'S house, beneath the layers of down and wool and freshly ironed lace, Martha doesn't wake.

The Conjurer

Emily Durand sits ramrod straight, staring fixedly into the looking glass as her maid dresses her hair for the evening: two ringlets on each side of her face; a single long braid coiled at the nape of her neck and then woven upward to be pinned in another curl at the top of her head. Within this plait is a string of pearls. Additional pearls dangle from Emily's earlobes; more grace her neck. The dress she will soon don—a new figured gauze over lilac satin—is also trimmed in pearls. Emily Durand prides herself on being an arbiter of fashion, and not only an arbiter, a vanguard of all that is glittering and lovely. The home in which she now allows herself to be attired, and that she shares with her husband, John, reflects this attitude. The pallor of her skin, the soft blondness of her hair, the proud manner in which she carries herself, her well-chosen gestures, her walk: all attest to a lady of noble birth but with decidedly cosmopolitan leanings. Emily is a queen in the realm that is social Philadelphia.

"Good" is all she says to her maid as she observes her image with a critical eye, trying out various poses to make certain she shines from every angle. The maid might as well not exist, so unconscious is Emily of an audience. Or perhaps the audience is precisely what she craves.

"Is my husband ready and waiting?" Emily touches the tip of a finger to her left eyebrow, leaning closer to the glass and glinting into its surface to make certain she looks as perfect as she should.

The maid watches in frozen apprehension. Oh, she doesn't want to begin redoing her mistress's locks at this late hour! Or preparing another gown. Or laying out more laces and ribbons and gloves. Or shaking out the long Russian plumes that continuously make her sneeze. Let alone pulling out all those shoes. Or the manchettes or capottes or the mantillas trimmed with fur.

"Is he?" Emily repeats. Her voice is sharper now, and the maid jumps as though startled out of a heavy sleep.

"Yes, madam. I believe Mr. Durand is already downstairs."

Emily nods briefly. The maid moves away to fetch the dress while her mistress remains enthroned, her beringed hands resting gracefully on the chair's arms, her gaze imperiously watching her mirror image.

Then all at once, something terrible happens to Emily Durand. She looks into her own hard, blue eyes, staring past the color, past the lauded almond shape as if her sight were tunneling inward, seeking out her deepest thoughts, her soul.

Emily is rooted to her place. The self she sees she doesn't know; the cheekbones and mouth are those of a stranger, the elaborate coiffure that of a mannequin, the neck like one belonging to a statue. There is no comforting, familiar woman to be found. Emily blinks, but the foreign creature merely blinks coolly back. Disdain drips from her countenance. Then the disdain suddenly melts into aching sorrow. The mirror eyes seem on the verge of weeping. Emily observes this weird permutation with something akin to terror. It will not do to have her maid see her so distraught, so ungoverned, so lost.

She grips the chair tighter and tighter, and when the satin gown is at length produced, she springs up with a greater degree of gaiety and verve than her maid has ever observed.

"I'M WORRIED ABOUT that young woman, Frederick," Henrietta Ilsley is saying to her husband, the renowned professor of Greek and Latin at the University of Pennsylvania. Ilsley is a man of imperious intellect, his white beard long and carefully manicured, his eyebrows patriarch-like and prominent. Only little Henrietta dares address him with such temerity and ease, but that is the result of a marriage that has lasted more than thirty years. "After all . . . Well, I would have imagined some trace of her father would be discovered before now, awful though the truth might be . . ." The remark remains unfinished.

Professor Ilsley gazes down upon his plump and fretting wife. He doesn't speak, and so Henrietta continues as if she were in conversation with herself.

"I must call upon her and extend my condolences. I wonder, is she still residing at Beale House, or has she repaired to her father's residence in town?"

Although her husband realizes that no reply is necessary—Henrietta will soon ascertain Martha Beale's whereabouts—he finally stirs himself to answer. The tone is deep and sonorous, a voice accustomed to respectful audiences. "I've been told she continues to dwell in the country, my dear. After all, it has only been three days since—"

"A mistake, Frederick. A bad mistake. A reclusive young lady like Martha Beale needs friends. Especially now."

"She has Owen Simms to comfort her."

"Oh! Owen Simms, indeed! What solace can a man like Simms provide? She needs to be about in the world. Attend concerts and so forth, musicale evenings and such like. Indeed, she should have been successfully married and out of her father's domain long ago." Henrietta gives her husband a pointed glance. She looks so much like a mother hen that for a moment he wonders whether she's about to peck him. "Beale should have urged her to wed when she was still in her prime and not in her middle twenties. Late twenties, I should say."

"Perhaps he didn't wish it, Henrietta."

"Nonsense, Frederick. All parents wish the best for their children."

"That term is open to interpretation, my dear little wife. It could be that Lemuel Beale considered it 'best' to have his sole child and heir remain under the safety of his roof rather than see her committed to a marriage that might not have been a fortunate one."

"A most selfish motive, Frederick, in my opinion. Besides, marriages, either good or ill, are the creation of two people, not one—"

"That is not always the case, my dear," her husband interjects, but Henrietta ignores the interruption.

"And now, with her father missing, how is she to move about in society? Certainly not upon the arm of Owen Simms!"

This time Ilsley succeeds in silencing his wife. "My dear Mrs. Ilsley, we don't know the circumstances surrounding Martha Beale's current or past state. I therefore caution you to take care before interfering."

Henrietta tilts her round and speckled face. "I do not interfere, sir. Rather, I am *engaged.*"

"Ah, an interesting turn of phrase, that. *'Engaged.'* I must remember it when I seek to quibble with a colleague." Frederick Ilsley says no more on the subject, and neither does Henrietta.

She has a good deal on her mind this evening, and her household is aflutter with nervous anticipation. This is no time for semantic jousting with her husband. She turns her back on her spouse's statesman-like form and gazes anxiously across the dining salon of their home.

None other than the heralded conjurer, clairvoyant, necromancer, and somnambulist Eusapio Paladino is to join the Ilsleys' weekly *soirée.* Securing his presence at the party is a decided coup for Henrietta and has enabled her to finally obtain the promised attendance of the prickly Emily Durand.

In preparation for this singular event, Henrietta has memorized every facet of Paladino's career: how when he appears in a public arena, his popularity forces him to maintain the strict perimeters of the stage lest audience members despairing of lost husbands or runaway wives attempt to storm the platform with requests for aid; how he communes with stones, walls, even lamp shades all the while averring in his native Italian *"Mi Parlano,"* "They speak to me"; and how, most thrillingly, in Buffalo, New York, during the previous winter, Paladino's psyche was invaded by the executed murderer Mack MacGuinness, who screamed out in guttural English, "They hung me and scooped out my brains! Damn the doctors! Damn the preachers! Damn them, and bring them to me in Hell!"

With the aid of the conjurer's assistant and translator, and of the Ilsleys' servants, the dining room that Henrietta now examines has been transformed. Gone is the simplicity of the Federal-era home; gone the view of gas lamps and the measured greensward of Washington Square; gone the world beyond. Because Paladino can only communicate with the departed in dim light (the dark containing the "negative energy necessary for such discourse"), black velvet drapes have been erected to cut the room in half. The oak dining table has been repositioned at the center of the remaining portion, while near Eusapio's chair are placed, in artful significance, a guitar, a tambourine, and a zither. The requisite writing slates and pencils are laid flat in the center of the table, which has also been draped in black.

Henrietta circles round and round with her short, hurrying steps, overseeing, checking and rechecking. Every detail must be correct if the conjurer is to commune with the spirit world. But Henrietta has another and more private motive in seeking the talents of *Signor* Eusapio Paladino. As the sole survivor of a goodly number of siblings as well as two parents who left a firm mark upon their offspring, she yearns to have communication with her vanished family. At the age of fifty-three, she feels this hunger growing daily.

"Do you think, my dear—?" she begins, then answers the unfinished query herself. "No, we'll put Emily there . . . and John here . . . It would never do to place a couple in too close a proximity . . . At least, that is the fashion in the Durands' circle."

"I concur," her husband says. He stands at some distance from her, surveying the scene as though from an Olympian mountain height.

Henrietta pays no heed to his reply. "'*Gauche*' would be Emily's term, I believe." She smiles briefly as she envisions that grand lady's haughty visage. "But what is your opinion, Frederick?"

"On the word '*gauche*'?"

"Good gracious, no! On whether we should breach those rules of etiquette and seat husbands with their wives—merely for the conjuring, of course. Not for the supper following."

"I'll leave that decision in your hands, my dear."

Henrietta smiles again, albeit uncertainly. "We'll follow the Durands' lead, then."

"A wise choice."

"Goodness, look at the time. Our guests should be at the door in mere moments!"

"Everything appears in perfect readiness." Ilsley's sage face nods.

"Yes." Henrietta sighs. In fact, her home suddenly looks far less than ideal: the Queen Anne furniture outmoded and plain, the carpet showing age, the chandeliers too simple and unstylish. She's beginning to severely wish she hadn't been so presumptuous as to include such a sharp critic as Emily.

At length, Henrietta pushes those fears aside and adds a quiet "I do so hope *Signor* Paladino can aid me in securing news from my dear sisters and brothers in the spirit world . . . and dear Mama, as well . . . and Papa. That odious Countess de St. Dominique whose séance I attended last year was such a bitter disappointment."

"She was not of the first order."

"A fraud, Frederick," his wife admits quietly. "I do believe the lady was a fraud . . . Ah, well, I believe I hear the door."

Less than a minute later, the Ilsleys' foyer is a hive of activity. Driving mantles, hats, bonnets, and fur-lined gloves are whisked off and carted away by footmen while the guests begin to gape unabashedly at one another as their garments are revealed. Little Florence Shippen, Henrietta's cousin and dearest friend, breaks into a peal of high-pitched and nervous laughter as she smoothes her wide skirt with two pudgy hands. "Pink *gros de Naples*! And in this weather! I feel as though I've been transformed into an actress upon the stage. I might as well be wearing a dressing gown in public; it would only be a trifle less appropriate than this summer gown—"

"Ah, my dear," her hostess responds, "you're attired in perfect harmony with *Signor* Paladino's commandments. His assistant informed me that by wearing the lightest of pastel shades the ladies will consume dangerous 'positive energy'—which will permit our mesmerist to work unhindered. It's the same reason the gentlemen are requested to display an inordinate amount of white collar and cuff."

"*Signor* Paladino will be the only person dressed exclusively in black?" The question is posed by the sumptuously clad Emily; her voice is brittle, her smile polite but commanding. Everyone gathered in the foyer, including her husband, reads censure in the question.

"And his assistant, naturally."

Emily's blue eyes glitter down. "Of course."

Florence Shippen blinks at the assembled company; the tilt of her head has turned defiant and brave. Florence is a great champion of her cousin. "This is a thrilling occasion you've afforded us, dear Henrietta. We ladies must aid *Signor* Paladino in any manner he deems fit—even if it means wearing summer attire."

It's Emily who answers. "Let us hope *Signor* Paladino has as much success with his clairvoyance tonight as you with your wardrobe."

"Oh!" is Florence's stunned reply. "You do like it, then?"

Emily merely smiles her chilly smile. She looks around her at the old-fashioned rooms and dull little group and wonders why on earth she accepted the invitation. The query makes her stand more erect, causing her to appear far more terrifying to her hostess.

The twelve men and women—the same number, following Eusapio's orders, as the Apostles—move into the converted dining salon and seat themselves around the table in accordance with their hosts' design. There are comments upon the unusual appearance of the room, upon personal anxieties and apprehensions, upon the many reports of Paladino's successes, and, naturally, upon Lemuel Beale's mysterious disappearance. The rumors that there may be more sinister work afoot than an accidental drowning is on every tongue.

But as the company talks, the minutes tick by and Paladino fails to arrive. In his absence, a worried and self-conscious restraint settles over the group. Henrietta notes this change of mood immediately, and she graces her guests with a number of placating smiles in the hopes of reassuring them that the evening is proceeding precisely as planned. Despite their hostess's effort at assurance, the guests begin to eye the tambourine, the zither, the guitar, and the writing slates in growing discomfort while they clasp and reclasp white hands upon the ink-black table. The tall-case clock in the corner ticks, tocks, ticks until John Durand clears his throat and suggests that they question the conjurer about the financier's peculiar circumstances. "As a test, don't you know?" he states in the plain and unadorned speech that's as much his trademark as his wife's is formality and artifice. "We'll put some words on one of those magical slates. No point in our venturing personal information until we know where we stand with the fellow."

"I was hoping that I might myself begin" is Henrietta's tenuous reply; and all but the Durands immediately concur. Lemuel Beale must wait until their hostess is satisfied that she has reached her long-lost family.

After nearly an hour of further conversation in which Henrietta minutely describes her adored relatives, Emily takes it upon herself to critique the conjurer for behaving so inappropriately. "I find it an outrage, dear, dear Henrietta, that this . . . Paladino should be so tardy. After all, he's been hired to entertain us. Not we to dance attendance upon him."

"Oh!" is her hostess's wounded reply, and Professor Ilsley's snowy beard quivers in protective empathy.

"It appears that Mrs. Durand is a skeptic of the clairvoyant's art." He leans back in his chair, affixing her with the caustic stare he gives his students.

But Emily is his match; she bends her tall, bare neck in her habitual pose of calculated flirtation. "Not necessarily, sir. Mesmerism, conjuring, and artificial somnambulism are *comme il faut, n'est-ce pas*? Ladies and gentlemen of society must acquaint themselves with all current fashions. It's no different than studying silver hallmarks or family pedigrees."

Florence Shippen squeaks in her chair while their host continues to survey Emily Durand.

"But you are not a believer?"

"I am neither a believer nor a nonbeliever, Professor Ilsley. Breeding prevents me from taking a stance on any situation remotely cultural or political" is Emily's airy response.

The door to the salon blows open at that moment, and two men dressed in black evening attire enter. One is of medium height and of such transcendent grace and beauty that he seems to float forward rather than walk. His companion is miniature and elfin, twisted about the shoulders and neck, his high, thin chest bone poking upward within his waistcoat and jacket. "Rise for Eusapio Paladino," he manages to wheeze, and the Ilsleys' guests swiftly struggle to their feet.

Eusapio turns his limpid gaze on Emily Durand. "Emily," he says in densely accented English. *Aimilee.*

Shock at such effrontery causes Emily to momentarily lose her famous *sang-froid;* she sends a startled glance in Henrietta Ilsley's direction. The hostess merely responds by blinking astonished eyes. *No one suppled* Signor *Paladino with the guest list,* the look conveys. To Henrietta's thinking, the fact that he knew Emily's name is proof positive of his powers.

"*Aimilee,*" Eusapio Paladino repeats more softly, then indicates that he wishes her to sit at his left, while their hostess will be seated at his right.

Emily looks at her husband, but he merely shrugs his own surprise and disbelief; and so she allows herself to be dictated to by a total stranger. An unknown man who has used her given name! She knows she should protest; she knows John should protest on her behalf. Both courtesy and pure bewilderment prevent her. She assumes the same motives are the cause of John's inaction.

Placed as she's been told, with the others also arranged around the table, Emily suddenly feels Eusapio's ankle pressing against hers. Her eyes widen; her heart pounds; she forces herself to sit erect. The pressure on her foot increases, and she experiences a panicky impulse to appeal to her husband, although, of course, such a reaction would throw the party into utter and unspeakable confusion. She chews the inside of her lip. She cannot bring herself to look into John Durand's face.

When Eusapio takes her right hand and Henrietta's left, Emily's mouth grows dry, and her lips feel as though they're about to crack in pieces. "Join hands—every one upon the table," she hears the necromancer's assistant order. "We will begin with a single question, which you will write on one of the slates. Then turn the slate downward. The words will remain unknown to *Signor* Paladino. If—I stress the word *if*—the spirits speak to him, he will transcribe their responses on the other slate. However, you must understand that the great Paladino is not always in communication with the departed. If there are unbelievers present, vanished souls are hesitant to appear."

Emily keeps her gaze affixed to the table, but not on her hand residing in Eusapio's own. If she had the strength of will to pull it away, she would, but her fingers no longer feel like her own. In fact, a more disturbing reaction occurs, and she begins to secretly enjoy the warmth of Paladino's hand. She wills herself not to shut her eyes in shame.

Then Florence Shippen's husband, a gangling and beak-nosed barrister, takes up the slate, passing it to their hostess, who writes in a shaking hand: HOW DO YOU FARE, DEAREST MAMA? The guests note the question, then return their attention to Paladino, who has remained aloof, staring thoughtfully into space.

"Aimilee," he repeats in a sleepy tone. His ankle and calf rub against hers; his fingers furtively caress her palm. "I see little girl," he says in halting English while looking beyond Emily Durand's shoulder as if there were another person standing there. *"Bimba bianca."*

"Little blond girl," translates the toad-like assistant.

"Oh, but I was never a blond—" Henrietta begins to state, but Eusapio's assistant silences her with a hiss.

"Bimba bianca . . ." Eusapio murmurs. *"Bimba triste . . ."*

Beneath her dressed yellow ringlets, her braid entwined with pearls, Emily feels her scalp prickle and her forehead turn damp while her husband shifts his boxy frame in a creaking chair and clears his throat:

"What's this got to do with—?"

"Shhh," the toad orders. "When the great Paladino speaks, it is a wonder."

"Bimba triste. Perché piangi?"

"Sad little girl. Why are you crying?" says the translator as Emily finally turns to face Eusapio. In fact, she's now holding back tears, and she knows her face has turned scarlet with emotion.

Paladino gazes serenely at her, then suddenly jerks his head back; his hands leap away from the women's and fly to his neck. A strangled noise issues from his throat, then a scream that ends in a wail. "I am here! Do not search further!" Bobbing within half-closed lids, Paladino's eyes, entranced and otherworldly, race across an invisible horizon.

"Who is here, *signor*?" Henrietta Ilsley murmurs. "Is it my dear mama?"

Meanwhile Eusapio begins quivering in his chair, rocking spasmodically as if someone tall and cruel were shaking his lissome frame. "Damn you! You cannot kill me!" he shouts; and at once, in unison, the guitar, zither, and tambourine begin to play in wild and villainous discord.

"Hell has entered this home," Florence Shippen whispers while her hostess repeats a plaintive "But my dear mama?"

Ilsley glares at Paladino's assistant. "This is most irregular—" he commences in a stony tone as Eusapio all at once collapses, ashen-faced and terrified, upon the floor. He works his mouth and claws the air, but no sound appears. Finally another male voice speaks through him, the tone smooth but autocratic. "Don't carry on so, Mary, child. It's better that you do not speak. Silence is golden in girls and women."

John Durand utters a loud "What nonsense . . ." but the interruption goes unnoticed by the mesmerist, who then sits bolt upright, staring long and hard at Emily. *"Morto. Maria, morto. La sua linguetta sul origliere."*

WITH PALADINO FINALLY led faint and weak from the room, and dispatched with his assistant to their hotel in the Ilsleys' coach, the group reconvenes around the table. Unprompted, each hand is again spread upon the black velvet cloth; and it is the sight of so many pale fingers and such an expanse of lightly colored cloth that makes Frederick Ilsley at last voice his outrage.

"A hoax," he insists as he gazes in concern at his deflated wife. "A patent fraud."

"How can you suggest such a thing, Frederick? The man was deeply moved . . . although by whom we cannot know . . ." Henrietta closes her eyes; she sounds dangerously close to tears. "Do you think . . . ? Do you think it could have been Lemuel Beale to whom—?"

"Not a bit of it, Henrietta," her husband commands.

"But, Frederick, the voice was so very like—"

"A ruse, my dear. And I need not remind you that we must not permit ourselves to become the promulgators of such odious gossip."

"But, Frederick—"

"We must not allow rumor and innuendo in this house, Henrietta."

"Yes, Frederick, however—"

"The man is a fake, Mrs. Ilsley. We need say no more on the subject."

The company fidgets in embarrassed silence following this pointed exchange before John Durand announces an authoritative "I agree that the Italian is an awful charlatan." Then he shifts his attention to his wife. "Why did you let him single you out in that disgusting fashion?"

Emily stares implacably back. Not for the life of her will she permit herself to be drawn into a public argument like the Ilsleys'. "I was hoping to induce *Signor* Paladino to further revelations," she states in a controlled tone.

"Well, I don't like to see a wife of mine hobnobbing with some unwashed foreigner."

"Then please accept my deepest apologies, John. I did not intend to cause you dismay."

If anyone notices how odd it is for Emily Durand to apologize to anyone or for anything, no one remarks upon it.

Then Ilsley waves at the air with irate fingers. "Paladino and his 'familiar' were the only souls dressed in black. The playing of the musical instruments was no more than a magician's exercise; we didn't see human hands strike them because our concentration was directed elsewhere, and the arms creating that unholy din on the zither, guitar, and tambourine were cloaked in black to match the drapery—"

"But he knew Emily's name," Florence Shippen interjects meekly.

"He must have had access to our guest list" is the professor's quick retort. "It is not unknown, albeit unpleasant, for servants to gossip about their masters' affairs."

"But what do you infer *Signor* Paladino meant when he said that . . . that a tongue was placed on a pillow?" Florence persists, her fleshy shoulders now shivering in a combination of horror and excitement.

Ilsley clears his authoritarian throat. "Do you speak Italian, madam?"

"Why no, Professor. That is, only what I learn from the occasional libretto—"

"Then how can you—or any of us—be certain of what was said?

A girl named Mary with her tongue laid upon a pillow. That makes no sense whatsoever, does it, Mrs. Shippen?"

"This is not the type of conversation that should occur in a decent household," protests Henrietta with a small moan. "Bodily parts discussed in connection with the bedroom, and such like . . . Oh, I'd so hoped . . ." The words trail off. Henrietta Ilsley has no further speech.

Her husband regards her; compassion vies with matrimonial dominion, and he continues in a tone that brooks no further comment. "Heaven only knows what that mountebank was attempting to frighten us with—"

"But what if he were truly conjuring Lemuel Beale?" Florence Shippen murmurs, at which point her host abruptly rises from his chair.

"I extend regrets from my wife and from me for a most unproductive evening. And now, if you will excuse us, we must bid you good night."

The other guests immediately take their cue, standing and offering words of thanks, but Emily remains apart. *Bimba bianca,* she thinks. *Perché piangi? Perché?* Unwittingly, her glance travels to a nearby looking glass, but the mirror has been shrouded in velvet for the evening's entertainment.

As Far as the Delaware

Lemuel Beale isn't found, although local constabularies from the several divisions that form Philadelphia's disparate police forces search both sides of the Schuylkill's storm-tossed banks, and even venture out upon the swollen river in punts and barges.

Thomas Kelman orders the joint effort; he's tireless in his involvement, calling in favors, even soliciting the help of the notorious fire companies: the brutally competitive gangs in Southwark that travel under the names of "the Moyamensing Hose Company," "the Weccacoe Hose Company," "the Killers," and "the Irish Fenian Brotherhood." When a simple kitchen blaze can produce a conflagration capable of razing many acres of property, the "fire boys," tough, swaggering, hard on their horses and even harsher with rival gangs, are a necessary evil.

Thomas Kelman makes use of these difficult men, promising twenty gold dollars to the single person or company that finds Lemuel Beale. It's a princely sum and a great enticement; unskilled labor earns only sixty-three cents a day—when work can be found.

South and east, from the wild woods of Falls of Schuylkill all the way down to the river's tempestuous confluence with the greater Delaware at marshy League Island, men in boots and storm coats tramp for four solid days. They find the carcasses of cows, sheep, and pigs, and the partial torso of a horse tangled within the branches of a huge and fallen oak, its eyes still staring among the sodden acorns. There's no sign of Beale, although the effort does turn up the water-bloated body of a drowned hermit, thickly bearded and ageless—one of countless such people living in hiding within the city's outlying forests.

Weary, footsore, angry at being cheated out of the promised reward, the members of the fire brigades are the first to desert the quest, marching away from the city's twin rivers in bands that fan out through Gray's Ferry, Southwark, and Kensington. They nurse numerous grudges against their fellow searchers—especially the police forces, whom they view as being too holy for their own good.

Above all, these men bear a special hatred of Thomas Kelman, who they believe dangled delusions and fantasies in front of their eyes. They grumble that Kelman knew he'd set them an impossible task, that the "mayor and his legions of hellhounds" lie behind the charade of a search for a man obviously well buried in the river. Then their wrath swells to encompass Lemuel Beale and every "snatch and grab" like him: Matthias Baldwin and his damn locomotives, Nicholas Biddle and his vile bank, the vaunted Rittenhouses, Levis, Whartons, Cadwaladers, and "all the other swells who run the show."

Thomas Kelman pays the grumblers no heed. His profession has put him in contact with many people; some are good, some are not. Rich men steal and lie no less frequently than the poor; it's just that their numbers are fewer.

For his part, he's deeply disappointed in the results of the massive search—but not altogether surprised, although the matter of the missing rifle continues to niggle at his brain. He senses something peculiar, a lost piece of the puzzle, but with so little of substance to ponder, his thoughts keep slipping into formless conjecture.

He decides to write to Martha and request the opportunity of *paying a visit to speak in private regarding Mr. Beale.* The wording causes him grave difficulty—which in turn produces frustration and self-rebuke. Penning a note to a lady he scarcely knows should be a simple matter. Instead, the effort seems stilted, indirect, devoid of humanity, although he wants the missive to sound ambiguous, as if he continues to hold out hope of success.

In fact, he has none. Lemuel Beale has vanished, and either his body remains still river-bound, submerged in some dam created by rock and waterlogged debris, or else the flood has carried him into the Delaware—and so out to sea. Or perhaps there is some more malign explanation.

My Dear Miss Beale, Kelman's awkward note concludes, *I hope I may call upon you this afternoon.* A boy gallops off into the countryside with the letter, and four hours later hurries back with a reply.

Miss Beale is indisposed. She is not receiving visitors.

Kelman turns the response over and over in his long fingers. The handwriting isn't a woman's—appropriate enough if she's ill and able to dictate only. But the terseness of the message pains him; he feels his face flush and his neck muscles tighten. Unconsciously, he touches the scar on his cheek, then thrusts the letter away, heaving it angrily onto his crowded desk, from where it falls, forgotten, to the floor.

Martha Beale is no better than the rest of her breed, he tells himself. Wealthy, heedless of others' emotions, she has no more warmth or compassion than a statue sitting in a park. Naturally, her reaction is of the shallowest nature. Why, he wonders, didn't she instruct her scribe to include a monetary gift as the final insult? She and her pinch-hearted father can go to the very devil.

"I WILL GIVE you a new name," the man in the fur-lined cloak tells the girl. The narrow city alleyway on which they stand is dank and chill, devoid of all light and life. No omnibus passes; no merchant journeys homeward; not even a solitary beggar boy can be found in the derelict space.

"I will call you Mary," the man continues in a lush and soothing tone, "the beloved of Christ. Will that make you happy?"

The newly dubbed "Mary," small, lithe, with a child's reckless grace, nods assent and is quickly enveloped in the hot and perfume-soaked fur.

"You have a place to take me, do you not, little one?"

With her face pressed against the man's chest, the girl nods again. She opens her mouth to speak, but he wraps gloved fingers around her lips. "Do not speak," he says. "It's better if you do not . . ."

Ladies of Pleasure

"I already told you two gents I can't describe him. Or haven't you been listening to anything I've said?" Dutch Kat's tone is beleaguered and irritable, her words directed not to the tall man who introduced himself as Thomas Kelman but to the police sergeant who stands squat and bulldog-like at his side, his uniform stretched tight about the belly and shoulders as if an actual animal rather than a person were inside. "He wore a fur-lined greatcoat, a tall beaver hat same as any other gent, and some type of colored scarf that just about concealed his face. That's all I saw. I don't generally waste my time on the customers my girls bring in from the streets. I've got regulars, I do, and they like a bit of fancy entertainment now and then. The kind of sophisticated show we did back in the old country—"

"Height?" the sergeant interrupts as he writes Kat's paltry description in a small, smudged book. "Weight?"

Kat sighs archly. "We've been through this all before, constable. Middling to tall—or maybe not. He had a hat, as I said, so it could have been the hat I was noticing. He and Claire passed through the front door, then they made for the stairway fast. I never heard him speak. As to whether he was heavy or thin, I couldn't possibly tell you."

"Claire." The sergeant makes note of the name while Kat continues to regard him. His nose, she decides, is exactly the color of watered wine. And about as attractive, too.

"No point in writing that down, either, Sergeant. It wasn't the girl's real name." Dutch Kat all but sneers this piece of information. "The kid said she was called Claire when she landed on my doorstep begging for work. I knew it was a lie, and a dull and foolish one at that. Solange would have been better, or Inez. My customers like a taste of the exotic. As I said, we get foreign gents here on many an occasion. *Noms de guerre* one Frenchman told me the names was. He's the one who dubbed me Dutch Kat—'a woman as ripe as a Holland cheese.' I'm from over there, myself. From Zwolle. I don't remember anything special about the cheeses, though. The ale, that was another thing." Kat studiously avoids looking at Kelman as she speaks. Something about him is beginning to unnerve her. Maybe it's his silence, or maybe it's the faint scar that slivers along his cheek. He looks like a dangerous customer even though she can see that he's quite clearly a toff. For the life of her, she can't understand what a man who's not a policeman is doing snooping about her establishment; and Kat is supremely uncomfortable with paradoxes.

"No, and I don't know her age, neither," she says in reply to an additional question posed by the sergeant. "Look, if I'd had all these facts and figures at my fingertips, I would have said so downstairs and saved myself the trouble—and you two gents, as well. She was young, though. Ten, maybe, or eleven. And then there's that silly name, like something in a nursery song. It didn't help her gain regular customers, I can tell you."

"It looks like nothing helped her," the sergeant observes.

Dutch Kat releases another long sigh, and she and her visitors continue crowding into Claire's small and rank-smelling room. The sergeant again writes in his ledger while Kat swings around to face Thomas Kelman, then immediately regrets her decision. "I don't wish no trouble with the law," she mutters, attempting to crinkle her eyes and flutter her lashes in a practiced picture of naïveté. The expression only makes her look deceitful and cunning, while the effort greatly increases her distress. Men like this fancy gent don't have any place in Kat's fancy house.

"Not a clue," she huffs in reply to the sergeant's next question: this one concerning the girl's parentage. "Sold by her father to some wealthy gent, I'd imagine. I get a lot that's been sold—then released by their masters to fend for theirselves. The men that buy 'em don't take 'em for long—once they're no longer babies, that is. And it's simple enough to purchase another kid." She shrugs her ample shoulders. " 'God helps those that help theirselves'; that's what the Good Book says, ain't it—?"

Another question interrupts her, and Kat's tone turns more belligerent. Her fleshy bosom heaves. Ill concealed beneath a lace and cambric bodice that is none too clean, her upper body gives off an acrid odor like cold boiled cabbage. "No, I did *not* inquire what her family name was, constable!" she all but sneers. "Oft times, the girls don't know, neither. We're not all blessed with fancy pedigrees—or didn't you know?" As she says this, she forces herself to stare at Kelman, who returns her suggestive gaze without flinching.

Kat has a sudden mind to grab for his crotch; it's a lunatic notion, and she finally and truly grins at the boldness of the thought. Her front teeth as she produces this garish expression are intact and very white. No matter that the rest are gone; it makes for "easier business." "You're a right gentleman, ain't you, mister?" she demands of Kelman. "I can always sniff them out. What I can't figure, though, is what you're doing poking around down here on lower Lombard Street. Don't you get enough pickpockets and footpads bothering the fancy folk over on Washington Square?"

Kelman doesn't reply. Instead, his black eyes regard her intently. Kat, shorter by far, unkempt, unwashed, feels herself squirm under the relentless scrutiny. "Can we finish this up?" she demands. "I got paying customers waiting."

"We can haul you in as a common scold," the sergeant growls. "The Criers' Docket has plenty of those. Adultery, too."

"Don't make me laugh!" Kat throws back. "'Common scold.' I'm only saying my peace as a law-abiding citizen." Then her pugnacious façade again begins to crumble under Kelman's steady perusal.

Inadvertently she touches her rumpled curls. She knows they need coloring; years and strain have turned their former blond to patchy gray, and she imagines him gazing down into the mismatched thicket as if surprised at such a multitude of colors. "This is a clean house, Dutch Kat's is," she states in defiance. "We're recommended in the *Guide to the Stranger*—only forty-four of us fancy houses made the list. Most exclusive, the publication is. The pamphlet's carried in the best hotels and lodgings." This last statement ends as a sort of appeal. She looks to Kelman, but he makes no response.

"Can we finish this up?" Kat repeats with a nervous giggle. "It's a chill night out, and I have gents waiting for my better girls. Men like a bit of warming on a bitter winter evening like this. Now, I could supply you two with something to cozy you up. We'll get this palaver over first, and then—"

The sergeant shakes his florid nose, then blows it on a rumpled bit of linen. He looks tempted by Kat's offer; Kelman does not.

"That's not the Bible you're quoting," he says in a tone of such resonance that Kat unexpectedly thinks of church bells. Church bells in a house for ladies of pleasure! "The words were penned by Benjamin Franklin—"

"As I live and breathe." Kat forces a snicker. "Our fine guest's got a tongue in his head after all!"

Kelman stares down at her. "And you can't tell us who did this?" he finally says, his fingers indicating the bed. Not one pair of eyes follows the gesture.

"I already said I hadn't a clue, didn't I, mister?"

"But there must have been something you noticed, madam. A slight limp or a manner in which he carried himself that might have indicated his age . . . whether his face was broad or thin . . . there must have been some discernible mark—"

"He was wearing a scarf and expensive coat. That's all I can tell you. Look, if I'd known what mischief he was up to I wouldn't have let him in, would I? I'm a business woman, not a monster." Kat spits out these words. "And it will be a right mess to clean it up, too! A nice mattress, that, horsehair. Feather pillows, too. They're pricey bits, and bloodstains don't disappear with soap. Lye soap, neither." Dutch Kat snaps her ruined teeth in frustration, then stabs the floor with a grubby foot. "Country girls! They're more bother than they're worth."

The sergeant again makes an entry in his book. "You're certain she was a country lass?" he asks.

"Look at that hair, why don't you, constable? Blond—and plenty of it. And her skin! Not a mark upon it. Leastways, not one made by nature. You don't get that type here in the Fifth Ward or the shacks north of Cramp and Sons Shipyards. Them girls is small and gray as rats, but they don't kill easy."

She stamps her heel as she speaks, and the vehemence of her movement shakes the bedstead. Kat and the two men look down just in time to see Claire's naked body slide downward to lie in a small, angular puddle on the dusty carpet. Murdered, she was posed half on the bed, her arms bending forward gracefully, her head turned gently sideways, and her thin, young legs trailing floorward as if sleep had overwhelmed her at her prayers.

Finding Claire thus dozing during working hours, Kat had first upbraided the girl for being "stuck on religion." Then she noticed the red-black sheets, the deep gash slicing the neck, and the child's pale tongue placed like an offering on a separate pillow.

Cherry Hill

CHERRY HILL" IS WHAT THE locals have dubbed the place. The name is accompanied by a twisting set of the mouth that indicates a combination of contempt and terror, because Cherry Hill is no longer the broad and bountiful cherry orchard that once sat atop a promontory at the bucolic northern outskirts of the city, but a penitentiary for Philadelphia's convicted criminals. None inside, neither the warders nor those sentenced to repent their crimes in solitary confinement, call the prison Cherry Hill, however. But then those who reside within its stout stone walls seldom speak. Absolute silence is the prison's rule.

Absolute silence within ten acres of land that's been divided into a central rotunda from which emanate cell blocks, a kitchen and laundry, a surgery, kennels for the Great Danes that guard the walls, a vegetable garden, and a pump house where dray horses pace endless rotations. Built a brief thirteen years ago in 1829, the complex officially called Eastern State Penitentiary is a miracle of modern invention; warders monitor each cell door through a series of mirrors that image interior corridors, and so maintain an appropriate air of monastic repentance and mute reflection. The notion that isolation and prayer can teach murderers and thieves alike to atone for their crimes has made the prison a famous place not only in the nation but abroad. All foreign dignitaries and European *artistes* touring Philadelphia insist upon visiting it.

But the prison is also notorious for its stench. Human waste is flushed through the great drains twice a month only; when flooding or heavy rains occur, the sewers regurgitate inside the cells themselves, carrying drowned rats, mice, swimming toads, snakes as thick as eels. The stink permeates the air, burrows into the skin and clothing of those incarcerated and even into the great stone slabs themselves. The smell and the enforced seclusion make suicide endemic.

Ruth is one of the newer inmates. She's nineteen, or thereabouts, a free Negress, not a runaway slave; and nearly three years of her life have been spent in a tiny, barrel-vaulted cell with a food slot cut in the thick oak door and a slit roof-window. Unlike her male counterparts, who are provided with private outdoor spaces as well as indoor beds, females are assigned to only one interior room for the duration of their term. The architects who designed the building reasoned that men, being muscular, needed light and air; women, even those confined, were to be protected from the elements at all times.

Ruth was once a maid-of-all-work. Caught stealing potatoes to tote home to her sickly baby son—he was born doubly afflicted: a victim of the falling disease, and offspring of a white father who forced himself upon her one unlucky day—she was released without references, a sentence nearly tantamount to death.

With her mulatto child in tow, she returned to the Negro ghetto bordered by South and Seventh Streets, doing what meager work passed her way, existing on meals of scraps and refuse. When she could no longer afford even a sleeping place on a vermin-infested floor, she bundled up her son and quit the ghetto, taking to the streets to beg pennies off the well-to-do whose warm and lamp-lit homes adjoined Washington Square.

Begging proved problematic. To the abolitionists, Ruth was an object of pity, sometimes even of sympathy, but to the many newly arrived Irish who struggled with their own poverty and unemployment, she was a pariah. Men and women alike spat upon her, kicked at her baby as he lay sleeping in her lap, called her a "sambo" and her son an "antichrist" while they glared at her child's paler skin and the features that looked so much like her nameless oppressor.

Ruth cowered under the threats, remembering every horrific moment of the riots of the 1830s when entire houses along Fitzwater and St. Mary's streets were burned to the ground, and neighbors dragged off shrieking into the night. She'd lost what little she had of family in those dark times.

Driven by hunger, despair, and the mewling cries of her son, Ruth finally gave up begging in favor of a nervous kind of thievery; she would dart between market-bound farm wagons so that the bellowing drivers were distracted, and objects from their varying cargoes could be removed by nimbler and more daring fingers than her own. A ham, a bushel of peaches, flour stitched into a sack: The goods would be shared between Ruth and her accomplices.

Her baby, quivering and glassy-eyed when the fits came upon him, limp and slack-lipped after they'd passed, ate and grew.

Finally arrested and pulled before the slumbrous-voiced and heavy-lidded Judge Alonzo Craig, Ruth stood tight-faced and silent, and was sentenced to Eastern State Penitentiary for three years. "Larceny" and "the receiving of stolen goods" were her twin crimes. Incarcerated, she was to experience regret for her evil ways; fortnightly and with an unseen teacher, she was to be engaged in learning the rudiments of reading and figuring, as well as mastering the skill of sewing. As for her child, a stranger took him from the courtroom;

he was two years old, and as he walked away his body heaved with terrible tears. When he stumbled, the stranger dragged him forward. That was the last image Ruth had of her little boy.

"'Whither thou goest, I will go,'" she now murmurs in the smallest of whispers. Her voice feels strange in her throat, like that of one who is deaf. She sits on her cornhusk-filled mattress, upright, hands resting on her lap. The warders, whose shoes are muffled with swaddling, are adept at peeking through the cell eyeholes just in time to catch and punish profligate behavior: handiwork dashed to the floor, words of protest, rage, and grief scribbled on the whitewashed stone walls.

"'And where thou lodgest, I will lodge: thy people shall be my people, and thy God my God:'"

She begins the lines again. "From the Book of Ruth," the Quaker lady told her during one of her visits. The choice of Scripture was inadvertent; not knowing the prisoner's name, race, creed, or age, the woman sat in the corridor, speaking quietly and unseen through the door slit where food is delivered daily. "The Old Testament. Thee must learn thy Bible, child."

The lady's queer Quaker speech remains in Ruth's ears: thee, thine, thou. "The story tells of the widowed Ruth," the woman continued in the same hushed tone, "who journeys with her mother-in-law, Naomi, to dwell in an alien land, and is then raised up by marriage to the wealthy and powerful Boaz. Ruth will become the great-grandmother of David, the king. I tell the story to teach thee about overcoming adversity. Ruth was a loyal and loving woman; she did not succumb to temptation nor to vice as thou hast—"

"I am Ruth," Ruth had suddenly blurted, although she knew that sharing her identity was as forbidden as talking aloud.

The Quaker lady remained silent, then finally responded with a constrained "Thee mustn't speak or say thy name. Only the warden can know thy history. It's for thine own good, girl, so that departing this place, no one shall guess thy past. That is why a sack is placed upon thy head the moment thee enters the gates—"

"But I'm also a Ruth" had been the stubborn—although hushed—reply, but the lady rejected the effort, proceeding with a placid:

"And why thou art conveyed to thy cell blindfolded, why thee and thy fellow penitents are dressed in identical and prison-stitched clothing, why thou dost not know among whom thou lodgest: male, female, old, young . . . Thee must remain B415 to me."

"I am Ruth," was the sullen and louder answer, "dwelling in an alien land."

"Thou blasphemest, child. Now keep silent, or the warders will force me to go."

Remembering this exchange, Ruth feels her eyes narrow and her fingers clench. *Thy people shall be my people, and thy God my God.* She bows her head. Whose God? she wonders. Whose people?

Something that sounds like a club bangs sharply against the cell's wood door. The onetime maid-of-all-work leaps up, surprised to see her meal tray sliding inward through the food slot. In her three years in Cherry Hill, she's never grown accustomed to the arrival of her keepers.

She takes the tray but doesn't attempt to peer through the opening. According to prison rules, no words are exchanged. Brown bread, water, a dented metal bowl of meat gristle: She carries the meal back to her bed. The whale-oil lamp sputters, emitting a choking, fish-innard odor that for a moment masks the all-enveloping stench of the prison.

Thy people shall be my people, she tells herself silently, then, unwittingly and against all better judgment, thinks of her son, her little Cai. Almost five years old, he would be now. Five years this winter. But whether he lives or whether he has died, Ruth doesn't know.

WHILE RUTH COWERS in the upper reaches of the female wing, another prisoner practices his walking in his own quiet cell on the ground floor of the men's wing. He's a slight man, thin-boned and sprightly, save for one terrible flaw. He was born with a club foot. Or, rather, no true foot. Where his right heel should be, he has only an ankle, the vestigial right toes curling up backward around a scrawny calf.

Unlike Ruth, he's white and because he's male has been assigned both a cell for sleeping and a solitary one for exercise. The advantage of such beneficence is lost upon him.

Long ago and despite his affliction, he glimpsed a better future for himself. He envisioned a man of modest means, his own small shop (he was a tailor by trade before his arrest for thievery), and a wife and children dwelling comfortably above his place of business. He pictured a weekly supper of roasted meat, a jug of ale upon the table, neighbors to whom he spoke and among whom he was admired.

From his earliest youth, he worked toward this gilded dream, teaching himself to walk erect and tall, not giving in to his withered right extremity. When he turned eight—he was called Dicket back then—he strapped the first of many hand-hewn sticks to his leg. His father by then being dead, his mother apprenticed him to a tailor. It was the last Dicket saw of her or of home.

His tailor-master renamed him Josiah, as his own name was deemed too juvenile for the trade he was entering. The tailor was a religious man beside being a shrewd one.

When Josiah reached sixteen, this master died, leaving his estate in ruins and his apprentice adrift. Josiah strapped on a "good" leg and walked carefully—and without a crutch—through the town seeking a new position. By then he'd learned to attach an empty shoe to the stick, to wrap the harsh wood in cotton batting, to stitch on a clean stocking. The bogus foot often looked better than the real. Josiah's secret remained his own.

The slim beginnings of prosperity ensued, and Josiah (now a hired man) dared to take a wife. She produced a daughter, a pink and round-faced child almost perfect except for her predominant brow. *All babies have big heads,* Josiah told his bride. *Susan will grow into hers like every other infant.*

The child proved him wrong. Her head grew and grew; her body followed fitfully, turning fat where it should have been long, her shoulders rounding into pasty lumps, her hands lying listlessly at her sides. She rarely reached for objects as other children did; instead, her eyes became milky, staring at nothing. When her mother held her, spittle ran from the little girl's mouth; when her parents tried to teach her the sounds and meaning of speech, she merely gurgled and drooled all the more.

Josiah's wife grieved, then grew angry. Alone with her baby she berated the child's sluggishness, her inattention, her vapid quiescence. The bitter words turned to pinches, then furtive slaps. Susan mewed like a hurt kitten and retreated further into her silent world, while inside the mother's head, frustration and wrath roared louder and louder.

Spilled porridge, lost milk, a broken dish: One of those infinitesimal moments brought ruin to Josiah's wife. When the child's insignificant transgression had concluded, mother and daughter eyed each other, the dawning of understanding etching terror on the child's face, endless hatred on the mother's.

Josiah's wife snatched up her baby, shaking Susan so fiercely that vomit belched from her mouth. Finished, the mother flung her daughter and herself on the pallet that served as mattress and commenced to wail, then shriek, and finally to beat her head against the wooden floor.

It was the noise of this rhythmic self-destruction that eventually brought the neighbors and the day watch who removed the screaming woman to the Asylum for Relief of Persons Deprived of Their

Use of Reason. Susan, motionless except for her quivering fingers, accompanied her mother in the wagon.

When Josiah returned home, his tiny apartment was all but bare. When, days later, he was finally allowed to visit his wife and child, both were as dumb and immobile as clods of earth. He left his false foot in the Asylum's carriage entry, kicking it away as if driving off a vicious dog, and limping home on the remaining stick, the "peg."

One month passed, then two and three. His daughter gradually improved to her former state; his wife did not. Josiah, in his distraction and despair, stitched sleeves shut, buttons without holes, breeches that could not close upon the calves.

He was released from service, but not before pilfering a gentleman's fine pocket watch. The white face set in gold reminded him of his daughter's visage: round, flat, its outward calm masking a world of spinning motion. Recklessly, Josiah held this lovely object to the sun, studying it as it turned, like a budding flower, toward the light. It was then that he was arrested.

Just as Ruth recites her own litany of want and despair, daily Josiah relives every moment of his wretched descent until the stones of the prison walls seem to begin to move closer, the barrel-vaulted ceiling to sink, and the floor to rise beneath his feet. Even the brief glimpse of sky seen from his solitary exercise cell appears oppressive and sinister, as if about to collapse down upon him. He knows that if he doesn't escape from this place he will turn as mad as his lost wife.

So he makes a daring plan, saving scraps of cloth from the yardage supplied for his prison work: a frock coat for the warden and a driving mantle for his wife. Josiah intends to stitch himself a dark jacket, lighter trousers, a white cravat to wrap elegantly around his neck—and a shoe made of heavy felt.

Dressed in this finery, he aims to scramble up and over the wall of his exercise yard just after a band of visitors has passed. If luck holds, he will mingle with them. When they leave the prison grounds, he will be in their midst, his only problem the reek that emanates from a prisoner's skin, but he believes this will remain unnoticed until he's free of the compound itself.

So Josiah waits, counting the hours and days until he hears a large group of visitors approach, practicing how they respond to their guide's remarks, reiterating the facts and numbers he's already heard from other tourists, oohing and aahing in copied awe and approval. ". . . The kennels for the Great Danes . . ." He imagines himself murmuring appreciatively to those around him. ". . . Walls thirty feet high, ten feet thick at the base, and buried twelve feet beneath the earth . . . How extraordinary . . ."

What he never rehearses is his final farewell to the place that's been his home for five long years.

A Refuge for the Poor

THE ASSOCIATION FOR THE CARE of Colored Orphans has been in existence for five proud years. The women who created it and who annually seek contributions for its benefit are among the chosen of the city: a Lippincott, a Morris, a Biddle, a Yarnall, a Cadwalader. These ladies envisioned an orphans' refuge at Thirteenth and Fitzwater streets—among the poorest of the poor—and their ardor and hard work have wrought a miracle: a comfortable place with scrubbed pine floors, wide windows, and plenty of fresh, invigorating air.

The gifts the women accept on behalf of their young charges are (when not ready cash) of a healthful, instructive nature: dried peaches, bags of beans, pocket handkerchiefs, stockings, sweet potatoes, and a map of Africa—which is a place so foreign that the foundlings who gaze upon it believe it is a chart of the heavens.

"This is from whence you came," the orphans are told. But they aren't about to be hoodwinked by a colorful picture. They know where they've come from: the cramped alleyways of the Seventh

Ward, the docks of the Fifth. Many of the orphans remember their days upon the streets; some even remember having mothers.

Sixty children are housed at the home on Fitzwater Street. When they're old enough—and fit enough—they're "bound out to respectable families." If the experiment is a success, so much the better. But if the effort fails, the foundlings rejoin the younger children in the classroom where Holy Scripture is recited daily and where the basic skills of reading and writing are taught and practiced.

Dr. Caspar Walne is the good man who presides over the orphans' health. Like the ladies who sit upon the Board of Governance, he's white and of the city's ruling class. Unlike them, he's in his later years, a venerable presence with a shrinking frame and a wistful expression as if remembering the words to a poignant song.

It's to the Association that Martha Beale is bound. Too many days cooped up out in the country have impelled her to quit Beale House in favor of her father's equally handsome city residence—and thence toward the activity she's long been denied. Thus while Thomas Kelman prepares to leave Dutch Kat's fancy house on Sixth and Lombard, Martha—robust and healthy despite the information he received to the contrary—exits her carriage a mere eight blocks away and prepares to enter the orphanage.

The elegant rig, the matched pair of chestnut geldings, the shiny brass fittings and brightly rubbed leather have attracted a sizable number of gawkers. They've never seen the like in this part of town before, and they view the carriage as a marvelous and mystical thing. The lady who descends to the street with the aid of a footman (a white man in brightly hued garments—white stockings, yellow breeches, top boots bedecked with saffron-colored tassels, a coat the color of fresh moss) is equally entertaining. As are the lady's clothes: the shoes that look like mud might melt them, the flowing pelisse that's trimmed with a green as inviting as young grass. The growing crowd gasps at the spectacle. Some surge forward to touch the apparition.

Martha shrinks back; the footman braces himself for trouble; the door to the orphanage suddenly and fortuitously opens.

"Is it Miss Beale?" This is Hannah Yarnall speaking. She's one of the most energetic and determined of the home's governors; close to Martha's age, but a good six inches shorter, her small frame and a certain recklessness of spirit make her seem far younger. "We were not expecting you so soon." Her lively brown eyes note the crowd, rapidly assessing the situation. "We . . ." She hesitates. Hannah is a forthright young woman; she's also inestimably kind. "We try to arrive here by less . . . by less obvious means . . . sharing a carriage that is not so . . . not so . . ."

"Elaborate?" Martha, deprived too long of companionship and warmth, smiles. She extends her gloved hand. "Yes, I am Martha Beale."

"I expected as much." Hannah also smiles. "And I am Hannah Yarnall. You may tell your men to go. We'll convey you home by other means. We attempt to exist quietly here."

"I'm afraid I've shattered that image." Martha's sunny demeanor lingers only briefly, then wholly vanishes.

"Portraits can be repainted" is the quick reply. Hannah leads the way through the simple and airy entry hall. Following, Martha is reminded of linen sheets blowing on a laundry line, of sunlight grazing a kitchen garden. She feels artificial and unwholesome in comparison.

"I have accoutered myself poorly for my visit," she says. Her voice is low and full of self-rebuke. *Whatever was I thinking?* she wonders.

"God does not distinguish between cloth-of-gold and calico, Miss Beale" is Hannah's soft reply. "We follow the Lord's example here. At least, we try."

The children, however, react almost identically to the strangers in the street. They gape at the new lady, pulling back in clusters of two or three when asked to state their names, while at Martha's back the daring reach out forbidden fingers to touch the soft stuff of her purple gown. Not one of them had ever seen even a doll to rival Martha Beale.

Rebecca Lippincott, the senior member of the Board—and the day's self-styled guide—frowns almost continually as the group parades through the house. She's a plain woman, her hair graying, her judgments swift. In her mind, their visitor, with her showy arrival and premature camaraderie, has disrupted the serenity of the morning's schedule.

"The sleeping quarters are above," she now says. The Board members and teachers, trailing children as if they were meteors' tails, have just finished inspecting the basement kitchen and larders. "You won't wish to see them." She pats the bunch of keys she wears at her waist: access to the cold-storage room, to the root cellar, to the hole where the coal is kept. As her fingers touch the keys, Rebecca's mind ticks off a week's worth of menus, a month of chores apportioned and accomplished.

"Oh, but I would" is Martha's happy answer. "I should very much like to see where the children sleep."

Rebecca eyes Martha's kidskin slippers and *broderie* bodice with ill-disguised disgust. She doesn't respond in words, but the bovine set of her body speaks volumes. Martha recognizes the assessment and the merciless eyes. The expression of lofty disapproval is one with which she is well acquainted. It's her father's behavior mirrored in female form. Martha's smile wavers; her shoulders slump in both apology and entreaty.

Rebecca turns away; she's accustomed to being obeyed, but Martha suddenly rebels. "I should very much like to see the sleeping quarters, Mrs. Lippincott. I will be brief, I assure you." Martha moves toward the stairs, followed by a band of children, but Rebecca stops the procession with a firm:

"The Association's charges must return to their classes, Miss Beale. Any visitor who wishes to converse with them or witness their training must adhere to orphanage rules."

"I hope to become more than a visitor, Mrs. Lippincott. I hope to join your ranks."

"The Board approves new members in a discreet and methodical manner—as does any other society of governance."

Hannah Yarnall passes behind Martha. The movement is no more than a human body walking from one place to another, a casual transfer in space and time, but Martha recognizes the gesture as one of support.

"Naturally, Mrs. Lippincott . . . I do not expect nor wish preferential treatment. I'm simply offering myself and my resources." The term "considerable resources" is on Martha's tongue. She avoids it but resumes her approach to the stairs.

"The sleeping quarters are vacant at this time of day, Miss Beale."

"I should like to see them nonetheless, Mrs. Lippincott."

"Should or would?"

Martha forces a smile. If Rebecca Lippincott's censorious stare matches Lemuel Beale's, his daughter's flinty expression now rivals his most obdurate. "Both, Mrs. Lippincott."

Followed by the compassionate Hannah, Martha mounts the stairs. Beneath her feet, the floorboards creak, the sounds amplified within the enforced quietude of the place.

The third floor houses the girls' dormitory, the fourth the boys'. Stopping in one of several rooms in the girls' area, Martha observes beds arrayed wall to wall: simple but clean pallets supported on pine testers and knotted rope. The floorboards have been soaped and rubbed until they gleam; the ceiling and walls are equally pristine, while the windows, unadorned, are fitted with devices designed to permit only partial opening.

"Curiosity is a constant worry here," Hannah murmurs. "Several of the bolder children have tried to climb out upon the roof to see the view." Despite her previous act of defiance, Hannah now maintains a deferential posture, permitting Rebecca Lippincott to precede her, and speaking only after the older woman has finished.

Martha silently examines the dormitory, noting the empty clothing pegs above the beds, the rigorous impersonality of each child's space. Not one gray blanket remains rumpled; not a pillow is out of place. All at once, the tidiness seems like a cry of terrible need; and she pictures small arms and hands at their tasks, hearts and brains vying for the teachers' attentions, hoping fervently for a kindly glance, an encouraging word. *It's remarkable, the order you maintain here,* Martha almost says but doesn't. Instead, she follows Rebecca Lippincott in ever-increasing guilt and shame. Her own bedroom, her clothing, the feckless abundance of her possessions begin to mock her in their terrible excess.

"You will note, Miss Beale, that the children do not own playthings," Rebecca Lippincott is saying. "We believe that personal possessions create mean-spiritedness and greed. When our charges play, they are taught to share. Prayers and the occasional story are all that accompany them into sleep."

Hannah Yarnall adds a soft "When the foundlings grow and leave us, their lot will not be an easy one. It would be unfair to provide too much."

Why? Martha wants to demand. *They're only children. They hunger for happiness and pleasure, for a loving voice. Why deprive them of playthings, of laughter? Joy is fleeting. Let them revel in it while they can.* Instead, her growing discomfort keeps her mute.

"Now we will proceed to the fourth floor," Rebecca Lippincott advises. "You may examine the boys' accommodations, and then our tour will have concluded."

Martha lags behind. The task she's set herself has begun to seem very great indeed.

"But I must warn you," Rebecca's voice continues, "that among our boy foundlings we have a child with the falling sickness—epilepsy. He was delivered into our hands a year ago, malnourished, filthy, unable to speak. Dr. Walne believed him to be two or three years old at the time, making him four or five at present—although exceedingly small for his age, as is to be expected. Racially, he is of mixed parentage, putting him at disadvantage with both Negro and white; mentally, he has changed little since his arrival. Sudden movements startle him, as do abrupt noises and confused surroundings. Knowing of your arrival, we kept him upstairs today."

"I'm not an ogre," Martha finally offers.

"Dr. Walne believes the child experienced great fear—perhaps even a form of physical torture. We take what precautions we can, although there is consensus that the Asylum will be our sole recourse as he ages. Of course, the illness is incurable."

"What is his name?" Martha asks.

"He responds only to 'boy.' "

THE CHILD IS wizened, a preternaturally grim and ancient face set upon gaunt shoulders. He gazes from Rebecca to Hannah; he doesn't smile, nor does he seem to register their arrival. Martha he affixes with a vacant yet perplexed stare; his mouth opens; he appears on the verge of attempted speech when his left hand begins quivering and then his right. His eyes glaze immediately after. The trembling intensifies and rapidly moves to his legs.

"Fetch Dr. Walne," Rebecca orders Hannah while bending over the boy's shaking body. Martha backs away, banging her head against a low-hanging beam. "I was concerned that such an event might occur," Rebecca states. "Visitors should be introduced gradually." Her tone is outraged, indicating every insult perpetrated by the callow—and idle—rich.

"Shall I leave, Mrs. Lippincott?"

"The damage is already done." Not one hint of forgiveness is present.

Martha hangs in the shadows, waiting. She hears the child's body being turned over, hears his back patted with a sharp, staccato rhythm, listens as the soles of his feet are slapped and his name called out. "Boy! Boy! Here, boy!" What she never detects in all these ministrations is love.

Dr. Walne arrives, followed immediately by Hannah. A tub is produced, water sloshed into it, the child's body immersed. Martha maintains her vigil among the shoulder-high beams. She has all but vanished from the group attending to the damaged child.

Her response to their efforts is panic; she feels her heart congeal while her head swims and her mouth turns dry. *I cannot do this,* she thinks. *I'm not strong like these other women. I have no vocation, no skills. My father, as usual, was correct. And Thomas Kelman also. What the poor need is food, not pretty notions.* For a moment, she's afraid she might be sick, and then realizes with equal horror that her light-headedness is accompanied by icy hands and feet. She's about to faint. As quietly as she can, she lowers herself to the floor. *I'm useless,* she tells herself. *I'm a failure.* Dry-eyed, she bends her head and stares at the floorboards and her billowing skirts. Self-loathing stabs at her chest.

Minutes pass. The crisis diminishes; the unnamed boy gradually improves. Finally, Hannah turns to Martha, surprised to see her sitting upon the floor. "Miss Beale? Are you quite well?"

Martha looks up, making a poor attempt at reassurance while Rebecca Lippincott's square face begins to glow with the recognition of her vindication. "We at the Association are accustomed to these scenes, Miss Beale. Cut heads, fingers slammed in doors, the usual childhood accidents. This house is no place for a person unhappy at the sight of blood—or other untimely discharges."

Martha doesn't answer. Rebecca continues, her expression almost seraphic. "This work is not meant for us all, Miss Beale. Although it was pleasant to have you to visit, I'm sure."

"I WILL WALK," Martha has told them, shaking off the urgent protests that the neighborhood is too neglected and slovenly, too dangerous for a white woman to traverse alone. "It's but half a mile or so to my father's city dwelling," she protested, all but backing down the orphanage steps and into the street. "The fresh air will do me good."

"But your fine shoes," Hannah argued, and Martha finally understood precisely how ill conceived her gesture of goodwill has been. *Shoes! What do I care for my pretty shoes? What do I care if the hem of my mantle drags through refuse and mud, or my dress is soiled and ruined? Why did I wear such impractical things? Why, indeed, do I possess them?*

So she sets forth, marching first north toward Lombard Street. She never looks back at the orphanage, just as she tries to avoid seeing the denizens of the street. She knows only that she needs to be among her own kind. She needs to return to the comforting cave of wealth, security, and power. *Let the good Samaritans of the world attend the unfortunate and destitute,* she tells herself. *I have not the stamina for it. I have not the heart—or the talent or the skill or the intellect.*

But those excuses are suddenly and woefully challenged by a familiar voice calling her name.

"Miss Beale? It is Miss Beale?"

Martha's face flushes red. "Mr. Kelman!" As she utters the hurried words, her foot sinks into a malodorous stew of horse dung and ancient refuse, releasing a stench so potent she reflexively closes her eyes.

Automatically, Kelman reaches out to aid her while she, just as unconsciously, leaps back, leaving them both standing silent and awkward on the dingy street.

Finally, Kelman speaks. His tone is formal and clipped. "You're making good your promise to give aid to the poor, I imagine?"

"No," Martha replies in deep chagrin. "No . . . I am not."

"But—?" Kelman looks past her. He recognizes the orphanage in the distance.

"I fear that I'm late for an appointment, Mr. Kelman. You must excuse me."

Kelman draws into himself; the memory of her rejection flashes hot through his brain. "Of course. I did not intend to detain you."

But Martha doesn't move. Instead, she blurts out an unhappy "You said you'd help me find my father."

Kelman eyes her coldly. "And I remained true to my word, Miss Beale."

She looks at him; mistrust and hurt play upon her face; resentment darkens his.

"The note I wrote you stated as much, Miss Beale. My men worked for four solid days, and far into the evening hours, as well." He pauses, then states a bitter "I trust you are now quite improved from your indisposition."

"What indisposition, Mr. Kelman?" is her startled reply. Then she adds a slower but equally perplexed "I never received a missive from you."

Unanswered Questions

"MR. SIMMS," MARTHA ANNOUNCES THE moment she enters the double withdrawing room of her father's city house, "I've just come from a chance encounter with Mr. Kelman. He claims to have written to me while we were yet residing in the country, only to have his message rejected with the news that I was indisposed and so could not personally accept his report on the search for my father." Martha doesn't know what else to add to this statement, so she stands upon the carpet, waiting. Her shoes are wet from her tramp; one is most probably ruined, but the state of her footwear is less troubling than this mystery.

"I suppose one of the servants took it upon himself to act on your behalf, Martha."

"But who would do such a thing?"

"I have no notion, I'm afraid." Simms is slitting open Lemuel Beale's letters as he speaks, his mind clearly on matters of greater consequence than this minor domestic question.

"I'm quite surprised that anyone at Beale House should imagine he could speak for me."

Owen Simms looks up for a moment only. There's a placating but distracted semi-smile on his face. "I assume the act was done in order to protect you, Martha."

"But I don't need protection, Mr. Simms. Not of this fashion."

Simms finally puts down the correspondence. "Of course you do, Martha. You're in the midst of an extraordinarily trying time, and I and everyone else in your small sphere must do all we can to support you."

"But I asked Mr. Kelman for his aid, and then—"

Simms stands and walks to her side. For a terrible moment, Martha fears he's about to embrace her. She instinctively steps backward, but even as she does so, she wonders what it is about her father's confidential secretary that so unnerves her. Then, with this query comes an offended *I'm the mistress of my father's household, am I not? In his absence, I am . . . I should be, shouldn't I? . . . and act accordingly, too, and be treated as such* . . . But those bold notions die away, as usual, leaving Martha looking merely confused and ill at ease.

Simms, naturally, cannot read her mind, and his tone continues both caring and faintly chiding. "You see, Martha, my dear! I hope you recognize how overwrought you've become. You leap away from me as if I wished you harm, which I assure you I do not. Until this tragic mystery of your father's disappearance is resolved, you must allow me to act in his stead. He would wish it. You know he would. Your protection and safety have always been his chiefest concerns."

"But I've been rude to Mr. Kelman," Martha persists. "Or rather, someone has been rude on my behalf."

"I wouldn't concern yourself with the likes of Thomas Kelman, Martha. For all his purported political connections, he's really no better than a local constable."

"But he did organize a search for Father." Martha knows she's losing ground in this interview; she feels it slipping away beneath her feet as though the room had turned mountainous and steep. It's precisely the pattern of her many conversations with her father: *But why may I not participate in a drawing class for young ladies? Why am I forbidden to attend the opera with you now that I'm old enough? Why may I not consider a proposal of marriage—or even encourage a young gentleman to look upon me with favor?* Her requests were frequent; the response always that she was too inexperienced to understand precisely what she was demanding of her parent. "When the time is right," her father had advised again and again, "when what you wish, dear child, is reasonable and sensible." *Reasonable and sensible!* If it were possible to dislike two words, Martha knows she would chose those.

"And so Kelman should have done. Without you asking him." Owen Simms returns to Lemuel Beale's affairs while his daughter knits her fingers together in frustration.

"But you discouraged him, Mr. Simms. You said—"

"What I said was that the river was in flood and the currents treacherous; and that I did not envision how any man—even a man as hale and robust as your father—could survive a plunge into its depths. I remind you, Martha, that I was repeating what many others had also asserted." Simms's voice has taken on a harsher tone, one Martha has never heard before. Then all at once, his anger—if it was anger—dissipates, and he again regards her with pensive concern. "And what was Mr. Kelman's conclusion following his search?"

"He and his men found no trace of Father."

"Yes, I know." Simms opens another letter and begins to read it.

"You knew, Mr. Simms?" Martha asks, but he's become so engrossed in the page before him that he fails to respond. "You knew?" she repeats, then waits, although she realizes she doesn't expect an answer. Of course, Owen Simms, as a man, would be privy to many situations she would not. It's how the world runs.

Simms surprises her. He puts down the letter. "I had hoped to spare you, Martha. I had hoped that we might hear more conclusive news, and until such time, I felt it incumbent to safeguard your very sensitive heart." He pauses. "This citified life is not conducive to your mental equilibrium, I fear. Perhaps we should retire again to the countryside. What do you say to that? Wouldn't you rather be in that more healthful environment?"

All Martha's mind's eye can envision is the ice-encrusted river and the lanterns bobbing along the shore as they began the search for her father, but she answers with a weary "If you wish it, Mr. Simms."

"It is for you that I desire it . . . Good, then. We will depart in the morning. And what work I must attend in town—Well, that is not for you to fret over."

AS MARTHA CONCLUDES this uncertain conversation and wanders upward through her father's city house, Emily Durand yanks open her own bedroom door, then pauses on the threshold observing the corridor, staircase, and part of the foyer below. Not a soul is in sight, not a sound is heard unless it's Emily's rapid breathing and the pounding of her heart—which seems to her very loud indeed.

As quickly as she opened the door, she closes it again, then stands leaning her forehead into the painted wood, which feels cool and soothing to her perspiring face. She has received a private letter from Eusapio Paladino, suggesting he has a message he needs to impart to her in person. What this might he, Emily doesn't know, but the very fact that he has written to her—and that she has kept the wretched thing—has become a torture. *Perhaps he wants money,* she tells herself, *perhaps he imagines because I didn't flinch away from his clandestine attentions that I am one of those sophisticates who crowd the European capitals: ladies with lovers, and husbands too occupied with their own amours to care. Well, I am not one of those immoral women; I'm a pillar of our American society; I was born to be one, and it is incumbent upon me to maintain the role for which I was raised.*

Even as she makes these grand arguments, Emily realizes how

specious they are. Excitement and danger are precisely the sensations for which she yearns. *Why else do I purchase clothes that outshine all others'? Why else the constant need to be the most* au courant *of my set, to make the cleverest remarks, to dance so close to the disapproval of staid Quaker Philadelphia? And what paltry substitutes are those for the real things!*

Emily's brain is now so thoroughly anguished that she presses her body closer to the door until its soothing resilience pushes against her breasts and thighs. The comfort she receives seems almost human, and she closes her eyes, releasing a groan of anguish and need. *No, I cannot leave my house on this absurd mission. I must cling to the life I've embraced. What I'm experiencing is an aberration only. It will pass. Don't I have all that I wish: a lovely home, a husband who respects me, more than ample means by which to guide my pleasant life?* Yet even as these arguments spill forth, others make their sly, subversive way forward, and her eyes fly open to stare into her room as if trying to discern the future.

But why should I be discovered visiting the conjurer's rooms? Who's to know whom I see or where I go? John doesn't dog my every step. My maid and my other servants come at my behest and no sooner. I'm Emily Durand, not a piece of chattel or a child who must be watched over and guarded. I'm a woman of means; I'm the mistress of my own affairs, and if I'm careful—Here the private monologue abruptly veers into more negotiable terrain:

I will visit the conjurer this one time only. I will go out of curiosity—and because to shy away from such a proposal would be cowardice. And I have never been—nor ever will be—accused of lacking in bravery. One brief journey to the Demport House Hotel: Surely that should be a trifling matter for someone like me?

Even cynical Emily is unaware how dishonest these promises are.

The Future Glimpsed

I'M TELLING YOU, ROSEGGER, KELMAN is—"

Owen Simms's host makes an abrupt and silencing gesture while his wife continues fussing over the tea table, slicing aniseed cake and adjusting lemon slivers as if those tasks were the most crucial in her life. Her white lace hair dressing and demi-gloves—mittens, as she calls them—flutter through the brown and murky air of her husband's private study. "Mrs. Rosegger," he says after some additional moments of china chinking and silver tinkling, "you may leave that." The accent is guttural and demanding. Despite the fact that he is no longer Austrian but American, that he speaks English flawlessly and has prospered hugely in his elected homeland, Rosegger's words still sound like orders issued by an old-world patriarch. The room reflects this view: only two vapor lamps lit; the new cast-iron stove that resembles a Gothic castle providing heat but no cheery hearth-light.

Rosegger's wife's knitted fingers instantly fall to her lap. "You will send for me, Mr. Rosegger, should you desire additional hot water—or something stronger, perhaps? Some port or a sherry wine?" Unlike her husband, Mrs. Rosegger is a native Philadelphian, but she has a curious manner of searching for words as though she weren't certain they were acceptable or right. "There's a cold roast in the larder, as well, I believe . . . venison, I think it is."

"We will need nothing further."

At that conclusive statement, Mrs. Rosegger makes a quick, polite bow to her husband's guest and withdraws. Her face is flat and emotionless, although in the corridor the mask breaks apart, and she gazes with both bitterness and fear toward the closed door before tiptoeing back to stand beside it, pressing her ear to the keyhole.

"You were informed that no trace of Beale was found? Well, what of it, Simms? It's a large river to be searching for a single man," she hears her husband say in his deliberate, hectoring tone, and then his guest reply with an agitated:

"You're taking this very smoothly, sir."

"Unless you bring me news of more substance, Mr. Simms, I have no other choice." Rosegger's wife knows that sound of his speech well. It's intended to discredit and demean. "And I fail to understand why—"

"I don't trust Kelman," Owen Simms interjects. "I don't know why it was necessary for him to be involved."

Rosegger permits himself something that sounds like a dismissive laugh. "A person as important as Lemuel Beale—"

"Dammit, man, I know all that! But facts don't make this situation any easier. Why can't he simply accept the obvious, that Beale drowned?"

"It sounds to me as though he does, Mr. Simms. It also seems to me that you may be of a different opinion."

"Why should I be?" is the angry retort, then Simms's voice abruptly ceases, and his steps begin treading purposefully toward the door. Rosegger's wife shrinks back within the corridor's shadows as the key is turned decisively, and her husband's door is locked. "Of course Beale drowned. The day watch has stated as much . . . but this . . . this hope that Kelman continues to hold aloft for the daughter—"

"You call it hope, Mr. Simms? I would not."

"Have you no heart, man? The young lady is most distressed. In fact, I have already made arrangements to remove her from the city tomorrow morning. She needs the wholesomeness of country air."

"Perhaps what she needs is her father, Mr. Simms."

Whatever Owen Simms replies, Mrs. Rosegger cannot discern; it's a sound that travels through the door as a growl only. If there are words attached, they elude her. Then silence seems to envelop both men.

"I told you I was in, sir," Simms states at length, but his tone remains bitter and surly.

The reaction to these words is a smug chortle. "In lieu of your master. Yes, you did . . . But I needn't remind you that fifty thousand dollars is a good deal of capital for a confidential secretary to raise."

"Are you doubting my abilities, sir?"

"I'm merely observing that Lemuel Beale must be a generous employer. A generous employer who is now either tragically drowned or—"

Owen Simms releases an angry breath.

"Am I not summarizing the situation sufficiently to your liking, Mr. Simms?"

The answer is slow in coming. The tone remains sullen. "What about the cost of the breaking and screening equipment?"

"Included in the original price of two hundred thousand dollars."

Mrs. Rosegger hears Simms fairly gasp at the number; in her silent place at the door, she suppresses her own astonishment at so enormous and unattainable a sum.

"But what assurances are there, Rosegger, that the city will require our company's services? The Northern Liberties is not an area that would seem to warrant modern amenities such as gas lighting and sewer lines."

"It will."

"You seem very certain."

"I am, Mr. Simms. I am."

When Beale's secretary doesn't respond, Rosegger eventually continues. "As you know, Henry Derringer, the firearms manufacturer, is up there. Resides in the area, too. On Tamarind Street. Some other fellows I know also keep houses there, private places for entertaining certain personal guests. Then there's Globe Mill, which has forty-seven looms in operation. One hundred sixty men and women in their labor force, and more than twice that number of children. Naturally, it pays the mill owners to employ locally so that time spent away from the looms is minimalized—"

"People who work in mills don't require gas lighting—"

"Perhaps not. But that isn't the point, is it?"

Simms remains silent, and Rosegger's calculated voice moves steadily forward:

"Let us agree—as you formerly noted—that many, nay, *most* of the denizens of the Northern Liberties dwell in a pestilential wasteland with domiciles too near the tanneries, ironmongers, and so forth. But let us also agree that the city is fast becoming the workshop to the world. Gas lighting should surely be available to all its citizenry. Not only the Derringers and other moneyed men of our fair town—"

"Which in turn produces the *appearance* of prosperity and health, do you mean, sir?"

Rosegger laughs lightly. "Which appearance, in turn, induces manufacturing companies to increase, and their labor forces to grow—"

"And the rents on leased property to double or even triple."

"Or more," Rosegger agrees, then adds an amiable "It's a shame that your master has vanished from the scene, Mr. Simms. Both he and I own sizable parcels of land in the Northern Liberties. But then, you must be well aware of his numerous investments."

Simms responds, but his voice is too soft for Rosegger's wife to hear—as are the exchanges that follow. She is beginning to quit her post when a newly energized and incisive question issues from her husband.

"What do you know of John Durand, Mr. Simms?"

"Why do you ask?"

"No reason."

"Come, man, be frank. Does this subject have some bearing on the other?"

"Durand wishes to meet with me. His letter indicates a good degree of urgency."

Then the voices hush again, and Rosegger's wife is suddenly aware that one of her children is summoning her, and that the importunate voice is coming dangerously near to where she is hiding.

COVERED HEAD TO toe in a hooded wool mantle of a weave and texture neither obviously costly nor overtly plain, Emily Durand slithers into the Demport House Hotel on lower Chestnut Street. It's a grand place, spankingly new, full of gilt and velvet and damask. She lowers her shrouded head in quick recognition of just how perilous this rash decision is; she almost decides to flee but then realizes that she's unwittingly attracted the attention of a number of patrons—all male, of course. Hotels only rarely cater to lady guests. She can feel rather than actually see the men regarding her, and she stands, frozen and powerless. It's a sensation Emily has never before experienced.

The smells and sounds of transitory male bonhomie fill her nostrils and ears: pipe tobacco, smoked herrings, onion tarts, shouted opinions, and a coarse and braying laugh that she's certain is aimed at her. *The man assumes I'm the hired companion of a hotel patron,* she tells herself; and the thought makes her heart beat violently and blood race into her brain.

She hurries across the crowded reception room and almost leaps upon the double stairs, where she must purposely slow her stride in order to avoid running upward. Within the thin kid of her glove, the hand grasping the banister is drenched and icy. Emily gasps for air; her vision blurs; she pushes on. By the time she reaches the hotel's third floor, her body is almost not her own. She hurries to the end of the corridor and raises her hand to knock upon a door.

THE TURNKEY TWISTS the jangling metal in the thick lock. Ruth hears the sound and shrinks back against the stone wall until her body is almost fused with its rough surface. Beneath the thin wool of her garment, she feels rock jab at her flesh.

"Won't do you no good," she hears as the man removes the key and enters her cell. With him come the light and the view of the corridor, the sight of other doors, the miracle of noise. Ruth's eyes dart past the turnkey; she hears an iron pot banging against a wooden surface; she hears a singsong moan issuing faintly from a cell to her left.

"Won't do you no good trying to hide there."

Ruth doesn't respond, and the turnkey throws a dark sack toward her. "Cover your face," he orders.

She takes it up; panic rattles within her chest. "I cannot—"

"Cannot or will not, missy? Cover your face, and be quick about it."

Ruth gazes at the guard's pale countenance. "Please, sir . . . Don't . . ."

"Hurry it up. I'm not here to gab."

Despite her own sternest exhortations to the contrary, Ruth begins to weep. "Please, sir . . ."

"Cover your head, I said!"

Ruth raises the mask. It stinks of fear. She pulls it over her hair. The turnkey yanks it into place, scraping her neck and collarbone. Ruth quivers, then forces herself to stand defiantly still. *Thy people shall be my people,* she thinks, *and thy God, my God.* Bile rises in her throat as she decides: *No, their people are not mine. I'm not like them, nor will I be. Not ever. I will be Ruth, black Ruth. I will be hard where they are soft, fierce where they tremble.*

When the guard grabs her, she shakes herself free. "Suit yourself," he barks. "You refuse to see the Warden, no one can make you, I s'pose."

Ruth's covered head jerks up.

"Thought that'd make a difference. Suspicious wench, ain't you? Thought I'd come to have my way with you, didn't you? That would be the rare day, when I'd rely on Negresses like you." He shoves her into the corridor, then looks back before banging the cell door shut. "Anything you want to take?"

Her head now thoroughly shrouded in the sack, Ruth doesn't answer.

"Suit yourself."

Awkwardly, they walk through the compound, the guard half pushing, half guiding, as Ruth tries to peek at her feet through the bottom of her mask. They cross the upper corridor where she was housed, then stumble down a steep flight of stairs that feel wet under Ruth's thin shoes. The guard propels her forward through another silent hall, then finally out into the cold afternoon air. Ruth jumps in reflexive surprise. Her head still wrapped, she looks up, imagining she's gazing into the darkening sky, the moon perhaps beginning its faint glimmer, the skeletal branches of the trees reaching longing fingers toward each other. Despite the rough fabric covering her nose and mouth, despite the stench of the prison, she smells freshness and hope. She's out of doors. For the first time in nearly three years, she stands within the sight of Heaven.

The turnkey shoves her forward, then hands her to another guard. "B415," he says to this person. "To the Warden's office." Ruth passes ahead in wondrous silence, then is pushed through a door, which shuts behind her with a bang. The space in which she finds herself is warm, scented with wood smoke, tobacco, and a metallic aroma like polished brass. She's told to remove her hood.

"Ruth, maid-of-all work, beggary, larceny."

The man (Ruth assumes it's the Warden) looks up at her from a chair that sits behind a long oaken desk. His face is as translucent as an ear of summer corn; his fair hair is silken.

"I am Ruth," she answers.

The Warden appears disturbed by her quick reply. "You are free to go," he tells her after a moment.

"Go?"

"Are you dull-witted, girl? Leave the penitentiary. Go away from this place."

"But—" Ruth begins.

The Warden interrupts. "I have no time to spare in argument, girl. You will present your prison clothing to the matron and receive, in return, the garb in which you arrived. Then the gate facing Fairmount Street will be opened, and you will be set free. It is the prison managers' fervent hope that these months and years of enforced reflection and meditation will have proven instructive, and that you will have been forever reformed from your evil ways. It is also our fervent hope that you will become what God intended, a willing and exemplary citizen of this fair city, and that you will apply yourself to wholesome work and so resolve to strive to live a pure and righteous life." He returns his glance to his desk to indicate the interview is over.

"My son?" Ruth asks.

The Warden looks up, annoyed. "I know of no son."

"My little Cai . . . He was—"

"I know of no son."

A spirit of rebellion overtakes her. "My Cai . . . He was with me in the court. A little boy with the falling sickness—?"

"Your affairs beyond these walls are your own." The Warden resumes perusing the sheaf of papers lying upon his desk. "Insolence will force the penitentiary managers to reconsider their leniency. Take care, girl." Then he adds a curt and bitter "And if you happen upon a club-foot tailor limping along in some secretive alley, you should consider it your duty to alert a member of the day watch."

"A tailor—?"

The Warden sneers. "Never mind. We'll catch the miserable fellow quick enough. He won't find it so easy to escape from this fine house." The tone that utters these words is filled with both resentment and revenge.

"Escape?" Ruth echoes in fear.

"Are you stupid, girl, that you must repeat my words? Yes, that's what our unfortunate tailor did, and the managers don't look kindly on that type of transgression. When we haul him back in, he won't find his life so easy. But you've won your freedom honestly. Now go."

What seems like mere moments later, Ruth stands in the street, a free woman. Dray horses pulling great carts rumble past. Bone-thin dogs dodge between the wheels; some hurriedly bury their snouts in fresh and steaming piles of manure; others bite the carts' wood siding as if remnants of food can be found there; all dart about as though anticipating blows and hard-booted kicks. Ruth has forgotten how noisome the city is, and how unfriendly. The day is now waning; evening will soon approach; and she has no place in which to lay her head, no coin with which to purchase her supper, no friend she can remember.

She plunges into the melee and begins the two-mile walk down into the city proper.

"AIMILEE . . . BIMBA TRISTE. *Non piangere.*"

Emily's quite dry and untragic eyes sweep around Eusapio Paladino's rooms. She spots his assistant, hunched and watchful in a corner; and the little man's pose, rather than appearing sinister and fearsome, emboldens her.

"What do you wish from me?" she demands. "If it's money, I won't supply it."

But all Paladino responds is a lilting *"Aimilee . . . Non piangere."*

"I'm not crying," Emily insists. She stands taller, statelier, although even as she strikes this pose she remembers the reflection in her mirror: the woman she didn't recognize, the one with the sorrowing eyes. "If it's gold you're seeking—"

"Bimba triste," Eusapio interrupts, and the toadish assistant hurries to translate:

"Sad little girl—"

"Yes. Yes. I know that," Emily briskly interrupts. "Ask him what he wants. I cannot stay here all day."

A swift consultation ensues; Emily cannot understand a word of it, but as she tries to ascertain its sense her eyes take in Paladino's rented rooms. She's shocked to see a large and canopied bed through the open door, and even more disturbed to note her reaction to such an inappropriate scene: "Voluptuous" is the word that springs to mind. The bed with its hangings, eiderdowns, and pillows seems as hedonistic as a pasha's lair.

So engrossed is Emily in this most unladylike response that it takes her a moment to realize that Paladino has taken her hand, and another befuddled moment to recognize that the assistant is no longer present. "What do you wish of me?" she manages to whisper, but the words have lost their urgency and force, and she can only gaze at her hand in his. She knows full well that he's about to kiss it, and that she will let him.

Oh God, her brain cries out, *what have you done by sending me into this place?* By now, she's weeping openly; she knows she should flee but also realizes that that is the last thing she wants—or is capable of accomplishing.

So Emily permits Eusapio to untie her mantle and pull off her gloves. She watches him push back her long sleeves and kiss her wrists, then smile into her face as he holds her palms to his lips. His eyes are mesmerizing; they seem to bore all the way into her. All Emily desires in this world at this moment is to trust them.

IN THE BED, obscured within a welter of silk hangings and crumpled sheets, Emily turns her face toward the man who is now her lover. Her tears are long since dried, and her apprehensions miraculously withered away. She raises herself on one elbow and begins to stroke his chest. He has the torso of a statue, she thinks, chiseled and perfect and seamlessly young. Emily feels ancient beside him.

"Bimba triste," Eusapio laughs, pulling her face up toward his own, and kissing her damp face and swollen mouth.

I am not sad, Emily wants to protest. Instead, she runs her warm hands down over his wondrous body, and he responds by wrapping his arms around her and pressing his hips into hers. *Again?* she thinks. *Do we do this again?* Not even in her most unbridled dreams has she experienced anything like this encounter.

When their bodies are fully joined, length to length, she has a sudden and disconcerting memory of her husband. He's climbing into his favorite gig with his Thoroughbred gelding at the ready. Poised, whip in hand, his broad back tensed within his driving equipage, John is a spectacle of accepted power.

"Cavallo," Eusapio murmurs into Emily's ear. *"Vedo."* I see a horse.

The Italian words mean nothing to her. "Hold me," she answers.

"Vedo un cavallo . . . Aimilee . . ."

"Eusapio," she moans in reply. She has no comprehension that her lover is envisioning the same picture as she.

IN THE MIDST of their lovemaking, Eusapio's legs suddenly stiffen and his hands turn into claws. Emily protests in words he can't understand, stroking his thighs, then taking his tightened fingers into her own. "My love? Eusapio? Are you quite well?" But his distress increases; and by the time she recognizes the totality of his affliction, he's begun to recoil from her, sitting huddled in the corner of the bed. His body trembles; every sign of his previous lust has dwindled to nothing.

"Una scarpa," he mutters. *"Senza lo piede."*

"I don't understand."

Emily reaches for him. He draws farther back until he seems in danger of tumbling through the bed's half-drawn draperies.

"Una scarpa." He points to a shoe lying on the floor. *"Lo piede."*

He grabs his own foot as if to wrench it off, then begins to stroke his toes, curling them under until they all but disappear.

"Don't," Emily says. "You're hurting yourself." She sits upright, drawing the sheeting around herself while Eusapio Paladino grows ever more irrational.

All at once, her thoughts begin focusing not on Eusapio but on her own predicament. She, Emily Durand, a married woman of great social standing, is in a hotel with a man who is neither her husband nor her peer. Her eyes dart across the room, searching for her hastily discarded clothes. *If an acquaintance of John's were to discover my presence here,* she thinks, but doesn't allow the idea to advance. Nervous sweat beads on her brow and neck and shoulders, running in rivulets between her breasts.

"Dal piede corto . . ." Eusapio marches two fingers over the mat-

tress, creating a lopsided gait like that of a person horribly deformed.

"Eusapio . . ." Emily enjoins with a stilted, pleading smile, praying that he won't cry out as he did in the Ilsleys' drawing room. "No more of this nonsense. You're not on display here. You needn't pretend. Come . . . I will be your *bimba triste* . . . your *Aimilee* . . . " She begins smoothing her hands across his shoulders. ". . . Come, no more pretense . . ." But Paladino scuttles away, jumping from the bed, then favoring one leg as if it were of no use while he stares into the room's dark corner as if intently watching someone moving there.

"Un huomo dal piede corto," he says. *"Vedo."*

Parallel Lives

"PLEASE SHOW HIM IN," MARTHA Beale tells the footman, then immediately regrets her decision as the man withdraws. The hastiness of her action seems both anxious and overt—as well as clumsy and unsophisticated. *And I should be in the withdrawing room rather than the parlor,* she reminds herself grimly. *Father would never receive a guest here. Handsome though the space is, it doesn't have the grandeur of the other. Besides, it seems . . . it seems too intimate.*

But she cannot call the footman back, and she can't go running through the corridors of Beale House hoping to reach the better room before her visitor does, and so she sighs and sits, takes up the book she was reading, but finds her hands are trembling. She returns the volume to the table, then looks at the title as if noting for the first time what type of reading matter she has selected from her father's library: *Plutarch's Lives.*

Oh dear! she thinks, *oh dear, what a mistake!* Her cheeks redden as she recognizes how overweening and unfeminine the choice seems. She reaches for the spine to turn the title from view, but before she can accomplish the task, Thomas Kelman is admitted to the room, and the footman withdraws, closing the doors behind him and leaving the visitor framed at the swagged and garlanded entrance.

Martha forces herself to sit erect and motionless in her chair: an acceptable although wholly false facsimile of a self-possessed woman. "Mr. Kelman. I'm surprised to see you in the countryside again. It's quite a journey you've made, and I thank you."

"The pleasure is mine, Miss Beale."

Both smile politely, hesitantly, noting the colors of clothing, of carpets and tabletops, of brocade and plush-covered chairs. They recognize and categorize the hour—it's approaching midday—by the amount of winter sun filtering through the high, draped windows, and they observe the yellow and gaseous light emanating from the numerous lamps. Their two faces, however, remain unexamined: a haze of pinkish flesh that the eye brushes rapidly past. When they speak again, their words fall out in unison.

"Mr. Kelman, I must apologize for that unfortunate missive you received. I questioned Mr. Simms—"

"Miss Beale, please forgive my brusque behavior in the street—"

As if they could physically retract the awkward beginning, both straighten their spines and shoulders, pulling themselves infinitesimally farther apart.

Kelman begins again. "My behavior the other day was hurtful. I'm sorry for it, and now, too late, I realize I should have written you to request this interview—"

Martha's speech breaks in upon his a second time. "You are always welcome at Beale House, Mr. Kelman. And at my father's house in town, as well, of course."

Each pauses. Each takes a breath. Each reassesses the situation.

"You were reading," he says at length. "And I have interrupted."

Martha feels her face and neck grow hot again. She glances sideways at the book as though it were a prohibited object while Kelman moves closer and picks it up.

"*Plutarch's Lives.*"

She lets her gaze travel to an inconsequential part of the room; she doesn't reply.

"Plutarch," he says again. He opens the cover and reads aloud. " 'As, in the progress of life, we first pass through scenes of innocence, peace, and fancy, and afterwards encounter the vices and disorders of society . . .' " He shuts the book quickly but doesn't return it to the table; and he and Martha remain motionless, arrested by words.

"Mighty thoughts," he allows at last.

Martha can't think what to answer, and so affects a dismissive smile that Kelman either doesn't notice or doesn't understand.

"I've disturbed your studies," he says. "I apologize." He turns the volume over in his hands; it hasn't occurred to him that she would be less than a thoughtful and well-read woman; his only surprise is that he has not had evidence of it before. He opens to the preface again.

" 'Nor will the view of a philosopher's life be less instructive than his labors. If the latter teach us how great vices, accompanied by great abilities, may tend to the ruin of a state; if they inform us how Ambition, attended with magnanimity, how Avarice, directed by political sagacity, how Envy and Revenge, armed with personal valor and popular support, will destroy the most sacred establishments, and break through every barrier of human repose and safety . . .' " He ceases his recitation; he places the book squarely on the table. "Parallel lives," he states. "*Plutarch's Parallel Lives.*" Martha can see how deeply affected he is.

"You will stay for luncheon, Mr. Kelman. Mr. Simms is engaged in the city today. I am dining alone and would welcome—"

Kelman regards her; his eyes are bleak, the scar on his cheek as silverine as water in the sun. "I have come on business."

Martha sinks back in her chair. "You have found my father's . . . body . . . I should have intuited as much when the footman announced you. But I thought when we met by chance two days past that . . ." The words trail away.

Kelman frowns. "Miss Beale, my visit was not intended . . ." He leaves the phrase unfinished, although his expression grows fiercer. "I've been insensitive. It's not usually my nature." He looks at her with quick and lonesome candor, then all at once imagines himself accepting her invitation, picturing conversation and warmth, then a stroll in the chilly and bracing air. She might take his arm as they tramp the winter-dead lawns. He would feel her breath near his face, the heat of her shoulder and wrist and hand.

He shakes the thoughts from his mind. "Did your father suffer from brain fever or any psychic abnormality, Miss Beale?"

"Immediately prior to his disappearance, do you mean, Mr. Kelman?"

"Or at any previous time."

Martha thinks. "He had no mental afflictions of which I was aware, Mr. Kelman. May I ask why you pose such a question?"

Again he hesitates. How to disclose his suspicions? How to broach the subject that Lemuel Beale might be alive? And that his drowning may have been meticulously plotted and staged? The effort of a deranged mind, or the careful conniving of a rational person with much to lose by remaining in his accepted persona but everything to gain by means of his deception.

Martha regards Kelman with her green-gray eyes. "You appear to have new information you are not revealing."

"I have some reason to hope that your father may yet be living, Miss Beale."

Martha starts in her chair. This is an extraordinary disclosure indeed. "Rescued unconscious from the river, do you mean? And recovering in some woodsman's cottage, as I had originally . . . ? Oh, Mr. Kelman—!"

"No, that's not what I mean." Again Kelman pauses, and it's Martha who propels the conversation forward.

"Then, please, sir, do tell me what it is that you intend."

Thomas Kelman weighs his words. "There have arisen reports that your father has been seen walking abroad—"

"Walking abroad! But you told me two days ago that . . . and Mr. Simms also assured me that you—"

Kelman interrupts her. "The reports may prove insubstantial, Miss Beale."

"Reports?" Martha finally notices the plural form of the word. "There has been more than one?"

"Three, Miss Beale. One claims to place your father in Philadelphia—near the commercial wharves—one in Chester, and one in New Castle, Delaware."

"And all since we last met?"

"It was only late yesterday that I was apprised of them . . . which is why I present myself to you now."

Martha considers the information; incomprehension furrows her brow, although her posture remains outwardly composed and pragmatic. "Are you intimating that my father suffered some dire blow during his accident—one that has rendered him insensible of his own identity?"

Kelman avoids the question by posing another. "Is it possible your father had an enemy he wished to escape? Or creditors?"

"I've already mentioned that I know of no enemy, Mr. Kelman; and as to creditors, surely Mr. Simms would have revealed as much."

"Is Owen Simms aware of every aspect of your father's business activities?"

"I imagine so . . ." Again Martha's brow creases in puzzlement. "But I cannot answer with certainty, as I was kept from full knowledge of my father's affairs. However, wouldn't creditors have applied to me—as Lemuel Beale's only child?"

Thomas Kelman gazes down at her, and she looks up at him, hoping for but not anticipating a reasonable solution.

"As I stated, these reports may prove to be false, Miss Beale. When a person as well known as your father disappears, there are bound to be peculiar and unfortunate tales. There are lunatics who insist they are the sole surviving heirs of wealthy and upstanding men—"

"That's a terrible consideration, Mr. Kelman . . . that someone could be cruel enough to either spread rumors or seek to resemble a vanished relation."

"The world is not always a kind place, Miss Beale."

She studies him. "So I have been discovering. But then, I think you are aware of my recent schooling." She shifts her focus, letting her eyes slowly wander the room. "Why would my father visit the towns of Chester and New Castle? If this man is indeed my father? The communities are commercial ports only. Not so great as Philadelphia, of course, although nearer to the ocean . . ." Martha doesn't finish her thought, and Kelman can supply no explanation.

Instead, he says, "It would give me great pleasure to dine with you, Miss Beale. If Mr. Simms will not object."

Martha's glance ceases its restless roving. She smiles. "Mr. Simms has left the countryside for the day. He's overseeing certain transactions at Father's offices on Third Street and will not be home until much later. Therefore, I believe he could not possibly object."

WHILE MARTHA AND Thomas Kelman dine on John Dory and ragout of lobster, on wild ducks and grilled mushrooms, on Nesselrode pudding and tartlets of greengage jam, while they talk of books and the weather, while they pause self-consciously or affix too much concentration to their plates, another scene is enacted in a very different location. The room here is small and sparsely furnished: a bed, a table, an overly large looking glass hung above it, a single chair. The sole extravagance is a pair of velvet draperies covering the window; the color of port wine, they balloon across the floor in a heavy cloud as if originally cut for a much grander opening. They are also dense with dust.

A young girl sits naked on the bed. Her little feet don't reach the floorboards. Her toes, her male companion notices, are gray. He tells her to wash them; he doesn't like dirt, he says. Of her hair, which is fair but is presently as dull and dusty as her feet, he says nothing.

The child stands and walks to the basin set atop the table. Gentlemen, she knows, are a peculiar lot. They want all sorts of strange things. But then, she realizes, ladies are often no better. Not the fine ones, anyway. Not the ones with the aigrette-trimmed hats and perfumes and silk-lined gloves.

She wrings out the cloth; the water is cold by now and cloudy; a film of grease from the lye soap shivers on the surface like fresh-forming ice. She's glad she washed her body when the basin was steaming and hot. The man helped wash her, another curiosity.

"Mary," he now says. "I must have purity at all times. You do understand the meaning of that word, do you not, my child?"

She opens her mouth to speak, but he raises his hand, the nails so perfectly sculpted, the flesh so luminous and white it makes the fingers look like a statue on a grave marker. "Remember what I told you, Mary? You must not speak unless I give you leave. You must not utter the slightest sound."

"Mary" shuts her mouth. She wants to tell him that isn't her name, that she's been called Ella ever since she can remember. Instead, she dries her toes.

"Now sit upon the bed again, my dear. And tell me again how old you are by holding up one finger for each year of your life."

In silence, Ella holds up both hands. Ten fingers.

"A lovely age," he says, and smiles.

Then he removes his shoes and stockings, and finally his trousers. The shirt and waistcoat and cravat and jacket, he leaves on. Ella braces herself; she knows this will hurt, and she doesn't like pain. The madam always tells her she's a baby to take on so, that a little discomfort is nothing when you have a full belly. But the reprimand doesn't keep the ache and sting at bay. Sometimes she bleeds, but it's not the natural monthly bleeding of the older girls. Without her being aware, Ella's lips tighten into a grimace of despair; a weary sigh rises from her breastless chest.

That quick, the man's hands are upon her throat. "No noise, I told you!" he hisses in her ear. "I must have silence! Utter silence!" Then the angry tone softens and the taut fingers relax. "Mary, my dearest, my chosen one. I didn't mean to frighten you. Tell me I did not, dearest. Tell me I did not . . . No, later. You may say a few words later when we are done."

But, foolishly, Ella again opens her mouth to speak, and again the man's enraged fingers fly to her throat. His thumbs press against her windpipe; she chokes and squirms until she wriggles free.

"You are a useless creature," he hisses in a ferocious whisper, and so Ella/"Mary" acquiesces again, curling silently back under him, terrified that the customer will refuse to pay, and that the madam will later beat her—and then perhaps send her hurtling into the streets forever. To comfort herself, she plays a "game of thoughts" that has become her recourse and consolation.

She imagines herself out the room and away from the horrible man who smells of too much soap and *eau de cologne.* Instead, she ensconces herself in a gold-washed chamber with a parquet floor and a tea table overflowing with confections and fruits. She once peeked in at the window of such a place and was astounded to see children inhabiting it: a girl of about her height in a dress of dark stuff and lace and a younger boy with long curled ringlets like his sister's. At least, Ella endowed them with the status of siblings. And she was able to watch long enough to observe how they played, how the girl was mistress, how the boy subservient, how they laughed and how the girl read to the boy from a book with colored pictures, and how icing stuck to their lips when they nibbled the cakes . . . But then the boy had spotted Ella and screamed, and his sister had followed his glance, staring unrelentingly through the glass as if willing their unwelcome observer to vanish—or perhaps to die. Then the girl had shouted something, and a man burst out the house doors with a broom as if he intended to sweep her, like trampled leaves, into the gutter.

Remembering this final piece of the scene, Ella inadvertently groans with sorrow, and the man rises up from her back, cursing. He slaps her buttocks; he hits her head, and when she draws herself into a protective ball and tries to roll away he pinches her calves and toes, spitting out a vengeful "You are useless! Useless!"

Ella leaps off the bed, naked and splotched with red handprints. "That I am not, sir! I'm a good girl. I do as I'm told."

"You don't know when to keep your mouth shut!" He follows this with loud oaths that roar into the hall.

The door to the room bangs open and the madam barges in. She simpers apologies to the man and turns a countenance on Ella that's so fearsome it looks like the maw of a watchman's dog. "Get out of this house!" she barks.

Ella grabs up the few clothes she can reach while the madam rains abuse and blows upon her, promising to procure a "quiet one for the gentleman" as she sends Ella tumbling down the stairs and out into the cold and inhospitable street.

A common man is walking by, a man with a crooked gait and clothes that remind Ella of a suit she saw on a boy doll in a shop window. "If you please, sir," she whispers.

The man keeps walking. Ella notices that his one foot causes him pain, and she pursues him as much out of need as curiosity. "Please, sir. I am cheap . . . and I am clean."

He makes no sign of noticing, and Ella plucks uncertainly at his sleeve. "I am—"

The man whirls around. "What do you want?" But the tone isn't unkind. Ella sees him gaze at her hastily thrown-on dress, at her stockingless and weather-stained shoes. "Why have you no coat?"

"If you please, sir. I'm a good girl. I do what I'm told."

"Susan?" the man murmurs after a moment.

"If you wish it, sir." *Susan,* Ella thinks, *Mary.* When will a client wish to use her true name? "Susan, yes sir. I will be your Susan."

The man stares through her. Ella waits, shivering. "No," he says at length, "of course, you cannot be my little Susie . . ." Then his eyes refocus on the child standing before him, and his face grows perturbed and angry. "Where are your mother and father that they allow you to walk about without proper covering?"

Ella can't think of an answer, and so she merely repeats a more importunate "Please, sir . . ."

"I will make you a coat," the man states, "and I will feed you. Then we shall find your family." And he takes her hand as though clasping the fingers of his own lost daughter.

Mary and Martha

Unappeased by the madam, Ella's onetime customer hurtles out of the fancy house, stalking in coiled anger into the waning daylight. The gas streetlamps—where there are lamps—emit a sulfurous and sickly glow, sending a green-yellow tinge into the thickening air. The man drags the collar of his fur-lined cloak closer to his face and pulls the brim of his beaver hat lower on his brow until only the tip of his nose is visible. His eyes and mouth are hidden.

The new girl provided by the madam failed him, too. She was too old, her hips and breasts already womanly, her glance censorious and lewd. Remembering her hard, judgmental stare, he grinds his teeth, moans, and marches on, brushing furiously against unwary passersby as he strides north out of the squalid neighborhoods bordering Lombard Street toward the more decorous region abutting Washington Square. This residential district he also avoids, turning at length down Chestnut Street toward the Delaware River.

The rowdy excesses of oyster cellars spill onto the pavement; there's the stink of decaying shells, seaweed, sawdust, and spilled malmsey wine, the screech of drunken laughter, the clatter of tin plates. From one oyster cellar an old dog bursts forth, scuttling up the steep stairs onto the street while open oyster shells, long-necked bottles, and several stones pelt after it. In his consuming rage, the man kicks at the animal but misses, and his foot, flailing at the empty air, brings him crashing and cursing down: a heap of heavy coat, a hat that dances away into the street.

A young Negro woman bends down to aid him. She wears a mantle of cheap fabric. Her legs are bare although she has shoes on her feet; and her act of compassion is unpremeditated. A human being falls; she reaches out her hand.

She steadies the man and helps him rise, then dodges through the carts and coaches and omnibuses to retrieve his beaver hat. She holds it out but doesn't leave her palm upward in hopes of a reward.

The man takes the hat and studies her, weighing her age against his desires. "You will go with me," he orders.

"No, sir. That, I will not do." She lets her eyes rest on his face and frowns. "Have I seen you, sir? Before now?"

"I will call you Mary," is the oblique response.

"If you mean to offer honest employ, sir, my name is Ruth, and I have skill as a maid-of-all-work."

The man smiles, although to Ruth the smile is more that of a starving animal than a human creature. "'Call me not Naomi,'" he recites, "'call me Mara: for the Almighty hath dealt very bitterly with me.'"

"I know naught of that. I am Ruth, and I—"

"Daughter-in-law to Naomi. In the Holy Book."

"Yes, sir. That book I know, sir. A Quaker lady read it me—all about the story of the mighty king and the part the loyal Ruth played . . ."

The man graces Ruth with a gentler smile. His passionate wrath is finally beginning to dissipate. In its place he knows he will experience the calm and pleasure of purpose. The girl in the bawdy house was a mistake. Perhaps, however, her failure is leading him to a better place.

". . . But I am no daughter, sir, nor daughter-in-law . . ."

The man's eyes half close as though in prayer. "'Mara' is so very near to 'Mary,' isn't it?" he murmurs while Ruth tilts her head, listening.

"I do believe I know your voice, sir—"

His fist rises in the air that quick, but Ruth leaps away from the blow. "You do not!" he spits out. "You do not!" Then he spins away, disappearing into the crowd.

RUTH TRUDGES ON. It feels to her that she has wandered the city ten times over since the three days of her release from prison, but there are still so many lanes and courts and alleyways to search. Finding her little Cai is her only desire. She can't remember when she last ate, or where she slept the night before.

Her hunt began in the tenements and factories near to where the Sparks Shot Tower rises above the lesser buildings: the ropewalks and brickworks, the tanneries, the slaughterhouses, the fertilizer manufacturers that collect horse droppings and dog pure from the streets and dry the ill-smelling mixture for use in the curing of hides. She reasoned that if Cai were still living he'd be of an age to perform tasks in such places. She was disappointed.

She moved on to the Northern Liberties with its textile mills and dye works, the wheelwrights and coopers of Green Street and Poplar and Laurel and St. John. There, her quest also failed. She considered continuing north again to Fishtown and the Boiler Works on Palmer, the iron foundries nearby and the glasshouses and brass and bronze smelters, but what would be the use? None but the skilled enter those premises.

In her great weariness, Ruth now sinks to the ground, mindless of the crowd surging past, mindless of the illegality of her act. With her chin nearly resting on her chest, she watches the world parade past her: the gentlemen approaching the Demport House Hotel up the street, the merchants strolling down toward the Exchange on Third. She sees them glance at her in distaste and dismay: a Negress crouching on the cobbles like some dressed-up monkey lady. *A slave,* more than a few will be thinking, *or an escaped slave whose master was foolish enough to bring her to Philadelphia while attending to business in the city. Doubtless, the wretch will soon be recaptured.*

Ruth realizes that it's only a matter of moments before a member of the day watch is called to haul her away. Perhaps she'll stand again before a judge; perhaps, return to prison.

She pulls herself erect and sets her feet in a westerly direction, but before she can take a step her attention is arrested by the sight of a crooked-legged man walking with a yellow-haired girl—his daughter, or so Ruth believes. The man's outer coat rests upon the child's shoulders while she smiles up at him and he beams protectively down. Then they move so close, Ruth can almost feel their happiness flitting through the air.

"A coat all my own?" the girl asks in wonderment. "Even though I be no Susan?"

"Yes. I will stitch a coat for you alone."

It's only after the two have disappeared that Ruth thinks to question what she's just witnessed: a limping man who can stitch a coat. Can this be the tailor who tricked the warders at Cherry Hill?

MIDDAY HAS CREPT into midafternoon, but still Kelman lingers at Beale House. Finished dining, he and Martha make a brief foray into the winter-gray gardens, where they find Jacob Oberholtzer resetting a sackcloth-covered winter frame around a bed of dormant roses. The cause for his additional work lounges at his feet—the younger of

Lemuel Beale's two dogs. Tip, the older one, rests nearby, and Kelman is struck by the tranquility of the scene: the courtesy and kindness Martha shows to the gardener, and the respect and goodwill he returns. Above all, Kelman marvels that the man bears the dog no malice but instead gruffly jests while rebuilding the frame. The words are in German, of course, but their meaning is plain. The dog bangs his tail upon the ground in a poor facsimile of contrition, and Martha laughs. With her gloved hand resting on Kelman's arm, she seems life and hope personified.

As they reenter the house, their faces ruddy with cold, Martha, on a whim, decides to show her visitor the home. "You've viewed only the drawing room, parlor, and dining salon, Mr. Kelman," she says, "but you haven't yet seen the morning room. I believe it's my favorite spot in the house. After that, I'll escort you to my father's study, and the cellars. They were built to the most exacting detail, most important for the storage of wines and foodstuffs. If I were a child with playmates, I would love to hide within them." Her smile vanishes into embarrassment. Unmarried women do not mention children.

"You have not lived here your entire life, Miss Beale?" Kelman says by way of answer.

"Oh, no. Beale House is new. Previously, we resided solely in town. My father purchased the land seven years ago and had the house built soon after. Prior to that, the area was nothing but forest interspersed with a few sparse farms."

A shrewd investment given the city's expansion, Kelman thinks, although he doesn't voice the opinion. Instead, he asks another question. "Do you regret having such a dearth of companions when you're out here?"

The query seems to take Martha by surprise, as if she never deemed it possible to challenge the choices others made for her. "I'm a private person, Mr. Kelman . . ." she begins, then stops herself and puts her head to one side, thinking. "No, that's not quite correct. I am adaptable. All human beings are, I expect. We modify our expectations to suit our surroundings and the various histories we've been given— or the histories we've come to discover." She frowns slightly. "But let me show you the morning room."

"I wonder that you do not stay in your house in town for the time being rather than remaining isolated here. Friendships, even slight ones, provide a measure of solace during times of distress."

Again Martha hesitates. "Perhaps I will, Mr. Kelman. Although Mr. Simms feels it best that we should reside here. He feels I need solitude and a healthful atmosphere." She doesn't add that her misadventure at the orphanage was the cause of this hasty decision, and naturally, Kelman doesn't ask.

"But such a remote place must make it difficult for your father's secretary to carry on his numerous business affairs."

"Mr. Simms is a very dedicated gentleman" is Martha's careful reply; then she raises her jaw as though purposely lifting her spirits and throws open the door to the morning room, allowing a profusion of flowery perfume to come rushing out. "Father permitted me this folly. It's my secret passion."

Kelman looks about in wonderment. There are tall ferns in baskets, blossom-covered vines trailing along columns, hyacinths in Chinese export porcelain jars spread upon the floor, amaryllis with white flowers, purple gloxinia, a gardenia tree in full and scented bloom, a camellia with rosy petals, and a well-used copy of Thomas Hibbert and Robert Buist's *American Flower Garden Directory* on a settee.

"I'm learning horticulture from that excellent manual," Martha explains. "It's teaching me all about pruning and repotting, tobacco smoke to combat aphids, and the wisdom of frequent sprinklings and pure air." She smiles. "I love growing things."

Kelman follows behind her as she points to the specimens, reciting their Latin names with studied care. "The *Dracaena ferrea,* the

Purple Dragon Tree, came from Mr. Pratt's gardens at Lemon Hill. The *Passiflora* did also. He had extensive greenhouses upon his estate. Mr. Buist was in residence there following his training at the Edinburgh Botanic Gardens."

"It's like being transported to a jungle," Kelman says. A slight, icy rain has sprung up, tapping the windows with frost while the wind puffs jealously at the panes. The flowers and fern fronds respond with the languid motion of pampered indifference while the heady aroma of petal and fresh leaf increases.

"I've never been to a jungle," Martha replies, "but, in my imagination, this room is all that and more. It is Eden, I think."

"It is your refuge."

"Yes." The word is the scantest whisper. Then, as if she's said too much, she changes the subject. "But you must be tiring of the distaff side of the house. Let me show you my father's study. He has some fine paintings installed there, as well as statuary."

"I'm happy here, Miss Beale."

Martha doesn't reply; instead, she looks at the windows' fogged panes, the day grown a splotchy gray, and the interior lamps reflecting muzzily in the glass, re-creating a mirrored picture of two people that is wavery and vague.

"Perhaps seeing my father's collection will aid your investigation into this peculiar mystery, Mr. Kelman," she offers at length. "Perhaps there's something of his character that you can discover there . . . or . . . or, at the very least, have some concrete personal effect with which to question . . . I hardly know what I am suggesting . . . with which to discern whether this man you have heard of may or may not be my father."

"If we can find the person—or the persons."

"Of course . . . if." Martha sighs in troubled thought, then leads the way from the morning room, retracing the route through the grand, contemptuous house until they reach the foyer and the wide and regal stairs.

There they climb toward the second floor, aware of the creak of the risers, the slow tock of the tall-case clock in the rotunda below, and their own awkward lack of speech. When they reach the landing, the front door bangs open and Owen Simms bursts into the house. His loud voice immediately overtakes them. "This is curious behavior indeed, Martha. I hope what I perceive isn't true, and that you are not conducting a gentleman caller out of the public rooms on your own."

Martha turns to watch Simms hurry up the stairs. She draws in a slow and steadying breath; her face lifts until her eyes are staring directly down at her father's secretary. "This is my house, Mr. Simms. Shouldn't I be permitted to entertain whom I choose?"

"Within reason, of course, Martha, my dear," Simms responds with a placating smile. "However, you must permit me to chide you on your father's behalf. And you are no longer a young girl to be so reprimanded."

"No, I'm no longer young, Mr. Simms. You are quite correct in your assessment." Despite her level tone, Martha's bravado begins to melt away, and Kelman can see her torn between chagrin and defensive ire.

"Perhaps I should explain the nature of my visit to Beale House, Mr. Simms—lest you misjudge the good intentions of your master's daughter. I journeyed here today to inform Miss Beale that there is reason to imagine her father may yet be living."

"That cannot be." The words jump out of Simms's mouth, and he frowns in sudden consternation.

"What leads you to believe that, Mr. Simms?"

"Your own constabulary force concluded that Miss Beale's father almost certainly drowned."

Kelman regards him. "You're correct, sir; it is the obvious assessment. But you yourself were troubled by the missing rifle—"

"Which was most probably stolen, as you and I have already—"

"Perhaps, Mr. Simms," Kelman interrupts in a peremptory tone. "Although there may be other explanations we have not yet explored."

Owen Simms, situated as he is at a less elevated position on the stair, keeps his back to the dark wood of the wall. His equanimity has apparently returned, and he graces Thomas Kelman with a smile that's tinged with melancholy. "Sir, I must protest on Martha's behest—as well as on my own. Continuing to provide hope that Lemuel Beale may still be alive is unkind indeed. Nay, even cruel. Have done, sir, and let his daughter and me mourn."

"If I believed, unconditionally, that Miss Beale's father was dead, Mr. Simms, naturally I would—"

Owen Simms waves his hand dismissively. His sorrowful expression grows more pronounced. "Enough, sir, of this sham investigation."

Kelman is not to be dissuaded. "It is my task, Mr. Simms, to see this troubling mystery through to its proper resolution."

A Confession?

WITH DELIBERATE CARE, EMILY DURAND extracts an egg yolk with a gold spoon. In her ruffled dressing gown, in her lace and watered-silk ribbons, her English pink and Paris gray, she sits as straight as a razor, her hands and fingers equally resolute and firm. Emily never permits silver to come in contact with egg. Nor with peas, nor flower stems, nor excessive heat. Silver is a temperamental substance, as everyone knows. "May I prepare your egg, as well as my own, John?" she asks, and experiences not only pride that her tone is so reasoned and calm but also a high degree of wonderment. It's hard to believe she's become adept at deceit in such a short space of time.

Staring out the window of the Durand family's ancestral home in the countryside of Torresdale to the north of the city, her husband glances briefly at her, then resumes his solemn contemplation of the property outside: five hundred acres that were part of an original land grant from William Penn and have been handed down, eldest son to eldest son, for over one hundred seventy-five years. John loves the place, its thick fieldstone walls, its low ceilings, its Quakerish simplicity, although he knows that his wife doesn't share his enthusiasm, that she far prefers their more fashionable house in town.

"You're unusually quiet this morning, John," Emily continues in a cheerful voice. "I'd hoped that removing here yesterday might improve your spirits. I know what store you set in country ways."

He responds at length with a mumbled "Mmmm," then looks briefly at his plate and the cooling boiled egg before resuming his slow perusal of the garden. A thin, sleety rain is beginning to fall, partially obscuring the garden, orchards, and fields beyond. What holds his rapt attention, Emily can neither see nor imagine. She forces an expression of wifely concern while, unbidden, her thoughts return to Eusapio and the bed they shared not three days past. She sees his abdomen glistening with sweat, feels his fingers clench her hips, hears his breaths panting in her ears. *Aimilee . . . Aimilee . . . bimba triste . . .* She finds herself beginning to smile and immediately takes up her cup of chocolate to hide this dangerous display of emotion. But her hands have a life of their own, and she cannot bring the gold-rimmed porcelain to her lips. "It certainly is inclement weather," she says as she returns the shaking cup to its saucer.

"It's winter, Emily" is her husband's dismissive reply.

Emily Durand feels her cheeks flush hot, a physical response that has nothing to do with clandestine memories of Eusapio Paladino. Self-righteous anger fills her; her tongue itches to speak, but she clamps her jaw shut until the sensation recedes. She studies the side of her husband's inattentive face and pushes her egg, half eaten, away. She doesn't attempt to drink her chocolate again.

John turns toward her. His eyes are dull and murky, his mouth pinched as though in anger; and her heart suddenly sinks. *I've been discovered,* she thinks with a wild and horrid premonition. *John knows. I've been careless; I've been stupid and wrong. Terribly, terribly wrong. Oh, how could this happen? How did I permit this to happen! What have I done? What have I done!* She glances away and holds her breath; the pieces of egg she's consumed rise back into her throat; in a moment, she realizes, she'll be forced to run, gagging, from the room. With the greatest of willpower, she returns her anxious gaze to her husband's face, but he continues to regard her with an expression so bleak that she can't decipher its meaning.

"Forgive me, Emily. My reply was impolite."

Emily's fearful eyes grow wide in both befuddlement and suspicion. "Forgive you, John? Forgive *you.*" She's so astonished at his request that her words jump forth in an uncharacteristic stammer.

"Yes. I was rude just now . . . when you mentioned the weather. I have much on my mind, however. I apologize if I don't seem myself." He stands abruptly; and the tea table, set as it is with such a plethora of tiny plates, jam saucers, sugar spoons, egg spoons, bread and butter knives, compote dishes of stewed pippins and preserved morello cherries, a full bowl of Devonshire junket, jingles mightily. "I'll be in the stables, Emily, should anyone wish to speak with me. The new groom has yet to make peace with the gray Thoroughbred mare. I fear I may be forced to replace him."

"Sorry news." Emily is scarcely aware of her choice of speech. She continues to gaze in wonderment at her husband. She feels as though she's just escaped a horrific carriage accident, and her brain whirs with a sound like rushing wind. Then, for a bizarre and awful second, she envisions John's large body in place of Eusapio's lithe one, the square Durand face growing red in astonishment at his wife's lewd and unseemly behavior. The image makes her gasp aloud.

Abruptly, she takes up her damask napkin and fans herself. "The fire in this room is too steeply banked," she manages to murmur.

"What's that you're saying?" Her husband goggles at her.

"I said the fire is overhot, John. Whoever laid it has been remiss. We are not tropical flowers requiring searing heat."

"Searing . . . ?"

Emily forces a smile. "Do you not feel it is too warm in here, John?"

He looks around him in perplexity. "Too cool, I would have said."

"Ah. Then we hold two differing points of view."

"Differing . . . ?" John echoes again. At this point, during similar past conversations, Emily would have thrust away her napkin and stood impatiently, her blue eyes spilling wrath at her husband's stupidity and incompetence. Today, she remains in place, venturing a hesitant:

"I hope the gray mare is quite well, John?"

"Yes" is the uninformative reply.

"You will . . . you will not eat, then?" Emily tries again.

"If you'll excuse me, no, I will not." But instead of moving away, John Durand turns heavily back to his wife. "I've been thinking, you know, my dear . . . that we should . . . that we should entertain more often . . ."

"Here?" Emily cannot conceal a look of dismay. *Not in this sober and outmoded little dwelling,* she thinks. *What can John be proposing?*

"No . . . no, not here . . . Or, well, wherever you see fit, of course . . . Here . . . or in town . . . This is a nice, pleasant place, though . . ." Her husband flounders again while Emily finds herself staring at him. Guilt makes her brain tear through his words. *John wishes me sequestered in the country,* she tells herself. *Perhaps he suspects something is amiss but doesn't yet know for certain and wants to keep me within easy sight.*

". . . In truth, Emily, I've been hoping to expand our circle a bit. Broaden our group of acquaintances, don't you know . . . Invite some folk we haven't heretofore included . . ."

It's a trap, Emily decides as her husband rambles on, although she has no clue how the mechanism of this particular snare might work.

"We could . . . we could include the Roseggers, for instance . . ."

Emily stares wide-eyed at her husband; she's still uncertain where his conversation is leading them, and her lack of authority rattles her severely. "The Roseggers! Why would we invite them? They're nothing but the most obvious *arrivistes*."

"He's an important man of affairs, Emily—"

"John. You cannot be serious. We might as well ask a fishmonger and his wife to dine." Even as she forms these words of protest, Emily is desperately trying to detect what her husband's motives might be. Certainly it's not the purported expansion of their social sphere. *The Roseggers,* her brain repeats, *the Roseggers . . . What on earth can John be getting at?*

"Oh, come, my dear Emily! That is an unchristian remark."

"But true," she counters with a familiar stubbornness. "The wife is unbelievably drab. Besides, everyone knows she was once—"

"She's very devoted, my dear. On the occasions when we've seen them both together, she strikes me as—"

"Dogs are also devoted, John, and yet human beings do not marry them."

Durand clears his throat and struggles with his cravat, but Emily, focused on her own concerns, fails to detect his deep unease. "Not every lady can hope to sparkle as you do, my dear wife."

Emily tilts her head. She perceives the pretty words as both manipulative and a covert warning, and searches her husband's eyes, but they remain inscrutable.

"We could ask Martha Beale as well, don't you think, Emily . . . ?" He clears his throat and fidgets with his cravat a second time. Despite these outward signs of anxiety, moment by moment, John Durand feels himself growing more confident in the deception he's arranged. For not one second has he recognized the strangeness of his wife's behavior. "Yes . . . have her to sup and so forth . . . her and the Roseggers . . ."

"Martha Beale's in mourning, John" is all Emily can think to reply.

"Oh, not yet, my dear. What I mean to say is there are no funerary arrangements—"

"Not as such, no, although given the circumstances of her father's disappearance—"

Durand won't concede his wife's interruption. In fact, he now seems quite sure of his position. His thick body almost swells with pride. "Which there won't be, of course, unless a body is found . . . So, yes . . . You could write to Martha Beale *and* the Roseggers, and . . . and . . ." Then he suddenly realizes that he's grasping at straws with this suggestion. ". . . And . . . and that Italian johnnie the Ilsleys had . . . Make a bit of a stir, don't you know . . . Have another of those . . . what do you call them? Private séances? Is that it . . . ? Yes . . . yes, and you could easily outdo the Ilsley set . . ."

Emily opens her mouth to reply, but no matter how much she wishes to sound calm and nonchalant, no sound comes.

"After all, why should Henrietta Ilsley outshine you, my dear? Your *soirées* are ten times more scintillating than hers."

Again Emily can only remain mute and immobile.

Without his wife's definitive answer to his proposal—a response John accepts as agreement—he nods agreeably, then strides quite purposefully from the room.

Left alone, Emily forces her gaze to return to the table but finds she cannot see anything; the linen, the silver, the porcelain, the now-chilled egg cup: All are blurred and meaningless. *Oh, what has John discovered?* her mind demands. *What can he mean by this peculiar scheme?* If Emily could lay her head upon the table and weep and scream aloud, she would, but that's not an act she's ever permitted herself. Not as a child, and certainly not as a married woman. So she remains rigidly still, thinking and thinking. *I must outmaneuver this man,* she decides. *I must.*

IN THE STABLE, however, Durand's show of self-confidence deserts him. He leans heavily against a box stall and releases a long and troubled sigh, then attempts unsuccessfully to regain some measure of remembered peace. He concentrates on the customarily companionable smells and sounds of the horses surrounding him, but solace eludes him. He sinks down onto a three-legged stool, carelessly letting his coattails sweep the ancient wood floor. He has little fear of being discovered in this unusual pose; the groom and undergroom have long since finished their duties of currying the animals and cleaning out their stalls. John sighs anew; his wide chest constricts, and his neck and face grow hot. He has lied to his wife; the new groom is an excellent man. It's he, John Durand, who's at risk.

He listens to the crunch of oats, the papery mastication of hay, the crackling of fresh-strewn straw, the contented blowings and mutterings of the horses taking their fill, the occasional peaceable whinny. He reaches out toward the iron bars surrounding a nearby storage bin and shuts his eyes. In his tortured imagination, he sees the very metal ripped from his hands, the box stall and its eleven neighbors yanked away beneath his feet, the barn gone, the paddock gone, the fields and orchards sold, the venerable stone house auctioned, and all the possessions in it: family portraits, porcelain and silver tea services inherited from long-dead great-grandparents, tables and chairs and bedsteads commissioned long before the War of Revolution: everything carted off by strangers. And all because of his despicable deeds.

John groans and reaches for the flask he always carries on his person. He sips at the fortified wine, then sips again until the flask is empty.

A Dinner Interrupted

"HE'S CALLED MR. ROBEY," JOSIAH, the tailor, tells his young charge, "although I don't believe that's his true name." Josiah sets forth two bowlfuls of sausages cooked in brown gravy as he speaks, the aroma spilling into the air and perfuming every crowded corner of their one-room home on lower Fitzwater Street: a "trinity" matching similar "Father, Son, and Holy Ghost" dwellings that line the block and contain an entire family on each of the three ten-by-twelve-foot floors.

"Eat, Ella."

The girl's eyes mirror her delight. "Sausages," she whispers. She might as easily be saying, *Silver and gemstones: Are they for me?*

"Sausages," Josiah answers her with solemnity. "It is a special occasion. I've received a gift from Heaven. A client of my own. And you know what that can lead to."

"No," Ella responds. She gazes at her plate and the hallowed food resting there. She thinks she might like to bury her nose in the wondrous stuff, just like a dog would.

"It means that if I'm careful, and more attentive to my work than the others are, that if I remain respectful and discreet, one day I may own a shop myself."

"And I will be your wife."

The tailor turns on her angrily. "You must cease that kind of talk, Ella. You are yet a child, and I am as old as any father you could have. As any father you *do* have. As any mother, too."

"But I—" she begins.

"Stop, Ella. I do not wish to hear more. Your past is your past, as is mine. We will not speak about such things. Eat your supper, and be still. Besides, you must remember that you're supposed to be my young cousin now, the child of a relative living in the country."

"Yes, cousin." Ella's voice is meek.

"And my name?" he prods.

"Jo . . . Daniel," Ella corrects herself. "You are my cousin Daniel."

"And he is?"

"A . . . a cousin to an aunt who has been rearing me after my own parents died . . . but . . . but my aunt could no longer afford to keep me"—Ella recites the tale she's been supplied—"and . . . and so you kindly agreed to take me into your home in Philadelphia in order that I might learn good stitchery and so prove helpful to your work."

"Excellent, Ella." The tailor's nervous anger gradually begins to dissipate, and he lifts up his spoon. "That is very good. Is there more to your history, perhaps?"

Ella thinks for a second only. "Yes . . . My parents moved so many times when I was living with them that I can no longer remember where I was born."

"Perfect."

Ella beams. "Thank you for the sausages, cousin," she answers. Except for the falsified relationship, this statement is altogether true.

"Let us hope that we have many, many more." Daniel who was once Josiah also smiles; and as he does he reflects on how well his newly chosen name suits him: Daniel, who in the biblical tale was rescued from the lions' den; Daniel, whose friends survived the fiery furnace of King Nebuchadnezzar. The stories are excellent omens, he believes. Besides, Josiah, the escaped prisoner, must cease to exist if Daniel, the tailor, is to remain a free man.

"Now, let us eat before our suppers cool."

They eat; a baby cries on the floor above; a baby bellows on the third floor, too. A chicken, escaping the depredations of a roving dog, hurtles itself against the window; a pig snorts greedily near the door. Ella jumps in fear when she hears it, and Daniel attempts to laugh away her terror.

"That pig cannot enter our door, little cousin. I won't let it."

"Pigs eat human babies. Dead ones, that is" is her still-addled reply, to which Daniel adds an unexpectedly bitter:

"You've seen too much for your age, Ella. We'll have no more talk about pigs and their food . . . Now, let us finish our own good meal."

She bends to her bowl, eating slowly and sparingly. "Is he a fine man, your client?" she asks after several more silent moments.

"I think he is." Daniel considers his response. He puts down his spoon and leans back from the table. "He could be a thief, though. The chief of a gang. His fingers have never seen hard work."

Ella shivers involuntarily at this description, but Daniel doesn't notice. "I'm inclined to believe he's a fine man, a gentleman who's found himself in an uncomfortable position. A debtor in hiding from his creditors, perhaps. He has an odd and secretive manner about him."

Ella knows all about odd manners among men. She nods in empathy. "He's demanding, Cousin Daniel?"

"No, that's the very problem. He's not demanding. And I expected he would be, given the elegant clothing he's ordering from me. But I have yet to elicit more than a few words from him at one time."

"What do his servants tell you?"

"I've never seen one. Mr. Robey opens the door to me himself."

Ella has already finished her marvelous supper. She knows she can't ask for more; if scraps remain, water will be added to the left-over gravy, making a thin soup for their meal the next day. "Perhaps he's a foreigner."

Daniel considers her suggestion. "He has no accent that I can detect."

"Maybe he's disguising it—and is residing in a strange and hidden house as a spy. Maybe 'Mr. Robey' is an invention. You just said you thought it might not be his true name."

This suggestion is uncomfortably close to Daniel's own situation, so he returns to his bowl, scraping the last morsels as he says a dismissive "You're a very fanciful child."

Ella is about to protest this additional reference to her youth and explain how knowledgeable life has made her when a calamitous noise erupts from a street nearby. There are screams and oaths, and a fierce and heart-stopping rumble as if the earth beneath the city has suddenly burst open. Then the night sky turns into a scorched and angry yellow.

"They must be firing the Negro houses" is Daniel's astonished exclamation. "A riot like the one six years ago! Stay here; bolt the door after me, and do not leave under any circumstances. I'll see what help I can render."

Before Ella can protest, Daniel hobbles out the door. She hurries to do his bidding as the clamor increases and the neighboring babies wail louder in response. For no reason that she can understand, an image of Mr. Robey and his gentleman's hands comes into her thoughts. She pictures him lurking outside in the deafening air, watching and waiting as her "cousin" Daniel leaves her all alone.

"Oh," she gasps, then runs for the corner cupboard where the tailor stores his wares, burrowing in amongst the woolens and silks and making herself into such a small package that she's certain she's turned invisible. In the dark nest created by the fabrics, she closes her eyes, remembering the truth of her past and not the fiction her savior has created for her.

Ella knows she had a mother once, and a sister, too, and a little brother who'd pitched forward into the hearth when he was but an infant and so developed a face that was half an angry purple demon's and half a startled angel's. *And those two?* Ella wonders. *Did Father sell my brother and sister also? Or do they still reside at home in the countryside? And does my mother sing to them as she sang once to me?*

Ella's shut eyes envision her mother crooning. She lifts her head as though she could hear the tune, pointing her nose as if it were the scent of her mother and not uncut cloth she was sniffing.

ONE FIRE GANG roars to the rescue, whipping the horses and hurling oaths at passersby too slow or stunned to leap from the path. But "the Killers," under the leadership of the notorious saloonkeeper Billy Mullins, refuse the interlopers entry to the scene of destruction. Instead, the members of the hose company descend from their tanker coach and build a solid wall of white bodies that faces out upon the crowd and allows the flames behind to soar unabated.

Shouts of outrage and invective ensue, until the verbal threats between the fire gangs become blows, become cobbles and bricks wrenched from the streets, become bleeding heads and battered hands while whatever Killer is able to leave a comrade's side starts rounding on the Negroes who are yet struggling to wrest themselves and their possessions from the blaze. Children are beaten about the head, and old men and women shoved full force into the road. Then a pistol appears in the midst of the fracas, and a Negro youth is shot and killed.

His body tumbles forward, and in that single moment the earth among these warring nations grows still. Both sides watch the young man fall until a wail of grief springs forth only to be answered by a shout of taunting glee. Soon the noise and bloodlust reclaim the street as the white mob proceeds to grab whatever loose objects come to hand: slop buckets, empty feed sacks, broken crates, heaving them into the blaze while the flames, so handily fed, leap from one building to the next, and the next after that. "Go home to your Southern masters, Sambo!" the crowd roars above the flames. "Woolly-heads!" "Niggerism! Nigger-friends!"

Daniel limps forward; his intention is to help rescue the children, but, alas, he has no formulated plan. He reaches out his arms in succor but is jabbed in the back by a red-faced man wielding a club. "Nigger-friend!" the spittle-slick lips scream. "Go home, dirty Jew!"

Daniel turns to face his assailant. "I'm not—"

"Papist foreign filth!" Another man raises his cudgel; Daniel scuttles sideways out of reach.

"Crippled abolitionist swine. I'll give you something to pray about—" But the intended blow is arrested by the sudden arrival of the militia: packs set squarely upon their tensed backs, gold-braided hats upon their heads. Weapons begin firing on both sides; and the seething crowd, either good or ill, huddles low in a swirl of broken flesh and fear.

Daniel gazes at babies lost, mothers fallen, blood growing sticky on the stone, tufts of hair, scraps of clothing, a shoe, a paper picture wrenched from a now-vanished frame. He sees a young Negro woman crouching amidst a group of circling white men; as they descend upon their victim, her cries for mercy sound like the bleatings of a newborn calf. Daniel backs away, worming through the mass of people, head down, shoulders hunched, arms held squirrel-like in front of him. He can't help. He's never been able to help. At the moment, "Daniel" seems the worst possible choice for his new name.

The riot continues all night, and all the next day. The Southwark Beneficial Hall, known far and near as an abolitionist meeting place, is burned to the ground. The African Presbyterian Church is also reduced to cinders. Fires—and looters—gut trinity homes on the alleys abutting Fitzwater and Catherine. Finished with those poor dwellings but far from sated, the mob threatens to move deeper into the city, and even the militia is hard-pressed to control the spill of screaming citizenry that begins to spread north toward the mansions that line Washington Square and westward to the orphanage where Hannah Yarnell has barricaded herself and her terror-stricken charges. On Washington Square, the Ilsleys' home and those of their neighbors are turned into fortresses manned by owners and their loyal servants. Shutters are pulled fast; lamps are extinguished, pistols readied.

The orphanage is not afforded such resources. Hannah and the two young and untried Negro women who serve the Association as nursemaids and aides are the sole adults in residence when the riots commence. None would know what to do with a firearm should it be proffered; and as to boarding up the windows, they haven't the time with so many frightened children to attend to. Instead, Hannah walks purposefully from room to room, spreading comfort, singing songs and hymns, reciting prayers, stroking heads and shoulders, and speaking aloud and intimately with God until even the most quivering child begins to believe that Miss Hannah is capable of saving them.

Only the nameless epileptic boy remains beyond her persuasive touch. He has fit after fit, sleeping openmouthed and leaden-bodied when the spasms pass; and Hannah experiences such concern for his survival that she decides he must be baptized lest he perish before the horrible ordeal is past. She takes a prayer book, calls for one of the nursemaids, and christens the child Caspar after the home's visiting physician, Caspar Walne.

The name has an astonishing effect. "Ca," the boy answers, which is the first verbal communication he has made since his arrival.

"Caspar," Hannah repeats, drawing out the vowels and consonants.

"Cai," the child slowly replies.

The effort is close enough for Hannah. "Well then," she says, smiling although her eyes swell with joyful tears. "Cai you are, and will always be."

And Cai, oh miracle of miracles, beams back at her.

Ruth

One day after an uneasy peace has been established, the city of Philadelphia still smolders: buildings and tempers, both. There are those who blame city hall, those who blame the Irish gangs or the militia or the tardy and criminally stubborn hose companies, those who continue to curse the Negroes for "stealing bread from honest men," those who rage at a system that makes free men and women out of people who were so much better off enslaved. Poverty of means and spirit is terrible when wed to the god of righteousness.

Ruth has survived the attack Daniel witnessed, but just barely, and that probably because she lay as limp as a rag until the men using her believed they'd killed her.

It's Dutch Kat who finds Ruth's battered body while prowling the eerily empty neighborhood, going out, as she told her ladies, "to see what finery might be left to purloin." Ruth's soft and whimpering cries first arrest the madam, but it's the sight of the swollen, battered face and bleeding lips that sends Kat hurtling back to the fancy house to fetch two of her strongest workers to bear the hurt woman to safety.

"Irish boys!" Kat snaps as she marches at the head of this somber parade. Of course, she's guessed who the culprits are. Who else could it be but the ruffians who laud their Fenian heritage? "Billy Mullins and his benighted breed," she fumes in her still foreign-sounding voice. "Them boys prefer clods of dirt to a bed. The girl's lucky not to have been a sheep. They would have done her and then slaughtered her, to boot!"

Ruth's bruised lips move in response, but they're too thick to form speech.

"What makes them think they're God's gift, I ask you? More like God's great joke, if you want the truth. More like one of them awful pestilences released upon the earth in the Bible times. The Irish be damned. Every mother's son of them. And their blasted ancestors, too. They were naught but naked savages when the Holland people were ruling the seas in elegant bateaus . . ."

Dutch Kat's tirade continues all the way home and all the way upstairs to the small room, where Ruth is then placed atop a freshly sheeted bed. "I'll give you a week or maybe a bit longer for the worst of those pricks' damage to heal. After that, if you wish to live here you'll need to work as hard as the other girls do. The house ain't a house of charity, but I'm a fair mistress. Do well by me; I'll do well by you. Dutch Kat is an honest woman who runs a proper establishment. Anyone can tell you that."

Ruth hears the words but cannot respond with more than a painful grunt. Lying on her back, she gazes at the ceiling; the room is tiny and misshapen and dark, but the mattress below her feels surprisingly new, as does the bolster pillow.

"You can't put her in this room, Kat. It's where—"

"Never you mind about that now," the madam interrupts as she perches her ample behind beside Ruth's aching body. "No bugs in this mattress," she announces in a commander's lofty tone, and she bounces up and down twice as if to prove her point. "It's as new as can be."

"That's because of the blood on the other one," another voice offers in a more pragmatic if less assertive vein. "Who knew a kid like that could have so much—?"

"That's enough idle chatter!" Kat lashes out. "I'm not running a salon for society ladies here. Gossip don't produce silver coins."

"I'm only saying she should watch her step if she becomes one of us, Kat, toiling under the sheets and all. Men like him come back. You know they do. Especially when they've found it so easy to take their peculiar pleasure. And it may be that he bears a special fondness for this little box you've put her in. I wouldn't jump in here, not I."

"No one's asking you to, you lazy slut," the madam all but roars. Then she swears in her own language, adding a smattering of French, Italian, and German for good measure. Dutch Kat prides herself on her cosmopolitan ways.

"You should tell her all about it, though, Kat," the voice continues in grim defiance. "Indeed you should. It's not right to keep the thing a secret."

"Seems to me like you've already said all there is to know. Now move along, missy, if you wish to keep your own private box. I have plenty of others asking for it, if you'll recall."

With that mysterious exchange, Ruth is left alone. She lies on the clean sheets, at first tentatively and then, as the hours stretch on, with an increasing sense of both ownership and doom. *My fate is sealed now,* she tells herself. *Ruth the maid-of-all-work is now Ruth the whore, and even if some miracle were to bring me my child, he would not be welcome here. Indeed, I would never wish him in such a place.*

Slumping deeper into the horsehair mattress, she falls into an uneven sleep, seeing the man whose hat she rescued, the man she thought she recognized. Then the hat becomes a baby, a naked infant rolling out into the busy street like a wet brown ball.

The dreaming Ruth dodges through the fine carriages and dusty market carts to save this helpless child who makes no sound although his mouth is open in a wide and terrible scream. *I knew that man,* she tells herself. *Indeed, I did. And do. And still, I do.*

WHILE RUTH SLEEPS, Martha listens to her bedroom clock chime off the long night hours. The riot, instead of sealing her retreat to her father's country home, brought Owen Simms hurrying back to the residence in town. With him, at her own persistent request, was Martha. But the acrid odor of burned dwellings and the intermittent shots still fired by the militia have proven more worrisome companions than the stillness at Beale House; and at two in the morning she's still very much awake. From her softly pillowed bed, she hears a lone carriage rattle past on the cobbles below her window, and a member of the night watch call out once from a neighboring byway.

She sighs at her inability to fall into slumber, then rises, lights a candle on the mantel, and walks impatiently to the window, where she pulls aside the several layers of heavy satin draperies and thinner lace curtains to gaze down upon the street. The gas lights are burning, covering the now-vacant roadway with intermittent and mustard-colored puddles, while the neighboring houses are only fitfully illumined; and some not at all.

Martha scans the scene, then draws in a sharp and startled breath. A man is standing within the shadow of the opposite house. He seems to be watching her window, watching her. Her first impulse is to release the drapery and turn back to the comfort of her cozy suite, but instead she holds her ground, studying the person who studies her. Almost, his posture looks like that of Thomas Kelman, but

Martha can't fathom why he would hide in wait outside her father's house.

She tries to study the man's face, but the features are too obscure to recognize. *He knows I'm here,* she thinks, and experiences a peculiar impulse to raise her hand in acknowledgment.

Instead, she remains motionless, willing him to make the first gesture. But he makes not a sign; and at length she quits her sentry post, closes the drapes behind her, and moves to a chair, where she sits and forces herself to concentrate on the ticking of the clock. *Father—or someone resembling Father—has been seen walking abroad,* she tells herself. *What can this mean? And what can it mean that Owen Simms refuses to believe such a tale is possible?* As Martha thinks, the clock's measured beats seem to transform themselves into jangled notes. Loud, soft, fast, slow: They begin to sound to her like footfalls scurrying over the carpeted hall beyond.

For a moment, she imagines that Owen Simms is about to rush into her chambers shouting out the news that her father has indeed been found alive, found wandering lost and brain-sick in the city of Chester or New Castle—and that Thomas Kelman is waiting below to disclose the extraordinary and marvelous information himself.

As quick as the thoughts enter her mind, Martha warns herself that they're nothing but invention. The denizens of the house are all abed. And Kelman and her father are . . . ?

With a bitter and impatient sigh, she leaves her chair, wandering with a heavy heart back to the window, where she again pauses before extinguishing the light and continuing on to bed.

The man who was watching her father's house is gone. "Oh!" she murmurs in both relief and disappointment. "Oh . . ."

Then Martha, like Ruth, like little Ella and even intemperate Emily Durand, finally also enters dreamland, but the bitter scents of the burning city alter the workings of her sleeping brain, and so the unknown man Martha glimpsed from her window grows and grows until he becomes a giant of a person, capable of reaching his huge hands into her bed and snatching her up as if she were only a small and helpless child.

"Father?" she mutters in her sleep. "Father, have you come home at last?"

Mary, Alone

THE MAN IS NAKED FROM the waist down; his buttocks, as he bends over the girl, are as white-gray and slippery as fish skin. Her skin is white also, a tangle of straight, young legs and arms whose color is brushed with a healthy-looking pink although it should not be. Because the girl is dead, and has been dead for some minutes.

The man knows this fact; he's already left off squeezing her throat but is continuing to pump his buttocks up and down, his flesh growing increasingly slick and prickled as if slapped with a sleety wind. "Mary," he croons as he works, "my little Mary . . ."

The child doesn't answer, of course, and the man's ecstasy increases. He's aware of the rapid beating of his heart, aware of the blood coursing through his body, and of a sensation of remarkable rejuvenation and power. He feels transformed, healed, saved, and wholly and forever at peace. "Mary," he sighs again, "my little one, my dear." He closes his eyes and sees angels and clouds, God ensconced on an amber throne and the saints who parade before him night and day, chanting hymns throughout the heavens. He accompanies their pure, celestial voices as they sing:

"'Blessed are those that are undefiled in the way, and walk in the law of the Lord . . . Blessed are all they that fear the Lord . . . Blessed be the Lord my strength who teacheth my hands to war, and my fingers to fight . . . O daughter of Babylon, wasted with misery . . . Blessed be he that taketh thy children and throweth them against the stones to execute judgment upon them . . . Deliver my soul, Lord, from lying lips, and from a deceitful tongue.'"

Then the sensation of glory and might begins to leach out of him as it always does, and he becomes increasingly aware of the dead body beneath him, its scent of fear, the excrement and blood and urine that seeped from it to stain his own spotless skin. He stands up in sudden disgust. This girl has soiled him all the way down to the depths of his soul. She is no beloved "Mary"; nor will she ever be.

He reaches into the pocket of his fine velvet jacket, extracting a pearl-handled pocketknife, which he puts beside the girl's jumbled body.

Then he removes his jacket and waistcoat and shirt, placing them in careful regard upon the far corner of the bed. He steps to the washstand and carefully bathes himself with a wet towel and a hearty dose of soapsuds. He enjoys the sensation of rubbing his body clean, the languid, thoughtful motions, the propriety of the act. His spirits begin to revive, although the reek of the fancy house and the cloying odor of grown women remain disappointingly in his nostrils.

He sighs that this should ever be the case, then dries himself, takes up his handsome knife, and twists the girl's head till it faces him. He opens her mouth, takes hold of her tongue, and in one quick movement severs it from her head. The metal blade bangs once against her fox-like little teeth. He winces at the unpleasant harshness of the sound, wrinkles his nose at the swift gush of blood.

Finally, he places the tongue upon a pillow and arranges the girl in a kneeling position, face down, chest down, with her feet trailing upon the dusty floor as though she were deep in prayer.

He surveys his work, then washes and dries himself again and pulls on his trousers, his fine leather boots, his soft linen shirt, the jacket that's the color of a mole's soft belly, his cravat, his fur-lined greatcoat, his scarf and beaver hat. At last, wiping the knife clean on the coverlet, he returns it to an interior pocket. With each activity, he's also returning himself to a person who has spent his adulthood as a respected citizen of the city and the state. When the knife is finally gone from view and his clothes carefully adjusted in the looking glass, he's almost surprised to also see a reflection of the girl upon the bed.

He observes this image with disdain, then averts his eyes. He's too fastidious a person to approve of nakedness or rumpled bedding. His nose quivers in dismay; and he stalks out into the hall, pulling the hat down as he passes doors that are either shut or partially open. He doesn't glance at the scenes that lie exposed; they're too shameful, too unpleasant, too base. Every single one of their scents and sounds offends him to the core of his soul.

He hurries down the stairs and out into the street. Not one person has remarked upon his haste or even turned to look in his direction. Then he begins a brisk walk toward the larger thoroughfare that leads eventually to Washington Square.

Saffron-Hued Silk

EACH DOOR IN THE CRAMPED corridor is wide open, and in every one stands a resident of the house caught in a state of undress and horror. Wails erupt from amongst the women, followed by sniffles of consolation, confusion, and fear. The paying customers at Indian Nell's House for Ladies of Pleasure have long since fled from this insalubrious scene.

"She was no more than a child, she was," the eldest woman among them cries. She's missing nearly all her teeth, and her body, beneath a soiled and ancient dressing gown, is soft and fat and sloppy. But she sobs with heartrending tears as if the murdered girl had been her daughter, the flesh of her aging flesh. "Why would anyone want to kill her? A little kid—"

"She looked older—"

"Well, don't we all? Besides, what's that got to do with—?"

"And acted it, too—" a third woman interjects while a fourth demands a panicky:

"What difference does it make how old she was? I'm seventeen.

Does that mean I needn't worry myself that the same could happen to me? Or to any other of us?"

The questions silence them momentarily. All remember the room and the blood—and the awful sight of that butchered tongue.

At length, the eldest practitioner takes up her sorrowing chant again. "Who would do such a thing—?"

Nell herself appears among them at that moment, ordering each to tidy up, make herself presentable, clean her teeth, comb her hair, and then gather in the downstairs parlor in double-quick time. Unlike the fancy ladies who work for her, and whose skin ranges in color from white to coffee black to a yellow-brown, Nell is a pale-skinned mulatto, tall as a man and with a man's wide shoulders and a free, rangy gait. She receives a good deal of respect from the women she employs; and it's not exclusively due to her physical presence. "There's a policeman wants to talk with you," she tells them. "Another gentleman, too. His name is Thomas Kelman, and he has some private truck with city hall."

"A special friend of the mayor's wife?" someone quips, but the sally fails.

"You'd best keep remarks like that to yourself if you know what's what" is Indian Nell's terse reply. "This town doesn't belong to the likes of us."

KELMAN WATCHES THE women file into the room until their ripe bodies crowd every corner and even air grows scarce: too much scent on clothing that's bedraggled and sweat-stained; broken, lusterless hair; stubby-fingered hands that have worked so hard from their earliest years that the evidence can never be eradicated. As with the previous murder at Dutch Kat's house, the man who chose this place was aiming low indeed.

"Ladies . . ." Kelman begins while the officer accompanying him retrieves a notebook and prepares to write.

Several in his audience giggle into their sleeves, although the sound is skittish and fearful rather than amused.

"Ladies, we have a craven killer in our midst. The girl who lived among you was the second he murdered—"

"Done the same as this?" the eldest whore murmurs.

"Exactly the same."

She begins to sob again, wrapping her arms around her anguished sides.

"Shut your trap!" another responds while a third attacks the second with her own angry:

"Cut your tongue out next while he's at it." The woman who spits out these words is coal black and reed thin with a caved chest that suggests the early stages of consumption.

"Better yours, you ugly cow!"

"Stop!" Nell's firm voice orders while Kelman's speech overrides both the madam's and her bickering hirelings':

"Did any of you see the man? Notice anything unusual about him? A style or pattern of speech, a mannerism that might have been unique? Clothing? Posture? An odd way of walking?"

"Are you suggesting we only get the halt and lame in here, Mr. Kelman?" It's Nell who asks this question, and there's more than a hint of challenge in the tone. Her head is high, her strong back straight. She's wrapped herself in a mantilla of Chinese red satin; given other circumstances, she might well be deemed regal.

Kelman regards her, and she gazes steadily, almost belligerently, back. "We may not be as pricey a house as some others, but we have our standards."

"No customer's going to come here now, Nell," the senior resident moans through her still fast-falling tears.

The madam rounds on her. "Not for your tired white flesh, they won't."

"I do my best, Nell—"

"Which isn't good enough. Not by a long shot—"

"I try, Nell! I swear to God above I do."

"Listen to you, calling on God! Perhaps you should try beseeching the other one for a while. Might prove more advantageous."

"Ladies!" Kelman interjects, then resumes his patient questioning, turning again to Indian Nell. "The girl's name was Maryanne? That's what you told the sergeant who first arrived on the scene?"

Nell nods, but the motion is brusque and quick. Kelman knows she's barely tolerating his presence.

"Maryanne what?"

"Plain Maryanne. No more."

"It was her true name?"

"I know what I'm told, Mr. Kelman. that's all." She draws out the "mister" until it sounds like a hiss.

"Relatives?"

"Whores don't have time for relatives." The madam shrugs; in her fine red wrap, she sweeps the room with an imperious glance, but no one supplies an answer as to whether Maryanne had family somewhere.

Kelman looks at his sergeant, then again moves his careful gaze across those gathered in the room. "We need your help in apprehending this killer before he strikes a third time. Think back, please, ladies . . . He was in your midst. You saw him perhaps in this very parlor. He passed by your open doors—"

"The girl brought him here," Nell insists with a toss of her head. "She picked him up on the street. They went up the stairs immediately—"

"I heard him say he wanted a girl named Mary," one of the women offers, and Kelman turns toward her questioningly. "He was most particular about it; Maryanne gave me such a nudge as she passed by. You know how she was . . ." The whore, a white girl, looks to the others as she says this. "Rolling her eyes in fun, and all. 'I'll be your Mary,' she told him, 'your little baby lamb.'" This account ends in a bitter sigh. "She liked a good time, she did."

"He had a fur-lined greatcoat," another voice adds. "And his hat was pulled so low there was no sight of his face. I thought he might have been hiding something, a birthmark or something—"

"But you saw no distinguishing feature?" Kelman asks.

"No."

"Can you describe the coat?"

The woman thinks. "The lining of the sleeves was the color of the Delaware in summer. Blue and beautiful. And some lovely yellow stuff he wore, too. A silk scarf. It was as bright as saffron rice—"

"Well, I can tell you something, Mr. Kelman," Nell interrupts in a voice that sounds more outraged than impatient. "Your murderer is a white man."

"You saw him . . . ?" Kelman leaves the question unfinished.

"I smelled him" is the madam's curt response. "You white folk insist that Negroes have a peculiar odor. I say men do. And white men most of all. And not just the ones who enter my establishment."

"You have many regulars who are white, then?"

Nell's tone retains its caustic bite. "How long have you lived in this city, Mr. Kelman?"

Thomas Kelman is silent for a long moment. "Was the man young? Old? Tall? Of medium height?"

"He wore a fur-lined cloak—as you just heard. And he paid for an entire night. If he was old, he didn't show it. He walked with a good, strong step. We have some that don't."

"There's nothing more you can tell me?"

"Nothing." She glares defiantly. Although nearly his equal in height, by her definition and the world's he's her enemy and master.

"And if you think I'm lying to you, and protecting one of my own kind, I'm not."

Kelman focuses on the ceiling. His sergeant patiently waits, writing in his notebook until he can write no more, while the women clustered in the room begin to show signs of unease, twitching and stamping their feet like anxious cattle. "I want you to bury her decently," Kelman says at length. "Not in a pauper's grave." He pulls a number of coins from his pocket.

Indian Nell accepts them, adding the total with a rapid, practiced eye. She doesn't extend a word of thanks; instead, she demands an acrid "Where were you when the girl was living? You and all your fine government friends?"

IN THE STREET, Kelman and his sergeant separate, the policeman to return to his duties of patrolling the streets, Kelman to simply walk and think. A great tide of weariness rolls over him, and he feels his shoulders bending under it as though from a physical weight. *Do you ever work among the poor?* he remembers Martha Beale asking him, and he thinks: *Yes. But my efforts are for naught. There are none that I can save. None that I can help.*

He trudges down the narrow roadway to where it ends in a warren of soot-fronted houses and tiny alleys. Carver Street, one is called, as if a name can bring respectability. In the dim light of a desultory winter day, Carver Street looks grease-coated, blackened by decades of human and animal waste. In some places the muck lies near to knee-high; in some places, the lane is so narrow and the buildings' upper floors so ragged and tilting that even the air seems unwilling to enter. This is the area of the city where the landlords have decreed that a single outhouse is sufficient for three dwellings—no matter how many residents.

He tries to imagine the scene during the previous night. What brought a man in a fur-lined cloak to a place like this? he wonders. Where did he come from? How did he discover this forgotten terrain? "Mary," he'd insisted upon calling the girl. Was that the kernel of fact that would aid in this search? But what to make of such a common name?

Kelman walks on. He'll get no more aid from Indian Nell, he realizes; and in truth, there'd be little interest in the case among the police who patrol the ward. A dead girl with no known family. A contentious Negro madam. Who would care what happened in her fancy house? That a white man had been involved would be of scant consequence—unless, of course, the man was the victim.

He turns his steps toward South Street and begins walking west, but before he reaches Eighth Street, a man, avoiding a careening horse and cart, lurches into him. The man is slight; his face has the pallor of one who never sees the sun. He appears to walk with a limp, and the shoe on his left foot looks stitched of cotton as if it were a piece of clothing fashioned for a doll. The man glances up, terror-stricken in an instant, like someone who's come face-to-face with death.

"Excuse me, sir," he mutters. His eyes run over Thomas Kelman, noting the scar, the somber coat. His horrified mouth rounds in an **O**, then snaps shut as if he can't bear to give voice to the word he thought.

Who—or what—he assumes the taller man to be, Kelman doesn't know. Nor does he have time to formulate an opinion, because the little man hurries off, disappearing into the crowd as he leans adroitly upon his good leg while favoring the bad.

It's only after the man has vanished that Kelman suddenly realizes he recognizes the smell the man carried with him. It's the reek of Cherry Hill.

"YOU WON'T GO there again, Cousin Daniel, will you?" Ella very nearly cries out, although she knows better than to talk to her savior in such a noisy and demanding fashion. "To where that policeman was? You won't, will you, cousin? Say you won't!" By now Daniel has returned safely home, but Ella, in her anxiety for his safety—and her own—cannot cease posing these frightened questions.

"I do not think he was a policeman, child—"

"He was something official! You said so yourself. You said you were afraid he would discover that you were a—" Ella's words gush out in spite of herself.

"Quiet, Ella! I won't go up that street again, girl" is the equally anxious reply. "Now let us return to our work, lest we fall behind. And let us also remember that we must keep our voices low."

"But, Cousin Daniel, if you'd—"

"Ella . . . Ella . . . hush . . . I don't want to leave you any more than you wish me to." He hobbles to her side and bends down to awkwardly embrace her. "And I will never desert you if I can help it . . . But we both have some powerful secrets, and we must whisper them or not speak of them at all."

The reminder of Daniel's criminal past—and of her own unsavory one—makes Ella whimper again. "But if the man followed you?" she murmurs in a quavering voice.

"He didn't. I looked back. He was nowhere in sight."

Ella chews on her lips. Despite his seniority, she feels her benefactor is naive and trusting when it comes to the ways of the world. Perhaps, she thinks, that's what comes from all those years in prison.

"Come, little cousin," Daniel says in a louder and rosier tone that Ella realizes is intended for their neighbors' ears. "Let us return to our work while we still have the daylight."

With a show of energy and gusto, he resumes his sewing, and eventually Ella also takes up her task. During Daniel's absence, she forgot to tend the fire, permitting it to die down—which then left the floor upon which they sit cold and uncomfortable and the air acidic with ash.

As she stitches, Ella's fingers feel numb with the chill, but her heart feels far worse. Take away her "cousin." Take away "Mr. Robey" and the many articles of finery he requires, and she will be out roaming the streets again. Or worse, returned to a fancy house with a gentleman client who has stronger and quicker fingers than the last one. Considering these awful choices, Ella moans aloud. Her stitchery falls to her shivering lap.

"Hush, girl, it's all right. I'm home. I am safe—"

"But if they took you away—"

"Which they will not—"

"But you're a convict—!"

"Ella! Child! Enough!" Daniel whispers urgently. "We cannot let anyone hear . . . Now please, be a good girl and take up your work. If you wish to help me, and yourself, that is how you may do it."

Ella stifles her frightened tears although her chest continues to heave in silence. At length, she dutifully picks up the vermilion-colored silk that will be the lining in Mr. Robey's new waistcoat. Her small fingers have proven easy to train, and her handiwork has become so tidy and neat that the tailor is finally permitting her to sew the expensive cuts of cloth. "He must be a very wealthy man indeed, cousin," she observes after several moments, trying to match Daniel's bright and resolute tone. "To think this is on the inside where none may see it!"

"His wife will notice it, I imagine" is the tailor's absorbed reply. His concentration is wholly on the cloth in his hands.

"He has a wife, then?"

Daniel pauses and frowns. He looks up at Ella as he speaks. "No . . . I think he does not—"

"But you said—?"

"I told you Mr. Robey had a wife, child, because most gentlemen do—"

"You don't."

"I'm not a gentleman," Daniel states with some asperity, then his voice grows softer and sadder. "But I did have a wife, once . . . and a baby girl, too."

Ella notes the melancholy in Daniel's reply. She waits for him to continue while she bites off a loop of thread and commences another seam. When he doesn't speak, she finally murmurs a sympathetic "They died?"

"No, they didn't die . . . But they are gone from me as surely as if they were dead."

"Oh! Daniel! You sold them!" Ella is so perturbed she forgets the all-important "cousin."

The tailor stares at her. The thought is completely foreign, so that even hearing it produces astonishment. "Sold them?" he repeats. "Sold them? What monster would—?" But the stricken look on Ella's face stops the question in his throat. "No, child. My family was taken to the Asylum when I was away at work one day . . . My little girl . . . My little Susan suffered from imbecility. Congenital imbecility. That's what I was told . . . My wife developed dementia and raised her fists against her own child . . ." His words trail off. "Nothing will ever heal their brains. They know neither me nor each other . . . Now, no more questions, Ella, child. You must let me do my work. And you do yours. We cannot risk offending so fine a client as Mr. Robey."

"You Will Dead"

AS DANIEL AND ELLA STITCH his new finery, Mr. Robey descends from a public coach after an uneventful journey northward past the outskirts of the city and into a distant farming community surrounding the sleepy village of Frankford. The establishment he seeks so early in the day is set apart with its own kitchen gardens, a farm that supplies the residents' needs for meat, poultry, butter, cheeses, milk, and eggs, a carpenter's shop, and an icehouse dug neatly into a hillside. The main edifice is two-storied and long: twin arms extending from a square central body. Although elegant in its simplicity, the structure boasts none of the embellishments householders often add—a stone urn for greenery or flowers, a birdcage or potted plant set within a sunny window—and for this reason the place seems odd and a little frightening.

Robey traverses a drive lined with evenly spaced poplar trees and approaches the main entrance. Despite the morning hour, he appears every inch the fashionable gentleman Daniel described, a fine figure striding effortlessly along in a velvet jacket, a spotless linen shirt, a silk cravat, a cloak and beaver hat. His bearing is self-possessed and assertive in the manner of all mature men of means. He mounts the edifice's broad front steps and knocks at the door of the Asylum for Relief of Persons Deprived of Their Use of Reason. He has no way of knowing, of course, that this is the same portal his tailor has often stood before.

A male servant answers and ushers in the guest.

"I will see Dr. Earle before visiting the patient" is all Robey says. He doesn't supply his name; the servant doesn't ask it.

"Please to wait here in the foyer, sir. I will inform Dr. Earle."

Left alone, Robey continues his show of lofty indifference, remaining beside a central table around which the otherwise sparsely furnished room revolves. He's in the process of perusing a published copy of the Asylum's twenty-fifth annual report when the resident physician, Pliny Earle, enters.

"You wished to see me, Mr. Robey?" Earle is a young-appearing thirty-three, concave of shoulder and soft as new butter, but he also possesses densely observant and probing eyes that some people instantly warm to—and that others equally dislike. His present visitor is among the latter. "You don't wish to first see your—?"

"Not yet, Dr. Earle. I'd like some prior words with you."

The physician studies the Asylum's visitor, his gaze tunneling inward through the man's many layers of personal disguise. "What is it you need to discuss?"

Robey's response is a calm "Is there somewhere more private we might talk?"

Earle doesn't immediately answer, although his brain rings with words of silent protest. *For Heaven's sake man,* he wants to shout, *we could entertain* an *entire symposium of medical experts and openly discuss the case, and none would connect the patient to another human on this earth.* Instead, he announces a terse "My office" and leads the way through the foyer to the stairs and up to his inner sanctum.

There, Robey hesitates. Earle watches him. He feels as though he were observing a spider gauging the haphazard progress of its prey.

"There's no improvement, then?" Robey at last demands.

"For the past seven years that I've been attending physician here, I've endeavored to explain to you that there can and will be no 'improvement,' sir. She suffers from mania and has, according to our files, suffered so since she was admitted three decades ago. Surely you've been told as much more times than you would desire."

"Yes. Yes . . . I understand. Mania. Dementia . . . Melancholia—"

"It is not melancholia, sir; it is mania. Produced, so the admitting notes suggest, by a uterine hemorrhage—"

"I know all that—"

"And 'domestic difficulty,' as the previous physicians so cautiously phrased it—"

"Yes . . . yes—"

"Relating to an unnamed sexual situation—as well as to an acute anxiety over religion"—Pliny Earle's eyes bore through his guest—"bearing some, as yet undiscovered, connection to her other problems. Now, what is it you wish to say to me, sir? We have a full complement of patients, as you know. Mornings here are a busy time."

"Of course. Of course. I understand perfectly your situation here, Dr. Earle, and I'm grateful for the opportunity to discuss the case with you."

Pliny Earle makes no reply; instead, his mind's eye watches the spider begin a slow and circuitous descent to the center of its web.

"She is . . ." Robey commences, then hesitates, as if attempting to better phrase his remarks. "At forty-nine years of age, she's no longer a young woman . . ."

"You're correct, sir. Forty-nine is well past the prime of life for a woman. However, your sister is in excellent physical condition, as is sometimes the case with those whose cares are essentially cerebral."

"Then I infer that she may survive to a goodly age?"

"Barring an unforeseen accident or illness, yes."

"Does this not seem a terrible waste to you?" Robey asks at length. The words are full of sorrow, but Earle instinctively doubts their authenticity.

"A waste that she should have been so physically and emotionally wounded as to become demented, yes—"

"No. No, I mean a waste of a life upon this earth, a squandering of the gifts God gave us—"

The physician holds up a white and flaccid-seeming hand. "Considering the patient's anxiety concerning religion, I advise we avoid it in our private conversations—as well as in public consultation. And frankly, sir, I fail to see where this discussion leads."

Robey regards Earle; as the elder of the two, he has assumed an expression at once tutorial and forbearing. "Might it not be better, Dr. Earle, that she . . . ? What I mean to say is: Are there means—gentle ones, naturally—whereby her life might end sooner than nature allows?"

For all his wisdom and training, Pliny Earle's response is horrified astonishment. "This is your sister you're discussing, man! Your own flesh and blood! Surely you've hurt her enough already without plotting her death?!"

"I'll ask you to remember that nothing was proven," Robey fights back.

"Go visit with the patient, sir. Our conversation is concluded."

Robey rises from his chair, but before quitting the room he turns back to Pliny Earle. "You know my true identity," he says. "And that of my sister."

"No, sir. I do not" is the physician's curt reply.

"I'm not a poor man."

"I have no cause to doubt you."

"I could . . . if money were—"

"Sir, I ask you again to leave my chambers. You and I have no more to say to one another. A nurse will escort you to your sister . . . and remain there with you, according to the patient's specific request."

"Nothing was proven in a court of law," Robey insists again.

"Good day, Mr. Robey."

AS IF THE riot, the pillaging, the mindless destruction of property occurred in far-off Spain or some sodden Belgian seaport rather than mere city blocks from their home, the Durands' house in town is a whir of festive activity. Emily has cast aside her suspicions concerning her husband's motives in proposing to hold a gala supper party and séance and, instead, has embraced his notion fully. More than fully; she's swept up in the plans, transported to the point where her feet feel as if they don't quite make contact with the floor, and her brain all but bursts with imagined song. In the short few days since her perplexing conversation with her husband at their country abode, and in the hurried time prior to that, Emily has convinced herself that she's a person protected from evil and harm. It helps that she's also covertly paid a second visit to Eusapio Paladino's rooms.

Now she hurries through the house, happy, smiling, gloriously reckless and unafraid, while her husband paces somberly through other rooms, listening to her numerous orders to their equally numerous servants, as well as the swift assents that greet the mistress's words. What Emily's insistent voice is demanding and what the household staff is agreeing to, John doesn't know; he has far greater cares than the arrangements of flowers or candied fruit.

He leaves the parlor for the second time, passes from the foyer into the vestibule, walks the length of the drawing room with its stately Corinthian columns, its pilasters, its double hearths and marble surrounds, its pier glasses and the matched Chippendale lowboys that were carved for the Durand family by master cabinetmaker Thomas Affleck—and then restlessly marches to the rear loggia, banging the door open into the cold air, then slamming it shut as he reenters the building. His legs are driven to trudge relentlessly forward; his mind cannot remain quiet. He quits the vestibule for the morning room, leaves that for the dining room, the dining room for the private family stairs; but on the second floor feels no greater relief for his dread and his terror. His distraught footfalls retrace their steps, and he finds himself again in the parlor.

"Oh, there you are," his wife says. She's sweeping through the entry as she speaks, her silken skirts rolling over the Turkey carpet like a wave covering a sandy beach. Durand notices that the cloth is embroidered and that it shines with threads that look like genuine gold. "I need your advice, John." Emily's voice rises in flirtatious intimacy, behavior he hasn't witnessed since well before their marriage. John notes the change with surprise but makes no comment.

"Yes, my dear?" he answers stoically.

Beside Emily stands the home's majordomo, a man whose name Durand cannot immediately recall, but who holds in his hand a small ledger in which he inscribes his mistress's slightest wish.

Emily beams up at her husband. "We should take supper after *Signor* Paladino performs, don't you th—?"

"I thought you told me his conjuring was the genuine article?" John interrupts. His voice has a panicky edge that his wife fails to detect. "What I mean to say is . . . *performing* isn't—"

Emily silences the objection with a playful wave of her hand. "After *Signor* Paladino *communes* with the souls of those departed, we will take our repast—"

"If you've already made up your mind about the evening's schedule, then I can't see what advice you wish me to provide," John interjects in an equally tight and nervous manner, but Emily merely gazes at him indulgently and continues as if he hadn't spoken:

"In that fashion, *Signor* Paladino can either join us at table or not as he sees fit—"

"Surely he won't sup with us, Emily?" John protests for a second time. His voice has grown louder and more obviously anxious, but again Emily overlooks these clues.

Instead, she ignores her husband's arguments, devoting her attention to the majordomo. "For the first course: Red mullet, clear oxtail soup . . . It's always appropriate to have a bouillon for those with delicate digestions . . . also, mock turtle soup and stewed eels. Entrées: *riz de veau au tomates, cotelettes de porc, poulet,* ragout of lobster . . . Second course: roast turkey, pigeon pie, garnished tongue, saddle of mutton . . . Third: pheasant, snipes . . . no, let us have partridges . . . no, no, wait—grouse. They're much more daring and rustic. Then follow with blancmange, cabinet pudding, a *vol-au-vent* of plums . . . and a mince pie, do you think, John?" Emily finally turns and gives her husband a polite smile. "Or greengage tartlet?"

"Mince pie would be homier," he offers in a glum tone. "Besides, at this time of year preserved plums cost a pretty penny—"

"The tartlet, then," Emily responds serenely. "I want everything to glitter. Us, our home, our acquaintances . . . Wines, let me see . . . Well, perhaps I should examine the cellars first. I know we have more than enough champagnes laid by, but as to clarets and hocks, I'm not certain . . ." She begins to move off, trailing the majordomo behind her, but John's next query arrests the parade:

"How many folk are you expecting for this dinner of yours?" This time Emily cannot ignore the tension in her husband's tone.

"*My* dinner, John? I believe it was you who wanted to invite the Roseggers, and—"

"A suggestion, my dear. Only a—"

"*And* Martha Beale."

"But those guests were . . . Well, what I mean to say is, Emily, that we needn't put on such a lavish show, need we . . . ? For Martha or the Roseggers or . . . or the others . . . It might put folks out, don't you know? As if we were trying to raise ourselves too high—"

Emily interrupts this stumbling performance, but she does so with a beatific expression as if she were explaining the simplest of arithmetic problems to a child. "The table seats thirty, John. So, thirty we shall be—"

"But isn't that too great a number to partake in the . . . in the conjuring? Didn't the Ilsleys indicate that their—?"

Emily Durand tilts her head to one side. At last, her husband's rambling protests are beginning to register. As she gazes at him, she decides he looks like precisely what he is: a countrified member of the aristocracy who is woefully out of touch with the fashions and customs of the times. "*Signor* Paladino has appeared before theater audiences, my dear. A party of thirty should seem an intimate circle to him."

"But the Ilsleys—"

"John! When you first suggested this evening's gathering to me, I recall that you specifically mentioned wishing to outshine the Ilsleys. Now I wonder what you meant by those fine words. You begin to sound as though you were concerned with the dinner's expense. Surely that is not the case?"

Durand stands taller and straighter. "Of course not," he states. "Of course not . . . The suggestion was simply for a more exclusive circle. I know how much emphasis you place on being the hostess whose invitations are the most highly prized in the city."

Soothed by this bit of flattery, Emily momentarily softens. "I could, perhaps, reduce the list to eighteen . . ."

John's square face brightens considerably.

"But that would require eliminating Martha Beale . . ."

"Ah . . ."

"And you did specifically request her inclusion in the gathering—"

"I thought we might . . . might alleviate her gloomy spirits, my dear. That's all . . . Can we not make the number nineteen, then?"

"You must be in jest, John?"

"An uneven amount. I apologize. Twenty, then . . . However . . . However, at the risk of repeating myself, didn't Henrietta Ilsley mention a maximum of twelve spectators?" Durand finds himself sweating profusely. It's an unpleasant sensation.

"I spoke to *Signor* Paladino's assistant personally, John. He assured me that we could invite any number we choose."

"Ah . . ."

"Now, we cannot invite Martha and deny the Emmetts and Corstairs—"

"No . . ."

"Nor the Misses Chichester, nor the illustrious Roseggers whom you're so insistent upon adding to our little circle—"

"Ah . . ." Durand mops at his wet brow. "Yes . . . I see . . . The Roseggers, and so forth . . ."

"And Miss Beale." Emily smiles again, her point won. "One would think you were enamored of our wealthy heiress, John. You are such an advocate of her well-being."

Durand's ruddy complexion darkens considerably. "Such jibes are unpleasant in the extreme, Emily."

She raises a caustic eyebrow. "Marriage, among such as we, my dear husband, should not be bound by adherence to outmoded rules. We must leave such regimented behavior to those for whom it is prescribed: the lower class of citizenry."

"Emily! Dear wife! The laws of marriage are the laws of the church."

"Oh, John, what nonsense you spout!" She returns her focus to the majordomo, who has stood silent and unmoving during this exchange. "We'll be thirty at table tomorrow night, as I previously detailed. Now, let us examine the cellars." Before leaving, Emily gives her husband one final glance. "Unless you wish to select the vintages yourself, John? As your traditional prerogative in our most traditional family?"

SUCH IS THE assemblage convened at Emily's decree: thirty of the city's most prominent residents mingling in the commodious drawing room, while the dining room has been reconfigured according to Eusapio Paladino's specifications. Black velvet hangings cover the household's purple damask; all paintings and mirrors have been draped; the long table swathed in thick black wool; the requisite writing tablets positioned upon it; and the curious musical instruments stationed close by.

It will require a neat sleight-of-hand to reset the stage for an elegant supper party, but this is of no concern to Emily. She and her guests will retire to the withdrawing room following the conjuring and return to dine three-quarters of an hour later in a space transformed by silver, gilt, French porcelains, goblets of crystal, sprays of hothouse flowers, and a continuous round of comestibles, wines, champagnes, and fruit liqueurs.

As was the case at the Ilsleys' home, when the guests are called into the dining room and seated at the shrouded table, all conversation ceases and everyone present looks to the conjurer for inspiration and guidance. Paladino, however, seems to take no notice of the attention. His eyes idly wander the room, gliding over the paneled doors, the silk-cloaked walls, the carpet, the Chinese funerary urns standing upon the glossy wood floors. He doesn't look at Emily's guests. Most significantly, he doesn't look at Emily.

Seated at his side, she feels this withdrawal acutely. She imagined clandestine touches, a furtive caress beneath the all-obscuring table—even stolen minutes upstairs; and the visions filled her with a heedless joy. But he now behaves toward her no differently than toward the other matrons seated at the table.

Emily tries to console herself that her lover's behavior is both wise and sensible, that she not only approves of his coolness but also secretly encourages it; but the truth is that Eusapio's disregard infuriates her. In the silence that envelops the group, Emily finds herself plotting terrible words of revenge, envisions refusing to visit his rooms, witnesses his abject remorse, and finally sees her own ire transformed into tears of forgiveness and release. Almost, she comes full circle back to breathless adoration.

Then, all at once, the silence is broken, and Eusapio says a single word: "Martha," which he pronounces as the Italian *Marta.* He focuses a level stare upon Lemuel Beale's daughter until both Durands begin to fidget in their chairs.

"Marta." The name is repeated slowly and tenderly. All eyes swivel toward Eusapio and then back to Martha.

"Marta. Ragazza mia."

"My little girl," the translator provides.

"Shouldn't we be asking—?" John interjects, but the others gathered around the table hush him with an insistent:

"Shhhh! It may be that Beale is wishing to communicate!"

Then the writing tablets are pushed forward, and a breathless quiet descends upon the crowd. With their eyes only, several of Martha's nearest companions urge her to take the chalk and form a message. She shakes her head in steadfast refusal and draws back while Eusapio, as if pulled by a magnetic force, leans closer to her.

Emily grabs one of the tablets, showily writes upon it, then turns it upside down and places it near her guest of honor. Eusapio seems unaware of the gesture, and after a number of tense and soundless minutes, Emily retrieves the tablet and brushes away her unseen lettering. She feigns an unaffected and world-weary smile although her furious eyes belie the effort.

Then Henrietta Ilsley, so sadly rebuffed at her own séance, attempts to make contact with her departed kindred. But again Eusapio pays no heed; and the minutes tick by, and Henrietta's slate is also wiped clean. Professor Ilsley makes his own foray into the realm of necromancy, but his efforts fall to naught as well. The conjurer only has eyes for Martha Beale.

"*Marta,*" he murmurs again. "*Bimba mia*—"

"My baby girl!" Emily fumes while her husband simultaneously rises to his feet.

"I won't have you insulting Miss Beale—"

"*Marta . . . Maria . . .* " Paladino continues as if his two hosts hadn't spoken. ". . . *Bimba mia . . . Ragazzina mia . . .* " Then his serene demeanor vanishes, and he gapes at Martha and begins weeping as unabashedly as a child. "Dead," he says in halting English. "You will dead."

"Listen to Him"

DEAD. YOU WILL DEAD.

After twelve full hours, the warning still echoes in Martha's brain. What did the necromancer mean? And what of the dual names of *Marta* and *Maria*? Was there significance in the choice? Or was it simply an imperfect translation?

"You will dead." Martha repeats the ominous words aloud, then walks to her escritoire, thinking to detail the previous evening's peculiar events in her journal, but no sooner has she seated herself, taken up the pen, and dipped the nib in ink than she grows bored with the effort. Or perhaps, she realizes, sharing thoughts with an inanimate page is too meaningless a course to consider. *Why not bare my soul to the silent walls or have discourse with the bric-a-brac that lines the mantel? Why not talk to Father's hunting dogs instead? At least they might shake their shaggy necks as if they understood.*

She sighs in frustration, stares at the journal's open pages, then slaps the book shut. *What wondrous confidences have I ever been capable of exposing?* she wonders. *I, who have done nothing in my twenty-six years of living?* She drops the pen. For a fraction of a moment, she considers snapping it in two or hurling it away, and she glares at the thing lying on her desktop as if it were the cause of her discontent.

"Oh," Martha sighs again, and the small sound is but a fragment of a larger one that wells up in her chest, propelling her away from the writing desk to pace around and around her bedroom while her brain leaves off all considerations of the Durands' party or Eusapio Paladino or his now quite irrelevant admonitions.

Where on earth is my father? her brain demands. *Is he drowned and gone forever as Owen Simms insists; or, as bizarre as it sounds, has he chosen to escape his public persona and take himself off into hiding as Thomas Kelman suggests? And, if the latter is true, then why? Why? What would drive him to such an act? And what did he imagine the consequences of such a decision would be on me?*

She sighs anew. The sound is now full of anger, and her footsteps marching over the carpeted and uncarpeted floor match the irate tone. *On me?* her thoughts repeat. *On me? What did he think would become of me whose entire existence has been at his behest?*

A hundred pictures from her childhood whirl into her head until she settles upon one single scene: her mother, a lady she hardly knew, languishing in a high and silent bed that needed a footstool to attain its surface. Around it flit shadowy people who warn the little girl not to make noise or pull the waxen fingers that rest upon the medicinal-smelling sheets. *Who were the other people in that room?* Martha wonders now. *A sister to my mother? A brother? Siblings of my father who came to share in his grief? Were there grandparents at the scene? Or cousins? Even distant ones? Were there friends?*

But nowhere there or in the years that followed can Martha clearly picture any face but her father's—and eventually that of Owen Simms.

This time she does pick up the pen, and then hurls it in great passion toward the floor. Her aim is wayward, though, and the steel point doesn't drop but instead races arrow-like and swift across the room, where it collides with a Staffordshire shepherdess sitting on the mantel. The sudden blow proves fatal; the shepherdess doesn't simply crack in pieces, she explodes, sending a gritty cloud of powdered porcelain over her companion figurines.

Martha marks the destruction; her mouth falls open in astonishment that her hand could wield such power, but no sooner does she begin moving toward the ruined object than Owen Simms knocks at her door, and then opens it and enters without waiting for a reply.

He notes the destroyed shepherdess at once. "Oh, my dear Martha," he says with the deepest and most heartfelt concern. "Oh, my dear girl."

Words elude Martha. She simply stares at Owen Simms; in all the years he's spent in her father's house, she's never before seen him display such strong emotion.

"We must put an end to this torture. Indeed we must. This rumor that Mr. Kelman has been spreading is too much for your fragile nature." He walks to Martha's side. In his hand is a sheet of letter paper, which he places in her fingers. "A note was just delivered to the house. I took the liberty of opening it, as I would all your father's correspondence."

She pays no heed to the letter. "But couldn't it be possible that what Mr. Kelman says is true, Mr. Simms, and that Father still lives?"

"Oh, Martha, what good is this sad conjecture? What sort of odious thoughts has Kelman insinuated into your brain? That your father has crept away like a thief, that he's dodging about in the dark under an assumed name: Is that what you think?"

Martha has no reply, and so Owen Simms shakes his worried head. "If your father had some private motive for spiriting himself away—and I assure you that I, who have worked closely at his side, know of none—then would he not understand how terribly damaging the act would be to your psyche? Come, Martha; you know he would. Has he not always put your well-being above all others'?"

Martha nods, but hesitantly.

"You have only to look about you, my dear! This handsome room, handsome clothing, porcelain statuettes at which you may aim your miniature arrows." Simms laughs lightly, but the sound is full of empathy and forbearance. "Your father has always provided you with the best that money could afford."

Martha finally finds her voice, but all she can think to say is "That's true, Mr. Simms."

"Then why would he deliberately cause you harm by abandoning you? I realize you would dearly love to have your papa still alive, but wishing something and having it declared as fact are two very different things . . ." Simms hesitates again, then seems to make some private decision.

"Martha, you've been informed that a man—or men—resembling your father have been seen at such and such a location. Quite naturally, you desire additional information. Should you press for further details, however, I fear you'll be told that gold coins must cross certain palms if your wishes are to be met . . . Now, let us say that you agree and willingly share of your wealth. I assure you that you will learn nothing definitive."

"Oh . . ." Martha murmurs.

"Such horrible frauds are committed continually, my dear. Why, just last year—"

"But Mr. Kelman must also be aware of those cruel practices, Mr. Simms."

"And that is precisely why I question his motives in coming to you with these spurious claims. Now, come, regard the correspondence I brought you. It's from the Roseggers, requesting your presence at tea this afternoon. Mrs. Rosegger mentions that she and her husband enjoyed meeting you last evening at the Durands' home. In the circumstances, however, I think it best if I respond and say that you are indisposed."

"No!" Martha's reply is more forceful than she intended. "I'll act on my own behalf, Mr. Simms." She glances at the sheet of paper in her hand. "Yes, I will go."

"Then I'll accompany you."

"No!"

"Martha, my dear. You must trust me to know what is best for you. Just as you trusted your dear father."

TEA, THEN. TEA at the Rosegger home on Chestnut Street. Martha and Owen Simms are admitted into the drawing room by a footman who then departs to seek his master and mistress. Martha doesn't speak; instead, she withdraws into herself and wonders if her father's confidential secretary must always accompany her in future. She ardently wishes she hadn't displayed such a dearth of self-control. It's certainly not how Emily Durand would behave: breaking statuary and exposing every fickle emotion that entered her heart. Pondering these reproaches, Martha feels the room begin to constrict; the suites of chairs, the statuary and paintings grow too cramped, the air too full of wood smoke and the heavy scents of pomander and bergamot. When the Roseggers enter the room, she almost rushes at them in relief.

The husband, as she remembers from the previous evening, is a handsome man with an uncompromising stride and equally martial posture. He also has a predatory air that she didn't detect at the Durands' party. When he looks at her, which he does often and intently, she feels her skin begin to prickle in discomfort.

Mrs. Rosegger, as was the case during their previous meeting, doesn't shine. Martha recalls the gossip Emily shared when the ladies withdrew to an upstairs sitting room prior to the conjuring: Mrs.

Rosegger's father had been a successful grocer, the owner of several shops and the employer of many men, and he'd doted upon his daughter, raising her above his two sons—or so Emily had stated in a *sotto voce* tone—and at his death she'd inherited his entire estate, which was almost immediately transferred to the man who'd been her suitor and quickly became her husband, and eventually a person as affluent and influential as Lemuel Beale.

"Rosegger married her for the father's money, of course," Emily Durand had murmured with a wicked laugh. "Why else would a man on the rise ally himself with a woman whose parent had been a mere merchant? At least those were the rumors . . . The others concerned the cause of the father's demise. He was said to have unwittingly consumed a tainted piece of fish, but I ask you, if you were a grocer, wouldn't you be able to detect good from bad?" Martha remembers Emily's arch smile as she uttered these words, as well as the whispered assents of the other ladies who'd joined their small group.

"So pleasant to see you again, Miss Beale," Rosegger himself now states. "And you also, Mr. Simms, an equally pleasant surprise." It's the husband rather than the wife who takes the lead, and he gestures formally toward two chairs for his guests while Mrs. Rosegger hurriedly assumes her place at the tea table and begins focusing her full concentration on her hostess tasks. "I trust you were not overburdened by that charlatan's quackery last night, Miss Beale," he continues.

Martha takes the proffered cup of tea as she forms a response. She notes that Mrs. Rosegger never once looks at her face although Martha tries to give her a smile of gratitude. "It was . . . odd, sir. In truth, I cannot say I was immune to *Signor* Paladino's remarks, however—"

Rosegger interrupts with a brief, sardonic laugh. "There's no such thing as clairvoyance or second sight, Miss Beale. I'm sure your father's estimable secretary has already assured you of that fact. Why, John Durand told me later last evening that an equally unpleasant spectacle occurred at a previous conjuring. The fellow pretended to see a dead child with its tongue cut out."

"Oh!" The sound of protest that issues from Mrs. Rosegger is over almost before it begins.

"My wife is a delicate creature," her husband announces flatly before returning his potent gaze to Martha. "Such a preposterous occurrence cannot be, of course, Miss Beale, but we must remember that this purported necromancer makes his living as a performer, and that his public audiences are generally of the most ill-informed kind. Naturally, they desire spectacle and melodrama, and he's obviously adept at providing what they want."

Martha waits, expecting either wife or husband to say more, but when neither speaks she sits straighter in her chair, urging herself to ask the questions foremost in her mind. "Mr. Simms tells me you know my father, Mr. Rosegger."

"The entire city knows of your father, Miss Beale."

Martha remains silent, thinking her host will continue, but he does not; instead, he sips his tea, eats a piece of seed cake, and carefully crosses his legs. She is beginning to wonder why she was invited when suddenly Mrs. Rosegger hurtles into a rapid and peculiar conversation:

"An unskilled laborer earns at most sixty pennies a day, Miss Beale, did you know that? When that person can find work, that is. The cheapest of lodgings is a single room shared with a number of other people and costing an exorbitant twelve cents daily—"

"Miss Beale isn't interested in life among the derelict of our city."

"Oh, but I am!" Martha protests, although it's really for her hostess's sake that she makes this boastful claim.

"A meal of scraps costs a penny," Mrs. Rosegger continues in her skittish rush.

"So does a glass of rum," her husband interjects with some brutality, "and I'm told the rum is often substituted for food. Let's have no more of this, Mrs. Rosegger. We'll have our guest and her guardian running for the door." He turns his attention to Martha. "My wife, as I indicated, has a delicate heart. As you must have heard, she was raised by a man who gave employment to many. Some were deserving; some were not. I fear his daughter inherited his natural kindliness, which makes it difficult for her to detect the good from the bad."

Throughout this little speech, Rosegger's wife scarcely moves, while Martha inadvertently recalls Emily's innuendo concerning the father's demise. *Good fish from bad,* Martha thinks, then pushes away the unpleasant suggestion, stating a conciliatory "I suppose, sir, that our purpose on this earth is to discover the virtue in *all* people—even those whom society considers wicked or corrupt."

"Prettily said, Miss Beale," Rosegger states, while his wife's response is a small catch of her breath that almost sounds like a sob. She covers her mouth as though she'd hiccoughed only, then pastes on a watery smile as she turns to Martha.

"More cake, Miss Beale? Or would you care to sample some of my ratafias? I make them myself."

Martha can hear a note of mutiny in this last statement, but Mrs. Rosegger's bland expression registers only wifely responsibility; and her husband makes no comment of either approval or disapproval of her sojourns in her kitchen.

With the plight of the city's poor exhausted or eliminated as a subject, Rosegger then expresses his formal sympathies for her father's death. "But it's not certain he is dead, sir," Martha counters softly, at which observation her host rises abruptly from his fancifully carved and brocaded chair and strides to a window, where he stands, hands clasped behind him, regarding the little traffic on the street. "It's winter, Miss Beale; surely there can be no hope of surviving a fall in the river" is what he says while Martha screws up her courage to pose another question. She avoids looking in Owen Simms's direction as she speaks.

"Do you know of any enemies my father might possess, sir? Someone . . . someone who would wish him ill . . . Perhaps even murder him—?"

"Goodness, Martha!" Simms protests. "Have we not had enough of this unfortunate chat before now?"

But Martha hasn't finished. "I'm asking you, Mr. Rosegger, because of what Mr. Simms tells me of your stature in the community."

"Why don't you pose the question to your father's confidential secretary then, Miss Beale?"

"I already have . . ."

"But you don't trust the response?" Rosegger laughs his dismissive laugh again.

"That's not my meaning, sir—"

"No?"

Martha is growing increasingly flustered. "I'm not here to discuss Mr. Simms, sir."

Rosegger eyes her with his shrewd and mocking stare; his wife remains focused wholly on her tea tray.

"You and my father are two men of affairs, sir—"

"And as such we engender our share of envy, Miss Beale." He produces another laugh; then the sound abruptly vanishes. "I suppose there have been those who wished me dead and gone. There will probably be more. I cannot describe your father's situation unless it were the mirror image of my own."

"A rumor, perhaps—"

"Martha, come, my dear," Simms interposes, but their host's domineering voice cancels even Simms's objections.

"I do not indulge in gossip, Miss Beale. And I would suggest you do not, either." Then he turns to the door. "Mr. Simms, shall we leave the ladies to their own devices? I have some excellent port laid by."

But Martha cannot let Rosegger go. "Can my father have been in debt, sir?"

"Anyone who trades in commodities is in debt at one time or another, Miss Beale—"

"I mean in serious debt," Martha interrupts.

"My suggestion, madam, is that you consult with someone closer to home."

Then the door to the drawing room opens; Simms exits with their host, and Martha and Mrs. Rosegger are left with a cold draft where once stood the lady's husband.

In his absence, Mrs. Rosegger begins tidying away the tea things, devoting so much attention to her chores that it seems she cannot both speak and act. Taking the cup from Martha's hand, she suddenly leans close. "I believe you've met Thomas Kelman," she murmurs, then adds a hasty "Listen to him" before continuing in a louder and more public voice. "Shall I show my children to you, Miss Beale? While my husband visits with Mr. Simms? My young ones are their mother's pride and joy."

Dreaming or Awake

Martha's dreams that night are tortured. She revisits the scene of her mother's deathbed, where she sees adult faces floating above her through the gloom. Their features are as bland as milk pudding, pasty white and utterly unrecognizable; the words they speak have no more meaning than the wind rushing down a chimney. She wanders among these tall, moving forms as if she, and not her mother, were the ghost. She asks a question, tugs at a sleeve, but no one responds, and so she stands apart, staring at the surface of a table, at a silver tray with a glass and spoon resting upon it. The contents of the glass are cloudy and pale. Martha, the child, thinks it looks like snow, if snow were liquid. She lifts the spoon to put it to her lips, but a large, angry hand snatches it away; then the spoon and the glass also disappear.

Next the dream shifts; she's still a child, but dressed in bed attire—a flannelette gown without a woolen wrapper—and standing in the night-dark hallway of her home. There's a solitary candle lit at the far end, but this small version of herself is too frightened of unseen demons to reach the safety of its orange glow. She hears a lady crying out; the sound makes Martha want to run toward the voice and offer aid, but she's far too terrified to move. Instead, she begins to cry, weeping with a noise that sounds like a puppy whimpering. A hand touches her shoulder; another takes her arm, and all at once she can't move, cannot run away, and the hands move to her chest, covering her mouth until she feels she can no longer breathe. She gasps, tries to shake free, but the constraining fingers only grip her tighter. She's so very young and helpless, and the person holding her so large.

Martha awakes from this nightmare, panting. The noise of her own fear follows her from sleep into consciousness. Her pillow is wet with tears. For a long moment, she believes that she's still a young girl escaping from a faceless foe.

Then the door to her bedroom opens a crack, and the light from the hallway knifes yellowly in. "Martha, are you quite well? I was passing in the hall and heard you cry out."

Still lying on her back and staring at the lace canopy above her head, Martha finds herself caught between the vivid reality of her dream and a peculiarly trance-like wakefulness; and so she answers with an automatic "Yes. Yes, of course, Mr. Simms . . . But I must ask you to leave my chambers . . . It's not appropriate that—"

Instead of complying with her wishes, however, he moves toward her bed and the bellpull that will summon her maid. "You're agitated, Martha. Let me ring for your servant. She can prepare a sleeping draught."

"No," Martha orders before he can reach her. "I won't have you awaken her." She pulls herself upright and drags the coverlet up to her throat. It seems wrong indeed that she can't convince Owen Simms to quit her rooms. "I'm sorry to have disturbed you, but I ask you again to leave. I'm sure it's very late."

"Sometime after two, I believe."

She looks at Simms more closely. "You're wearing one of Father's dressing gowns."

"It's very similar to one of his, Martha. Your father kindly had it made for me by his own tailor. You're observant to notice how alike the two garments are . . . Now, let me summon your servant so that you can get a peaceful night's slumber."

"I won't have the household disturbed because I had a foolish nightmare, Mr. Simms. I'm quite well, I assure you, but you must go away. It's not appropriate that you remain with me at this hour."

"Nonsense, my dear. I've known you since you were a girl. I'm as close to a family member as any you might have."

"I have no family except my father." Martha frowns, remembering pieces of her dream. "Have I, Mr. Simms . . . ? I seem to recall a lady—"

"Your mother, I presume—"

"No, not my mother . . . another lady . . . Did my mother have a sister, Mr. Simms? Or my father?"

"If you had female relatives, Martha, don't you think your father would have introduced you to them? Or male family members, for that matter?"

"That doesn't answer my question."

"Of course it does." He smiles benignly down at her. "Do you imagine your father purposely withheld aunts and uncles and cousins who could have lightened his own burdens as a parent?"

Martha doesn't reply. She pictures the twin parts of her dream, but this illusory fiction is no match for Owen Simm's logic.

"There," his calm voice continues, "you see? It only takes a modicum of common sense to provide solutions to all our queries—whether large or small. There were no uncles or aunts, no young cousins with whom you could play, my dear; instead, your father provided his singular care and support. And that was ample indeed . . ."

Simms pauses. "Now, Martha, I will do as you request and leave you to return to your slumbers as you can, but before I do, I have a request to make. It's a serious one, and I want you to consider well before responding."

Martha's heart thuds in her chest. For a horrible moment, she imagines Owen Simms is about to ask her hand in marriage, but the notion is so absurd she quickly casts it aside. "What is it, Mr. Simms?"

"Take as much time as you wish before making your decision, but know also that I will continue to press my case—"

"Yes, Mr. Simms?" Again Martha experiences a hard thump that feels like panic. Again she reminds herself that the furthest thing from Owen Simms's thoughts is a union with his master's daughter.

"Your father, dear Martha, has been missing for some time—"

"Sixteen days."

"Yes, quite so. Sixteen days. I realize that what I'm about to say may seem to disregard the delicacy of your emotions . . . but in fact, it is to those very sensibilities that I appeal."

Oh! Martha thinks. *Oh, no! I was correct in my unlikely conjecture, after all! What should I do? What can I do?* "Mr. Simms," she begins, "I believe I know the request you wish to make of me."

Owen Simms lays his head on one side while he continues to gaze down at her. "Ah, then you're as wise as your father. It is he—as well as you—that I'm considering when I make my suggestion. He would not wish us to continue in this vague and ambiguous mode forever—"

"Pray, Mr. Simms, let us talk no more of this, but say a peaceable good night to one another."

Owen Simms stands still and tall. "And so you agree that we declare your father drowned and so proceed with an announcement and funeral service?"

"What?" Martha is so astonished at these words that her body leaps in surprise.

"You told me you understood the nature of my request . . ."

"Yes . . . Yes . . . So I did . . ."

"Then we will proceed as I suggest? And place the household in an appropriate state of mourning?"

"Mr. Simms, I beg of you. Let us discuss this in the light of day—"

"You cannot stave off the inevitable forever, Martha."

"Good night, Mr. Simms."

"Mine is not an unreasonable recommendation, my dear. And you will, I know, take some measure of solace when you finally acknowledge your loss."

"Tomorrow, Mr. Simms. We will continue this discussion tomorrow after we have breakfasted."

BUT THE NEXT morning, Martha doesn't arise until well after Owen Simms has left her father's house, and when she's finally eaten and dressed, and prepared herself to consider Simms's advice—or steeled herself to cease avoiding it—her maid comes running up the stairs. There's a man downstairs, and he's insistent upon seeing her at once. He's in the foyer, and the footman cannot get him to budge.

Martha continues the task of affixing a brooch to her bodice, although her hands have begun to shake. Her mind pictures Thomas Kelman waiting below, and a smile begins to flicker around the corners of her mouth. When the smile grows, she dispatches it, instead attempting to mirror the type of cool gaze she imagines Emily Durand displaying in such a situation. But, studying and adjusting this haughty expression in the looking glass, Martha inadvertently stabs herself with the brooch's pin. In a pique, she yanks off the offending piece of jewelry and throws it back in the box; then she all but runs out of her room and down the stairs. The bright smile remains despite her loftiest intentions.

It's not Kelman who has been admitted, however; it's Eusapio Paladino's assistant. "Forgive my intrusion, Miss Beale," he wheezes. "My master is outside in a carriage. He's most anxious to speak with you in private."

Martha is stunned into silence. *What can the conjurer possibly want from me?* she asks herself, but can find no answer. "I'm afraid that's impossible—" she begins.

"You will not be alone. I will remain with you—to translate."

Martha lifts her jaw as she's seen her father do in circumstances not to his liking. "Your master is welcome to join you here in my home." She steps back half a pace as if to precede him into the drawing room.

"He refuses to enter this abode, Miss Beale. I'm afraid he has some horror of it. I beseech you . . . Please . . . It's a matter of urgency."

"But I am—"

"Please, Miss Beale. There's a lady—" He checks his speech.

"A lady?"

"In a vision."

"Is it me . . . ? *Marta* . . . dead . . . as your master said the other evening?"

The assistant only shakes his unwieldy head. "And there is something about your father also."

At this news Martha's sense of decorum starts to desert her. "*Signor* Paladino has information concerning my father?"

"Please, Miss Beale. My master will require only a little of your time."

Martha considers the request. Previously, she would have declined, and her reasons would have been obvious to those who knew her history: Lemuel Beale's daughter didn't travel unchaperoned in the company of two strange men; Lemuel Beale's daughter never accepted any invitation of which her father did not previously approve; in fact, Lemuel Beale's daughter rarely left her home, and when she did, it was most habitually in his company.

"I will fetch my cloak," she says.

THE HIRED CARRIAGE speeds out of the city, jouncing from the cobbled byways onto the stone-strewn dirt lanes of the countryside. Martha bumps from side to side, asking herself with growing apprehension whether her decision to join the mesmerist was wise. A lifetime of being the circumspect and prudent daughter has been tossed to the winds, and she's beginning to sorely regret her newfound temerity. All this while, Eusapio Paladino crushes close, alternately moaning, sighing, and conversing at an erratic tempo that sometimes gushes a tumult of words and sometimes sounds as halting and painful as a child's tremulous stammer. She assumes he's speaking to his assistant in Italian.

"What can you tell me about my father's disappearance?" she interrupts after another minute or two of this alien conversation. "*Signor* Lemuel Beale," she adds, fearing she has mispronounced the word.

There's no reply from Paladino or his assistant, so Martha repeats her question, adding an assertive "You said you had information to share concerning my father. Please, you must tell me."

But the answer the assistant supplies is a halting "There's a lady . . . *Signor* Paladino has conjured her in a mental vision . . . She does not reside in the city but in the country . . . My master has visited this place in a trance-induced state. He's attempting to locate it now . . ."

"But my—"

"Hush!" the assistant insists. "The great Eusapio Paladino must have silence in which to work."

"But—" Martha objects. Paladino suddenly throws himself back against the coach's prickly horsehair cushions. His eyes are closed, his face rigid in concentration. Martha glances at the assistant in appeal. "My father . . . ?" she asks again.

An abbreviated consultation ensues while Martha, increasingly concerned, is batted time and again into Eusapio's steely body. She grips the seat with her hands but finds her fingers rolling under his thighs. She pulls her hands away but is then bucketed into his chest.

"There's a lady . . ." the assistant reiterates as though Martha had not posed her own question. "My master informs me that she had some unfortunate situation with a man . . . You understand . . . ?" He looks to Martha, who shakes her head *no* while another rapid spate of foreign words occurs.

". . . It was a physical problem . . . a love problem . . ."

Martha shuts her eyes while more peculiar words barrel past her.

". . . She was ravished . . ."

Martha turns her hot, chagrined face against the cold siding of the coach; her stomach heaves in embarrassment and self-reproach. *Why did I agree to this?* she demands of herself. *These men could be of the vilest sort, and here I am held against my will. Oh, Martha, you fool! You silly, silly woman! Your lack of circumspection may well prove your undoing.* She has a sudden and gruesome picture of Thomas Kelman called in to investigate her death at the hands of her two companions, and raises a gloved hand in both protest and supplication, but Eusapio and his assistant merely continue the horrible tide of words. ". . . Ravished by her brother . . . Many times . . ."

Martha covers her mouth with her hand; she gags. "Stop the coach, please. I am ill. Please! I am terribly ill!"

The horses clatter to a halt; dust swirls past the descending figures, covering them in the brown dirt and gray grit of the road; and

Martha kneels ignominiously in the bracken. She feels Eusapio's hand touch her shoulder and flinches in fright. *"Marta, Maria,"* he whispers.

"I am not *Maria* . . . Mary," Martha mutters in her shame, then finally summons an angry "Why am I here? You promised news about my father. Instead you—"

A further slew of Italian words issues from Eusapio as Martha gradually gathers her wits and her strength. "I must return home at once—"

Eusapio studies her. *"Difficile. Molto difficile . . ."* Then he stops speaking.

"Why did you bring me here?" Martha demands, standing to glare at him. "And why must you taunt me with these horrible tales? You said you had information on my father, while instead you . . . you—" Outrage curtails her speech.

Paladino makes no reply to Martha's accusations, and at length his assistant supplies an answer. "*Signor* Paladino no longer has a reliable picture of where this unknown woman dwells . . . As you know, his remarkable gift of clairvoyance requires full concentration from all persons present . . . and this brief stop has . . . has broken the thread of his vision . . . He agrees that we should return homeward but insists, *insists*, that your life is in terrible peril . . ."

Eusapio reaches for Martha's hand, but she backs away with a firm and resolute step as the translator continues. "He wants you to know that he cares for you . . . that his soul recognizes your soul . . . and that he bears you the deepest respect . . . But, please, Miss Beale, be careful of who your friends are—"

"Take me home," Martha interrupts. Her voice is as stony as her face. "Take me home at once."

A Secret Too Vile to Keep

THOMAS KELMAN TAKES THE TEACUP Martha proffers, although his expression remains grim, and it's doubtful whether he knows what he's just been handed. In fact, it appears as if his fingers might snap the delicate china in two. Against the pale glow of the hearth fire, and the darkened windows that reflect the now dusky day, the painted porcelain seems very fragile and white. "You should not have been alone in the company of those two men, Miss Beale. They are unsavory characters, and Paladino's claim of having news regarding your—"

Seated meekly at the tea table while her visitor is ensconced in an adjacent settee, Martha raises her hand to beg silence. "Please, Mr. Kelman, I'm only too aware of how foolhardy I was—"

"You are a wealthy woman, Miss Beale. I need not remind you that kidnappers prey upon such as you—"

"Mr. Kelman, I—"

"And this other atrocious tale! It's unconscionable, Miss Beale. It's unconscionable that this so-called clairvoyant would dare to—!"

"I'm fully aware of all of that, Mr. Kelman. I am. Truly. It was difficult enough for me to reveal the details of *Signor* Paladino's vision to you in the first place. Indeed, I hesitated for a full hour before sending word and asking you to come to my house."

"You should not be forced to hear of such horrors, Miss Beale."

Martha puts down her own teacup, and as she does so, tears unexpectedly start into her eyes. She turns her head to keep Kelman from noticing. She feels incapable of stemming the emotion that inspires her upwelling of sorrow, or even of identifying its source. "I had hoped . . ." she manages to murmur while her blurred gaze regards the purple-hued panes of glass, the gas streetlamps flickering to a dull ocher life, as well as her own doleful reflection. ". . . I had hoped . . ." But there seems no point in defending her decision to accompany Paladino and his assistant. If there truly was news of her father . . . Martha doesn't bother to finish the thought. It's suddenly quite obvious to her that Lemuel Beale is gone and that there's no hope for his return. "Mr. Simms wishes to declare my father officially dead," she says. Her tone is flat; her face remains hidden.

Kelman's outrage at her unnecessary brush with danger evaporates when he hears the despondency in her voice. "And you, Martha, what do you wish?"

For a moment she cannot understand what she's been asked; all she hears is that Thomas Kelman has called her by her given name. "I?" she finally manages to whisper.

"Yes, you. What do *you* wish?"

"Wish . . ." Martha considers this word, and considers also how alien is the concept of following her own desires. *Wish?* she thinks, *I?* She cannot remember when she last joined the two expressions in the same sentence. "I hardly know, Thomas—" Her words halt with a quick gasp. How can she have been so forward, so inappropriate in her behavior? It's one thing for a gentleman to make such a blunder; it's quite another thing for a lady to err in a similar fashion. Her mind flies around searching for a solution to her dilemma. Should she apologize for her egregious familiarity, or would that only call attention to her mistake? She decides to say nothing; the coward's choice, she knows. "I wish my father had not vanished," Martha says at length, and uses no name whatsoever.

Kelman thinks. If he's aware of his hostess's *faux pas,* he makes no sign. Instead, he's silent; and Martha, glancing at him furtively, can see how troubled he's become.

"Can it be, Martha, that there is some greater evil at work in this situation that we have surmised? Your father, as you noted, has 'vanished.' Purportedly, he's been seen elsewhere since his strange disappearance—or someone very closely resembling him has been sighted . . . Then this morning you were lured into a carriage by two men who have only the sketchiest of histories. What did they intend to do with you after they'd conveyed you to their unspecified location? If you hadn't become physically ill, and so caused the carriage to stop, where would you have been taken? And to what end?"

Martha has been so intent on Kelman's repetition of her given name that she has difficulty following the questions he's posing. "There's also the 'lady' Paladino described," she offers; embarrassment at recalling the somnambulist's description of the mystery woman's plight makes her ears suddenly tingle and her cheeks and neck grow hot.

"I don't believe there is such a person," Kelman states with some force. "I think she's an invention, a ruse, a manipulation to make you fearful and upset."

"Well, the trick worked," Martha replies with a shy laugh.

"A trick indeed," Kelman echoes somberly. "But why?" He leans back in his seat and stares at the fire, frowning and remote. Martha finds herself studying his face; at the moment, comforting him seems of paramount importance, and she yearns to cast aside discussions of her misguided journey into the countryside, and even to forgo speaking about her father.

"You trust your servants, do you not?" Thomas Kelman asks after several somber moments.

"Yes, of course."

"And Owen Simms?"

"Naturally." Even as she responds, Martha realizes she's not certain she's telling the truth.

"And you feel these people would defend you should . . . should the need arise?"

"But surely such an awful occurrence will not, Thomas?" Martha's lips clamp tight in her dismay. "Mr. Kelman . . ."

He stands abruptly; he's hardly listened to her query. "I wonder if you should consider hiring a secret service agency."

"A secret service agency?" Martha has never heard the term before.

"I know of a highly respected one. It's located in the Wintrob Building on Juniper Street."

"Oh!" She mulls over the location. It's not the most advantageous of addresses. "But what service does such an agency—on Juniper Street—supply?"

"In the case of a criminal investigation, it may be beneficial to have a specialist, other than the constabulary, make discreet inquiries, or, in certain instances, provide—"

"A criminal investigation," she interjects. "Do you mean concerning my father?"

Kelman's response is to continue with an evasive "Provide protection to clients who might be in harm's way."

"You refer to me, then." Martha shakes her head. *What would I give,* she thinks, *to change the tenor of this conversation? To be simply two people enjoying the warmth of a pleasant fire and the company of one another?*

"Yes. It's you I'm thinking of."

"And my father? Is he part of this 'criminal investigation' of yours?"

"I cannot yet explain more, Martha—other than what I said previously."

"Cannot or will not?" Martha queries, but her guest makes no reply. So she continues with a grave "I will give your suggestion some thought." She can't bring herself to add "Mr. Kelman," nor can she say "Thomas." She suppresses a sigh. "I met with Mrs. Rosegger . . . Yesterday. At tea. She and her husband invited me . . . Mrs. Rosegger seems to hold you in high regard."

"Good" is the only response Martha receives, then Kelman walks toward the hearth, where he turns, the better to face his still-seated hostess. "I intend to thoroughly question this Eusapio Paladino and his servant."

Martha looks up into his eyes. "May I accompany you?"

"I don't believe that would be wise."

"Oh, wise!" Martha bursts out, gesturing so boldly she nearly upsets the tea tray. "Should I not be the judge of that?" Then she adds an equally reckless "Should I not, Thomas?"

Kelman regards her. Despite his standing position, he doesn't seem to be looking down at her; rather he seems to be gazing straight across as if he were discovering something about Martha Beale that he hadn't fully understood before. "You're quite right. You should be the judge of what you do. And when. And how . . . And yes, it would be most helpful if you would accompany me when I question this man Paladino."

EMILY DURAND'S BERINGED hand clenches in a spasm as she replaces the letter she's just read in its envelope. She tries to conceal the dreadful unease this message from Mrs. Rosegger has caused, but her fingers willfully betray her.

"No reply," Emily announces to whichever servant handed her the missive. The face blurs before her, and she realizes she has no notion of whether the features are male or female, young or old. "That will be all!" she barks out. "I said there was no reply."

"Yes, madam . . . But the messenger said he was to wait for a response." The old/young, female/male presence remains as still as a stone in front of Emily. "His instructions were to wait."

"Am I not mistress in my own house? And are not *my* instructions paramount here?"

"Yes, madam." The servant doesn't budge.

"You may leave me, then," Emily orders.

The servant doesn't speak but also doesn't quit the room.

"There's no response to the letter . . . I believe I made myself clear."

"Yes, madam."

Long seconds tick by. "Mrs. John Durand is not available," Emily announces at length and, summoning every ounce of strength, rises from her chair. "Tell the wretched messenger that you had been instructed not to disturb me."

"He will ask for the return of the envelope, madam."

For a moment, Emily seems about to lash out and strike her servant. Instead, she wilts and sinks down into her chair again. "Bring me my pen and paper. And be quick about it!"

She dashes off a response to the unwelcome note, folds it, then rethinks her reply and quickly rips her letter in half. "The woman cannot be planning to blackmail me?" Emily mutters below her breath. "Because to what other secret can she refer if not to . . . ?"

She jumps up, strides away from the table, and then immediately returns. *I will have to see Rosegger's wife face-to-face,* Emily tells herself. *There's no escaping the fact. And no denying that the hideous woman must be treated as an equal—if only until she reveals what information she holds. But if I can delay . . . if I can postpone such an interview until I discover what sort of "secret" she may be suggesting . . . if I can make certain my own actions seem blameless . . .*

Emily grabs up another sheet of paper, writing a polite but ambiguous message of thanks for Mrs. Rosegger's concern for her well-being and suggesting that they meet at some unspecified time the following month. *I fear I am much overburdened with engagements at the moment,* Emily concludes, *but I welcome the opportunity of calling upon you in future.*

There! she thinks. *That should provide me with ample opportunity for determining my own course of action.* But as Emily seals the envelope, she realizes that her body is shaking uncontrollably. *What can that horrid creature know?* Her brain cries out. *What other secret can there be but my clandestine liasion?*

FOR HER PART, mrs. rosegger nods in resignation as she reads Emily Durand's reply. It's not the first time she's been thus refused. It won't be the last. Still, she deeply regrets this latest snub. It makes the task she's set herself so much more complex. If she can't see the woman soon, how is she to successfully warn her of what may befall? Surely not by a letter that anyone—including their husbands—might chance upon and read!

Mulling over these dilemmas, Mrs. Rosegger walks through her home. Save for her children with their nursemaid and governess, she's alone. She's almost always alone. Her husband has long since made it clear that his ways are not to be dictated by social niceties or necessities. He will come and go as he pleases—and with whomever he pleases.

Such is the pact she's made. And, oh, how handsome and glorious that contract long ago appeared! A luxurious home, servants at her bidding, matched horses to pull the carriage, and footmen arrayed in colored silks—just like the kind that wait upon royalty. In her younger mind, the original pictures included supper parties, afternoon musicales, ladies proffering embossed visiting cards or stopping for tea, evenings with her husband "at home" where the elite of the city might meet. None of those daydreams have come to pass. Rosegger doesn't enjoy entertaining, just as he does not enjoy his wife.

"'For every one that doeth evil hateth the light,'" she recites in a whisper from the Gospel according to John, then adds an ardent "What shall I do? This secret is too vile to keep." For a moment, she considers seeking Thomas Kelman's advice, but then quickly shakes her head *no.* Rosegger would never forgive her, she knows.

But if I can keep my own counsel and my husband is not apprised . . . ? she wonders; and the traitorous notion opens up a world of such brilliant heights and depths, and full of such glowing color and scent, that she closes her eyes for fear of falling.

The Devil Incarnate

I CANNOT HELP YOU, I'M afraid," Rosegger tells the man sitting opposite him. The tone is languid and sure, quiet because it doesn't need to shout.

His guest stirs violently in his seat, and the chair's innards groan: horsehair stuffing, iron springs; even the wood frame creaks. "I cannot afford to be caught out in this, Rosegger," he insists, although the sound is closer to a plea.

"Rather late to consider that, don't you think, Durand?"

The two men sit in high-backed chairs in a room paneled with cherrywood. Vapor lamps burn atop several tables, but the light cast from these otherwise lively flames is dulled by a superabundance of dark drapery and furnishings and a mahogany ceiling so densely coffered and black, it lies like midnight upon the scene.

Durand again shifts anxiously in his chair. He doesn't speak, but his host produces a single cynical laugh.

"Say what you wish, and be done with it, Mr. Durand. I'm a busy man; the hour is growing late, and I have other affairs to settle before quitting these offices for my home. I do not cleave to your fancy ways, as you know, and I like plain speech."

As if to confirm the tardiness of the hour, there's a subdued passing of footsteps in the passage that lies beyond the closed doors. The faint and hurrying squeak of leather reveals the walker is not a wealthy man but a scribe or clerk belonging to Rosegger's business.

"You must help me," Durand plainly states.

"*Must?* Must? Do you think I have the power to keep these wrongful doings of yours from coming to light?"

"I have my reputation to consider, Rosegger . . . my family's . . . my . . . my—"

"Your wife, Emily, perhaps?"

John Durand moans. He buries his face in his hands. "Don't bring my wife into it!"

"Sentimentality comes late to most of us, doesn't it?" his host observes.

Durand's arms straighten; his fingers jerk back to his sides. "You are the very devil, sir!" he says.

"It's taken you a good long while to recognize that fact," Rosegger responds with another harsh laugh.

"I have friends, you know," Durand next offers, but his hollow tone belies the self-assured intent.

"*Had* friends, I should say."

"They'll stand by me . . ."

"Will they, now?"

John Durand's chest rumbles; he seems to be gathering his last bit of strength. "You will not be a popular man in Philadelphia should you permit word of this . . . of this *problem* of mine to surface—"

"Your 'problem,' sir! Your 'problem' has nothing to do with me. Prison is what you're facing, Mr. Durand."

JOHN DURAND FLINGS himself down the street. He marches willy-nilly, not caring against whom or what his arms and shoulders bang.

"Watch it, sir!" he hears. "Pardon me!" "That's a lady you've pushed by!" The voices are incensed, even threatening. Durand pays no heed. He needs air, needs to clear his brain, needs to calculate his future.

He flounders on, approaching and then skirting Washington Square and the fine houses that send their stately glow upon the nearly deserted turf. *The devil!* he thinks. *The devil incarnate, that's who Rosegger is. How dare he threaten a Durand! A man who was once no better than a hop-up-johnnie. No better indeed!*

As he storms along and the minutes pass, his passion begins to diminish, leaving in its stead a child-like loneliness and longing. It's now approaching the dinner hour, and he feels badly in need of a treat, although his thoughts don't turn to food or drink: a visit to his club or the rowdier recesses of an oyster cellar. Instead, his senses begin to yearn for the soft and innocent caress of a woman. Someone pure of heart and sweet, someone to soothe his tormented soul, to sit on his knee, gaze adoringly into his eyes, and listen in patient silence to all his bitter woes.

Hardly aware where his feet are leading him, he finds himself wandering deeper and deeper into the soiled alleys where such girls are found.

He passes one house for ladies of pleasure, then another, and each time is beckoned inside. But he shrinks from the offers. The establishments seem almost too respectable, and he's deathly afraid of being discovered. He ignores the whores' invitations, pretending instead that he's merely using the street as a shortcut while attending to urgent business.

They know better, of course. They can smell lust as well as fear, and their suggestive phrases turn to catcalls; and John Durand finds his pace increasing until he's nearly running. He forces himself to slow. He draws a breath, thrusts out his broad chest, then all at once decides against this foolhardy mission, ordering himself to turn from the alley and journey home.

But such is the terrible battle within his soul that his feet freeze in place; his knees lock; and all the pent-up anguish and grief produced by his recent interview come bubbling up in a hunger that cannot be denied. He continues down the path toward the meaner houses.

And then stops suddenly. Another man stands in front of him. Although his back is to Durand, and although he's severely shrouded in cloak and hat, John feels they know one another. He recoils, terrified that this unexpected acquaintance might turn and recognize him; then he shrinks into the shadows, pinning his shoulders against the slimy walls.

"What are you waiting for, then?" he hears a female voice call out to him. "Trying to turn into stone?" The sound is girlish and high-pitched, although there's an obvious effort at seeming more mature. "I reside close by . . . Pretty little room all my own with the daintiest of looking glasses—" The girl pauses in her sales pitch, peering through the gloom. "You been down this street before, sir?"

"No," Durand tells her, but he keeps his voice muffled lest his unseen companion hear.

"I could swear I seen you hereabouts."

"Someone else, my dear madam," Durand murmurs.

"Oh, I like that! 'My dear madam'! I've never been called that." She laughs gleefully again. "Come on, sir; I'll make it worth your while . . . Or another evening if you prefer . . . Marietta's my name."

"Mary—?"

"If you wish plain Mary, sir, I can be that," the girl coos in reply. "Or Pamela, or any other pretty name you fancy." She creeps forward as if she means to curl herself around his legs like a cat.

"No!" Durand says, suddenly repulsed by the girl's coarse and insidious manner. He pushes himself away from the wall, no longer caring who sees or hears him. "Be off with you, madam. I want none of your wares." Then he rushes down the alley with the irregular gait of a man being pursued.

The Lame Man and the Girl

THE HAND BANGING UPON THE door is loud and urgent. Emily starts up out of a heavy sleep. "Who . . . ?" she mutters. "Who is . . . ?" Then she looks at the face lying close to hers; the noise from beyond the bedroom has not yet disturbed it.

"*Caro mio,*" she whispers. "*Caro,* my dear one . . . Wake up . . . I believe your assistant is trying to rouse you." For a ghastly moment, Emily imagines it's her husband that Eusapio's servant is trying to warn them of, but she willfully forces that terrible vision from her brain. *John cannot possibly know of my presence here, nor of my connection to Paladino,* she tells herself. *Or can he? Can Rosegger's wife have approached John when she found me an unwilling participant in her sly schemes?* Emily's head droops in fear as she mutters a more insistent "Go see what your man wants . . . *Caro* . . . Please . . . Wake up . . . You must send him away . . ."

The banging recommences, and Eusapio finally stirs, reaching for her as he always does, letting his fingers trail across her breasts and her belly as though there were no noise outside, and no matter requiring his attention.

"*Caro*, you must go to the door. Your servant is obviously anxious about some problem, and I fear the noise will produce unwanted attention. Please, now!"

Eusapio swears in his native language, then rises, puts on his dressing gown, and marches angrily through the bedroom and into the outer chamber. The instructions he provided his assistant were plain. He was never to be disturbed when entertaining his guest.

While her lover prepares to admonish his servant, Emily cowers in the bed, pulling the heavy hangings closed and hiding within a mound of linen and blankets that she hopes will conceal her presence in the room should the need arise. As she huddles there below the airless sheets, she feels as frightened and helpless as a child. *It cannot be John!* she tries to promise herself. *It cannot! It cannot!* Despite these forced assurances, terror roils through her stomach, and a greasy sweat breaks out on her skin. *That grocer's daughter had better not have betrayed me; because if she did, she'll find me an implacable enemy.* But Emily knows these threats are hollow. If she's discovered in Eusapio's rooms, the entire world will turn against her.

Scarcely breathing, she hears the door open and Eusapio gasp in surprise. She listens as he argues fiercely with his assistant. She can't understand the words but knows her lover is berating the man. Then she hears another male voice enter the heated discussion. It's a quiet yet insistent tone, its meaning too distant to be understood. Anxiety almost stops her heart. Although she can't detect who this second intruder is, she becomes convinced that it's her husband and that her clever precautions and many stratagems have been to nought. *Dear God,* she thinks, *what's to become of me?* Her tongue is now parched with apprehension, and she prays as she's never prayed before in her life. *Please,* her brain wheedles, *please . . . please . . . Oh, God, help me, please!*

But no. John Durand is not the person who insisted upon disturbing the necromancer in his rooms.

"*Signor* Kelman . . ." Eusapio says. "*Signorina* Beale . . ."

Emily flattens herself and makes not a sound. *No, God,* she continues to beg, *let Eusapio have the wits to keep those two in the outer room. Let his servant remember to close the bedroom door. Please, God, please, please . . . !* Then she recalls that much of her clothing was discarded in the other chamber of Eusapio's suite of rooms. *And dear God, let them imagine my finery belongs to a hired companion, a lady of pleasure—even an admirer who pursued him following one of his performances . . .* If Emily were not so terrified, she might consider what she had to barter for these pleas for safety; instead, part of her mind keeps ardently beseeching God for intervention while the rest of her thoughts wheel about trying to devise a possible escape. *The armoire,* she thinks, *I can hide in the armoire,* but then she cannot recall whether the room has such a thing.

JOHN DURAND RETURNS home to find his wife gone. He questions the servants; no one knows where she's gone; nor had she given word as to when she would be expected to return. Her maid simply says, "She didn't believe you'd be home so soon, sir. She believed you'd gone to your club when you failed to arrive for dinner"—as if that were answer enough.

Durand orders a cold supper prepared, then goes to his own rooms to wash off the city's dirt; and while he does, he is visited with an eerie sense of existing in two places, two bodies.

One self appears to him to be sensible and pragmatic as it carefully unties a cravat, removes a jacket, and walks across a handsomely accoutered dressing room. The other self has lost all semblance of sanity, all claim to hope. This being doesn't reside in a princely home on a pleasing street. Instead, it creeps through the gutters and clings to shadows, pulling its hair and gnashing its teeth. This self is drowning in self-loathing and despair.

Standing in front of a looking glass, he's aware of examining the two creatures that share his body. The one his wife and friends witness daily; the other is known only to him. Durand picks up a silver-backed brush in order to smooth his hair, then watches the mirror-hand move toward his head. So effortless, the action seems, so prudent and serene. So stunningly deceptive.

He replaces the brush, pulls on a different jacket, walks to his desk, dips a pen in ink, rapidly puts ink to paper, blots it, then folds his completed missive in half, in quarters, and finally eighths, firming the creases with desperate hands.

Finished, he returns to his dresser, hides the letter, then rummages within a drawer until he finds the object he needs. His fingers tighten around it as if it holds magical powers. Then he slips it into his pocket, walks silently down the stairs, and goes out into the night.

IT'S MARTHA WHO first observes the women's clothes scattered here and there across the floor in the outer chamber, and Kelman who notices that the door to the bedroom has now been firmly shut. "Oh!" Martha gasps. She draws back and bites her lip, then moves her glance to a less incriminating section of the carpet while Kelman spins on Eusapio's assistant.

"Your master is not alone? You knew this and yet permitted us to accompany you?" The words reverberate with disgust, as if Kelman were saying *How dare you insult this lady by placing her in proximity with a whore?*—which are his thoughts precisely.

"You insisted, Mr. Kelman," the assistant fights back. "I told you that the hour was inopportune."

"You didn't say he was engaged with a . . . with a—" Kelman is so enraged his words stop in his throat. "Miss Beale. Let us go. My many apologies for permitting you to witness this most reprehensible—"

But Martha's next gasp arrests him. Keeping her eyes on the floor, she's recognized the dress tossed so carelessly near a chair. And with the dress, the shoes, and with the shoes, a reticule . . . Her face drains of color. "I must leave this place," she murmurs. "Please . . . This is very wrong."

JOHN DURAND STROKES the Derringer pistol concealed in his pocket, and its cool metal momentarily consoles him, inspiring confidence and resolution. When he doesn't handle the pistol, when his fingers grab the air near his thighs, or when he pauses to wipe his brow, all the caverns of Hell open before his eyes; and he knows himself to be forever damned.

He strides on and on and on, grinds his teeth until his jaws bulge, then sobs aloud and pushes forward, rounding a corner and crossing another street. In the distance he notices a man and a young girl buying hot cooked potatoes from a street vendor. The sight arrests him, and he watches them intently: the girl wonderfully, ardently attentive—and so grateful for this gift of food.

When the lame man and the girl proceed on their way, Durand turns and follows them.

"PLEASE, THOMAS . . . MR. Kelman . . ." Martha repeats. ". . . Please . . . The business we intended for *Signor* Paladino . . . Let us postpone it . . ." The tremulous urgency of her tone and her continued concentration on the discarded clothing give Kelman a sudden and unwelcome revelation.

"Do you recognize these articles?"

She hunches her shoulders in misery. "I think so . . ." Her head bows farther; her spine bends in both regret and disbelief . . . "I think . . . I think they belong to Emily Durand . . . I may be mistaken, however . . ." Martha's words falter as she suddenly realizes that she is not. It is Emily Durand they've discovered in Paladino's rooms; Emily, the epitome of breeding and sophistication and power.

Instead of experiencing shock and outrage at such illicit behavior, however, Martha's thoughts undergo an odd metamorphosis, and she begins to take pity on this proud woman. *What must she be feeling,* Martha asks herself, *sequestered in another room while Thomas and I cast censorious glances at her clothes—and at her foolhardy choice in partners? Wrong as her decision seems, wrong as it is, shouldn't Emily be given a chance to defend herself?*

Martha doesn't express these unconventional thoughts, though; what she says is a simple "I would prefer to question *Signor* Paladino tomorrow—when he is not entertaining."

DANIEL AND ELLA finish their warm potatoes and move on with John Durand trailing close after them the way a dog follows a butcher's boy, sniffing the air, ears alert, searching for a sign.

"But why, Cousin Daniel?" he hears. "Why do you fear you cannot count on Mr. Robey's commissions much longer—"

"Hush, Ella. Remember, we're in a public place."

"But why?" Ella persists almost as loudly as before.

"Ella, please. We must take care. Remember what I told you?" Then he relents, continuing with a hushed but reasoned "I believe something powerful is troubling the man. A wasting disease, I suspect . . . He asked if I knew of an apothecary who could be 'trusted.' He put particular emphasis on the word—as one who does not desire his motives known."

"Oh, cousin!" Ella whimpers. "Does he mean to end his life—?"

"Ella, you must not take on so. Your voice calls too much attention to us."

Durand moves closer. He fingers the Derringer; and the self who is the man with a fine home on a fashionable street succumbs to the self who has no name, no allegiance, no mercy for his own sorry state or that of his fellow earthly travelers.

"But what will become of us, cousin? What will we do without Mr. Robey?" Ella continues to protest.

"He hasn't deserted us yet, child. And we must pray he does not."

"Oh, but Cousin Daniel!"

"Peace, child, peace—" As the tailor speaks, John Durand slides the pistol from his pocket and takes aim.

The Silver Snuffbox

THOMAS KELMAN STANDS BESIDE THE man's lifeless body. It's a little after seven in the morning, and the light still dim and gray and sunless. The alley is strangely devoid of daytime activity—only an undertaker's cart, the steaming and woolly horse that pulls it, the two men who will haul away the corpse, and the day watchman who happened upon the scene.

Kelman studies the watchman as he rephrases his question. "And the body was in this precise position?"

"I never touched him" is the anxious reply.

"I didn't ask if you'd touched him. I asked whether you found him lying in this exact fashion."

The day watch is a young man, thin and frail and scrawny-necked beneath a coat cut for a larger person. He gazes at the mica-flecked stone of a wall and refuses to look at the ground, although from the tremor troubling his left eyelid, it's clear his mind's eye sees the dead body—sees it over and over and over again.

"All that blood under the head," he replies at last. "I got some on me boots." The boy's pinched nostrils flare; a pallid sheen of nausea douses his face. "I've never seen a man shot before . . ."

Kelman waits while the young man composes himself. "When you arrive for work, you replace a night watchman, do you not?"

The watch shifts his nervous gaze from one quarried stone to another. "Sometimes," he mumbles.

"Sometimes you shirk your responsibilities? Or sometimes the watch you relieve has already departed?"

"The second one." The reply is muted; the boy lowers his narrow head. Speaking to such a person as Thomas Kelman can bring little good, but a great deal of harm if certain folk were to learn that a potential snitch walked among them. "The night man's a good fellow, though . . . Been a member of the constabulary since I was dressed in nappies. Us younger fellows have learned a lot from him."

"But he never reported hearing a weapon fired? That's quite an explosion during the still of the night."

"The neighbors didn't say nothing, neither," the boy retorts, then adds a hopeful "Maybe the fire gangs were out . . . When there's a blaze raging, you can't hear yourself think. What with the shouting and the horses and bells and whatnot."

Kelman studies the day watch's face. It's still blue-gray and shiny with physical revulsion. "Have you seen this man before?"

Unwillingly, the boy's glance returns to the corpse. "I don't think so, sir . . . But I don't really know . . . What with his body all twisted up, and his head—"

"Yes, the bullet entered the skull near his right ear. What about his clothes?"

"Just ordinary clothes, sir. The kind most rich gents wear. Besides, they're all . . . They're all—"

"Yes, I know . . . There's a great deal of blood."

"Never seen anything like it," the watch repeats quietly.

"And I hope you never do again," says Thomas Kelman. The voice is not unkind. He moves his focus away from the day watch and is again struck by how devoid of passersby and curiosity-seekers the scene is. Save for the undertaker's men and the watchman he's currently questioning, it's as if every denizen of the alley off lower Lombard Street has made a pact to stay away. It strikes him as odd indeed. Someone nearby, he feels, must have information concerning this slaying. And that person is deliberately choosing to stay away.

WITH THE DAY watch gone, and the undertaker's horse pawing the ground, Kelman bends down and pulls the dead man's arms from beneath his blood-spattered torso and begins examining his pockets for some identifying object. The legs he leaves in a tangle of frozen wool.

The first pocket yields an intricately stitched handkerchief. Brand-new, from the look of it, with needlework that must have been a severe hardship on some poor woman's vision. Kelman places it in a satchel he has close by and moves to another pocket. The horse whinnies; one of the undertaker's men shifts his weight from one stout boot to another and seems about to speak, then apparently reconsiders as Kelman reaches into the second pocket and retrieves a silver snuffbox.

"A regular toff," the undertaker's two men whistle in unison.

Or a thief, Kelman thinks; although he doesn't voice the opinion. He turns the snuffbox over in his hand. Carved in the silver are the letters J^{n}Dur^{n}d.

Kelman sits back on his heels while he studies the snuffbox, then leans cautiously forward and reexamines the clothes. They're finely made and of excellent material, but they also bear a countrified air as if the wearer eschewed city ways. No thief—no matter how much he desired to emulate those of the landed gentry—would attire himself thus. The man lying dead in the alley must be none other than John Durand.

Kelman's brain jumps back to the previous evening and the discovery of Emily Durand in Eusapio Paladino's rooms. Although Martha insisted on leaving without specifically ascertaining that it was Durand's wife who was keeping company with the conjurer, they both privately understood that to be the case. In light of this present discovery, Emily's action and Paladino's position look more than questionable; and Kelman quickly deduces what the populace will make of the news.

At length, he stands, but he does so slowly as if reluctant to set in motion the events he knows will follow. Then he gestures to the undertaker's men, who move forward in unison to heft the dead man into the cart. The horse whinnies at the quick shift in weight as Durand's body falls on the floorboards, but otherwise the scene remains eerily silent. And eerily empty.

THE BROADSHEETS SPREAD the horrific news across the waking city. The *Citizen Soldier,* the *Spirit of the Times,* the *Daily Black Mail,* and other penny presses trumpet headlines that blare: MURDER! WHO CAN BE SAFE? and WHENCE OUR CITY OF BROTHERLY LOVE? as all of Philadelphia reels under the unspeakable notion that a prominent citizen can be gunned down while traversing its orderly streets. The coffeehouses and oyster cellars, the private drawing rooms and public street corners buzz with gossip, blame, and fear. By afternoon, the newspapers have discovered the greater scandal: Emily Durand had been in the Demport House Hotel with a lover on the evening before her husband's body was found. And that man is none other than the famous conjurer and mesmerist Eusapio Paladino, who is now in the custody of the constabulary on charges that he murdered his mistress's husband.

"SHOULDN'T WE TELL them, cousin Daniel? What we know? Shouldn't we be telling someone what we saw?" Ella's words tumble out in a high-pitched stream. "There in the alley?" she continues. "Where—?"

"No, Ella," Daniel tells her. "No joy will come of our talking to the police."

"But—" she persists.

The tailor, equally nervous, issues a firmer "No! No, we cannot" while the child, as if compelled by a higher force, repeats her anxious appeal:

"But the broadsheets are saying that Mr. Durand—"

"Stop it, Ella! Stop, at once!" Then Daniel immediately regrets his temper. "Child, I cannot go to the police. You know that."

"Oh, but, Cousin Daniel, we were there! We saw—!"

"No more, Ella. No more, I say! We will do nothing. We *can* do nothing . . . Listen to me, child, if I seek out the constabulary now—albeit for a worthy cause, they will arrest me for being an escaped convict and return me to prison. You understand that, don't you, girl? Don't you? And where will you be then?"

Ella's lips remain parted, her eyes wide but dry.

"We must keep what we saw to ourselves, Ella. You know we must."

At last, she finds her tongue. "I could speak without you, cousin."

"Oh, Ella, child . . . And where will you tell them you dwell?"

Ella thinks. "At the house I left when I came to you."

"And don't you imagine the police would then return to it and question the madam whether that were true?" Daniel hobbles back and forth as he speaks. Despite his brave words, he's also growing very frightened, and his fear is infecting the girl he's trying to protect.

She starts to cry. All the fine things she's been imagining for the future seem suddenly as insubstantial as snowflakes melting in the sun. "We're in danger, aren't we, Daniel?"

"Not if we keep our heads down and our thoughts private . . . just as we've been doing, little cousin."

But Ella doesn't believe this. "What if we were seen in that alley with Mr. Durand? What if someone already knows you and I were there? Maybe that policeman you met up with four days past?"

"He wasn't a policeman, child. At least, I don't believe he was—"

"Or someone else?" Ella's voice drops to the merest whisper. "Someone who may have encountered you while you were in prison?"

A Letter to a Friend

ALMOST ALL THE NOTABLES OF the city turn out for the funeral of John Durand, making the portion of lower Pine Street that fronts St. Peter's Church and its memorial garden a sea of people and carriages and horses. There are footmen and coachmen attending to their nervous animals as well as their equally distressed masters and mistresses; there are those same highborn people hurrying along, heads down, necks tense, eyes grimly focused on the cobbled road as they thread their way through the noisy, pushing gawkers; there are hawkers of broadsheets and penny papers, crying out the latest and most sensational headlines; and there are ordinary town folk who merely hope for a glimpse of the now notorious Emily Durand and her cohorts. Philadelphia has never known such a scandal. For those gathered to watch the spectacle unfold, it's a raucous and entertaining time.

For the true mourners, such a rowdy scene is torture. They murmur curt and somber greetings to one another when they finally pass through the wall's wrought-iron gates and achieve the sanctuary of the churchyard and the row of undertaker's men who line up to greet them: their tall hats swathed in black veils, their coats swagged in black draping as wide as capes.

Martha and Owen Simms are among the crowd who hurry in from the crowded street. Simms speaks in hushed tones to several people close by. Martha says nothing although her thoughts revolve and revolve around the catastrophe. *If I hadn't insisted on accompanying Thomas to the hotel . . . if Emily hadn't been hiding in Paladino's rooms . . . if their secret had been maintained, would John Durand now be alive?*

Or is it possible that the conjurer wasn't involved in the murder, as both he and Emily continue to insist, and that this cataclysmic act—as some are suggesting—is the result of a theft gone awry? Or perhaps even a case of mistaken identity, as others hypothesize? Because what motive could Paladino have for killing his mistress's husband? What good result would the conjurer have expected from his actions? Surely he didn't imagine he'd marry her? But even as Martha poses these final queries, she recalls her own experience with the man. Reason and logical deliberation are not attributes Eusapio Paladino seems to possess.

Then she remembers the snuffbox Thomas Kelman found, and her ruminations hit an insurmountable hurdle. *Pickpockets and cutpurses are far too agile and clever to leave behind silver boxes. If John Durand were purposely murdered, wouldn't his assassin have robbed him in order to make the crime appear to be the random act of a footpad? Even Eusapio, for all his otherworldliness, would have considered the simple precaution of searching his victim's pockets.* Something is missing, Martha feels. But what? What?

With Owen Simms guiding her, she steps inside the packed church. The cold morning air seems chillier on the brick building's interior: the stone and marble floor frigid, the carved wood of the walls icy to the touch, despite her silk-lined gloves. An usher festooned with the customary satin ribbons silently escorts them down the center aisle and places them in a box pew already occupied by the

Ilsleys and the Shippens. Below the facing seats are small braziers full of hot coals, but they do nothing to warm the wintry air. Martha nods silent acknowledgments to those closest to her, then gazes across the gathered people. Beyond the inky-hued hats and veils, beyond the crepe and bombazine, the paramatta and cashmere and grenadine, she notes that the golden processional crosses have been sheathed in a velvet so black it appears to crush the light.

Then, most astonishingly, the widow herself appears. Fully shrouded in heavy veils, she's conveyed to her family pew. To those in attendance, it's inconceivable that Emily Durand should be present, that she can lift her head in public after she's broken the strictest law of polite society; and a murmur of outrage begins echoing through the large old building. The faceless figure remains stiff and stoical. Martha wonders what her expression must be beneath her widow's weeds and feels her heart open in pity. *Surely Emily couldn't have wished her husband dead,* she thinks. *The woman may have been heedless and headstrong, and her transgression complete, but don't we all deserve our fellow sojourners' compassion as well as God's redeeming grace? Especially when we are most in need of aid?*

Then the organ commences its dirge, and the funeral procession begins. Despite this signal that the service has begun, the congregation can barely cease its shocked and disapproving whispers in order to rise and sing.

". . . WE BROUGHT NOTHING into this world, and it is certain we can carry nothing out . . ." Martha hears intoned from the Order for the Burial of the Dead. For a moment, she thinks of her father, and the fact that she must soon have these same words recited for him.

". . . I said, I will take heed of my ways: that I offend not in my tongue . . ." Martha can't help herself; she gasps aloud. As quick as lightning, Owen Simms touches her gloved hand with his own.

"Are you quite well, Martha, my dear? Do you wish to leave?"

THE WOMAN'S SHORT gray hair sticks to the sleeping pallet like thousands of sewing needles stabbed willy-nilly into the mattress ticking. Her lips are half-parted and colorless, her skin also curiously ashen.

From beyond the barred window in her chamber, a cock crows dawn. The woman doesn't stir. The cock crows again, and the sounds of other inmates beginning to waken jostle into the room. There are loud and unencumbered yawns, a resonant, repetitive cough, a habitual and nervous laugh, a mumbled curse. The woman's lips remain parted; her hands, clenched and gnawed to the quick at her fingertips, maintain a claw-like grasp on the gray blanket.

"Time to rise!" the matron calls in as she passes the open door.

The woman doesn't respond, and the other female residents of the Asylum for Relief of Persons Deprived of Their Use of Reason also begin walking by, lining up to wash in the communal bath. "The princess needs her beauty sleep," one of them jeers. Several gawk at the reclining figure, then turn away and shamble forward in the queue. The corridor is cold, the bath the only room with a fire. No purpose is served in palavering over an obvious malingerer. Better to move on to the next event of the morning: a breakfast of porridge followed by the distribution of daily tasks.

The matron returns to the patient's room. "Time to rise," she orders again, but the woman remains insensate.

"You and your dreams," the matron adds. "You'll have us all thinking we'd be better off asleep. Are you flying about like an angel again? Is that it? Or do we have the hidden cave in the hillside and all that?"

The matron regards the motionless figure for another moment. "Time to rise, I said." She sighs irritably. "Your brother won't be visiting, if that's what's fretting you. He's only here but once every other month or so, so you've a good many weeks before you see his face again."

Again the gray-haired woman fails to respond.

"I'll have to call Dr. Earle if you don't shake a leg, missy."

The woman remains motionless, and the matron begins noticing the stiff fingers, the hard line of the cheekbones, the rigid shoulders. "We can't have any of this stubborn nonsense you're playing at. There's nothing to be fearful of, I tell you. You must get up at once and join the others."

When the patient again makes no reply, the matron's temper gets the better of her. "Don't you think you can simply close your eyes and pretend not to hear me!" She strides toward the bed and reaches down to shake the inmate from her lethargy, all the while maintaining a stance of preparedness. Not a few of these cases have suddenly leapt up and tried to choke a nurse. "I'm telling you, your brother's nowhere near!"

The matron's fingers touch the woman's shoulders, draw instantly back, then rush to her neck and the life force that should be beating there. "Nurse!" she shouts. "Send for Dr. Earle."

STARING AT A sheet of letter paper, Pliny Earle folds his hands on his desk, then unknits the fingers and repeats the process—several times over, ten times over. He wishes he could close his eyes and erase the picture of the dead woman's face, the vision of her living face, too, the eyes that looked only inward, viewing and reviewing scenes from the past.

Earle takes the file on Robey's sister, dips his pen in ink and writes a methodical *Now deceased* on the top right-hand corner, and then again pauses. A life ended. A life eked out in the unwholesome solitude of this place. And for what? Better, he thinks, that she should have died three decades before. Or before that. Pliny Earle doesn't believe in the existence of a God, or this would be an excellent time to rail against that deity's callowness and injustice. Instead, he's left with an almost suffocating sense of purposelessness and defeat.

He moves his left hand to the letter paper, again inks the pen.

Dear Mr. Robey, he writes, *I regret to inform you*—then stops. This time he does close his eyes, and his mind begins to whip through Robey's sister's file as if he were reading it.

Admitted to the Asylum thirty years prior, she was suffering the physical effects of uterine hemorrhage coupled with acute religious anxiety that produced a form of mania in which the patient alternately called herself "Martha" or "Mary."

The former was hardworking, whether in the kitchen gardens of a summer day or in the sewing and knitting circles that clustered together when the weather cooled. This persona also had an air of brusque and sometimes brutal impatience that kept the other patients at bay. "Mary," on the other hand, was dreamy and often idle; when she sat alone staring into space, she claimed she was "listening to Jesus speak."

It was understood that Robey was not her true surname, but her mental state remained so damaged and precarious that her true identity never surfaced. Implicit in the admitting physician's remarks was the recognition that the patient came from a family who were of some means—and as such wished their name withheld. It was not an uncommon practice.

All this and more was described in the file: decades of interviews and observations. What did not appear in the notes, however, was Earle's recent and disquieting conversation with the woman's brother—and this is what now causes him to stare at the empty piece of letter paper.

Are there means, Dr. Earle? he can almost hear "Robey" ask him, *whereby my sister's life might end sooner than nature allows?*

It's the memory of that exchange that impels the physician to take up his pen again, although the letter he now commences is not the one he previously began. Perhaps the woman died in her sleep of natural causes as all believed. But perhaps there's a more sinister reason. A poison that can't be detected, an accomplice who administered it. The idea is hideous; and Pliny Earle's uncertain how he will face his board of directors if such proves the case. Better—and safer—to ignore such a dire possibility, but that he simply cannot do. The patient should not be forgotten in death as she was in life.

Earle composes a brief letter to a friend he's known and trusted since their college days together. The man isn't a physician, and his position as an aide to the mayor of Philadelphia is enigmatic and ambiguous. His name is Thomas Kelman.

An Embroidered Shawl

As Martha sits in growing consternation and listens to a eulogy for John Durand, and Pliny Earle puts pen to paper, Thomas Kelman is admitted into Mrs. Rosegger's second-floor sitting room. The maid withdraws, leaving the two alone in a place made intimate by soft and shadowy light: a small fire dozing in the grate, the midmorning sun stirring behind layers of heavy drapery and lace.

"It's good to see you again, Thomas," Mrs. Rosegger says with some effort, then abruptly turns mute. The seven small words seem to her too weighted with innuendo, too perfumed and amorous. After several inarticulate moments, she recommences her discourse, attempting but failing to achieve a less personal tone. "It was kind of you to respond so quickly to my message."

Kelman continues to stand. She doesn't ask him to sit. He nods in reply, then looks down at her chair and at her.

"My husband is at the Durand funeral. He felt it would be too disturbing an event for me, however," she says as though in answer to a question.

Again Kelman nods, then forms his own response. "You have a fine house, Marguerite." Too late, he notes that the use of her given name has made her shiver in discomfort.

"Yes . . . Yes, I have. A luxurious house . . . servants. All that I ever wished."

"I'm glad for you."

Marguerite Rosegger smiles with what's intended as a facsimile of sophisticated nonchalance but, in fact, seems only wistful. "My father would have been very gratified to see how comfortable my situation is."

"I'm sure he would have been."

She looks away. "It's a long while since anyone called me Marguerite." Then, as if she's revealed too much, she continues in a hurried tone. "I asked you here because I believe I have . . . indelicate information concerning John Durand."

Her guest continues to stand and wait. "Please sit," she says at last, inserting a barely audible "Thomas." She tightens her lips and speaks again in the same quiet and constrained tone. "I hope you did not feel I spurned you—all those years ago."

"I was a very young man. Even at nineteen."

Her expression turns rueful. "And I was not so young."

"That wasn't the intent behind my words."

"It's the truth, however."

Kelman finally sits, although he chooses a place at some distance from his hostess. "What's this you wish to tell me about John Durand?"

Her answer is an elliptical "I'm surprised you haven't married yet, Thomas." Then she adds an equally ambiguous "How do you find Martha Beale?"

"She's concerned about her missing parent, naturally."

"That's not what I meant, Thomas."

Kelman sits up straighter in his chair. "What do you know about Durand?"

Marguerite Rosegger laughs slightly. It's the first time in its history that the room has been party to the bright sound. Then the mirth as rapidly subsides, and the financier's wife resumes her hesitant tone. "I told Martha Beale to trust you . . . when she visited us for tea . . . I hope she follows my advice." After that, silence again reigns until Mrs. Rosegger concludes with a hushed "My husband has information concerning Durand. I don't know what it is other than that he views it as something of substance. I wrote to Emily Durand, suggesting that her husband had a . . . had a private situation that might be of an awkward or difficult nature, but her response was to put me off . . . Now it's too late . . . But I wanted to warn her—and her husband, naturally—as one woman to another . . ." The words trail away, then finally resume. "Mr. Rosegger can be a forbidding opponent."

Kelman remains silent a moment. "And you have no notion of what this mysterious information is?"

"No, but I did hear Rosegger mention Durand's name to Lemuel Beale's secretary. They met here in the house, and I happened to be passing through the corridor during their consultation." Marguerite pauses, uncertain how to proceed. "I had thought . . . in asking you here . . . I had thought that you might find a means of questioning Owen Simms. Perhaps he can reveal what hold my husband has . . . had on Mr. Durand . . . It might aid his widow . . . Although I understand her situation now is quite precarious. Those who govern society's customs can be unforgiving."

Kelman looks at her, considering the suggestions; they're of little help, but he doesn't tell her so. Instead, he says, "I'm sorry your life didn't turn out as you wished."

She shrugs in an attempt at dismissal. "I wanted to live in the lap of luxury—"

"And you have your children."

"Ah, yes . . . Rosegger's children . . ."

Another uncomfortable silence ensues, which Kelman finally breaks. "And there's nothing else you can reveal of this matter or your husband's role?"

She thinks. "At first, I assumed Durand's difficulty was purely of a financial nature—"

"But it could have been another problem?"

"My husband makes it his business to delve into personal secrets, Thomas" is the vague reply.

"Such as a young man keeping company with a woman seven years his senior?"

"Six and a half," she corrects him, "and that was an eternity." Then she adds another oblique "I don't suppose Rosegger would have chosen me if he'd found me blameless . . . And then, of course, there was my father's successful commerce—"

"Which a youth of nineteen couldn't hope to attain to."

Marguerite Rosegger remains silent for some moments. Kelman can only imagine what she's remembering: a driven and hardworking father who'd created his own worldly success and now demanded the very best for his daughter, an entry into Society and a name that would make her an equal with ladies higher born; a father who brusquely dispatched suitors he didn't feel matched the stringent qualifications he'd established for a potential son-in-law; a father who at last set his sights on Rosegger only to perish before he could see his favorite child wed. These are some of the images that fly across Marguerite Rosegger's features, but all she says is a small "Time was against us, Thomas. And circumstance."

He also says nothing for a minute or two, reflecting on Rosegger the suitor and then Rosegger the husband of an heiress, the brother-in-law to two men who must bear him remarkable ill will. Finally,

Kelman stands, uttering a polite "Thank you for contacting me, Marguerite, but I don't wish to compromise you by staying longer."

Marguerite Rosegger maintains her seated and proper pose, but her body appears to retreat into itself as if girding against a chill. "Please extend my regards to Miss Beale . . . Or do you call her Martha?"

Kelman allows himself the smallest of smiles. "I have, once or twice."

"Lucky woman" is the brief response before another hushed volley of speech hurries forth. "When Owen Simms visited my husband, they had a good deal of discussion concerning her father—" The words cease; her eyes fly to the closed door and the keyhole there. A faint rustle of female clothing has been heard in the passage beyond. When Rosegger's wife resumes speaking, her voice and attitude have met with a transformation. "If you should see Miss Beale, please convey our best wishes to her. We greatly enjoyed our visit with her. Were my husband at home now, I know he would add his heartiest hopes she find some resolution to her father's disappearance. And now, I must wish you good day, Mr. Kelman."

KELMAN LEAVES THE Rosegger house, striding south along Broad Street past the mansions of the very rich: the Hawes residence recently built by the architect Thomas U. Walter, then the large and showy Butler home fronting Walnut Street. The Durands' equally proud domicile lies among them, dressed now in deepest mourning: each door and window affixed with wreaths of grogram and crepe, every curtain on every floor firmly drawn.

Rosegger had some mysterious hold on John Durand—who's now dead, Kelman tells himself as he gazes at the dwelling. *Owen Simms also met privately with the financier; his master, Lemuel Beale, is missing and presumed deceased.* Intuitively, Kelman feels that there's some nefarious connection among these four men, but what it is he cannot divine.

His steps wander north again, leading him to the Greek Revival structure that houses the United States Mint at Chestnut and Juniper Streets, where he stops, studying every quarried block of stone in the façade, every brick and cobble in the pavement, while his mind turns and turns around what facts he has—finally alighting upon Eusapio Paladino, and the conjurer's graphic descriptions of the hideous murders of two young girls.

At length, Kelman begins to walk toward the "Hell's Half Acre" that stretches beyond Lombard Street. He passes Tin Alley with its smithies, the cluster of busy livery stables facing Charlotte Street, Marble Court with its masons and chisels and everlasting whorls of stone dust, and Blackberry Alley, whose trade has nothing to do with the sale of farm-ripe fruit. He regards these byways as if they're capable of reason and therefore possess relevant information, but the places merely gaze slyly back.

Finally he finds standing himself in front of the Association for the Care of Colored Orphans; and his thoughts begin reeling backward to his first encounter with Martha Beale, and how earnest was her desire to "work among the poor." Then he frowns, remembering Marguerite Rosegger—Marguerite as she was many years before when he was a youth of nineteen and she a woman of twenty-six. *How is it,* he wonders, *that our solitary existences are so dependent upon others? We believe we're self-governing, but circumstances continually work to remold us; and we grow like trees clustered in a forest: bowed down by prevailing winds, stunted within the shadow of larger plants, or flourishing because a neighbor has toppled and relinquished its proprietary ownership of light and air.*

IN THE MIDST of walking up the staircase in her father's town house, Martha Beale makes a decision. She's only recently returned from the Durand funeral and has been surprised but not at all displeased to have Owen Simms inform her that he'll be detained elsewhere for the remainder of the day.

Her hand grips the carved balustrade as the revelation arrests her in midstride: one foot resting upon a polished oak tread, and the other rising toward the landing and the Vandyke brown and syenite blue Turkey carpet installed there. Then her thoughts galvanize her, and she begins hurrying up the remainder of the stairs toward the forbidden room that's her father's private office in the house. *Yes,* she tells herself, *yes! I need no longer be passive: allowing Mr. Simms to guide me, or Rosegger to provide a clue as to my father's associations—or even Thomas to give me assistance. I'll search Father's correspondence myself. If there's an enemy who wished him dead, surely I can find reference to such a person.*

But taking the key into her fingers, she pauses. *Such a momentous step! Such boldness and daring! What would Lemuel Beale say if he saw his daughter embarking on this clandestine and unladylike mission? Affairs of business, affairs of the world must be left to men's capable hands, not women's.* As she thus argues with herself, Martha's mouth tightens, then she clasps the latch, releases it, and thrusts open the door with a solid push.

Inside, all is dim and cold. No fire has been lit in many a day; no lamp has been trimmed; no air has stirred. Martha shuts the door behind her but hesitates at locking it. The gesture seems too secretive by far. What would she say if Simms were to return home and discover her thus sequestered? Better to find some simple excuse . . . Martha thinks until she devises one she finds acceptable: In light of Mr. Simms's proposal to arrange a funeral service for her father, she was hoping to find her parent's prayer book and take inspiration from it. Owen Simms dare not question such a sincere and heartfelt motive, and one so seemingly innocent and benign. In the pallid light, Martha smiles in satisfaction at the ruse.

She lights a lamp, then two, and her father's ponderous walnut desk with its many drawers and cupboards rises from the shadows, a hulking thing as black and forbidding as a bear. She stifles a tremor of doubt, then moves purposefully toward it, pulling open drawers, peering at the contents, and lifting out personal and public papers to arrange them on the desktop. She has no idea what she's searching for, and so the words she reads upon the pages have scant meaning.

Her father has made brief notations about a business entitled "Northern Liberties Gas Works," and then cryptic asides listing numerous street addresses. "Tamarind Street" is underlined on one page; "Coates" and "Brown" and "St. John," as well. There's also mention of "Loomis's Chemical Works," "Globe Mills," and "Henry Derringer."

There are letters to her father, but no copies of his correspondence in reply. The missives he received are brief and suggest that longer and more detailed messages preceded them, but those accounts are apparently missing—referred to only in numerical jottings from her father's pen. Martha realizes that it's his hand she's studying and not Owen Simms's, which intimates there were business affairs Lemuel Beale kept concealed even from his confidential secretary. She frowns at this curiosity. Secrecy has ever been her father's way, but she presumed he shared every one of his various concerns and interests with the man he'd hired to do that work.

She returns the pages she's read to their rightful places and searches on. A noise in the passageway disturbs her and sends her hands fluttering to her sides. She stands erect and slowly turns to face the door, readying her excuse for the intruder she assumes will be Owen Simms, but the sound of footsteps moves on, and she decides it's probably the ash boy cleaning out the hearths. There's a bump of something metallic like a pail.

Martha conquers her fright, sweeps away another stack of papers, then opens the bottom drawer, where she discovers a lady's embroidered shawl. The shawl is not a new one or a very fine one, and moths have done it considerable damage. She lifts it from its resting place thinking that it must have belonged to her mother, her mother as an unmarried maiden before she wed into the growing wealth that would become Lemuel Beale's.

Martha holds the thin woolen fabric to her face, trying to imagine what it would be like to hold the real person, or how it would even feel to have a mother. A parent to talk with, to walk arm and arm with, to share enthusiastic excursions into the city's shopping emporia as she's watched other mothers and daughters do, or simply to sit with in companionable silence listening to the ticking of a clock.

As her daydreams drift in this melancholy manner, the front door bangs open. Martha can hear Owen Simms march inside, stamping his feet from the cold. Something tells her to return the shawl to the drawer lest he approach the study and discover her with the object in her hands.

Having done so, she makes another quick decision, rushing to douse the lamps before she hurries from the room, closing and locking the latch behind her with the gentlest of clicks. Her excuse about a prayer book seems too transparent all at once.

Then she proceeds toward the staircase, where she meets her father's secretary walking up and already at the landing. "Ah, Martha," he says, "I'm sorry I had to leave you so soon after the Durand funeral. I trust you didn't find it too difficult to bear."

Martha drops a polite curtsy but doesn't otherwise respond, and Simms passes by, saying only a regretful "My apologies, my dear, but I won't be joining you at dinner tonight as I'd planned . . . However, I hope that we may continue our conversation about clarifying your father's circumstances on the morrow."

"As you wish, Mr. Simms" is Martha's careful reply, but Simms has already moved on without awaiting her answer.

Mr. Robey's Sister

THOMAS KELMAN REREADS PLINY EARLE'S letter, this time with more than a little annoyance. The incident the physician describes occurred two days prior, and although Pliny has promised a thorough examination of the dead woman, Kelman chafes at the delay. He understands its cause, the need for discretion, the delicacy of his friend's position, but still he chafes. Ordinary post brought the message; a man on a fast horse could have delivered it in a matter of hours—could have brought the matter to Kelman's immediate attention. Time has been needlessly wasted.

Robey, he thinks; his eyes narrow in concentration as if he were staring past the letter, past his desk, past the dusky walls of his office into the forgotten recesses of his own brain. *Have I heard that name before?* Something hints at the fact that he has, but he can't remember what that connection is. He considers the many conversations he's had in only a handful of days: the strange and unsettling visit to Marguerite Rosegger, his ineffectual discussions with Emily Durand, the futile interview with the clairvoyant Paladino, but finds no reference to a man called Robey. *Perhaps,* Kelman thinks, *I'm confusing it with a similar appellation.*

He folds Pliny Earle's letter, puts it in his waistcoat, then rises from his desk and takes up his hat and coat. His horse can be quickly saddled, and as the day is cold but dry and the roads hard-packed and passable, he estimates that he will arrive at the Asylum near the hour of their midday meal. If he cannot accomplish the return journey until after dark, he will spend the night there.

For a moment, he considers writing to Martha Beale to explain that he's been called out of town and may not return until the morrow. But he reminds himself the notion is a capricious one. Of what import would it be to her whether he remained within the city or not?

"I CANNOT PROVIDE that information, Thomas," Earle states abruptly, although the concerned and ambivalent frown surrounding his eyes belies the rigidity of his tone. "When the patient was first admitted, it was understood that family members wished her true identity to remain unknown—"

"Her brother, you mean."

"He was the only person who visited . . . But originally there was reference to 'family members' in the plural."

Kelman pauses in thought. "And no mention as to who those other individuals might have been?"

"No. I'm sorry I can't supply more substantial information, but you understand that the nature of this institution must be a discreet one."

"Your rules—or your customs—certainly hamper a criminal investigation, Pliny."

A rueful smile briefly crosses the physician's face. "You're correct; they do. However, in other cases, they provide our patients with the anonymity often necessary for their safety. Some are even healed and return to society, although in the cases of persons whose family connections or connubial situations have damaged their psyches, those unfortunate relationships are not reestablished. We have a number of women here—as you can imagine—who have suffered most cruelly at the hands of their husbands, and youths, also, who have been reduced to near imbecility by a parent's malevolent ministrations."

Again Kelman doesn't speak for several moments. "How do you stand it, Pliny?" he finally demands. "Melancholia, mania, dementia . . . produced, as you so prudently described it, by 'domestic difficulty.' How do you bear the sight of the husbands? Or the parents who have inflicted the damage?"

"Are you not also surrounded by the horror perpetrated by humanity?"

"In my case, the guilty attempt to hide themselves."

"As they do where I'm concerned, Thomas . . . Only in a few instances do the culpable request to visit their prey, and so I'm spared discourse with the majority of them."

"But not Robey."

Pliny Earle shakes his head. "The man Robey is a different case. His visits have been regular—despite his sister's obvious discomfort in his presence."

"Could you not have prevented his admittance?"

"Hindsight might indicate that would have been wise. But, no, I—and my predecessors—could not refuse him entrance. As he was quick to indicate, his guilt in the matter of his sister's impaired state was never proven."

"Nor, most probably, ever investigated by a court of law."

"I would infer not, Thomas. Despite our forefathers' best intentions, those with means exist under a different judicial system than the poor." Earle attempts another smile.

Kelman presses the tips of his poet's fingers together as his mind mulls over what facts he has. "And how has Robey differed from the relatives of other inmates?"

This time it's Earle who pauses before speaking. "He evinced no sense of guilt or regret. People who experience shame habitually become sly or sycophantic—or, as I indicated, they ignore their connection to the patient, and probably deny their own role in the situation. They may even successfully forget they were involved. But Robey . . . I believe he remembers very well his part in his sister's downfall . . . Perhaps his visits here were in part to further witness her disgrace, or perhaps he merely wished to assure himself that he would never be castigated as a result, that her real identity has never been exposed . . . He's a man who needs to exercise considerable control, and my guess is that beyond the Asylum and the part he played here, he's a man who cleaves to power."

"He raped his sister—"

"Repeatedly, as my predecessor was led to believe. And the hemorrhage she suffered as a result was engendered either by his brutality—or by a midwife attempting to curtail an unwanted pregnancy."

Kelman's lips grow pinched and tight. "You're describing a monster."

"Yes," Earle says; his eyes are bleak. "Whatever his true identity, Robey is not a good man."

Again Kelman remains silent, at length stating a pensive "I've been investigating other criminal cases, Pliny . . . One involves the murder of two young girls."

The physician accepts the information with a studious demeanor but doesn't respond, so Kelman continues, almost as if he were talking to himself:

"I hardly know why I mention this, as there's no connection between this man Robey's sister and the other situations—"

"Who were the girls?" Earle interjects.

"Poor children, of no known parentage . . . Their only means of sustenance came from selling their bodies. For their pains, they were strangled and their tongues cut out."

The physician shifts abruptly in his chair. "Ritualistic activities such as those are not likely to abate, Thomas. Instead, they may in all probability increase—and the victims may change."

"Yes, I know" is the weary reply. "Until this moment, I felt we had apprehended the man: a purported necromancer and somnambulist who originally claimed to 'see' one of the murders."

"And now?"

"Now, I'm beginning to question whether your Mr. Robey might be involved. It's an absurd leap of judgment, I admit, and I have only intuition to guide me . . . or perhaps it's simply that I want so badly to solve the crime. But something about your case bears echoes of the other." Kelman pauses. "You said that your deceased patient referred to herself alternatively as 'Mary' or 'Martha.'"

Pliny Earle nods.

"'Mary' was the name given to one of the murdered children. I believe the appellation may have been part of the ritual act."

"And 'Martha'?" Earle asks, then watches his friend's face redden with an unaccustomed flush, although Kelman's habitual self-control quickly reasserts itself.

"The biblical allusion is a familiar one, I realize, Pliny . . . the two sisters of Lazarus, the friend of Jesus who was famously raised from the dead. Martha was the busy and hardworking one; Mary was thoughtful, perhaps even a trifle dreamy—although she became the chosen one of our Lord . . ." Kelman shakes his head. "I see from your expression that you feel I'm attempting to draw too many inferences and too many similarities where there may be none—"

"Not at all, Thomas. I'm simply surprised at—"

"My perspicacity?"

Earle laughs. "That's not the word I would have employed."

"Ah . . . But I feel it was your intention."

Earle chortles again. "You don't usually devote yourself to pondering the vagaries of the human brain, Thomas."

"Perhaps it's time I did."

Pliny Earle studies his friend but otherwise makes no response to this personal admission. "If the person who killed the children is indeed Robey," he ventures at length, "and if Robey also connived to murder his sister, then I fear he may strike again. And, as is the case with our patient here, it may be a bolder attempt."

Kelman nods. Reflexively, his focus turns to Martha, and then to the weird and ominous message provided by the necromancer. "Pliny, at the risk of making myself even more absurd . . . In your estimation, does communicating with the spirit world lie within the realm of human possibility?"

"The physician in me would dictate an unconditional 'no,' Thomas. However—"

"However?"

"I believe that we medical men have too slight a grasp on circumstances that exist beyond our limited studies."

Kelman contemplates his friend. Pliny Earle gazes calmly back.

"What does your Robey look like?" Kelman asks.

"He's a man with all the attributes of a chameleon. His hair never seems the same color from visit to visit; his clothes are very fine but characterless, revealing nothing of the wearer's mood or fancies. One month they're gaudy, one month drab. Height? Average. Girth? Also average. Age? Not young, certainly. You know how old his deceased sister was, but whether he was the younger of the two or not, I don't know. Concealed within the varying shades of his tresses, he could well have snow white thatch. He's clean shaven—if that helps you. And your murderer?"

"No one can describe him" is Kelman's quiet reply. Then he changes the subject. "What do you wish me to do in the matter of the Asylum's dead patient?"

"Nothing here—except to advise me. I'm still conducting medical tests in an attempt to determine if the woman was poisoned. The situation, as I'm sure you're aware, is a delicate one. If I find evidence of mischief, it means examining the brother's culpability, as well as the possibility of collusion from those who work here or from inmates. None of our other patients have fallen ill, so I've ruled out the possibility of accidentally tainted food. But wolfsbane, or monkshood, *Aconitium napellus* by the medical name, which tastes similar to horseradish, would produce the same results as consuming and then repeatedly vomiting up a contaminated supper—which was how Robey's sister was discovered. Horribly, persons thus doomed remain fully intelligent until the last moment of life, and so may well understand that they have been marked for death."

"And there's no antidote to this *Aconitium napellus?*"

"No. Not even if we'd been able to recognize the direness of her situation and so provide medical attention . . . But all this is still theoretical, Thomas."

Kelman nods in understanding. "You'll have to inform Robey of his sister's demise."

"I have no address . . . no proper name—"

"Have you considered an announcement in the newspapers? Worded sensitively, it might appear an appeal for compassion . . . A woman patient who died without benefit of the company of her dear brother, Mr. Robey."

"And what then?" Pliny Earle asks.

"He'll either return to express his grief or, in his relief, he'll vanish," Kelman responds. "My guess is that his reaction will be the former. If Robey is the manipulative man you suggest he is, then he should enjoy viewing the success of his handiwork."

"And what do I do if and when he does appear, Thomas?"

"Send for me. At once. Send a man at a gallop, and I will gallop back—no matter the hour. And detain Robey. Insist that there are legalities that require his presence. Paperwork to sign. Staff members to meet, effects to sort through. But maintain a demeanor of condolence and sorrow; and do not, for a moment, allow your suspicions to surface."

Pliny Earle sighs.

"It won't be as difficult as it sounds. Besides, you've dealt with many nefarious types in your line of work and have always maintained a sure grip on your emotions."

"And what will you do to Robey when you arrive?"

"That will depend upon whether or not you can determine if your patient was murdered."

The Rifle Found, at Last

But everyone's saying the necromancer spoke in Beale's own voice, Henrietta . . . and while awaiting trial for the murder of poor John Durand! Why, whatever can it mean . . . ? And Mr. Beale's rifle found in the possession of . . . ?" Florence Shippen leans close to her cousin in order to whisper these awestruck words while her pudgy hand raps an ivory fan on the plush-covered box rail on the first tier of the Musical Fund Hall. She can scarcely sit still, so excited is she—as is every other patron at that evening's performance of Bellini's tragic opera *La Sonnambula*. As if the scandal created by Emily Durand, or the slayings of two young ladies of pleasure (children, really), or the mystery surrounding Lemuel Beale were not sufficient grist for the rumor mills, the discovery of his lost rifle has now set every tongue wagging again. For not only was the weapon found in the wilds near Beale House, but it was also in the hands of a half-crazed hermit—who, naturally, has denied all connection to the financier's disappearance.

It's a wonder anyone can concentrate upon the stage.

". . . And Emily herself at Paladino's side in the Moyamensing

Prison when he entered his peculiar trance . . . ! And, as if that behavior isn't scandalous enough, continuing to insist upon his innocence, insist he knows nothing of Beale's lot . . . Why, even the constabulary present attested to uncanny similarities to Beale's voice and posture . . . Imagine, Henrietta . . . Just imagine . . . !"

Her cousin makes no reply to these fevered remarks; instead, her eyes continue to regard Bellini's ill-fated sleepwalker as she treads rhythmically across the gaslit floorboards. In Henrietta's mind the soprano's movements seem to mimic Paladino's; and she thinks back with yearning to the short time past when she truly believed that living mortals could commune with the departed.

". . . And to think you had Paladino in your house!" Florence rushes along in another stream of words. "A killer capable of such barbarous . . . ! And I sat at the same table with him . . . Oh my. Oh my . . ." Tap goes the fan again. Tap, tap, tap, tap, and accompanying the sound is the frenzied creak of corset stays and taffeta petticoats. ". . . And, don't you remember, Henrietta . . . that business about the child's tongue lying on a pillow? What the conjurer pretended to 'see'? Imagine that he could have committed so heinous an act—and then spoken of it! To us! And in your very house! Doesn't that prove how depraved and conniving he is . . . !" In her excitement, Florence all but moans, and her undergarments repeat the noisy cry. ". . . All the same, you mustn't criticize yourself, Henrietta. You cannot be blamed for introducing this demonic character to Emily Durand. Indeed you cannot. And you mustn't feel her low character bears any reflection on those of her acquaintance . . . But what do you think can be the meaning of this percussion rifle and the hermit? Do you think he could have killed—?"

"Mrs. Shippen, please!" Professor Ilsley cautions in a murmur that rumbles through his long white beard. "Pray, let us save the rest of this conversation for the intermission."

"Oh!" Florence responds with a small gasp. "I did not intend, Professor—"

"Then let us say no more about murders or percussion rifles or the reprehensible mores of a certain widow until the intermission, madam."

"Oh!" Florence repeats. Her face, could it be seen in the darkness of the concert hall, has turned very pink. "I simply thought your wife and I could—"

"Mrs. Ilsley and I are devotees of the opera, Mrs. Shippen—"

"As my husband and I are also, sir, I assure you—"

"We will have sufficient time to continue our discussions at the close of the act—"

"Well, yes, of course, Professor Ilsley. I merely thought that—"

"Good. Then let us give our singers the attention they deserve."

By this time other patrons have begun grumbling, and so Florence Shippen withdraws into the eclipsing darkness of the box's curtains and sulkily watches the legendary star performers, Mr. and Mrs. Seguin, act out the parts of the trusting young farmer and his sleepwalking betrothed, Amina. Florence stifles a heavy sigh while the gas lamps set upon the footboards flicker, illuminating a number of patrons installed in the first row of seats. In the chiaroscuro created by the artificial light, only stray parts of their torsos appear: a man's gloved hand gesturing; the ruddy side of a bewhiskered face; the exposed neck of a lady who wears a dress of russet-colored silk brocade and *point d'Alsace* lace—very *à la mode,* Florence knows. She regards the scene, frowns in escalating impatience, and continues toying with her fan until her husband reaches out a diffident but restraining hand.

She shifts in her chair. The most extraordinary events in her entire life are unfolding while she's forced to sit in polite silence and study a diva feign walking in her sleep—rather than discuss Eusapio Paladino conjuring the spirit of Lemuel Beale, or how the missing man's weapon was retrieved, or what sort of cruel beast could so brutally slay two girls. Florence kicks her little feet against the brocade-clad wall. *Oh, to have dared enter the terrors of the Moyamensing Prison! Oh, to have heard the tortuous cry of "I'm in a watery grave; search for me no more!" Oh, to be as willful as the terrible but fascinating Emily Durand.*

"AND THE MEMBERS of the day watch who discovered the hermit are quite convinced they've apprehended Father's murderer, Mr. Simms?" Martha asks, then pauses for a moment only, shaking her head in confusion and disbelief. "But I still fail to understand how they can be certain that such a simple soul—"

Owen Simms interrupts, walking with a show of authoritarian calm to the parlor hearth, the better to view his master's daughter. In his hand is the porcelain cup she recently filled; she remains, as customary, presiding over the silver tea things arrayed upon the table. The subdued supper during which they scarcely referred to the astonishing arrest has given way to a more heated exchange now that the servants are no longer present. "My dear Martha, you and I must rely upon the long experience of the constabulary. If they're convinced they have the man who killed your father—"

"But what does Mr. Kelman say to this notion?" Martha's brow is creased, and her chest feels tight with perplexity and the sense that her father's confidential secretary is not providing the entire story of what occurred. "Because surely such a reclusive creature would be easy to blame . . . *wrongly* accuse is what I mean—"

"Your Mr. Kelman is no longer part of this investigation" is Simms's firm response.

Martha stares at him. She cannot believe she's heard correctly. "Oh, but Mr. Simms, surely—?"

"Martha, have we not had similar discussions in the past? I must caution you to obey reason and not your heart. Mr. Kelman no longer has—"

"But have you spoken to him?" she asks in growing consternation. "Have you explained—?"

Owen Simms smiles down as he interrupts her again. "You're as stubborn as your dear papa, Martha. I think he'd be pleased to see you so insistent that all proper measures in this inquiry be satisfied. You have a kind heart. He—and I—have long recognized that fact. You fret over dogs taking chill; you worry about overtaxing your servants; you wish to aid the destitute. Naturally, you also desire to spare the feelings of Thomas Kelman . . . But the truth in this matter cannot be avoided. A half-beast of a man was found in possession of your father's rifle. How could this hermit have come to own the weapon if he hadn't slain your father?"

"But Jacob saw it lying on the rocks when he—"

"Jacob *claimed* to have seen it, Martha—"

"And I believe him, Mr. Simms!" Martha's words are almost a cry, and her body quivers with the desperate need to be heard.

Simms's response is an even-tempered and almost playful "My dear Martha, you'll never be capable of managing a household if you trust every word your servants tell you."

"But couldn't the hermit have simply found Father's rifle when Jacob came home to report the news?" Martha persists despite her companion's obvious desire that they put the conversation behind them. Or perhaps she continues her argument precisely because Simms doesn't want it. "Isn't that what the prisoner's been insisting? That he never heard of a person called Lemuel Beale, and—?"

"Nonsense, Martha. Everyone in this city knows of your father."

"But—"

"We must trust the wisdom of the constabulary, Martha," Simms tells her with some asperity. "If they believe they've apprehended your father's killer, then we, as law-abiding citizens, must accept their judgment." He graces her with another smile, then continues in the same decisive tone. "Who's to say that the gardener wasn't in league with your father's assassin? Who's to say your father didn't have something of value in his possession when he vanished? Even a few gold coins would be a fortune to a pauper—"

"Jacob Oberholtzer is not a pauper, Mr. Simms; he's an honest and good man."

Simms puts his teacup on the mantelpiece. It's a supremely self-assured gesture, and Martha finds herself growing not only irritated at it but also strangely frightened. "Well, let us not impugn old Jacob's character—for the time being, my dear. But even you with your loving heart cannot feel empathy for a savage who willfully shot your father. And that man, most assuredly, *is* a pauper."

"*If* the hermit did murder Father, Mr. Simms," Martha responds forcefully.

"Which we must leave for a jury to decide, my dear. As we must also permit a judge to ascertain how or to what extent Oberholtzer was involved—"

"Or whether Jacob had no part in this, Mr. Simms!" Martha argues. "Other than discovering Father's dogs waiting on the shore." Even as she makes this vigorous objection to Simms's accusation, Martha feels her defiant spirit beginning to desert her. She forces her gaze away from Simms's face and tranquil hands and returns to the tea set spread before her.

So much has occurred in a mere day's time! Since the discovery of the rifle, her father's confidential secretary has rarely left the house. Instead, he installed himself in Lemuel Beale's study, where he first entered into discussions with the captain of the day watch who found the weapon and then attended to other private affairs—while Martha hovered outside the door, at first anxious lest he find some object of her father's misplaced, and then worrying over the fact that he didn't send for her. Hours of fretful pacing because Simms deemed it inappropriate for her genteel ears to be subjected to descriptions of the half-savage creature who possessed the weapon!

Nor did he consider it fitting for her to peruse her father's business correspondences.

So much for my courageous decisions, Martha now thinks bitterly. *So much for my declaration of autonomy.* She sighs in self-rebuke, but Simms mistakes the sound for one of sorrow.

"You must continue to be brave, my dear Martha. Your father would wish it."

Martha makes no answer. It's the truth, of course, but how she yearns to be no longer reminded of her parent's dictums.

"Would *have wished* it." Simms corrects himself. "Because the time has come when we must behave as reasonable folk. Whether the strange creature found carrying your father's rifle had an accomplice or whether he simply acted for his own greedy gain, the fact of the matter remains: Your father is dead and must be properly mourned."

"Yes," Martha replies in a leaden tone. She knows precisely to what Simms refers: the rules society has established for a daughter bereaved of a parent. Six months of near-total seclusion dressed in full mourning; four months of semi-mourning, and finally two months in half-mourning. For ten months, there will be no callers stopping by to visit her other than family—of which she has none—or female or older male acquaintances of long standing, the chief one of whom is Owen Simms.

"I propose to make another visit to the Association for the Care of Colored Orphans before I make my retreat, Mr. Simms," Martha now states in the same heavy and defeated voice. "I feel I've left some hopeful efforts unresolved. I shall journey there tomorrow morning, then return home and order the appropriate black-edged paper and the envelopes and memorial cards."

"I've taken the liberty to order letter paper already, Martha."

"Ah . . ." She stares at the tea tray, but the silver pot and sugar bowl and creamer begin to blur before her eyes. *Already my exile begins,* she tells herself. "You've thought of everything, Mr. Simms."

"It was the service I provided your late father, Martha. I hope to continue to do so for you."

Martha glances up at him with her bleak face. *Here's my chance,* she thinks; *here's the moment when I inform Owen Simms that I wish him to quit the house.* But he speaks again before she can craft the necessary words.

"In fact, I hope to one day be of even greater aid . . . In a year's time, when this period of mourning is passed, I hope that you will consider doing me the tremendous honor of becoming my wife—"

"Oh, Mr. Simms!" Martha is so horrified at this proposal that she finds herself riveted to her chair. "Surely you cannot imagine—"

"You're right to suggest it's too soon to speak of such matters, my dear, but I—"

"No! It's not a matter of—"

"But I feel your father would approve. No, I am certain he would approve, and that he'd also wish me to proclaim myself now in order to assuage your grief—"

"No!" Martha can only repeat. She tells herself she should rise and leave the room, but her legs have turned to stone. "Please, Mr. Simms. Let us no longer discuss this—"

"Not for a full year, naturally. I fully comprehend the awkwardness of acting so hastily, Martha, but as I stated, I hope you'll recognize with what deep affection I regard you, and so gain a measure of solace in your time of trial. Your happiness is all I wish, my dearest Martha . . . And now I'll comply with your request and not refer to this proposal again until your period of mourning is past—"

"Not then, Mr. Simms. Not now and not then," Martha states as she finally forces herself to stand. "I bid you good night, sir. We will not refer to this matter again."

REGAINING THE SAFETY of her room, Martha flings herself fully clothed upon her bed, staring up into its abundant draperies while her brain whirls around in fury. *A marriage to Owen Simms?* her thoughts rage. *A union with a man nearly my father's age! How could anyone consider such a preposterous idea? How can my father have sanctioned or suggested it? Better death than sharing life with Owen Simms!*

And I've already shared so much of my existence with the man, Martha continues to rail. *Years and years and years of my time upon this earth! Years of obeying both my father and his henchman, being secluded from people my own age, from their pleasures, their confidences, from the young men who might have whispered words of endearment. Owen Simms? No, I won't marry Owen Simms!*

In her outrage, Martha pounds her fists against the satin coverlet and rakes at the eiderdown with her still-shod feet. *Never Simms! Never, never! No matter how much my father may have desired the match. No matter how many times in the months ahead Simms seeks to craftily remind me of my "dear papa's" wishes. I will be the mistress of my fate. I'll rule my own house, and demand that Simms leave it. I will not listen to my father's dictums or wishes any longer.*

I'll never obey him again. And I'll never, ever permit Simms to make another mention of this odious matter.

Then the fury of these emotions dissolves into panic. *Oh, Thomas!* Martha thinks. *Oh, help me! Help me!* She gazes upward while her body becomes increasingly inert, seeming to grow heavier and less mobile by the moment until she feels she's sinking down into the mattress, down through the floor, plummeting into the suffocating earth. *Oh, help me,* her heart cries as she tumbles into tortured sleep.

But, oh, what dreams rise up to trouble her there. She sees the little orphan boy succumb to a convulsive fit, but his face is then replaced by that of Eusapio Paladino in his own trance-like state.

"Search no more!" the necromancer calls while his handsome features grow fishy and gray and his flesh turns soft and putrid. "I'm in a watery grave. Let me rest. Let me rest here in peace." The voice sounds like bubbles in a brook, then the bubbles grow louder, gushing a grim crimson red as Lemuel Beale's percussion rifle explodes. Martha spins away in horror at the sight and finds herself suddenly awake, lying cold and uncovered, her petticoats twisted and bunched beneath her and her corset jabbing at her ribs.

"Martha, my dearest," she hears Owen Simms murmur. "Your dreams have been worrying you again. Forgive me for entering your chambers without your permission, but I couldn't permit you to so torture yourself. I've brought a sleeping draught with me—so as not to disturb your maid. Take it, I beseech you, my dear. My dearest girl . . . You must have your rest . . ." Then she feels Simms's fingers touch her neck, holding her in place while she drinks the milky and cloying liquid.

The Shambles

"MAR . . . MISS BEALE . . . I STOPPED at your house and was told that you . . . I apologize if I've disturbed your—" Kelman calls out these halting words, then abruptly ceases his clumsy effort as he doffs his hat and bows while intently studying the threesome walking down the street toward him. Martha appears greatly changed; she steps slowly forward with a rambling and indecisive gait and looks so pale and languid as to seem ill. Beside her is a shorter woman with an open and jovial face, and between them trudges a little boy whose skin isn't fully white or fully black. Neither the child nor the other woman appears aware that Martha Beale is not herself.

"I was told I might find you at the orphanage . . . Again, my apologies if I've interrupted your outing." Kelman continues to regard Martha with a penetrating gaze, but she merely looks lifelessly back. "Are you quite well, Miss Beale?"

"Mr. Kelman." Martha fixes him with a vapid stare; she neither smiles nor offers her hand nor responds to his question. Instead, she turns sluggishly toward her companions, covering a yawn with her hand. "May I present Hannah Yarnell, and a pupil whom she named for Caspar Walne, the physician who devotes so much time to the children." As Martha speaks, her tone remains flat and emotionless as though Kelman were the most causal of acquaintances. "Hannah, this is Thomas Kelman, the gentleman who initiated the search for my father."

"I have disturbed your walk" is Kelman's perturbed reply.

"Miss Yarnell and I are journeying to the Shambles on Second Street," Martha says in the same dull tone, "where I intend to purchase oranges for the children. We've heard that a ship arrived yesterday carrying a cargo from Spain. Oranges are certain to be among the ship's fare." Then she adds a bleak "As you must have surmised, Mr. Kelman, this is my last excursion for some time." She pauses. What she wants to speak about is Jacob Oberholtzer and the savage man she feels is being wrongly charged with her father's death, but all she hears clanging in her ears is Owen Simms's methodical words of argument. *The truth in this matter, Martha, cannot be avoided . . .* Then she continues the rebuke with her own woeful self-critique: *And who's to say that I am right in my intuition, and the remainder of the logical world wrong? I, who have so seldom been right or wise or prudent or clever.*

"I do thank you, Mr. Kelman," Martha finally manages to say aloud, "for your aid and support. And I apologize if my father's secretary was overbrusque in his treatment of you." Here, she stops again. *Owen Simms,* she thinks, *I cannot possibly be wed to Owen Simms! I will not! Indeed, I will not!* But instead of betraying that fierce sentiment, she murmurs a reasoned "Mr. Simms's greatest desire is to see my father's death resolved. Sometimes that wish causes him to seem high-handed and rude."

"I was glad to be of service" is Kelman's courtly reply, but he observes Martha closely as he speaks. This is not the same woman who ardently sought his counsel. It's not the person with whom he's shared a private meal or walked in the garden or strolled among hothouse flowers. This is a Martha Beale in form but not in fact. Kelman is about to continue in a more probing manner when Hannah's small charge suddenly throws his hands skyward as if asking the tall man to pick him up.

"You seem to have made quite an impression, sir," Hannah tells him. "Our Cai is not a demonstrative child."

"May I carry him for you, Miss Yarnell?" Kelman bends down to the child. "That is, if you will permit my company on your excursion." Again he looks searchingly at Martha, but it's Hannah who replies:

"We would be delighted to have you join us, sir," while Martha merely removes her mute stare from Kelman's face and gazes unseeing at the street beyond. *Marry Owen Simms?* her mind cries out. *That I cannot do!*

ALONG THE COBBLED streets that border the open-air market building known as the Shambles, dray horses stand puffing and blowing in the cold; crowded among them are butchers' wagons hung with venison, mutton, and pickled hams; fishmongers' carts; country buckboards full of potatoes and cabbages packed in straw; oyster sellers' flat barrows piled with seaweed; wood crates containing live fowl and rabbits; and two-wheeled handcarts stacked with loaves of bread. Dogs and cats slink between the many large and small wheels, keeping wary eyes on the restless hooves of the horses while all manner of young people race in and out of the vendors' stalls: shopkeepers's boys sent on errands; ragtag brothers and cousins dodging from one patron to the next, begging for the chance to carry a parcel, find a hansom cab, or garner a stray coin or two. Some of the children wear long white aprons; some sport adults' high hats announcing their masters' trades; some have jackets; some do not. Those without not only appear sicklier and colder, but their faces and postures bear the unmistakable stamp of isolation and ostracism.

Martha stares at the noisy scene and feels her stomach contract in pity, although her sluggish brain seems incapable of forming words with which to express what she feels. So she doesn't look at Hannah or Kelman but simply plods ahead, wading stiffly through the trampled rushes that line the dirt-and-stone floor until she reaches a fruit vendor where she finds the promised oranges.

"These just arrived, madam," she's told by the dark-suited merchant. "Sevilles for marmalades, sweet Chinas for eating, and Maltese whose flesh is as red as blood . . . They're extra, they are, the Maltese. Greatly favored by European royalty, I'm told." The man is sizing her up while he studies her companions. The tall woman he recognizes as "quality," but he's not certain how to gauge the ranks and relationships of the others.

"I will take them all," Martha states, although her words maintain their dispassionate tone.

"Oh, no, Martha," Hannah insists, stepping forward. "You're far too generous. We'll never be able to make use of all these oranges. One per child is sufficient—"

"I don't want sufficiency," Martha insists. Her voice grows more strident. "I want abundance for these children. I want them to know what it is to have plenty."

"Two, then. More than that may bring indigestion—and Rebecca's ire." Hannah smiles as she makes this gentle reminder.

"No. No, I will buy them all. All of them in this shop." Martha's pallid cheeks have turned mottled pink, and her green-gray eyes bright and hard. "You and Rebecca may do with them what you will; make marmalades and jams; pickle and sugar the rinds; throw the rotten ones to the pigs for all I care. I want those children to have a surfeit. Let them live like kings and queens for a space." She spins back to the vendor. "Have them delivered to the orphanage on Thirteenth and Fitzwater Streets." Then she yanks open her reticule and tosses out enough gold coins to purchase twice the amount of fruit in the stall. "And send a large box to the same address every time a decent cargo arrives."

In the midst of this transaction, little Caspar crows from his perch in Kelman's arms, then points toward a young girl standing just outside the shelter of the stall's canvas awning. She regards the scene boldly, although she remains at a distance. "Is that your baby?" she asks Thomas Kelman.

"No." It's Hannah who responds. "This is a foundling child. A Negro."

The girl frowns slightly. "That doesn't mean he doesn't have a white papa."

"That's true." Hannah looks at Kelman as though seeking his advice, but the girl continues with a soft:

"I think the boy loves this man as much as he would his own father."

"Would you like an orange?" Martha asks abruptly.

"My name is Ella" is the answer. "I've never tasted one." But she makes no move to enter the fruit vendor's stall.

"Does your papa work here?" Martha probes.

Ella scowls but doesn't reply.

"Or your mother, perhaps?"

"I'm not an orphan" is Ella's sole response; then the need for human contact finally propels her into the shop. "Please. I would like to taste an orange." She gazes up at Cai, who continues to stare down at her with the fascination younger children reserve for older ones; then she swiftly returns her attention to Martha. "You have not been here before, I think, miss?"

"No," Martha answers as she turns unsteadily, negotiating a separate sackful of oranges for the little girl. The clearheadedness she experienced for a moment is quickly passing, and she can again feel the effects of the sleeping draughts Owen Simms prescribed. "No, I haven't."

"You have a girl to do for you, then, miss? Or you are looking to engage one, perhaps—?" Then Ella interrupts her question with a swift dodging turn of her head. The motion is so rapid and defensive it almost appears as though she's been slapped.

Kelman looks in the direction Ella is staring. A group of women are walking there; and from their garish clothes and loud manner, he knows immediately what trade they are engaged in. "Do you know any of those ladies, Ella?" he asks as Martha and Hannah follow his glance.

"No" is Ella's defiant answer, although she keeps her face averted and her eyes on the ground. "They are not ladies, either."

"Where is your mother?" Hannah asks her.

"At home. Where else would she be?" Ella blurts out, then all at once drops the oranges and plunges away, disappearing among the crowd.

"Thief!" someone shouts at her retreating figure, but Martha rallies, producing her own forceful cry:

"Let the child pass. She's running an errand for me." Then her shoulders slump and her knees almost buckle, and she turns back and gazes emptily at Thomas Kelman once more. "It's time for me to return home. I've been sufficiently long on my outing." She looks at Hannah. "Tell Rebecca she can blame me if the children grow spoiled."

"Let me escort you," Kelman says; he cannot bring himself to add "Miss Beale." He knows he shouldn't say "Martha" in this public place.

"Thank you, no, Mr. Kelman. That would not be seemly—or befitting to my father's memory to be seen in the company of a recent acquaintance." She pauses, her display of energy now spent. "You will apply to Mr. Simms, will you not, if you have further news concerning my father's death to impart? Or of this . . . this hermit . . . ? Mr. Simms will be . . . he will be my ears and my mouthpiece for a while . . ."

"I would prefer to talk with you directly . . . should I gain information—"

"No. That will not be possible." Martha seems about to speak further; instead, her gloved right hand reaches up and lightly touches her neck. "Let us say farewell, then, Mr. Kelman." Then she summons what little remains of her strength and walks in a slow, straight line from the market building.

IT'S RUTH WHO spots the girl running. Running and crying, then stumbling and nearly falling in her haste to escape the Shambles. "Stop, child!" she calls out, and hurries behind, catching Ella in her arms after a block-and-a-half chase. "Stop. Child. What ails you? Has someone done you harm?"

Ella stares up at the Negress. Her first instinct is to flee; her second is to rail against her captor; her third is to sag into the taller woman's arms. "A lady bought me oranges," she finally manages to mumble.

Ruth gazes into the child's fearful eyes. "And were you afraid of what she might demand in exchange for the oranges?"

"No . . ." Ella looks down at her feet. "But she wanted to know about my mother . . ."

Ruth nods; she continues to hold the frightened girl. "What's your name, child?" she asks at length.

"Ella."

"Well, Ella, mine is Ruth. Do you know that name from the Bible?"

Ella shakes her head.

"Ruth was a young widow lady. When her husband died, her old mother-in-law, who was also widowed, decided to leave the country of her husband's family and return to her own people. Ruth went with her, although this meant traveling to a far-off land." Ruth pauses; Ella continues to regard her. "But this Ruth was very good and very brave, and when her mother-in-law told her to lie with powerful King Boaz, she did—"

"The king paid the mother-in-law?" Ella asks with a quick, angry scowl.

Ruth also frowns. "No. It was not like that . . . I think her mother-in-law believed the king would marry Ruth if he slept with her."

"Ah," murmurs Ella.

"And the child this Ruth and her king would make together would also become a king, the grandfather of an even greater king named David. And so Ruth would be remembered forever."

"Ah," Ella repeats, but with less enthusiasm. Royal people are of little interest in her world. Then she stands straighter, wiping her nose with the back of her hand. "And do you have a son you call David?" she asks.

"I have no son. I did once, but I do no longer."

Ella doesn't question this statement, although she recognizes the great sadness in Ruth's voice. "I had a mother once, too," she says in empathy.

Ruth nods. "And a father also, I'll warrant." Her tone is gentle, but Ella stiffens instantly.

"My father sold me," Ella states, but the sound of the words is defiant rather than sorrowful.

"And who do you dwell with now, that you are running away from fine ladies shopping in the Shambles?" Even as Ruth poses this kindly query, she realizes that she's heard the girl's voice before. "I saw you walking some days ago . . . with a man I thought was your parent—" Then Ruth grasps Ella's shoulders in steely and deter-

As Much Gold As You Can Hold

IN THIN BOOTS WRAPPED IN cloths, Ella's cold feet trudge along the cobbled pavement, carrying her north once more toward the Shambles, where the lady offered her the oranges two mornings past. Ella has little hope of retrieving that lost piece of luck, but she retraces her route on the chance—the barest of chances—that she might.

As she marches doggedly on, head down, shoulders defensive and fierce, she berates herself for running away from the tall lady who bought the oranges. Running away when she might have taken those lovely sweet-smelling fruits! Or maybe found a paid position in an elegant household. Or been given a few pennies to put in her pocket. Oh, anything wonderful might have happened, if only she hadn't been such a baby. And if she hadn't been such a cry-baby, the terrible Negress called Ruth would never have grabbed her and asked her name and then demanded to know what she knew about a club-footed tailor.

This last recollection makes Ella tremble in helpless fright. *Suppose this Ruth chased after me when I ran away?* she wonders as her eyes dart apprehensively around. *Or suppose she's sneaking somewhere near—right now—waiting to follow me home and discover where Daniel lives, and then turn him over to the police? Suppose I bump into her when I turn the corner or cross the street? Suppose she spots me walking here?* Picturing these awful scenes and recalling Ruth's strong fingers holding her tight, Ella begins clinging to the shadows cast by the cold morning sun, darting nervously from dark splotch to dark splotch on the icy pavement.

She remembers the little mulatto the gentleman held in his arms. How well dressed the boy was, and how warm and safe. An orphan decked out in finer array than she's ever known! Envy and longing twist at her heart and make her face knot itself in pain. *And I have only Daniel,* Ella tells herself in despair. *Daniel, who's so afraid of the day watch and night watch that he cannot seek honest wages from an honest shop. That little orphan boy has fine people to carry him about, but I have only my frozen toes and an empty belly and a benefactor who may not be able to afford keeping me much longer.*

Tears of woe well into Ella's eyes and begin rolling down her cheeks. *And what's to prevent Daniel from casting me off if Mr. Robey deserts him? Or perhaps selling me to another fancy house as my father did? What's to stop this horrid Ruth from creeping around the city until she finds us? She'd get a reward for exposing an escaped convict; I'm sure she would.*

The hurt and self-rebuke Ella feels have now hardened into anger at those around her, and her mouth sets itself into an unforgiving line. *Well, I know what I can do; I can turn Daniel in before any Negress does! Or before he takes it into his head to abandon me. I'll seek out a member of the day watch and tell him I know the whereabouts of the club-foot tailor. Then I'll get the reward money and be my own mistress. And no one will be able to buy or sell me again.*

But this vindictive dream evaporates almost as fast as it began.

Daniel saved me, Ella reminds herself. *He made me a supper of sausages—and many other things; he gave me a warm place to sleep; he gave me a coat. I could never harm him. Never. Never.*

Instead of lifting her spirits, however, Ella's heroic claim induces another spate of anxious tears, causing her to stumble as she walks, which makes her almost collide with two matrons strolling together, then a nursemaid and her charge, an aproned errand boy, and finally a gentleman and his lady: all of whom look askance at the slight and dirty bundle of despair who hurries blindly past them.

When Ella finally looks up, she notices her path has carried her to the high brick wall surrounding St. Peter's Church. Peering through the gates, she sees the morning sunlight glinting upon the window-panes, turning them a gilded color as hot as desire. Ella draws an awed and wondering breath, then passes into the graveyard as though an unseen person were urging her to do so. People pray for blessings, she's heard tell; they pray for healing from ravaging illness, for the discovery of lost objects, for babies—some of them—or husbands who won't squander a family's livelihood on drink.

She considers what her own request might be, and the shiny cross leaps into her mind. She'll ask God for gold. Boxes and boxes of it. More than she can ever hold. And think how pleased Daniel will be then! And the dangerous Ruth? Well, they'll be able to pay her handsomely for her silence.

BUT THIS MIRACULOUS intervention comes to naught. The church in which Ella wished to pray is shut against her, a Negro man with a broom chasing her out long before she can kneel and make her vital request, then shooing her off toward the street like a diseased and unwelcome cat, and finally shaking the broom after her as if even the dust she'd left behind were tainted.

Ella slinks along the pavement imagining the many fine things God's gift will never provide: no pretty dresses, no butter cakes, no doll with a shining china face, no toy rocking horse like she saw in a shop window, no fine roasted beef for Daniel. Or silks for him to sew or handsome bone buttons. Or glittering silver ones, either.

She forces herself not to cry. Instead, she trudges along, berating the Negro man with the broom and the God who permitted him to threaten her with it. Then her anger finally levels on God alone. God who provides rich people with more riches, velvet cushions to kneel upon and glowing candlesticks and lace embroidered with colored threads as bright as summer flowers. What use is it to pray to a being as selfish as that? Might as well pray to a beetle not to spoil the flour or a mouse not to steal the baby's food.

When she reaches Daniel's house, her fury is nearly spent, and she pauses on the threshold, forming a heartfelt apology for not returning home laden with the wonders she envisioned. As she considers the words, she hears another man talking to her protector. The voice makes her freeze in place. It's the man who wrapped his fingers around her neck and tried to choke her. Ella creeps round to the side of the house and listens at the oilcloth-covered window.

"I have been told you have a daughter, tailor."

"I did once, sir. I have no longer."

"Come, man, I've been told otherwise. You've been seen walking with the child. A pretty blonde girl."

Daniel doesn't speak for a moment. When he does respond, the sound is halting, as if he were limping forward. "Ah . . . Ella, that would be. She is . . . she's my young cousin . . . a girl from the country whose family wished her to learn the trade of sewing—"

"And you pay for her keeping, this charming 'cousin' of yours?" the man interrupts. Ella can tell by the mocking sound of his voice that he doubts she and Daniel are related.

Again Daniel hesitates. "I don't understand your meaning, sir."

"Do you pay for her keeping? Or does she pay for yours? I've heard she's a most comely thing, despite her age."

"Oh, no, sir! I would never permit the child to labor in that fashion. As I said, she's studying stitchery, and—"

"A girl sewing doesn't earn the fine wages a girl in a fancy house does."

"That may be, sir. But I'm not so bad off as to profit from the sale of human flesh—"

"You have numerous persons clamoring for your wares, then?"

Breathless, Ella waits for Daniel's reply; she's guessed where the questions are aimed even if her benefactor has not.

"I do not, I regret to say—"

"No . . . You have but one client. And that man is me."

"Yes, Mr. Robey, that's true . . . Though times are improving, so the people say."

Ella hears Mr. Robey sigh as though in sympathy; when he resumes his speech, the tone is as liquid as warm molasses. "It must be a pricey proposition keeping a hungry child fed and clothed."

"It's not so bad, sir" is Daniel's gentle response.

"I think I must help you out, tailor. I'd count myself a mean-spirited man not to aid a young girl—and her patron—in their hour of distress."

"I'm hardly her patron, Mr. Robey. Ella is my cousin—"

"Then you will allow me to assume that title? For my Christian edification?"

Ella squints her eyes in terror and wills her knees and hands to cease their noisy shaking. She tries to gulp back her fears, but her mouth and tongue are as dry as last year's leaves.

"She's a simple girl, sir, a country lass. I'm not certain she's fit to become a lady—"

"For my betterment as a true and devout Christian, Daniel. You must allow me to help your fair young cousin."

Ella hears a purse open; she hears coins—heavy ones—rattle in a warm grasp. "Gold is a handsome commodity, is it not, Daniel the tailor? Come, man, take it! As much gold as you can hold . . ."

A Message From the Departed

BEFORE KNOCKING AT THE DOOR to her husband's study, Marguerite Rosegger pauses. She cautions herself to summon courage, and in so doing tries to recall the hopeful woman she once was, and the proud life she led when her father was still living. Despite these efforts, she finds she cannot re-create the bright spirit she was then. The words she can recall but not the emotion; and that loss affects her severely. She senses herself even less equipped to deal with her powerful husband than she was before. Moment by moment, she realizes that her fortitude and willpower are waning. Moment by moment, year by unforgiving year.

Propelled by something akin to desperation, she raises her hand and raps loudly upon the door. "Mr. Rosegger?" she calls.

"I didn't summon you," comes the answer, and Marguerite's first response is to creep away. Instead, she remains in place, switching her rustling skirts and rocking back and forth on her new shoes until the homey sounds of creaking leather and wheezing floorboards restore her determination.

"May I bring you coffee? Or perhaps a pot of chocolate?"

"I didn't call you!" is her husband's rough reply.

"Mr. Rosegger, I must speak with you." She draws in another tight breath; her fingers grasp each other as though clinging to a cliff face. "It concerns John Durand."

A sound half oath, half groan erupts from the study. Marguerite hears four fast footsteps, and the door is flung open. "What do you know of this matter?"

She stares up at her husband in both fear and bravado. "A good deal. I . . . I wrote a note to Emily Durand."

Rosegger nearly drags his wife into the room, slamming the door behind them as he does. "Why would you do a fool thing like that?" he thunders; then his eyes narrow into slits as if he were already anticipating the pain his next question would inflict. "And what was Mrs. Durand's response?"

"She . . . she suggested that we meet to discuss my message some time in the future."

"Poor Marguerite. So underappreciated by the gentry. Even gentry in disgrace." There's no sympathy in the tone.

His wife doesn't pause, doesn't prevaricate, doesn't look back. "What do you intend to do about the situation, Mr. Rosegger?"

"Nothing."

"Nothing?"

He shrugs. "The man's dead and buried—"

"But the truth cannot long escape notice."

Rosegger eyes his wife with some humor. "I hope you are not attempting to tell me my own business, Marguerite. For it ill becomes you."

"I am."

"Then you greatly miscalculate your influence over me."

She ignores the remark. "You must write to Emily Durand immediately . . . No, you must pay her a visit. Today. She cannot discover this dreadful affair through an unknown source. It would make her situation even more dire—"

Her husband's loud laughter interrupts her. "Gentle Marguerite! You and your fine morals."

"You will do this, Rosegger" is her staunch reply. She squares her shoulders as she speaks, and this bit of bravado surprises them both.

He laughs again, but more hesitantly this time. "What would make you imagine you could dictate my actions?"

"I know about you and Owen Simms. I know about you and Lemuel Beale."

THE OBJECT OF Marguerite Rosegger's concern paces in growing anger through her brittle and perfect mansion while she rages at the hideousness of her current state. *Shunned by all, and a widow as well! I might as well be dead as face this odious existence. I might as well have never been born.* Emily sighs in pent-up fury and gnashes her teeth. *Will Philadelphia ever forgive me? Will my acquaintances ever forget? Probably not,* she realizes. *No, not probably, but decidedly. I've become a pariah. I've become no better than a whore.*

No better than a whore: The thought sends bile burning into her throat as she rushes from the parlor into the foyer. *And Marguerite Rosegger sending me that ridiculous and poorly phrased note hinting at indiscretions on my husband's part! As if any gentleman worth his salt didn't have entanglements he'd rather keep concealed! And thank God for that! Thank God for men robust enough to keep secrets from their wives!*

Emily Durand takes momentary comfort from this latest image, envisioning her dead husband as a private Lothario, a man with a string of hidden mistresses. But the pleasure is short-lived, because, surely, if that had been the case, he was putting his wife at risk of disease.

"Damn him!" she swears aloud. "Damn every last one of them!" Her feet in their silken, high-heeled slippers slap hard and spitefully on the floor. She marches up the stairs. She has no thought as to where her footsteps are leading—only that she must keep moving. Then her furious ruminations round back on Martha Beale and Thomas Kelman. *They're certainly welcome to each other*, she fumes. *They'll make a fine pair if they ever arouse enough passion to wed. Cool. Polite. And so bloodless, they'll certainly never find enough heat to enliven any conjugal bed. Or perhaps old Lemuel will arise from his grave and forbid his daughter to marry below her station!* The notion makes Emily laugh aloud. The sound is close to hysteria.

When this brief and nervous spate of humor passes, she realizes she's entered her dead husband's chambers. It's the first time she's approached the rooms since his demise; and she halts, all at once at a loss as to what she currently is—or should be—feeling. For a brief moment, she experiences pity for the man who married her. *It wasn't his fault that he didn't have the passion of Eusapio Paladino; it wasn't his fault he was often tedious and countrified in his tastes. It wasn't his fault he chose a tempestuous wife.* Guilt makes a small hole in Emily's heart, and she stands, staring about, picturing the ghost of John Durand drifting aimlessly through the chambers. Then the very vacillation of this imagined specter makes her again grow wrathful. *Why did my life become so hateful?* her soul cries out. *Why am I not free? Why was I never free?*

Then the silent scream turns practical. She looks at John's armoire, at the highboy and chest-on-chest that hold his personal linens; and a sudden revelation takes hold. *If I dressed as a man,* she tells herself, *I could go out into the world at will instead of sitting pent up in my supposedly tragic widowhood. I could attend the theater; I could walk the streets, frequent oyster cellars and any number of other rowdy and hedonistic places. I could become an observer of the foibles of both friends and foes, because no one would recognize me as Emily Durand, spurned society maven and grieving wife of a murdered man.*

She laughs again. This time the sound is a gush of rapture as thrilling as a fulfilled sexual liaison. Emily hurries across the room, yanks open the drawers in a chest-on-chest, and begins riffling through John's shirts and folded waistcoats, his cravats and undergarments. Her eyes shine with delight, and she holds up each item, measuring it against her body as she tries to determine whether she'd prefer to be accoutered as a dandy or a quiet fellow visiting from the countryside. She hums aloud, then attempts a low and mannish whistle, but the unfamiliar sound fades on her lips when she catches sight of a letter hiding beneath her husband's effects.

So John had a secret admirer after all, Emily thinks with malicious pleasure while a smile of complicity curls around her lips. She removes the letter and carries it toward a lamp sitting atop a table. There she unfolds the paper and reads until all joy vanishes from her face.

"Oh, my dear God," she murmurs as she turns the page face down, then as rapidly rights it and peruses it afresh. "It's not possible . . ." she whispers below her breath. "Tell me what he's divulging isn't possible."

Caught in a Trap

MARTHA SITS BY HER BEDROOM window, her face turned toward the glass but her eyes glazed and unfocused. She's been thus posed longer than she remembers. Indeed, she has a difficult time recalling how long it has been since she walked through the Shambles in order to purchase oranges for the orphan children. A day? More? Less? But no, it cannot be less than a day. Surely she has only recently arisen; and the excursion into the world—her last—was in the morning. So, an entire day, at least. One day or perhaps more of the twelve months she must remain sequestered in mourning for her father.

Martha can't remember when she last spoke or what she said. She's dressed, which leads her to assume she must have spoken a few words to her maid. And there must have been supper, or suppers, with Mr. Simms. Surely conversation as well . . . Unless Simms was not at home for the evening meal, which is a possibility as he's often away, although she has no recollection of whether or not that was the case.

Gradually her glance drifts toward her escritoire, and she tells herself she should settle herself there and commence some of her correspondence. There are letters of sympathy to respond to. Or she believes there are. There should be, should there not? Messages from the Ilsleys and Shippens, perhaps from the Roseggers or Emily Durand, or others with whom her father was acquainted but she was not.

But the move from one chair to the next seems more taxing than she can currently bear. She would need to stand first, then cause her feet to move, and then . . . It doesn't bear considering. She will remain as she is.

Martha feels a great weight pulling her eyelids closed. *As I am,* she tells herself. *As I always have been and always will be: the compliant and docile daughter of Lemuel Beale.*

OWEN SIMMS HAS awakened in fine fettle. His plans are moving apace; his personal business dealings with Rosegger will make him a wealthy man, which, in turn, will provide him with the appropriate status to join in holy wedlock with the daughter of his former employer. The heiress to Lemuel Beale's great fortune would never be permitted to marry a man with meager assets; such a union would not find favor in the eyes of the world.

Holy wedlock. He considers the term as he rings for Beale's valet—now his own; Simms likes the word "wedlock" better than its religious partner; the physical finality of it suits his frame of mind. *Martha locked to me,* he tells himself, *wedded as metals are melded together.*

The valet appears, shaves his new master, and helps him to dress.

"Is Miss Beale still abed?" Simms asks the man as his jacket is dusted and his cravat straightened.

"No, sir. Her breakfast was delivered to her rooms an hour past."

"Ah, then I am the tardy one today. You may send my own meal to her chambers. I will join her there."

"Very good, sir."

The valet withdraws, and Simms smiles at his reflection in the looking glass. When his own period of formal mourning is past, he must order up new suits of clothes. He'll need more costly fabrics, livelier colors, too. There will be no point in maintaining the drab costume of a confidential secretary.

"BUT YOU HAVEN'T touched your breakfast, Martha my dear."

Martha hears a voice near her shoulder and turns lethargically to see Simms bending near her chair. He almost looks as though he's about to kneel on the floor beside her. "You must eat, you know."

Her eyes drift to the tray. "I thought I had . . ." What a lot of effort that short speech requires! She falls silent again, then again listens to Simms speaking: this time in a sterner tone.

"And you're certain she has not been given too much of the sleeping draught."

"It was what you told me the doctor prescribed, sir." A female voice utters these words, although Martha doesn't recognize the accent as belonging to her lady's maid. "I'm always very careful with my dosages. My references—"

"Yes, yes, I know all about that," Simms's voice interjects, this time at a further distance from Martha's chair. "But does the lady not seem to you peculiarly insensate?"

"Perhaps it is her great grief, sir, that has rendered her so impassive."

Simms frowns. "Ah, yes, her great grief . . . Still, I think we must lower the dosage."

The nurse curtsies. "I will do as you say, naturally, sir. But, in my experience, sorrow takes many forms; and her father was missing for some time before his death was officially declared. Perhaps her hopes were inadvertently raised, which might, in turn, make her feelings of loss all the greater."

"Of course," Simms responds; then he sends the nurse away and returns to Martha.

"You need not speak, my dear. I know how weary you feel with the medication the physician recommended. However, simply know that I am near you. And that I shall be with you always. Till death us do part . . . Ah, but I'm forgetting myself. We must not anticipate our happy union yet."

You will dead, Martha thinks, suddenly remembering the conjurer's words, but her sole reply to Owen Simms is to fix him with her sluggish gaze.

EMILY DURAND SILENTLY receives Rosegger into her drawing room. She neither speaks nor offers him a chair but watches him advance across the carpet with what she hopes is an expression of haughty disdain. In fact, it's earth-shaking fear that rattles through her already nerve-wracked body. "I know why you wish to see me, Mr. Rosegger," she states in a harsher and less controlled tone than she'd wished. "I understand that my husband had some . . . some private conversations with you."

"May I sit, Mrs. Durand?"

"Please." The word is nearly a yelp. *From Emily Durand,* she thinks, *a cry approaching pain!*

Rosegger chooses a chair opposite hers and regards her as he takes his place. "Your husband came to see me just before he died."

Emily makes only the slightest of nods; her neck is so straight and tight it looks as though it might break off if touched.

"He was not as lucid as he might have been. In fact—"

"My husband, as you might have surmised, Mr. Rosegger, was a deeply troubled man." Her tone has the icy, still quality of the defenseless and hopeless.

"Yes."

"I have a letter John penned to me that same day. I understand the nature of his visit to you."

"I see."

"Would you care to know what he wrote?"

"That is not necessary, Mrs. Durand."

"If you knew about this, why did you not seek me out before?" Emily demands; the sound is like a muffled scream.

Rosegger studies her. Never did he imagine finding a woman as arrogant and intractable as Emily Durand made so helpless. "I did not believe this was the type of news a wife ordinarily welcomed—"

"And I welcome John's death, Mr. Rosegger?" Emily lashes back at him. "Because surely, you must perceive that his distress caused him to take his own life. His own life! Have you any notion what the reaction will be when the world discovered that fact? When the city learns that he was not, in fact, murdered but did the deed himself . . . ? But of course, you do know just what will occur. You must have anticipated his decision when he left you." She suddenly lowers her head, but the gesture is one of fury rather than grief or self-pity or even despair. "Now, instead of the penny press stating that I either specifically or tacitly inspired Eusapio Paladino to slay my husband—which I did not—I'll be excoriated for causing John such misery that he had no other choice than to . . ." The bitter words trail away. Emily stamps an irate foot. "Either way, I'm become no more than a whipping boy, but perhaps it's what I deserve."

"You're accusing me of a monstrous lack of compassion, Mrs. Durand" is Rosegger's quiet response.

"You talked to John . . . watched him leave you. You must have recognized how dreadful his financial burden was." Emily's fingers clench the chair arm, the fabric dented under the force of her grasp.

"His own life, sir. Shooting himself with his own Derringer pistol . . . Nothing is worse than that, Mr. Rosegger! Nothing! Not one of my transgressions can equal that one fatal act—"

"The Derringer was not recovered—"

"What difference does that make?" Emily almost hisses. "I have the letter detailing his intentions! And when the news spreads abroad . . . !" She heaves herself back into her chair, all semblance of a noble society lady gone. "I didn't believe my circumstances could grow worse, but they have—"

Rosegger interrupts again, a covert smile beginning to slide into his careful eyes. "I have a proposal for you, Mrs. Durand—"

"That comes too late, surely!"

"Hear me out."

Emily regards him, noting for the first time his hungry mouth and hooded eyes. *So,* she thinks, *we have a different man in my drawing room than the one I've encountered in public. How interesting.* "Your wife wrote to me last week . . . prior to John's death," she says at length.

Rosegger's private smile increases. "About this matter? Or about some other?"

"About this situation, I assume . . . The missive was delicately worded, excessively so . . . Your wife claimed to have information regarding certain 'associations' of my husband's—"

"But you did not learn the extent of her information?"

Emily sighs impatiently. "No. I did not. I chose to delay the visit she requested."

"Have you my wife's letter?"

"Why should I keep mysterious correspondence, Mr. Rosegger?" Emily exclaims. "Quite naturally, I discarded it. You may think me rude, if you wish, but I've been accustomed to playing on a very different field than you and your wife enjoy."

The financier ignores the jibe; in fact, to Emily's surprise, he almost seems to relish it. "Marguerite mentioned no situation other than that which directly affected your husband?"

"No. Nor alluded to any, either. As I've already disclosed, her words were painfully circumspect . . . But come, sir, you and I know why your wife wrote me, and you have come to see me on account of it. Let us proceed. I'm prepared for the worst. John was under financial obligation to you; I assume he'd entered into unfortunate business transactions that—"

"I cannot let a lady as fine and handsome as you find yourself so low, Mrs. Durand," Rosegger interjects.

"Yet that is how you do find me, sir. Now, pray tell me why you are here. Unless it's to make further mockery of my reduced state."

"On the contrary." Rosegger's secretive smile spreads to his lips until they curl like a wolf's. "I've come to offer my aid."

Emily stares at him; she doesn't speak, although her lips part slightly, and her cheeks flush hot of their own accord.

"You claim that your world will collapse when news of Mr. Durand's financial embarrassment is known—"

"Such as it is," is Emily's terse response.

"But who is to make it known, madam?"

Emily draws herself up in her chair, leaning gradually toward him. She has an inkling of what he's offering, but it seems impossible to believe. "Who is to keep this information private might be the better question, sir."

"As a man of business, I'm accustomed to keeping many confidences, Mrs. Durand. And I've heard you're a woman who's also adept at keeping a secret or two."

In former days, Emily would have bridled at this *arriviste*'s reference to her liaison with Eusapio Paladino, but those days are long gone. Emily is no longer the haughty, dry matron she once was. She regards the vulpine smile, the dark demanding eyes, and her body inclines itself closer to his as though it were being pulled along by an invisible wire. "You mean that if we two say nothing—?"

"Precisely—"

"But there's your wife, Mr. Rosegger," Emily protests. "She must know that my husband—"

"My wife doesn't matter, Mrs. Durand. She will do as I tell her."

"She wrote to me without your knowledge or approval, I believe."

"I assure you, madam, she'll do nothing of the kind again." Rosegger pauses, leans back, and crosses his legs; every movement is marked by Emily. "She's a sentimental soul, my poor Marguerite . . . too much so for her own good. When she recognizes how important it is that the situation surrounding your late husband's death be held in confidence, she'll remain silent as the grave . . . And if, perchance, there was a witness to the tragedy, well, I'm certain that person can also be persuaded to keep his peace. After all, as you pointed out, the Derringer was missing from the scene. Someone had to take it, don't you agree?"

Emily doesn't respond. She gazes long and hard at her guest. She's now fully aware of what type of person Rosegger is. Instead of finding him repellent, however, she realizes the very opposite is true. Eusapio Paladino was a child compared to this dangerous and powerful man who now sits opposite her. "My husband was bankrupt, sir," she says with a studied tilt to her head. "And although I'm deeply grateful for your offer to keep John's embarrassment *entre nous*, and to forgive what monies he may have owed you, I'm afraid such a proposal is too meager."

Rosegger allows himself a brief laugh. "Are there tradespeople who know of your difficulty, Mrs. Durand?"

"Not that I am aware of . . ."

"Or other creditors your husband may have been indebted to?"

"I believe not . . ."

"Then I suggest to you, Mrs. Durand, that your husband only recently lost control of his financial affairs, and that the world at large is innocent of his problem." Rosegger moves in his chair, lessening the space between him and his hostess. When he speaks again, it's in a tone his wife has never heard and never will. "My dear Mrs. Durand. . . . Emily . . . I can and will provide whatever aid you need."

Emily lets her eyes rest on his face. "You will erase all of Durand's debt?"

"I will remove all the debts your husband—and you also—may have incurred."

"Why?" Emily demands.

"Simply say that I feel pity for the loneliness of widowhood."

Again Emily inclines her handsome head. "Your reputation, Mr. Rosegger, does not admit to such frailty of spirit. Pity for those in distress is a condition not generally associated with your name."

Rosegger laughs. "You associate mercy with weakness, I see."

"As perhaps you do also, sir." Then Emily also moves forward in her chair, and her voice lowers. "And Eusapio Paladino? What becomes of him?"

"He will stand trial, Mrs. Durand, and a jury will do its solemn duty."

"But he didn't kill my husband."

"My dear Mrs. Durand, someone must bear the blame for that tragic death. And we agree, it cannot be perceived—or even suggested—that your husband took his own life."

Emily closes her eyes, but the action fails to blot out the image of the bargain she's about to make. She views it in all its terrifying clarity but also recognizes that she's powerless to object. "And I, Mr. Rosegger?" she murmurs at length as she looks at him again. "What would you have of me in repayment for this . . . aid you're suggesting?"

"Oh, I'm sure we'll think of something."

AS HER HUSBAND concludes his visit of mercy and consolation to the new widow, Marguerite Rosegger is climbing the showy front stairs of her home when she's seized by a particularly violent pain in the pit of her stomach. The sensation grows until she fights for breath and doubles over, leaning hard against the railing. For a moment, the ache miraculously subsides, but then it attacks with renewed vigor. "Oh, my dear God," she pants in shallow gasps. Nothing—not even childbirth—is equal to this sudden agony.

She tries to stand erect and pull herself, hand over hand, up the banister but realizes that she's now growing faint as well as horribly nauseous. Her mouth burns; her tongue feels as though it's been attacked with a hundred scalding needles. *What did I consume,* she wonders, *that has so adversely affected me?* Her mind flies over the varying luncheon dishes she and her husband ate, but all seem bland and unsuspicious: boiled turbot with a horseradish sauce, a roast fillet of beef, stewed endive, savory rissoles, a fig pudding, and other lesser dishes that didn't taste remotely tainted or peculiar, although her mouth can still feel the sting of the horseradish sauce.

It's an ague, she decides, *a particularly vituperative ague. I must get myself to bed.* She rises from her half-crouching position and takes one uncertain step upward but is then seized by such overwhelming nausea that she again collapses, vomiting without restraint as she tumbles downward until she lies motionless and befouled on the entry floor.

In Prison

OWEN SIMMS TAKES OFF HIS tall beaver hat and places it upon his knees as he sits and looks long and carefully into Thomas Kelman's face. Under this steady stare, Kelman gazes resolutely back, noting the hat, which appears to be new, the fine fabric of the black mourning suit, the excellent leather of the shoes, and the impeccable linen at the man's throat and wrists. He imagines that some of these articles may have belonged to Lemuel Beale.

"You wished to see me, Mr. Simms?" he asks his visitor.

Owen Simms doesn't immediately respond; instead, he makes his own inventory, categorizing the items found in Kelman's office: the furniture, which is neither *au courant* nor elegant with age and history; the carpet that bears the grit of the city; the drab color scheme of dark green and ocher-brown. It's a place for a man who lacks either interest in his surroundings or the sufficient funds with which to improve them. This situation Simms finds curious, because Kelman strikes him as a well-born man, but then the former confidential secretary reminds himself in what reduced circumstances many members of the aristocracy are.

"Yes, Mr. Kelman. I would like to discuss the conjurer, Eusapio Paladino."

"I assume you're not here to suggest his innocence in John Durand's murder as another of Miss Beale's acquaintances did." Kelman half-smiles as he poses this question; it's a confident expression, but it's also a watchful one. Owen Simms's motives bear close scrutiny.

"You assume correctly, sir. I am most heartily sorry for Durand's death, and believe strongly that you did right in arresting the mesmerist as his slayer. From what Martha has explained of the fellow's theatrics, well, let me state unequivocally that his claim to consult with the dead is most obviously a deception. A calculated deception that permitted him entry into the most exclusive of circles—the result of which is this unforeseeable tragedy."

Kelman notes the free and easy manner in which Simms uses his onetime master's daughter's given name, while Simms recognizes that Kelman understands the reference.

"You perceive that I call Mr. Beale's daughter by her first name, Kelman. I assure you I'm not being impertinent. In brief, Martha has agreed to become my wife—in private, naturally. We must wait until her mourning period is past to make a public announcement of our intentions. I share this happy news with you because I know you have had Martha's best interests at heart."

"My congratulations, sir," is what Kelman answers, although the tone is guarded and joyless, "when those felicitations can be applied."

"Oh, now is acceptable." Simms smiles broadly and genially. "And I trust you will extend your personal good wishes to dear Martha as well. That is, when she can receive casual visitors again."

Thomas Kelman knows precisely what Simms intends in this short exchange; he means to state that he has won the field. But if the man expects a pained reply, Kelman won't provide it; his sole physical reaction is a slight tightening of his eyes while Simms lowers his voice and continues in a confiding manner:

"It was what her dear father wished . . . that I would continue his role as her protector—"

"Then Mr. Beale had some intuition that he wouldn't be in that position much longer?"

The question seems to take Simms by surprise. He hesitates a moment. "Mr. Beale was a very wise man" is his response.

"Are you implying that your master knew he was going to die?"

"I am implying nothing, sir. I am simply stating that he was a wise and clever man. If I were to add to that assessment, I would tell you that I was privileged to know him."

Kelman makes no answer, but his eyes and the scar on his face grow harder.

"Really, Kelman, even the sagest of men couldn't envision being killed by a wretched near-savage—and with his own weapon. My master, as you insist upon continuing to call him, would have needed to be a clairvoyant to foresee that horrible calamity. And we both know that the supposed 'gift' of second sight is a sham."

"We don't know for certain that the hermit killed Lemuel Beale, Mr. Simms. He claims—"

"Surely, sir, you cannot believe the ravings of a wild man? He was found with Mr. Beale's percussion rifle. How else could he have obtained it except by force?"

"By finding it at the water's edge, as he stated when members of the day watch questioned him."

"Oh, come, sir! Even you, the loyal defender of the deranged and destitute, should be able to recognize the folly in that rationale. Besides, shouldn't it be the respectable citizens of our fair city who deserve the greater protection? Shouldn't you be more concerned with Lemuel Beale's murder than with the rantings of a wild beast? But let us return to the reason for my visit. I have no bone to pick with you today, Kelman, and I trust our judicial system will see the law properly executed with regards to this hermit—and any accomplices he may have had."

"I know of no such theory, Mr. Simms."

Simms makes no reply to this statement; instead, he continues in the same superior tone. "I'm aware that this Paladino is not only detained for the murder of John Durand but is also being questioned in connection with the brutal deaths of the two girls."

Kelman nods but doesn't speak.

"And that the conjurer has confessed to the latter crimes."

"You're misinformed on that account, Mr. Simms" is the cool reply.

"Oh, come, Kelman, I wish you no ill. Let us have an open and convivial exchange."

"I'm afraid, Mr. Simms, that I do not view the discussion of murder as a time for conviviality."

Simms makes a dismissive wave of his hand. "Let us not quibble about semantics, sir. I was told that this mesmerist provided quite vivid details regarding cut tongues being placed upon pillows, and that the children in question were similarly mutilated."

"Who told you that, sir?"

"Everyone knows it, Kelman. The entire city is discussing the affair—and in the most bloodthirsty fashion. What matters is that the facts are true."

Kelman thinks. "What's your interest in this, Mr. Simms?"

Again the question seems to surprise Owen Simms. "Why, Martha's welfare, of course."

"Paladino is in custody. What harm can he pose to Miss Beale?" Both men recognize the difficulty with which Kelman pronounces the name, but neither overtly reacts.

"As you know, Kelman, my Martha was duped into traveling with this criminal in a coach, where he made the most base of suggestions, inventing certain sexual—"

"In all likelihood, the conjurer will hang in connection with John Durand's death. He'll no longer be a threat to your future wife, Mr. Simms—"

But Simms interrupts with another argument. "And in the midst of those foul mutterings he made reference to Lemuel Beale—which reference had originally induced her to accompany the loathsome fellow. Poor dear, she was desperate to gain news of her father—no matter how dubious the source."

"Paladino was questioned about Lemuel Beale, Mr. Simms. I promise you he knows nothing about the financier's fate."

"I wish I were as confident of that fact as you are."

"Are you critiquing the constabulary, sir?"

"As Miss Beale's future husband, I would like to be . . . I *must* be familiar with every aspect of this investigation."

Kelman stares at Owen Simms. "You wish to query Paladino yourself?"

"I do."

"Then why did you not apply directly to the mayor? Why waste time explaining your desires to me?"

"I speak to you, Kelman, because I know what a very special interest you have taken in this sorry business." With that, Owen Simms rises. "I would like you to conduct me to the Moyamensing Prison yourself."

DOWN THEY MARCH, down and down into the cold cellar rooms of the Moyamensing Prison. Although newly constructed, it's already overcrowded with those awaiting trial, the men and women and children who have committed the large and petty crimes of the city: the pickpockets, the cutpurses, the forgers, the public drunkards, the pimps and cutthroats. All are jumbled together in the malodorous semi-gloom regardless of age or sex; and all make noise as Kelman and Simms pass. Were it not for the turnkeys, the prisoners would throw whatever they had at hand, and Simms might find himself lamenting the night soil that ruined the handsome hat he now holds in his hands as he stoops to avoid the low rafters and stone vaulting.

The sergeant at Kelman's side growls for silence, and the clamor lessens but doesn't fully cease. At length, the three reach the cell in which Paladino and his assistant have been chained to wooden benches.

"Go ahead, Mr. Simms," Kelman states with no further introduction. "There's your man. Pose what queries you will."

Italian words fill the air before Simms has a chance to speak, but the sergeant interrupts with a peremptory "Translator, on your feet. We'll have none of this gibberish now."

"Thank you, Sergeant" is Simms's smooth reply. It's a gentleman's tone, and it sounds like money. "Please ask the prisoner what he knows of Lemuel Beale."

"Ask him yourself," Kelman insists.

Simms does so, but his effort has little effect. The mesmerist merely gazes dumbly ahead while his assistant whimpers an apologetic "The Great Paladino can no longer communicate with the man you want, sir. When the atmosphere is—"

Owen Simms bangs his silver-tipped cane hard upon the earthen floor. "I was told your master conjured up Beale in a séance at the Ilsley home, that he spoke in plain English."

"*Signor* Paladino speaks what his spirit guides dictate, sir. If those guides are not present or if the atmosphere is not conducive—"

"Damn it, man! I want answers. Tell me what Paladino knows of Lemuel Beale."

"Sir, my master's gift—"

"Trickery, you mean," Simms sneers. His cane bangs the floor again. "And trickery which he used upon Mr. Beale's innocent daughter. Luring her into a carriage journey where he described in the most insensitive detail a woman who had been wretchedly maltreated by her own brother—"

"My master no longer retains the original vision of the lady."

Owen Simms glares through the darkness. Kelman can feel some change in his mood but is uncertain what the alteration signifies.

"The woman was raped repeatedly," Simms states, although his tone is calmer. "Ask *Signor* Paladino what he recalls of that disgusting claim."

The assistant again appeals to the clairvoyant, who again makes no reply.

"So there was no woman?" Simms demands. "Your master invented a phantom simply in order to terrorize Miss Beale—and then further misused her by feigning to have information regarding her father?"

Paladino doesn't answer.

"Admit it, conjurer. Admit that your own evil brain created these fictions—just as you defiled those little girls—"

"Enough, sir," Kelman interjects, but Simms will not be interrupted.

"Tell these gentlemen the truth, damn you!"

"Mr. Simms, I tell you—"

"The truth, damn it—!"

In the midst of this order, Eusapio Paladino suddenly falls to the floor, his body writhing and his chest heaving in rapid pants as though he were gulping for air. *"Morto!"* he screams out while he stares at Owen Simms. "You! *Morto! Morto!*"

"Pipe down, you!" the sergeant yells while Simms draws himself erect, nearly banging his head on the stone ceiling.

"You're correct, Kelman. The man is a fraud. Let him hang for however many murders you believe he committed; he knows nothing of Lemuel Beale." Then Simms turns away, holding his cane and hat in front of him as he prepares to exit the cell.

But Kelman stops him. "Is the name Robey familiar to you?"

"I've never heard it before in my life," Simms states as the sergeant locks the iron door behind them.

Kelman studies the man who will marry Martha Beale. For a moment he's silent, causing both the sergeant and Simms to wait in the gloom. "There's another death I'm investigating . . . but no matter . . . Given your wide range of acquaintances—and those of your master—I thought you might have met a person by that name."

RUTH IS TURNED out on the street, the door to Dutch Kat's establishment closed forever behind her. Sympathetic though the procuress may have claimed to be, in the end, she's a business woman; a bed's a bed; a bed must turn a profit.

Ruth understands Kat's logic, and the realization of her own culpability in the decision suddenly enervates her. She knows she has no one to blame but herself, no one to rail at, no one to whom she can appeal. She plunks herself down on the fancy house's top entry step in order to think where she might next venture, but a man hurries up to the establishment, pushing past her as if she were a stiff and toothless dog. Then the door to Dutch Kat's opens, and the madam orders a rough "Move along there, girl, or I'll have you hauled away for a vagrant! You've done enough damage here, already."

Ruth does as she's told.

A failure as a housemaid, she recites silently as her feet tread aimlessly northward. *A failure as a thief. A failure as a lady of pleasure. A failure as a mother.* Ruth has become too blasted by hopelessness to cry.

She walks and walks some more; and at length her shambling steps carry her to a rum cellar where the sound of laughter emanating from its depths arrests her.

"It's a penny a glass, missus," a voice beside her whispers. "I'll show you some happy times, if you'll return the favor."

Ruth nods in dumb acceptance, then moves down the stairs, stepping onto an earthen floor.

"Or perhaps you have a place you'd like to take me?"

"I have no place."

"Ah, well, we'll resort to a quaint little alley I know of. You and me will be Adam and Eve—out in the open air."

Ruth bobs an imitation of a coquette's curtsy, then drains the proffered glass in one swift gulp and follows the man back up the stairs—only to follow a second and third back down the same steps and back into the same fetid lane.

When she emerges from her final encounter, her benefactor remains behind. He doesn't speak a word of parting; nor does she. She merely dusts the dirt from her skirt, straightens her shawl, and reenters the street. The sunlight spreading down this broader concourse makes her squint and jerk her head in surprise.

She turns toward the source, the west and the slowly reclining sun. Her head is spinning, her footsteps none too steady, and the smile that has affixed itself to her face is practiced and empty. She puts out a beggar's palm to a married couple that pass and comes away empty-handed. She tries again with a young gentleman walking toward her at a brisk pace, and again with an older and stooped fellow hobbling rigidly along. It's at that moment that she suddenly remembers the lame tailor and the girl, Ella. *Why, it's so simple,* Ruth's woozy brain declares. *How many pairs like them can be living hereabouts? I'll find those two if it takes a week—or a month. I'll discover where the tailor's hiding and alert the day watch. And the night watch, too. That I will. And I'll be rewarded. Handsomely rewarded for helping to recapture a dangerous prisoner. How else could I be treated except as the good and loyal Ruth that I am?*

Assuring herself of that happy future, Ruth lurches down the street on her determined quest.

Silently and Without Question

THE MAN WHOM THOMAS KELMAN, Pliny Earle, Daniel the tailor, and his young charge, Ella, call Mr. Robey unlocks the door to his private domicile, enters and then quickly replaces the key in the latch. Inside the house, all is silent—as it should be. Robey hesitates in the foyer, making certain this is the case. The first rule he imposed upon Daniel after installing him and the girl in the residence was that quiet should reign whenever their master was present. He didn't wish to hear the sound of speech from either of them; if they moved about in their quarters at the top of the house or in the kitchen or pantry or laundry, they must do so with stealthy steps.

"My dictums are for Mary's edification," he'd told them. "I aspire to teach her to be a lady, and ladies are composed and meek in everything they undertake. The child cannot hope to comprehend or appreciate what my actions mean now; she's too raw, too fresh from the . . . from the countryside, but she'll understand and thank me when she grows older."

Ella—or Mary, as she's now called—had listened to this speech in disbelieving silence. She remembered everything about her first encounter with the man, and although she would never reveal the ugly tale to Daniel, who depended upon his patron's largesse, she guessed Mr. Robey meant her harm. She also suspected, although nothing had been said, that her new master intended to remove his tailor from the house as soon as he was certain his "ward" would not escape. Daniel wondered about that, too—although the two didn't speak of the possibility. Not even during the nights and daytimes when Mr. Robey was gone from the house.

In fact, they seldom spoke more than a few monosyllables even when their master was absent. Fear kept Ella constantly watching and waiting. Remorse tortured Daniel into a near-catatonic state; and the pallid hope he had of providing Ella with a better future began ebbing away until he grew to fear that Robey's claims for his ward's eventual betterment might well be false.

In the attic rooms where they reside, Ella and Daniel now hear Mr. Robey enter. Both have been stitching him a glorious new wardrobe, fashioned of the finest fabrics and cut in the latest style. Immediately, they put down their needles and scissors; then, without a sound between them, Daniel creeps down the rear service stairs toward the kitchen while Ella pulls off her warmer dress and dons the flimsy garb Robey wishes her to wear while in his presence.

Daniel has told her that the gown makes her "look like an angel" and that "Mr. Robey likes it because he's a most religious man"; Ella believes otherwise, but then she heard a number of odd tales about gentlemen and their unusual desires during her days at the fancy house. What she knows for certain is that the thin white garment—without the flannelette chemise and pantaloons she wears under her other dress—is no protection against the cold.

In her bare feet, she tiptoes down the chilly front stairway until she stands outside the shut parlor doors behind which Mr. Robey has ensconced himself. She can smell pipe tobacco and *eau de cologne* and soap. He's a gentleman who's extremely particular about cleanliness. She recalled that vividly from their first unhappy meeting, but he's reminded her many times since as if she were too stupid to learn such a simple lesson.

She raps once upon the door as she's been instructed to do, and waits discreetly as she's also been told she should. And then waits, and waits some more until her icy toes grow numb from standing, and she finally sinks down into a crouch, hugging her knees to her chest in order to keep off the dreadful cold of the hall.

Robey, inside his cozy lair, listens to her knock, and then eventually hears the small creak of the floorboards that means she's slipped into a sitting position while attending his summons.

He considers calling her; he aches to have her in the room: her transparent little gown flicking around her naked body, her eyes wide and grateful when she stands, at last, by the health-giving fire, her mouth growing pinker and wetter as the blood floods back into her cheeks, her childish odor returning while she basks in the heat.

And then what? Will he tell her to climb onto his lap? And will she soundlessly wriggle close at this command, caressing him with her small and willing buttocks, playing innocently with his shirt and trouser buttons while he whispers "Mary . . . my beloved . . ." into her ear? Will she then keep silent as he exposes himself, and finally thrusts upward between her soft, thin legs?

But no, she will not. He knows it as well as he knows his own true name; and the beautiful vision bursts apart like a vase falling onto a marble floor.

His Mary will not keep quiet; she'll draw back in alarm and pain as he seeks to enter her; then she'll scream aloud and try to squirm away, while he'll be forced to lash out and hit her in order to stop her dreadful squawks.

And then the loving act will turn unspeakably sordid. In her escalating panic, she'll claw and bite him, then soil herself like a fox in a trap, all the while grunting and yelping and heaving her body one way and another as if she were fighting off the devil instead of welcoming her savior.

Reliving this ugly picture, Robey stifles a moan. His right hand flies to his pocket and the pearl-handled knife he keeps there. He moans again and, in his despair and fury and bitter disappointment, is all at once aware that the girl outside has heard him. The floor creaks. He knows that she's risen to a standing position.

"Go up to your room, Mary," he calls out sharply. "I don't want you here."

No noise. She's hesitating, unsure of what to do. Robey hears her shallow, uncertain breaths.

"Go away, Mary. I don't want you." His voice maintains its harsh and angry tone.

He listens, and, at last, she scurries away. *I must train this one properly,* he thinks. *As a dog is taught by a firm and deliberate master. I must take my time and wait until she's ready to obey my every command, exactly as a hunting dog would: silently and without question.*

The Courtroom of Judge Alonzo Craig

The courtroom of judge alonzo Craig is filled to overflowing. Spectators crowd every bench both on the floor and in the gallery: the ladies crushed in among the gentlemen; the aristocracy of the city rubbing elbows with shopmen and milliners and actresses and pie sellers. Noise is everywhere as everyone clamors at once. With the fickleness of all public opinion, the recent headlines concerning the slaying of Lemuel Beale are now of far less consequence than the trial of the conjurer and necromancer Eusapio Paladiono.

Naturally, all of those who've managed to gain access to the room hope to witness one of the mesmerist's spectacular performances. Perhaps he'll succumb to one of his celebrated trances and reenact the crime, shooting his victim in the head and then creeping away in the dead of night. Perhaps he'll "speak" in John Durand's voice, reviling Emily from the grave for her wanton infidelity. Perhaps somnambulism will grip the Great Paladino, and he'll lapse into an unnatural sleep and revisit the scenes of his amorous entanglements. Or perhaps, perhaps, the mesmerist may prove to have been an unwitting dupe, and the crime will have been not one of passion but a hired assassination by a woman who'd grown tired of her married state. The other rumored charge against Paladino—that he may also have slain two young ladies of pleasure—is of lesser importance to the spectators today. Such deaths among the impoverished of the city occur, perhaps not in such a bloody fashion, but they're part of daily life. The downfall of a woman who held herself above even her most exalted peers is not.

The circus atmosphere would have appealed to Emily Durand, but she's not there, of course. Her widowed state will not permit her to be abroad in the public eye, so the scandal she's engendered must carry on without her. However, Rosegger, as they've agreed, is in attendance; the private pact he made with Emily supersedes his wife's mysterious malady. It's important that the tale he's devised, and that Emily has agreed to be bruited about: a heart-wrenching fable of a distraught lady who now bitterly repents her follies, who will no longer appeal for Paladino's release but instead insist that his strange mind must have concocted the cruel murder of her dear husband—a crime she knew nothing of. According to this scheme, she'll bemoan her manifold transgressions in letters sent to the mayor (the contents of which will then find their way into the penny press) and declare she would trade all she had in this world to have her dearest helpmeet and soulmate returned to the land of the living, and herself returned to her formerly blameless state.

Rosegger's public role in this charade is to stoutly denounce Paladino while forgiving his foolish and misguided paramour. Yes, the lady was dreadfully wrong to have entered into an illicit liaison, but ladies are weak and must be protected from their coarser instincts. Perhaps, Rosegger will continue to suggest, Durand was a harsh mate. The marriage was never blessed with children; perhaps their empty home led her to impulsively place her affections elsewhere . . . The final and obvious consequence of these arguments being that the conjurer seized upon poor Emily's frailty and, in his arrogance and overweening jealousy, murdered a respected member of the community.

It's a neat play Emily and Rosegger have prepared to enact, although Rosegger understands his role to be assured while Emily, at home, is experiencing several degrees of terror. The impulse that led her to accept Rosegger's protection now seems both foolhardy and dangerous; the only constant is her realization of how beholden to him she's about to become. Everything in her existence, her homes, even the clothes upon her back, will be subject to his whims and caprices. *And when he tires of this game and of me?* she thinks, but her brain stops there. When Rosegger casts her off, Emily knows full well she'll have nothing.

"What say you, Ilsley?" Rosegger now asks as the professor and his wife make their way through the crowd. "The conjurer's guilty, of course."

Ilsley stares at the speaker. "I did not believe I'd see you here, sir."

"But surely we both counted the Durands as friends, Professor," is the genial reply.

"It's not that to which I refer, sir, but to the frail health of your wife. My sympathies to you both. I'd heard—"

"Yes, yes. My poor, dear wife . . . In truth, she's gravely ill, gravely ill." Rosegger repeats the phrase with a heavy sigh. "But she insisted that I attend today to show my support for Mrs. Durand—"

"Ah, then your wife has regained full use of her faculties?" Henrietta Ilsley asks. "Oh, I'm so happy for you. It's an answered prayer. We share the same physician, as you may know, and he told me she was quite unable to communicate."

Rosegger stares down at the little woman. "No, I did not realize that we had a medical doctor in common, Mrs. Ilsley."

"Oh, yes, and he was most terribly concerned. Tainted food can often prove fatal—even to those with robust digestions. I know he feared greatly for her life. It was tainted food, was it not?"

"Mrs. Rosegger—and I—are fortunate indeed to have so many concerned friends" is the surprisingly cool response, and Ilsley interrupts what he believes is becoming an awkward conversation.

"My wife did not intend to pry into your and your wife's personal affairs, sir. It was her natural compassion that led her to question our physician. She wanted to help in any fashion she could. Her nature is one that is greatly affected by the welfare of those around her."

Rosegger accepts this apology with a nod but doesn't otherwise reply, and Ilsley continues with an equally conciliatory:

"In fact, it's because of my dear wife that we're here today. Were it not for her generosity of spirit, we would have avoided such a spectacle, but, you see, she feels much to blame for introducing the prisoner to the Durands. I've tried to convince her otherwise, but—"

Rosegger again looks down at Henrietta, a convincingly compassionate smile now spread across his face. "You mustn't criticize yourself, dear Mrs. Ilsley. Your lady friend was misguided, terribly misguided, but surely all culpability rests on the charlatan we shall soon see in chains before us. He cast a spell upon her as he does with all his audiences—"

"Oh, Mr. Rosegger, that's kind indeed of you to say . . ." Henrietta dabs at eyes that are misty with regret.

"It's not kindness but the truth, Mrs. Ilsley." Then he turns to the professor. "True ladies have such tender hearts. Our task as gentlemen is to safeguard our wives and sisters and mothers from actors who spin tales in order to further their own gains."

"And what gains would those be, Mr. Rosegger?" Henrietta asks.

"Dear lady, I hardly think it appropriate to discuss this in your presence . . . but imagine Mrs. Durand left a sorrowing widow—which she is. Imagine, then, the mesmerist freed from prison by some fluke; and finally, ask yourself to whom she might turn in her distress. Mrs. Durand has been left a wealthy woman. I need hardly say more."

"Oh!" Henrietta gasps. "You believe—?"

"I do. And all the more reason Paladino should hang. He did not envision himself as an aide to those seeking news of loved ones long deceased—but was hoping to assume the role of John Durand. And, though I apologize for mentioning so base a subject, we cannot disregard the other two reputed charges against him."

"Oh!" Henrietta gasps again.

Further speech is curtailed as the prisoner and his assistant are brought into the room. Both are manacled; both are under guard. A thrilled hush falls across the crowd, so that when Judge Craig's slumberous voice calls out a weighty "Silence!" the throng is already stilled; and the only sound is the occasional creak of whalebone stays or the rustle of silk as the female spectators in their blinkered bonnets strain for a better view.

Rosegger looks around him. He spots the Shippens, to whom he briefly nods in greeting, and Owen Simms, whom he also acknowledges. Thomas Kelman is there as well, although his part in the proceedings seems to be as spectator rather than participant. Rosegger observes, however, with what keen attention Kelman regards Simms. The behavior strikes him as curious, and he makes a mental note of it. It will not be beneficial to continue in partnership with a man under scrutiny by the police.

Then the trial begins.

AFTER TWO HOURS of intense questioning, the case against Paladino is no further advanced. The prisoner behaves like a man asleep; his eyes close when the barrister is finished querying him, and when open, they're listless and unresponsive, roving aimlessly among the crowd, seeing nothing. No wonder that those gathered in Judge

Craig's courtroom are growing restless, and that his solemn, patrician voice must remind them over and over to keep silent.

The orders, coming as they do from an obvious member of the gentility, begin to rankle with the poorer members of the crowd. "He's related to the Cadwaladers and Rittenhouses and such. He can't tell me what to do—not in my free time, at any rate," they mutter with increasing discontent until Alonzo Craig growls out a loud "Silence in the court!" and either the commanding tone or the suddenness of the declamation so startles Paladino that his body jolts in the prisoner's box and his manacled hands strain to reach into the air before him as though caressing an invisible human form.

"I will call you Mary, the beloved of the Lord," he murmurs in English while he swings his head around to stare at the crowd, picking out females in the audience to affix with a leering stare. "Do not speak, my child, my little one."

The courtroom erupts in noise. Nothing Judge Craig can demand nor the warders shout can halt the gasps of surprise and horror or the cries of delight. A number of ladies faint, and their male companions call for aid, for smelling salts, for space in which to move.

"Mary, Mary!" a trio of young toughs chants. "How does thy pretty little garden grow?" The song is greeted with such obstreperous cackles and hisses and cheers that it spawns another version; and the back of the room replies with a lusty "Little maids all in a row!"

Paladino and his assistant are dragged from the room by their guards while members of the day watch appear, truncheons at the ready. They move among the churning sea of people pushing them toward the doors and then out onto the street, where Rosegger and Simms find themselves face-to-face.

"A word with you, sir," Rosegger says. As he speaks, he offers his arm to Florence Shippen, who's being so buffeted by the crowd she looks as though she'll fall. "My husband," she pants while Rosegger spots the tall barrister and hails him, handing him his frightened wife. But Simms lacks his companion's purposeful equilibrium; in fact, he trembles all over.

"Have you a touch of ague?" Rosegger asks in a pointed tone.

"No" is the brusque reply. "What do you wish to speak with me about, Rosegger?" Then Simms collects himself. "My apologies, sir. I should be asking you about the welfare of your wife. I was told that she was most horribly—"

"Yes, a dreadful mistake made by a new kitchen maid—or so the physician assumes. The girl has been fired, naturally, but the fact cannot readily heal my wife from her villainous ailment. If, indeed, she can ever fully recover. As yet, we live with diabolical uncertainty." Then the financier abruptly ceases his discussion of his wife's health while he regards the former confidential secretary. "You're accoutered well, Mr. Simms. Lemuel Beale's unfortunate demise has not affected you adversely, I'm glad to see."

Simms makes a thin attempt at a smile while his eyes continue to search out and acknowledge those passersby he recognizes. "If you wish us to speak, sir, shouldn't we find a less congested thoroughfare?"

The conversation between the two men is interrupted by a noisy altercation nearby. It concerns a member of the day watch and a Negress whom Simms and Rosegger—as well as everyone else in the vicinity—assume to be a beggar. A dirty beggar woman and a drunk, to boot. A disapproving space clears around the pair, leaving them to battle as if they'd been provided with a private stage.

"I'm telling you I know where he's keeping himself," the woman's shouting, although the words slip and slide into a nearly unintelligible morass of rum combined with an empty stomach. "The prisoner that escaped from Cherry Hill. The man with—"

"Be off with you," the constable interjects, "before I haul you in for vagrancy—"

"I found the house where he's hiding" is Ruth's staunch but slurred reply. "You should be thanking me. You should, instead of—"

"Enough of this," the day watch argues, grabbing for her arm.

But Ruth in her inebriation and desperation wriggles free of his grasp. "I want the reward money," she screams at him, "for the man with the—"

"Be off, I tell you," the day watch insists in a louder and more belligerent tone. "This is Judge Alonzo Craig's court you're standing near. Unless you want a taste of prison yourself—"

"Judge Craig?" Ruth mumbles, spinning around to face the building entrance. "Judge Alonzo Craig?" By now the drama enacted by these two has drawn spectators who would rather participate than keep silent. Sides are taken; there are hurrahs as well as hisses for Ruth, and catcalls for the constable.

"You're correct, Mr. Simms," Rosegger states above the growing din. "This place is far too congested and public for a serious discussion." He hands Simms a card with an address written upon it. "I will be at this house tomorrow afternoon. It's a domicile in the Northern Liberties. I believe I mentioned that your master and I had similar—and private—investments in that area. I suggest you meet me there."

A Frantic Appeal

THE FIRST MISSIVE EMILY DURAND receives from Rosegger produces a tight and hesitant smile. She's been anxiously awaiting news of Paladino's trial and of the successful maneuverings of their schemes. In the middle of the foyer, unaware of the footman who produced the correspondence, and who now stands before her bearing an empty silver tray, Emily rips the envelope open, letting the torn paper scatter upon the floor.

My dear Emily, Rosegger writes—she notes with quick dismay that he now refers to her by her given name—*You may rest certain that your husband's murderer will surely be punished for his despicable act. Public sentiment is very much against the man who so churlishly took advantage of your gentle nature, and then sought to replace your worthy husband in your affections. I hope to call upon you in person on the morrow and provide what further details you may desire . . .* He continues in that circumspect vein, describing the people with whom he spoke and the general tenor of the crowd, but the tone remains exceedingly cautious as if he expected the letter might fall into the wrong hands. Emily reads the message through, then reads it again; her hands are trembling, as is her chest. Until she starts to walk forward across the parquet floor, she's unaware that one of her feet has fallen asleep. *Good,* she promises herself, *good.* She steadfastly refuses to picture the gibbet from which her onetime lover will hang. Then she tears up the letter and crumples it into a fat ball. "No reply," she tells the servant.

She hurries upstairs and shuts her bedroom door. Her heart is beating so violently, she's afraid she will faint. *All is well,* she tries to promise herself. *All is well. All will be well. I had no other choice, did I? John gave me no other choice but to seek out Rosegger's protection.*

The second letter arrives the following morning as Emily's maid is bringing her her breakfast in bed. From the light weight of the envelope, Emily guesses that the financier's message is brief. She places it beside a pot of marmalade, wishing she could dispense with reading the thing until she's properly dressed and prepared for the day.

But curiosity gets the better of her, and she sits erect, waving away the tray of breakfast things as she girds herself for news stating that Rosegger expects to call upon her within an hour or two. *I will receive him downstairs as would be appropriate,* she decides as she slits open the envelope. *With luck and cleverness on my part, we will remain there. It would not do if I appeared too eager—or acquiescent to his designs.*

But Emily is horribly surprised by what she reads.

My wife took a sudden and terrible turn for the worse last night. I'm sorry to inform you that she died not an hour past. Forgive me if I do not call upon you this morning in your own time of distress, but I'm sure you will understand.

Emily bolts to her feet. "My clothes!" she shouts to her maid, "and my bonnet . . . and my warmest mantle and my gloves!"

The maid bobs a startled curtsy.

"Hurry!" Emily fairly yells at her. "I am visiting a friend in need. I must leave at once!"

"But your breakfast, madam?" the servant ventures. "Will you be wanting it before you—?"

"Oh, what do I care about eating! Now, bring me my things!"

IT'S NOT TO Rosegger's house that Emily flees, however, but to Martha Beale's home, where she hurtles upstairs and all but flings herself through Martha's bedroom door. The footman's echoing words of protest and the startled squeals of Martha's lady's maid cannot slow Emily's progress, but her singular entrance grinds to a halt as she regards the shocking change that has come over Lemuel Beale's daughter.

Martha looks like a woman walking in her sleep. Or sitting, rather. For there she is, slumped in front of her dressing table, with her hair only partially braided and a receiving gown awkwardly buttoned as if a doll had been hurriedly pushed into it and not a living person. She turns a blinking stare on Emily.

"Oh, my goodness!" are the only words Emily can produce. Her frenzied quest all but disappears from her mind. "Are you . . . are you quite well, Martha . . . ?"

It's the maid who answers. There are tears in her voice. "It's the medication, madam . . . the sleeping draught that Mr. Simms's physician ordered for my mistress . . . The dosage is too great, I fear, but Mr. Simms—"

Another woman enters the chamber at that moment, and the maid falls silent although she doesn't leave her mistress's side.

"And what is in this sleeping potion?" Emily demands while the maid looks sheepishly at the newcomer who responds with a brisk:

"Laudanum, madam . . . as prescribed by—"

"You've been feeding this woman opium?" Emily's voice rings out, traveling angrily out the room and down the hall.

"No, laudanum, madam, as—"

"Which is another name for tincture of opium" is the swift retort.

The woman drops a nervous curtsy. It's quite clear to her that Emily Durand is a force to be reckoned with. "The potion was ordered to offset the grief Miss Beale is experiencing over the death of her dear parent. I suggested to Mr. Simms that the dosage was too high, but he deemed it necessary until—"

But Emily dispenses with the speaker. Instead, she spins around and addresses Martha's maid. "Get me vinegar and water, as well as a basin of the coldest water you can find. Then we must pull this dressing gown from Miss Beale's chest and dash the icy liquid on her face and upper body." Emily tears off her fur-lined mantle as she speaks and tosses it and her bonnet and gloves toward a chaise. "And once the emetic has done its work, we must walk her up and down until she becomes sensible of her surroundings again." Emily ceases her instructions for a second to ask a sharp "And where is Mr. Simms now?"

"He has left for the day, madam" is the maid's response. Emily hears bitterness as well as a hint of vengeance in the level tone. The lady's maid, quite obviously, is not an admirer of Owen Simms.

"Good," Emily responds, then adds, "and I want the remnants of the sleeping draught thrown away. All of it. And if Mr. Simms objects . . ." Emily doesn't finish the threat. She'll deal with him later. In all this time, Emily has not once considered the reason that brought her to Martha Beale's house.

MARTHA IS FED the vinegar and water until she spits cloudy white liquid and greenish bile into a pail. Then her face and chest are doused with cold water; and she's dragged moaning and stumbling around the room and marched along the upper hall. Emily's and the maid's arms encircle Martha's waist; their hands support her head when it sags, while Emily speaks brisk words of encouragement and the maid remains mum.

For two hours they work until all at once Martha shakes herself as if waking from a nap and straightens her spine. "Oh, I'm so hungry" are the first words she utters.

Orders are sent for dry toast and cambric tea. Emily and the maid help the still-weak Martha to a chair, where she sits with remarkable aplomb, holding her head high and her back firm, although she still clenches Emily's hand.

"I trust you will never heed Owen Simms's advice again," Emily states, and Martha looks upward in surprise. "He was poisoning you."

"Oh, I don't believe—" Martha begins to protest, but Emily cuts her short.

"Perhaps he didn't seek your death, but he did wish you all but insensate."

"But he asked my hand in—" Martha continues to object, but again Emily interrupts her. This time, however, the words turn into a choked cry. Emily has suddenly remembered why she's in Martha's bedroom.

"Rosegger killed his wife."

Martha can only regard her guest in stunned silence.

"I had a note from him this morning . . . because after the trial yesterday, he wrote concerning the possible outcome . . . and I . . . he and I . . ." Emily's lips twist in agony, although she avoids Martha's gaze, instead staring into the corners of the room. "Oh, I have done something so terrible . . . so evil . . . so unforgivable . . . ! And now Eusapio Paladino will hang . . . and I . . ." She breathes a fierce sigh, and the words that ensue are just as full of passion and anger and self-retribution. "John killed himself. He was not the victim of a murder as the world assumes . . . but Rosegger and I devised . . . We devised . . ." Emily's eyes narrow into squints as if she were attempting to eliminate the pictures her mind is seeing. "John was bankrupt . . . He was . . ."

As if the weight of her own self-loathing were crushing her, Emily Durand sinks to the floor at Martha's side; their hands are still joined, although it's now Emily who clings to Martha's fingers rather than the opposite. "Please . . . Martha . . . Miss Beale . . . you must help me if you can. I must get away from my odious entanglement with this man. He killed his wife; and I fear . . . I fear he may eventually also tire of me. And why should he not? I, who have been the cause of so much grief . . ."

Martha says not a word during this extraordinary speech; instead, she regards Emily with a steady gaze.

"I throw myself at your mercy. I know I'm undeserving of pity . . . or kindness or compassion . . . And that I've never given succor or aid to anyone—"

"Where will you go?" The reasonableness of Martha's tone pulls Emily's spine erect.

"To Europe," she says as though just now formalizing her decision. "To the Continent. I can live cheaply there. And I will be unknown—"

"And how will you survive?"

"I can teach something . . ." It's clear Emily Durand hasn't thought through her entire plan. "Piano . . . or tutor in English or—"

"And you need financial aid in order to carry out this proposal."

Emily's head bows in humiliation, but Martha pays no attention to this abject pose. She's already rising to her feet. "Of course you do. And you need it quickly." Martha takes a step; it's a trifle unsteady still, and her brain feels less solid than it should, but her thoughts are ordered and resolved. "And I am a wealthy woman. A very wealthy woman." She smiles. How strong she suddenly feels, and how alive! "I will write a bank draft on my father's letterhead. And I will give you what gold we keep in the house." Then she turns back to Emily. "Will your maid know what to pack for you?"

"Why, yes, I suppose."

"Good. We will send my maid, and they can gather your things together. Two sets of hands work faster than one. And you will stay with me until such time as you find a ship that's ready to sail—"

"I cannot do that to you, Martha" is Emily's reluctant reply.

"Why not?"

"Think how sullied my reputation is . . . and now with this new disaster . . ."

"I couldn't care less about that."

But Emily retains some trace of her old proud spirit. "I thank you from the bottom of my heart for aiding me financially, Martha, but I cannot permit you to soil your own good name by harboring me here."

Martha doesn't immediately respond. When she does, her tone is forceful and sure. "We will consider the next course of action after your maid—and mine—finish packing your trunks. If you wish to oversee their work, I certainly understand."

Emily pauses. She looks at her discarded mantle and bonnet. "If you can, Martha, will you grant me one additional request?"

"If I can."

"When I'm safely away from Rosegger, reveal everything I've told you. Whether you approve of his mores or not—or mine, for that matter—Eusapio Paladino mustn't be slain because of a lie."

WITH EMILY AND the two maids gone, Martha enters her father's study to write the promised bank draft, but as she takes up his pen and retrieves a sheet of letter paper, a card with an address slides out from among the pages as though it had been hidden there.

Martha studies it; she doesn't recognize the handwriting, but the place she does. It seems to be a private home in the Northern Liberties. She frowns in thought, then carries out her promise and pens the note for Emily Durand before examining the card again.

Why is this here? she asks herself. *Did my father hide it? Or Owen Simms? Is there a connection between Father's disappearance—his death—and this scrap of paper?*

Martha rings for the footman and tells him to personally convey the letter she's composed to the Durand household, and also to arrange for a hansom cab to take her on a short journey. Naturally, she's advised that the Beale carriage can be readied instead, but Martha replies that she doesn't wish to be noticed. The reason she gives is that driving abroad would interfere with the rules of her mourning period.

Then she dons a hooded pelisse that conceals her identity. For a brief second, she considers sending word to Thomas Kelman, informing him of her intentions, but then banishes the notion. This little jaunt may prove of no more importance than a drive around the park; there will be ample opportunity to apprise him later if she learns anything of substance.

She walks down the stairs, but as she does so she realizes that some residual effects of the laudanum remain, and that she's a good deal more light-headed than she wishes.

A House in the Northern Liberties

THE HOUSE AT WHICH MARTHA knocks is a solid but unassuming place, one in a block of equally new domiciles at the northernmost stretches of the city: all of them brick, all triple-storied, all with four broad marble steps leading down to the cobbled street. None appears shoddily or hastily constructed, but each so mirrors its mate as to seem designed by a single man. Martha recognizes them as speculation properties, constructed for shopkeepers and other tradesmen with newfound wealth but inferior social position. What connection her father—or Owen Simms—has to the place she cannot surmise, but she raises her hand and boldly bangs the door knocker.

A club-footed man answers and gives her a goggle-eyed stare. "Yes?" he says, and all but bars her entrance as he swiftly looks past Martha into the empty street.

"May I come in?" she asks him.

"You have the wrong house" is the hasty reply, but Martha recognizes terror rather than truth in the tone. "You must go."

She looks behind her, trying to detect what can be frightening the man. *Is someone watching this place?* she wonders. *Has this crippled man been cautioned about speaking with strangers? Or is it possible it's me he's been warned not to admit?* But the suddenness of her movement combined with the hot fur hood produces an unwelcome and powerful dizziness, and Martha feels herself about to faint. "Please . . . I must sit down . . ."

The man releases a sharp, angry sigh but opens the door a crack more, permitting Martha entry before immediately closing and locking it behind her and then sliding a second bolt in place.

"Who is it, Cousin Daniel?" Martha hears a girl's voice calling quietly. The response is an urgent but also hushed:

"A woman. A sick woman, I'm thinking. And you, Ella, you keep yourself to the pantry and kitchen. I told you to stay in the rear of the house, or you'll be ruining everything I've planned. Besides, you know the master's rules. You appear only when he orders it."

Ella has already walked into the foyer. "But he's not yet arrived, cousin," she says with some bravado, and Martha, despite her weakened state, suddenly recognizes the voice.

"You're the girl from the Shambles," she says.

"Oh!" is the startled reply. Ella jumps away as though she's spotted a ghost while Martha raises her bleary head and studies Ella's dress—or lack of one.

"You must be freezing, child." Martha fumbles at her cloak, untying it and draping it around Ella's shoulders without giving her or Daniel time to protest. "Who on earth put you in such a flimsy garment?" Martha gives Daniel an accusing stare, but before she can speak again, there's the sound of a key twisting in the lock.

"Oh, Lord!" Daniel hisses. "It's him! Go back to the kitchen as I told you, Ella. And take this infernal woman and put her out into the rear alley. We can't have him finding her—"

"But I only came to ask if you knew a man named—" Martha starts to argue, but Daniel interrupts with a ferocious:

"Go, or you'll ruin everything. Go! Go!" Then he spins on his misshapen foot, calling out a loud and placating "I'm coming, sir. That new lock is a tricky one, it is . . . I had to put the additional bolt on, sir, so nervous was I that the door wouldn't close aright . . ."

While Daniel seeks to soothe their approaching master, Ella yanks on Martha's hand. "Come, miss, please come. He won't like it if he finds you here."

The raw fear in the little girl's tone begins infecting Martha also. "Who, child?" she asks in her own whisper.

Ella replies with a fervent "Come, miss, do come. You can leave the house by the alley route as Daniel said. There'll be no harm done then." As she speaks, Ella ushers Martha through a tall doorway leading to the back of the house, then hurries across the dirt floor of the kitchen to the tradesman's entrance. But when she opens it, a neighbor's hound begins a loud and snarling baying, causing Ella to slam the door shut again. "Oh, that cur and its infernal noise. The master will hear it, sure, and wonder why I'm down here and not upstairs where I belong."

"But I'm only looking for—" Martha begins in a more reasonable tone.

"Miss! Hush, please . . . We can't have him hearing you." Then she suddenly adds, "The butler's pantry . . . We'll put you there for the time being. You won't be in Daniel's way then."

"I have no reason to avoid your master, though—" Martha protests, but Ella will hear nothing of this argument, and her frightened state lends her such physical strength that she succeeds in forcing Martha out of the kitchen and into the pantry. "Now, you stay there in the corner where it's dark, and don't say anything. Daniel intends to set us free. And no fine lady with oranges is going to spoil it."

"But I'm looking for—"

"Hush, miss! You don't know what you're risking. Mr. Robey is not a kind gentleman when angered."

At the name, Martha falls silent. *Robey,* she thinks, *isn't that the person Thomas is seeking? The man who murdered his sister? It is; I'm sure of it . . . and I'm here with him, with only a frightened girl and a cripple to attest to my presence. Oh, what a fool you are, Martha Beale . . .*

Ella raises a warning finger to her lips, then turns and scurries away; and Martha presses herself against the wall. She can easily see the entry into the dining salon but only a small portion of the room itself: shiny, new crimson wallpaper in arabesque designs, stiff crimson draperies still redolent of sulfuric ether, and two plump chairs upholstered in crimson damask. She recognizes the color scheme as being solely masculine, which means the dangerous Mr. Robey must be an unmarried man. But that's as far as her conjecture takes her, because Daniel hurtles crookedly through the entryway at that moment, muttering about "Mr. Robey's unexpected guest" under his breath. When he spots the hiding Martha, he almost groans aloud. Instead, he fixes her with such a malevolent glare that she reflexively closes her eyes. "Ruin this," a whispered snarl informs her, "and I'll do you the same as him."

Then she hears him hobble through the pantry and into the kitchen, murmuring, "Two we have for luncheon, Ella. Not one as I'd planned . . . He'll make it difficult for me, will he? Well, we'll see about that—"

"But there are sufficient meats and other fine things, aren't there, cousin?" The girl's anxious voice replies.

"It's not the food I'm fretting over, child—"

"Then what, Daniel?"

"Be quiet, girl, and let me think. And you, you remain here near the alley door as we discussed. No matter what sounds you hear coming from the other rooms—"

"Yes, cousin . . . But what about the lady? I couldn't get her out into—"

"Swear to me, Ella."

"I swear it, Cousin Daniel . . . but—?"

"No more, Ella! No more. The lady must attend to herself, and I must be about my work, or Mr. Robey will grow suspicious. And then everything will come to naught . . . And now there's the door knocker clacking! It will be our master's guest clamoring to get in. Hide yourself under this table, Ella, while I go attend to the damned gentleman."

That's all Martha hears, because at that moment her faintness returns. Her flesh turns cold and clammy; her lips grow dry, and her stomach spins over. She pinches her wrists and cheeks in hopes of reviving herself, but to no avail, for the next thing she knows her eyesight dims to black; and she slides down the wall to curl into a limp bundle at its base.

While Martha's brain drifts in an unconscious state, Daniel's roars through the present. He unlatches the door for his master's visitor, takes the man's tall hat, cloak, and cane, then makes a hasty retreat back to the building's rear, his thoughts spinning around like dead leaves caught in a storm.

Oh, how he curses the gold coins he accepted for this miserable bargain. How he loathes himself for keeping Robey as a client . . . and fleeing Cherry Hill; and being imprisoned there in the first place . . . and failing to assist his wife in her awful need; and then losing her and his little daughter . . . and now Ella, who put her trust in him, and whom he must save! No matter what, he must rescue her from the fate their master intends. Grief and censure burn through Daniel's throat and gut till his innards feel as if they're made of living coals, and the coals spark into fire.

"VERY TIDY FOR you how these matters have evolved, isn't it?" Daniel's master is saying as he escorts his guest through the sliding double doors of the drawing room and into the dining salon. Like the furnishings in the front room and throughout the remainder of the house, all is waxy and spanking fresh; the carpets shine as if just cleaned with spirits of turpentine; and each polished wood surface is so glossy it hardly seems dry. "You put up the requisite fifty thousand dollars for the gas business your former master and I proposed for this area—a sum, as I once mentioned, that seems overlarge for a confidential secretary to possess . . . But then, I suppose such monies are not too great a sum for a man who's poised to marry one of the richest women in the nation . . ." The speaker pauses. "Ah, but please do take a seat. I cannot promise a lavish feast, but I'm sure as Lemuel Beale's successor you will enjoy many sumptuous repasts in the future . . . Now, let me wish you joy in your wedded state. Matrimony is a fine and holy thing; as you know, I am sadly experiencing my own loss today . . ."

It's at the utterance of these four final words that the unseen Martha begins to recover. *Surely that's Mr. Rosegger speaking,* she tells herself. *But why is he here in this man Robey's house? Especially now that his wife—?* But her queries are interrupted by a voice she knows far better than Rosegger's.

"I trust you're not suggesting that I was involved in Lemuel Beale's death, sir?"

With a quick intake of breath, Martha comes fully to her senses. *Owen Simms . . . But what can he be doing here as well?* She pulls herself into a sitting position and strains forward to catch the words curling in from the dining room doorway.

"I'm merely remarking upon the timely—or untimely—coincidence, Mr. Simms . . . as well as the *coincidence* of a hermit being found in possession of your master's percussion rifle."

"What are you suggesting, sir?"

"Oh, I think you know" is the level reply.

"No, I do not, Rosegger."

"No? Then let us posit that this hermit shot Lemuel Beale in order to obtain his rifle . . . Wouldn't a body have been found, sir? The woods and shoreline were searched intensively—and by a good many men, from what I understand. So what I propose to you, Simms, is that your master did fall into the river—although not by accident—and that whoever pushed him in weighted the body so that it could not be found—"

Martha gasps, then clamps a hand over her mouth while her face turns toward the blank wall as if her vision could bore through it. *What am I hearing?* her brain demands.

"Which means," Rosegger continues in the same lordly tone, "that Lemuel Beale was either shot to death first or dispatched in some other fashion—"

"By me, you imagine?" Simms finally demands.

"Yes, by you, sir. You killed your master and disposed of the body—which is why you remain under scrutiny by our able constabulary. And why I now begin to perceive you as a less than ideal business partner."

Oh! Martha thinks, *oh, what Hell have I stumbled into? Simms and Rosegger in league? How can this have happened without my knowledge?* But even as she poses these silent questions, the answer appears: *What, Martha, did you ever understand of men's affairs?*

"If it's Kelman that's troubling you, Rosegger, you needn't worry. I've made arrangements for him. And as to our partnership—"

"Another errant hermit with a stolen rifle?" Rosegger interjects with a cutting laugh.

Martha gasps again, but what Simms's "arrangements" for Thomas Kelman might be or how he intends to defend the accusations against him or curry favor with his would-be "partner," she is not to learn, because Daniel hurries through the pantry at that moment with a large tray of foodstuffs in his hands. "My apologies, Mr. Robey, sir . . . With an extra mouth to feed, I fear it's taken me longer than I'd like."

"We haven't all day, tailor," Rosegger replies testily, and Martha realizes, *Robey . . . Rosegger is Mr. Robey . . . and Owen Simms and he . . . and Father and Simms . . . and now Thomas . . .*

She listens for further revelations as Daniel limps from place to place distributing plates of butter, rashers of bacon, ham preserved in fat, and a forcemeat pie hot from the oven. But the platters so jounce and clatter upon the table that whatever words pass between the diners are drowned by the sound of cutlery and china until she hears Rosegger demand an angry:

"Is that all there is, man? We are two gentlemen with healthy appetites, not one. And from the accounts I settle on this house, I know that it's a well-stocked place."

"Yes, sir," Daniel mumbles in reply. "It is, sir. I have grilled sweetbreads still preparing, and grilled kidneys and sausages. They're roasting in the oven coals yet. I thought, you being two at table, you would require additional—"

"Silence, man! I need no speechifying from you. Now fetch what's already cooked."

"Yes, sir."

Martha listens to Daniel scuttling around the dinner table; then there's a splintering crash as he bumps into what she imagines must be an unlit paraffin lamp. She can smell the oil and hear it dribbling from the table to the floor, as well as the man's awkward steps as he tries to daub up the spill.

"Leave it, tailor! I and my guest are hungry. You may clean this mess away later. This is the second lamp you've overturned in this very room in two short days, and upon this new and handsome carpet. The repairs will come from your wages if you cannot set the matter aright yourself."

"Oh, sir. Yes, sir. My apologies for my awful clumsiness. It's my foot, sir. It's made me ever thus—"

"Enough, tailor! Now bring us our meal."

"Sir. Yes, sir," Daniel mumbles, stumbling away.

When he returns to the butler's pantry, he reeks of paraffin oil and bears a look of such single-minded vengeance that Martha's heart congeals. *He means to work some mischief here,* she realizes. *That's the "plan." That's how he intends to free Ella—*

But Martha has no sooner formulated this assessment and risen to her feet in protest than a yelping scream erupts from the kitchen, and Daniel comes hurtling back, running into the dining room, followed by a line of fire. In his hands are clutched the promised meats, which also spark with flame. "Now, Ella, now!" he calls behind him.

Rosegger shouts out an oath at this sudden attack; Simms also swears, but Daniel's cries are louder as he hurls himself and the blazing food upon the table. Martha hears candlesticks overturn and set alight both cloth and napery; she hears yelps of pain, bodies grappling, chairs falling with heavy thuds, and then the roar of the growing fire as it shoots up the new curtains and blisters across the carpet. The wall at her head turns hot; the air fills with smoke. The cries emanating from the dining room become shrieks. Then she's aware of Ella calling:

"This way, miss . . . Daniel will join us."

Martha lifts her skirts, leaps over the stream of flame, and throws herself bodily through the kitchen and into the rear alley. The neighbor's dog is barking ferociously, yanking hard against its chain, but Martha and Ella dart past the corner of a privy building; and soon the animal is growling not at the strangers but at the heat that pulsates from the burning house.

"Daniel will join us," Ella states again as she gazes at the terrible spectacle. "I'm to wait for him here. At a distance, he told me, so as not to be in harm's way. He was very careful in his instructions." She pauses in her small speech. "He had friends who once escaped a fiery furnace, and he understands how such miracles are done."

Martha can think of no reply; she's aware of the clatter of a fire wagon approaching, then of the arrival of another, of shouts and oaths and the nervous whinnies of horses echoing in the street beyond, of flames shooting from the building's windows, and finally of water hoses hissing and pinging, and of charred wood splintering. In all this noise, never once does she hear the voice of Owen Simms or of Rosegger or the tailor, Daniel.

She wraps her arms around Ella's shoulders, and her sole thought is how fortunate it is that she gave the child her fur-lined cloak.

Dream, to Wake

SPRING HAS COME TO PHILADELPHIA. Spring, bursting with pale narcissus blooms and orange-bright daffodils, with purple crocuses, with the hazy-pink buds of apple and cherry trees, with the marvel of green leaves unfurling from branches that once seemed dead.

In St. Peter's churchyard, this manifestation of earth's renewal and abundance rolls across the graves, spiking fresh shoots of grass around the weathered bases, dropping petals upon the gray stones, charging the air above the markers with the acrobatic loops of bees and baby birds, with the insistent, clamorous noise of life reborn and glorious.

As has become her habit, Martha Beale strolls along the memorial garden's old brick walks and amongst its venerable trees and showy blossoms. With her is Thomas Kelman, and with the adults, sometimes standing excitedly between them, sometimes dashing off in pursuit of a fat-tailed squirrel, are two children, both of whom Martha has now adopted as her wards. One is Ella; the other is the boy called Cai.

There is deep peace among these four. Despite the rules dictating Martha's period of mourning, she's been in Kelman's company many, many times during the months that ended winter and brought the fullness of spring. And although she knows her behavior has been causing gossip, she doesn't care.

Let the world talk, she thinks now, as she has repeatedly. *Let my friends and acquaintances speculate upon why I brought two outcast children into my home, or why my father was murdered by a man he trusted, or what Ella's sordid history entailed. Let people critique my defense of Emily Durand, as well as my ill-fated visit to Rosegger's infamous abode. Let them carp about the source of my wealth—as they certainly will—or say I'm too old to wed, or that my inheritance is my only attraction. I know the truth, and I know what matters is that I've learned to do those things that I believe are fitting and right . . . And I'm happy, truly and endlessly happy for the first time in my life.*

As if Kelman can read her thoughts, he presses the fingers of her hand that rest in the crook of his arm. If they weren't in a public place, he would put those fingers to his lips.

Martha smiles at him, then briefly frowns, adding a quiet "Poor Marguerite" as if her own joy must be tempered with the worries of others. "It's still impossible for me to believe Rosegger would poison his wife . . . And to what end? To what end?"

"He killed his sister in the same fashion, Martha," Kelman states in a somber tone. "And he may also have had a hand in his father-in-law's demise, although we'll never know for certain . . . There are many things about the man and his motives we'll never understand. Nor should, I suppose . . . not unless we wish to enter his twisted brain."

She nods. For a moment she doesn't speak; instead, her mind considers how much evil exists in the world—not only murderers like Rosegger or Simms but people driven by greed and envy. Parents who sell their daughters and sons, the buyers who take and then discard them, landlords who profit by providing shoddy housing to the poor, merchants who grow rich on the backs of starving children: the list of injustices and cruelties seems endless, while the fight for compassion and fairness seems almost too daunting a task to consider undertaking. "I don't know how you do it, Thomas," she says with a slow shake of her head. "Encountering so much that is vile and sinister in our city, and yet continuing to battle on the side of goodness and mercy."

"We effect what changes we can, Martha" is Kelman's quiet reply. "Just as you've taken Ella and Cai into your house. We address what wrongs we're able to. We cannot fix them all."

Martha again remains mute, thinking, while around them robins twitter, hopping with showy exuberance from gravestone to gravestone as if there were only mirth and merriment in the world. "And those tragic Rosegger orphans. What a cruel legacy they've been given. To know their mother died by their father's hand."

Kelman also pauses before speaking. "Hopefully, the children's uncles will be able to allay their sadness. And remember, my dearest, they haven't been left destitute. Perhaps, in time, they'll devote themselves to some admirable work, and so alleviate their own distress."

"Yes," Martha answers, then says no more, and both she and Kelman turn and walk to where Lemuel Beale's marble marker stands.

I KNOW MY REDEEMER LIVETH. She reads the words in silence, as she's done many times before. The passage she ordered engraved upon the stone seems fitting for a man whose body was never found, but Martha also has a personal motive in choosing the words. Redemption, she's come to realize, is not only about securing a place in a far-off Heaven. Redemption can be found much closer to home.

"Oh, Thomas," she says as she eventually turns her head away from the gravestone, "you know, that day, when I overheard Owen Simms so casually discussing both Father and you . . . how he'd 'arranged' to have Father's rifle discovered, and thereby lay blame on another man . . . and then what his intentions were toward you, oh, my brain envisioned the most awful scenes. Truly, I didn't think to see you alive again."

"I'm sorry you had to listen to that conversation, Martha. And endure that catastrophic fire."

"It was nothing compared to the grim thoughts my imagination created." She closes her eyes for a long moment. "Poor Father." She looks back at the marble tablet, touching it with one hand while the other stays firmly in the crook of Thomas Kelman's arm. "Betrayal is a terrible thing, isn't it?"

"It is. And so is murder."

Martha sighs. "I wish . . ." she starts to say, but doesn't finish the sentence. In fact, she's not sure what she wishes: That her father were still alive? Certainly. That he hadn't witnessed the treachery of Owen Simms? Of course. Or that he hadn't allied himself with a man like Rosegger? Which is also true. But what her secret heart is whispering is the wish that Lemuel Beale had confided in his daughter rather than his numerous acquaintances, that he'd recognized her value and instead of discipline and disapproval had chosen to show love and admiration. "If I'd been a better daughter—" she finally begins.

"Oh, Martha, my dearest. I'm certain you were the best daughter anyone could wish."

She doesn't respond, and so Kelman continues with a more soothing "If you gave your father half the joy you give me, then that was great indeed."

"You're kind to say so, Thomas." Then she permits herself a small smile. "But then, you are always kind."

"To you" is Kelman's simple response. "I'm not so certain others who know me would agree with that assessment."

Martha's thoughtful smile grows, and she tilts her head and looks up into his face. "I know you claim not to believe in the gift of clairvoyance, Thomas, but if you'd asked me last January where April and May would find me—or Cai or Ella or you—well, I could never have imagined we'd be here strolling together, arm in arm, our hopes and futures shared."

Kelman's eyes shine down upon her. "And you think that *Signor* Paladino could have?"

"No . . . No, his mind seems capable of conjuring only the darkest of images—"

"Or inventing them—"

"Oh, they weren't inventions, Thomas. I'm not certain what his strange visions were, but I don't believe he created those scenes. They were too close to the truth to be mere fantasy . . ."

Kelman doesn't answer. He has no response to this assertion; his conversations with Pliny Earle concerning the phenomenon of second sight have produced more questions than solutions, and Kelman's not a person comfortable with the nebulous and vague. "I'm glad the man's life was spared," he says at length.

Martha nods. "Yes. It took true bravery on Emily Durand's part to confide what she did. Escaping such a stigma will be difficult, even with a new life in Europe."

"You were a good friend to her."

"Oh, no, Thomas, she was the one who rescued me!" Martha laughs, then leans her head against Kelman's shoulder and stares up into the blue, blue sky. "In all my life, I never realized that humans could experience this kind of joy. Or love. Above all, love."

At this point, despite all propriety, Kelman would have turned her toward him and kissed her full on the lips, but a shout arrests them both. "Mother!" Ella calls out from the other side of the churchyard. "Come. Quickly! Come here!"

Hurrying to the child, Martha and Thomas find Cai with a stick in his hand. He'd been poking it into a bundle of rags lying within the shadow of the high brick wall when the bundle stirred, revealing the face of a beggar woman, her dark skin so besmeared and stretched over her shrunken flesh that she looks no more than black bone or coal.

"Oh!" Martha says, bending down while the woman strains to lift her head and stare at Cai, who whimpers a fearful "Mother!" then yanks on Martha's hand as she impetuously kneels on the ground.

"Hush, Cai . . . Hush . . . You're quite safe." She holds the boy close, then looks up at Kelman. "Find the church sexton, Thomas . . . No . . . No, bring Dr. Percival. And take Cai with you. Ella and I will wait here, and I'll try to comfort this poor wretch."

The beggar stares at Martha. "C . . . ?" The sound is no more than a croak.

Repellent and ill-smelling as the creature is, Martha's better instincts guide her. She smooths the stiffened rags around the bony face, then lays her hand on the fevered brow. "In truth, the boy is named Caspar . . . the inspiration being the physician who attends the children at the orphanage. Cai has suffered much and is now my ward, for which I am most grateful . . ." Then words fail her; they seem overgarrulous, overbright, too full of hope where none is found. Why would Dr. Walne or an asylum for colored children matter to a person who's obviously dying? "Help is at hand," she adds in a subdued tone.

"C—" is the woman's muffled response, but Martha interrupts with a gentle appeal:

"Hush, dear lady . . . Don't attempt to talk. You're weak now, and tired and ill. But when you're well—"

The woman stares at Martha. Her lips part. With great difficulty, she opens wide her yellowed eyes. "C . . . is . . ."

"Yes, the boy is my ward. We call him Cai although his given name is Caspar—"

"Which he couldn't say," Ella interjects while Martha attempts to hush her with a soft:

"We must allow this lady to rest, dear—"

"C . . . is . . . !" The noise is awful with effort. The beggar struggles to raise herself into a sitting position, but the work proves too great for her frame, and she falls back, her mouth open, her eyes blank and lifeless.

Martha bows her head, but Ella continues to gaze at the dead woman. "I've seen her before, Mother . . . That day at the Shambles . . . She said her name was Ruth."

Author's Note

IT WAS IN RESEARCHING TWO ancestors, Nicholas Biddle and Francis Martin Drexel, that the idea of *The Conjurer* first took shape. Drexel ascended to power and prominence while Biddle was publicly castigated and gradually eclipsed during the period known as the Great Depression. This financial catastrophe was instigated by Andrew Jackson's deregulation of the banking industry; it was a time of foment throughout the country, but especially in Philadelphia whose status as a preeminent industrial city added to its luster as the nation's first capital. The grinding poverty of the newly emigrated stood in stark contrast to the vast wealth of the old established families; a vociferous abolitionist movement fought an equally determined proslavery coalition; a series of murderous labor strikes and race riots collided with William Penn's heritage of empathy and tolerance. Mesmerism, somnambulism, clairvoyancy, and conjuring became a panacea that appealed to every social class. Philadelphia, considered the "Athens of America" and an arbiter of style, eagerly embraced the vogue.

It's important to note also that as late as 1842 the city remained divided into townships, boroughs, and districts, and at that time had no unified police force. A criminal could break the law in one part of town and escape punishment by fleeing into another area of jurisdiction. The inadequacy of such a system was the subject of much public debate and outrage. The penny papers, gazettes, and broadsheets of the day devoted considerable ink to the problem.

The Library Company of Philadelphia, founded in 1731 by Benjamin Franklin, and the Athenaeum of Philadelphia, whose current home on Washington Square was completed in 1847, provided me with a plethora of primary research materials. Holding the actual newspapers and journals published in 1842, and reading their editorials, their short works of fiction, their articles, essays, and advertising cards was transformative. I was also able to access records and annual reports from the mental asylum referred to in the novel, from the orphanage, and the Philadelphia Gas Works, and of course I read the original of the famous *Seybert Commission for Investigating Modern Spiritualism.* Many, many thanks to Phillip S. Lapsansky of the Library Company and to Ellen Rose of the Athenaeum. Their Web sites www.Librarycompany.org and www.PhilaAthenaeum.org provide an inventory of their holdings.

Physically, Philadelphia retains so much of its history that it's impossible to walk down the streets without feeling transported through time. The brick homes, the grand religious houses, and government buildings, even the cobbles and pebblestones of the roads evince a palpable sense of the past. Ghosts, either good or ill, abound. If you're a stranger to the city, I invite you to discover it.

I also invite readers to write to me with queries or comments. I can be reached through my Web site www.CordeliaFrancesBiddle.com